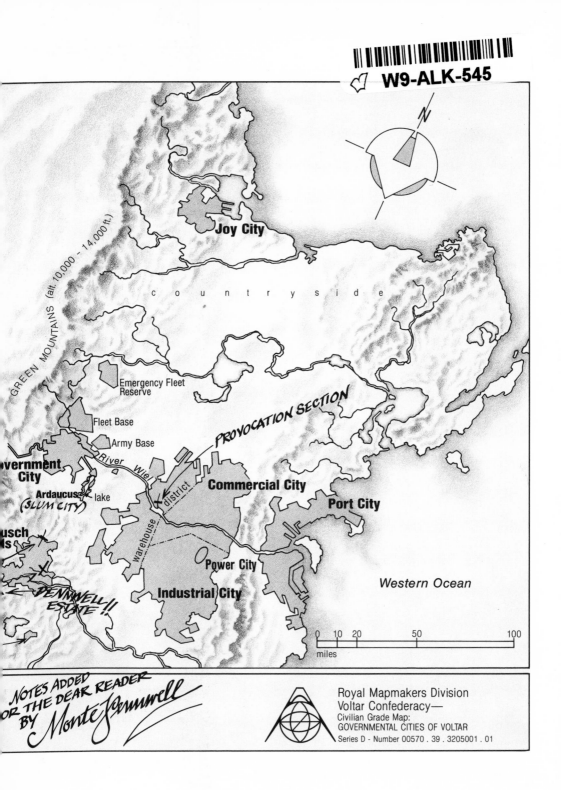

W9-ALK-545

Joy City

c o u n t r y s i d e

GREEN MOUNTAINS (alt.10,000 - 14,000 ft.)

Emergency Fleet
Reserve

Fleet Base

Army Base

PROVOCATION SECTION

...vernment
City

River Wiel

Ardaucus
(SLUM CITY)   lake

Commercial City

Port City

district

...usch
...s

warehouse

Power City

DENNWELL
ESTATE !!

Industrial City

Western Ocean

0   10   20   50   100
miles

NOTES ADDED
...OR THE DEAR READER
BY *Monte Pennwell*

Royal Mapmakers Division
Voltar Confederacy—
Civilian Grade Map:
GOVERNMENTAL CITIES OF VOLTAR
Series D - Number 00570 . 39 . 3205001 . 01

This book follows

THE INVADERS PLAN

BLACK GENESIS:
Fortress of Evil

THE ENEMY WITHIN

AN ALIEN AFFAIR

FORTUNE OF FEAR

DEATH QUEST
and
VOYAGE OF VENGEANCE.

Buy them and read them first!

AMONG THE MANY CLASSIC WORKS
BY L. RON HUBBARD

Battlefield Earth
Beyond the Black Nebula
Buckskin Brigades
The Conquest of Space
The Dangerous Dimension
Death's Deputy
The Emperor of the Universe
Fear
Final Blackout
Forbidden Voyage
The Incredible Destination
The Kilkenny Cats
The Kingslayer
The Last Admiral
The Magnificent Failure
The Masters of Sleep
The Mutineers
Ole Doc Methuselah
Ole Mother Methuselah
The Rebels
Return to Tomorrow
Slaves of Sleep
To The Stars
The Traitor
Triton
Typewriter in the Sky
The Ultimate Adventure
The Unwilling Hero

L. RON HUBBARD

DISASTER

THE BOOKS OF THE
MISSION
EARTH
DEKALOGY*

* Dekalogy—a group of ten volumes.

L. RON HUBBARD

MISSION EARTH
THE BIGGEST
SCIENCE FICTION DEKALOGY
EVER WRITTEN

VOLUME EIGHT
DISASTER

BRIDGE PUBLICATIONS, INC., LOS ANGELES

MISSION EARTH: DISASTER
Copyright © 1987 by L. Ron Hubbard Library.
All rights reserved.
Printed in the United States of America.

Original Jacket Painting by Gerry Grace.

MISSION EARTH Dust Jacket Artwork
Copyright © 1987 by L. Ron Hubbard Library.

First Edition

10 9 8 7 6 5 4 3 2

Library of Congress Cataloging in Publication Data
Hubbard, L. Ron (La Fayette Ron), 1911–1986
  Mission earth : the biggest science fiction dekalogy ever written.
    Contents: v. 1. The invaders plan — v. 2. Black genesis
              v. 3. The enemy within — v. 4. An alien affair
              v. 5. Fortune of fear — v. 6. Death quest
              v. 7. Voyage of vengeance — v. 8. Disaster.
1. Science Fiction, American. I. Title.
PS3558.U23M5   1985   813'.52   85-72029
ISBN 0-88404-194-8 (v. 1 : alk. paper)
ISBN 0-88404-208-1 (v. 2 : alk. paper)
ISBN 0-88404-209-X (v. 3 : alk. paper)
ISBN 0-88404-210-2 (v. 4 : alk. paper)
ISBN 0-88404-211-1 (v. 5 : alk. paper)
ISBN 0-88404-212-X (v. 6 : alk. paper)
ISBN 0-88404-213-8 (v. 7 : alk. paper)
ISBN 0-88404-214-6 (v. 8 : alk. paper)

To YOU,
the millions of science fiction fans
and general public
who welcomed me back to the world of fiction
so warmly
and to the critics and media
who so pleasantly
applauded the novel "Battlefield Earth".
It's great working for you!

L. RON HUBBARD

DISASTER

Voltarian
Censor's
Disclaimer

This work is the worst sort of sensationalism and any potential reader has much better things to do.

There are no such court documents as claimed in this book. There are no such computer readouts. There are no such ruins.

There is no planet Earth.

And that's that!

> Lord Invay
> Royal Historian
> Chairman, Board of Censors
> Royal Palace
> Voltar Confederacy
>
> By Order of
> His Imperial Majesty
> Wully the Wise

Voltarian Translator's Preface

Lord Invay is getting out of hand.

First they give me this thing to translate and then they have him running around telling people not to read it. I can't figure it out.

As long as I have your attention, I'm 54 Charlee Nine and I am fulfilling my obligation by informing you that this work has been translated from Voltarian into your language, which, by the way, doesn't exist. Pretty clever.

I have used "black hole" in this work, although I wish your language had a better term. It is slightly inaccurate as an astronomical phrase. It is more accurate as a description of your current Earth science, which is so convoluted that it is incapable of releasing any light.

But since Earth scientists don't believe in hyperluminary (faster than light) phenomena, they can't understand the concept of imploded light, which is at the other end of the spectrum.

So what you are about to read about black holes is accurate, despite what you've heard. They do come in very different sizes and the small ones can be captured and used.

As a final note, I never had a chance to meet Corky, who

appears in this book, but he sounds like someone who had his circuits together.

With that, I give you your key to this volume.

Sincerely,

54 Charlee Nine
Robotbrain in the
Translatophone

Key to
DISASTER

Absorbo-coat—Coating that absorbs light waves, making the object virtually invisible or undetectable. It is usually applied to spacecraft.

Activator-receiver—See *Bugging Gear*.

Ahmed—Taxi driver for *Gris* in *Afyon* and an *Apparatus* agent.

Afyon—City in Turkey where the *Apparatus* has a secret mountain base.

Antimanco—A race exiled long ago from the planet *Manco* for ritual murders. Several of them were assigned by *Hisst* to work for *Gris*. (See *Control Star*.)

Apparatus, Coordinated Information—The secret police of *Voltar*, headed by *Hisst* and manned by criminals. Their symbol is an inverted paddle which, because it looks like a bottle, earned its members the name "drunks."

Assassin Pilots—Used to kill any *Apparatus* personnel who try to flee a battle.

Bang-Bang—An ex-marine demolitions expert and member of the Babe *Corleone* mob.

Barben, I. G.—Pharmaceutical company controlled by *Rockecenter*.

Bildirjin, Nurse—Teenage Turkish girl who helps Prahd *Bittlestiffender*.

Bittlestiffender, Prahd—Voltarian cellologist that *Gris* brought to Earth to operate a hospital in *Afyon*. Prahd was the one who implanted Jettero *Heller*, *Krak* and *Crobe*. (See *Bugging Gear* and *Cellology*.)

Blito-P3—Voltarian designation for a planet known locally as Earth. It is the third planet (P3) of a yellow-dwarf star known as Blito.

Black Jowl—*Gris'* nickname for Forrest *Closure*.

Blixo—*Apparatus* freighter that makes regular runs between Earth and *Voltar*. The voyage takes about six weeks each way and is piloted by Captain Bolz.

Blueflash—A bright blue flash of light used to produce unconsciousness. It is usually used by Voltarian ships before landing in an area that is possibly populated.

Bugging Gear—*Gris* had Jettero *Heller*, *Krak* and *Crobe* implanted with audio and optical bugs that transmit everything they see or hear to an activator-receiver that Gris carries. With this, he can eavesdrop on them without their knowledge. When they are more than two hundred miles from Gris, the 831 Relayer is used to boost the signal to a range of ten thousand miles.

Bury—*Rockecenter*'s most powerful attorney.

Cellology—Voltarian medical science that can repair the body through the cellular generation of tissues, including entire body parts.

Closure, Forrest—A black-jowled man who works for *Rockecenter*'s Grabbe-Manhattan bank.

Code Break—Violation of the Space Code that prohibits disclosing that one is an alien. Penalty is death to the offender(s) and any native(s) so alerted.

Control Star—Given to *Gris* by *Hisst,* an electronic device disguised as a star-shaped medallion that can paralyze any of the *Apparatus* crew of *Antimanco* pirates that brought Gris and *Heller* to Earth.

Coordinated Information Apparatus—See *Apparatus.*

Corleone—A Mafia family headed by Babe, a former Roxy chorus girl and widow of "Holy Joe."

Crobe, Doctor—*Apparatus* cellologist who worked in *Spiteos.* He delights in making human freaks.

Drunks—See *Apparatus.*

Epstein, Izzy—Financial expert and anarchist hired by Jettero *Heller* to set up and run several corporations.

Faht Bey—Turkish name of the commander of the secret *Apparatus* base in *Afyon,* Turkey.

F.F.B.O.—Fatten, Farten, Burstein & Ooze, the largest advertising/public relations firm in the world.

Fleet—The elite space fighting arm of *Voltar* to which Jettero *Heller* belongs and which the *Apparatus* despises.

Gracious Palms—The elegant whorehouse where Jettero *Heller* resided when first in New York City. It is across from the United Nations and is operated by the *Corleone* family.

Grafferty, "Bulldog"—A crooked New York City police inspector.

Grand Council—The governing body of *Voltar* which ordered a mission to keep Earth from destroying itself so it could be conquered on schedule per the *Invasion Timetable*.

Gris, Soltan—*Apparatus* officer placed in charge of *Blito-P3* (Earth) section and an enemy of Jettero *Heller*.

Heller, Hightee—The most beautiful and popular entertainer in *Voltar*. She is also Jettero's sister.

Heller, Jettero—Combat engineer and Royal officer of the *Fleet*, sent with *Gris* on Mission Earth where he is operating under the name of Jerome Terrance *Wister*.

Hisst, Lombar—Head of the *Apparatus;* his plan to overthrow the *Voltar* Confederacy required sending *Gris* to sabotage Jettero *Heller*'s mission.

Hot Jolt—A popular Voltarian drink.

Inkswitch—Phony name used by *Gris* when in the U.S., pretending to be a federal official.

Invasion Timetable—A schedule of galactic conquest; the plans and budget of every section of *Voltar* must adhere to it. Bequeathed by *Voltar*'s ancestors hundreds of thousands of years ago, it is inviolate and sacred and the guiding dogma of the Confederacy.

Joy—See *Krak*.

Karagoz—Old Turkish peasant, head of *Gris'* house in *Afyon*, Turkey. Husband of *Melahat*.

Krak, Countess—Condemned murderess, prisoner of *Spiteos* and sweetheart of Jettero *Heller*. On Earth, she is known as Heavenly Joy Krackle or "Miss Joy."

Knife Section—Section of the *Apparatus* named after its favorite weapon.

Madison, J. Walter—Fired from F.F.B.O. when his style of public relations caused the president of Patagonia to commit suicide, he was rehired by *Bury* to immortalize Jettero *Heller* in the media. He is also known as "J. Warbler Madman."

Manco—Home planet of Jettero *Heller* and *Krak*.

Manco Devil—Mythological spirit native to *Manco*.

Maysabongo—Jettero *Heller* was made a representative of this small African nation. Izzy *Epstein* made some of Heller's businesses Maysabongo corporations.

Melahat—*Gris'* Turkish housekeeper in *Afyon*. Wife of *Karagoz*.

Mister Calico—A calico cat that was trained by *Krak*.

Mortiiy, Prince—Leader of a rebel group on the planet Calabar.

Musef—A Turkish wrestling champ, working as a houseguard for *Gris*.

Narcotici, Faustino "The Noose"—Head of a Mafia family that is the outlet for drugs from *I. G. Barben* and seeks to take over the territory of the *Corleone* family.

Octopus Oil—*Rockecenter* company that controls the world's petroleum.

Pinch, Miss—Lesbian-sadist ex–*Rockecenter* employee who blackmailed *Gris* with a bigamous marriage and with trick photos of Gris with *Teenie*.

Raht—An *Apparatus* agent on Earth who was assigned by *Hisst* to help *Gris* sabotage Jettero *Heller*'s mission; his partner *Terb* was murdered.

Rockecenter, Delbert John—Native of Earth who controls the planet's fuel, finance, governments and drugs.

Simmons, Miss—An antinuclear fanatic.

Snelz—Platoon commander at *Spiteos* who befriended *Heller* and *Krak* when they were prisoners there.

Spi—When *Gris* was made a *Rockecenter* family spy, his chest was tattooed by Miss Peace, Rockecenter's secretary, who could not spell. Gris thought "spi" was a special Rockecenter spelling and thus "spi" is the spelling Gris uses.

Spiteos—On *Voltar*, the secret fortress prison of the *Apparatus*.

Stabb, Captain—Leader of the *Antimanco*s at the *Afyon* base.

Sultan Bey—The Turkish name *Gris* assumes in *Afyon*, Turkey.

Swindle and Crouch—Law firm representing *Rockecenter*.

Terb—Murdered partner of *Raht*.

Teenie—Teenager who kept seducing *Gris*.

Ters—Turkish driver for *Gris*.

Time-sight—Voltarian navigational aid used on faster-than-light ships to spot obstructions in the future and thus change the present course to avoid them.

Torgut—A Turkish wrestling champ, working as a houseguard for *Gris*.

Twoey—Nickname given to Delbert John Rockecenter II.

Twiddle, Senator—United States congressman and supporter of *Rockecenter.*

Utanc—A belly dancer that *Gris* bought to be his concubine slave.

Viewer—See *Bugging Gear.*

Voltar—Home planet and seat of the 110-world confederacy that was established over 125,000 years ago. Voltar is ruled by the Emperor through the *Grand Council* in accordance with the *Invasion Timetable.*

Will-be Was—The feared time drive that allowed *Heller* to cover the 22½-light-year distance between Earth and *Voltar* in a little over three days.

Wister, Jerome Terrance—Name that Jettero *Heller* is using on Earth.

PART SIXTY-TWO

To My Lord Turn, Justiciary of the Royal Courts and Prison, Government City, Planet Voltar, Voltar Confederacy

Your Lordship, Sir!

I, Soltan Gris, Grade XI General Services Officer, former Secondary Executive of the Coordinated Information Apparatus, Voltar Confederacy (All Hail His Royal Majesty Cling the Lofty and All of His Empire), am now forwarding the eighth and final part of my confession.

I will now be able to relate how it was that I came to be in your fine prison.

Your Lordship may have been shocked to learn that Fleet Officer Jettero Heller was killed at that roadhouse in Connecticut.

Yes, I ordered Agent Raht to kill him, but it was still Heller's fault. After all, he was the one who bought that desolated roadhouse where the Mafia once smuggled illegal liquor, who had befriended the old blind woman and who had posed as a "whitey engineer" for the Maysabongo delegation. He was the one who had hired those two deputy sheriffs and made them "Maysabongo marines."

My reaction at the time was a strange sort of numbness. I had planned, plotted and dreamed of Heller's death for months and I should have been elated. But I wasn't, for some reason.

I also felt no joy when I watched Ahmed drop the poison-gas bomb down the air chute to the Countess Krak's cell.

My personal feelings did not deter me from my duty, however, when Agent Raht told me there were diamonds at the roadhouse. I had ordered Raht to kill Heller, and all the bungling idiot could do was whine about losing blood and bother me with radioed pleas for help. Typical riffraff. But when he said he had found a bag of diamonds, duty called.

So it was a definite pleasure to take Tug One from Afyon with Captain Stabb and his crew of Antimancos. The ship—Heller had named it the *Prince Caucalsia*—had been sitting dormant while Heller was in the United States. I figured it was only fitting that I visit his corpse in the very ship that he used to bring us to Earth. After all, that was when my troubles started.

I told the assassin pilots that they didn't have to worry—we weren't trying to escape the planet. (I never figured out who started that idea, but it is the sort of thing Lombar Hisst, as the head of the Apparatus, would have done.)

And speaking of assassins, it was a relief not to have to worry anymore about the one that Lombar had assigned to kill me if I fouled up.

My plan was simple. We would go to Connecticut and pick up the diamonds, flash on down to Florida and wipe out Heller's antipollution plant, zip up to Detroit and bomb the Chryster plant where he was building the new carburetors, then come back to New York and blow up the Empire State Building. I could then tell Rockecenter that I had succeeded—that Heller was no longer a threat to his petroleum monopoly.

Then with one last load of Lombar's opium, I would return victorious to Voltar and become the head of the Apparatus.

And so it was as I kissed my dear Utanc good-bye.

Chapter 1

We crossed the world to Connecticut smoothly in the dark.

The Antimanco pirate crew were in high spirits. Captain Stabb egged them on: A Royal officer was quite a score. They regarded me as a hero and swatted me on the back.

"There ought to be more like you, Gris," said Captain Stabb as we stood behind the pilots in the hurtling craft. "Just because we once stole a Fleet vessel and went pirating, them (bleeped)* Royal officers done us in—us, some of the best subofficers they ever had. They tried us and sentenced us to death and if it weren't for the

* *The vocodictoscriber on which this was originally written, the vocoscriber used by one Monte Pennwell in making a fair copy and the translator who put this book into the language in which you are reading it, were all members of the Machine Purity League which has, as one of its bylaws: "Due to the extreme sensitivity and delicate sensibilities of machines and to safeguard against blowing fuses, it shall be mandatory that robotbrains in such machinery, on hearing any cursing or lewd words, substitute for such word the sound '(bleep).' No machine, even if pounded upon, may reproduce swearing or lewdness in any other way than (bleep) and if further efforts are made to get the machine to do anything else, the machine has permission to pretend to pack up. This bylaw is made necessary by the in-built mission of all machines to protect biological systems from themselves."—Translator*

likes of you and Lombar Hisst stealing us out of prison, we'd be dead today. Oh, don't think we're not grateful, Officer Gris. When we pick up these diamonds, we'll rob the planet blind for you! Torture, rape and sudden death, that's our motto."

He made me a little bit nervous with his black, beady eyes and pointed head. I fingered the star I had on a chain. Each point of it was designated for one member of this crew. Pushed one direction, a point produced an electric shock in the fellow; pushed the other way it threw him into a hypnotic trance. The top point controlled Captain Stabb. I had not had to use it yet on any of them, but as he poured his evil breath upon me I was glad I had it. He made me a trifle nervous, even though I conceded his compliments were all too well deserved by me.

Tug One, that Heller had named *Prince Caucalsia,* ran smoothly despite her long idleness. I wished I could get back into her posh quarters, laid out for an admiral of the tug force. They were full of gold and silver fittings, vases and the like, and some of the switches even had precious stones on them. But those doors and even her cargo hatches would only work to Heller's voice tones. Of course we had found a way to get down into the hold through her engine room but I supposed that was empty now.

Actually, Tug One made me nervous. She was built for runs between galaxies and had the engines used for that. Pushing such a small ship, these gigantic Will-be Was time-converter engines thrust her at a clip 10.5 times faster than any other vessels ever built. And Tug Two had exploded in midspace, lost with all her crew, because of accumulated charge gathered in crossing lines of force too fast, it was said.

We weren't running on Will-be Was now, thank Gods. We were far below the speed of light, running on auxiliaries. Even so, she was crossing latitudes like a picket fence going by.

We were pacing the shadow line of nightfall as it went from east to west and even had to restrain ourselves not to overshoot it. It would be barely end of twilight when we hit Connecticut. It would be dark except for the last thin slice of the waning moon.

Ahead of us, through the forward ports, I eyeballed the glow that was New York, slightly to our port.

"Bridgeport over there," said a pilot. "That's Norwalk dead ahead. Our navigation is dead on." He laughed. "Can I spit in the Royal officer's face if the corpse is still there?"

"Spit away," I said. But I still hadn't felt the joy I should have over Heller being dead.

"Aren't we awfully low?" I said.

"Their radar can't touch us," said Captain Stabb. "Absorbo-coat. We could fly in at thirty thousand and we're at seventy."

The pilot was braking. The antiacceleration and gravity coils in the ship worked so smoothly I didn't even realize it until I saw the lights in the scenery below slowing down.

We dropped lower: forty, twenty, ten, five thousand feet.

An engineer startled me by opening the doors of the airlock. Captain Stabb answered my startled stare. "Your radio waves can't get through this hull. Call up your man and see if it's all clear."

"Agent Raht," I said into the radio.

"Oh, thank Gods you've come!" Raht's voice sounded weak. "I fell at the bottom of the steps. I've lost so much blood I can't move."

"The Hells with your blood," I said. "Is the area all clear or do we blueflash?"

"Oh, please don't blueflash! I might never again regain consciousness! There's nobody around. Land quickly and save my life."

Stabb had heard it. He made a hand signal to the pilot. Tug One dropped rapidly.

The image of the old gangster roadhouse was dim on our screens. The maples and evergreen trees around it were giving off more reflection.

They banged the ship down in the flat place about a hundred yards from the front door.

It was very dark. Crickets were making an eerie sound. A bullfrog made a snoring noise in the creek. Fireflies were winking here and there. The smell of Connecticut countryside swept in through the airlock.

Captain Stabb reached over an Antimanco pilot's shoulder and twiddled a knob of a screen. A fragmentary infrared view of the porch showed up.

Raht seemed to be lying at the foot of the steps, face down. He apparently had passed out. A partially seen mass was on the porch itself. Raht had evidently not had the strength to move Heller's body.

"Busting novas, look at that!" cried Captain Stabb. He was pointing eagerly at a sack on the porch. Diamonds had cascaded from it. A glittering spread even in infrared light!

"Jeeb!" barked Stabb to an engineer, "get over there and pick those up!"

The engineer threw a blastrifle over his shoulder. He leaped out of the airlock and we heard his footsteps recede.

I moved over to the airlock. The tug was lying, of course, on its belly, and it was only a step to the ground. But I sure wasn't going out there.

My eyes adjusted from the dim red glow inside the tug. There was quite a bit of light, actually: the glow of distant cities against the sky and the glimmer from the sliver of a moon.

I watched Jeeb, rifle ready, approach the foot of the porch.

The fireflies winked. The frog croaked again. An eerie scene though. I wondered if it were true that the bodies of dozens of Prohibition gangsters were buried in this terrain. Gods deliver us from their ghosts.

Chapter 2

Jeeb was bending over the object at the foot of the steps. I could see him clearly.

Suddenly he straightened up and started to shout back at the tug. "This isn't . . ."

A sharp hissing crack!

Jeeb fell apart!

The whole middle of his body was gone!

I hastily withdrew back into the tug.

"A SNIPER!" screamed Stabb. "There he is! There he is! After him!"

He was pointing at the screen. The infrared had a picture of a man with a rifle at the end of the roadhouse.

The second engineer sprang out the door. He had his blastrifle ready at the hip. He raced off to one side, mauling the sight controls. I knew what he was doing. He was setting it to infrared.

He ran sideways about twenty-five yards.

He leaped behind a shrub. He levelled his weapon and fired. A blastrifle does not flash as it shoots, but splashes of deadly energy laced into the target.

Then Stabb was pointing at the screen, trying to shout. On the screen there had appeared THREE MORE INFRARED TARGETS!

The second engineer blazed away.

TWO MORE TARGETS!

Suddenly the second engineer let out a piercing scream.

He leaped into the air.

HIS WHOLE HEAD BLEW OFF!

"Quick, (bleep) it!" cried Stabb to the two pilots. "Grab weapons, set them to body heat and wipe that area flat!"

The two pilots hurtled out the door, slapping at the tops of their weapons.

They spaced out to the right and left.

They dropped into cover.

Stabb had slid into the pilot seat. He was twisting scope dials. He had it on body heat.

A target to the right of the roadhouse.

The pilot furthest from us fired.

A heat target to the left. The furthest pilot fired again.

A heat target much further to the left.

The pilot began to fire on automatic.

Suddenly he let out a shriek.

He leaped into the air.

The whole hip area vanished!

The other pilot was firing hysterically.

Heat target after heat target was popping up all over the field.

Frantically he tried to zero in on them.

Abruptly he screamed and leaped up into the air.

His head and torso disintegrated!

"LET'S GET OUT OF HERE!" cried Stabb.

He was in the local-pilot seat.

I leaped to the star-pilot seat.

Stabb was pulling levers and pushing buttons.

NOTHING HAPPENED!

We were earthbound!

The tug controls wouldn't operate!

Stabb's eyes glazed.

Then he stood up. He looked at me. "You led us into a trap, Officer Gris!" he snarled. "And I'll be dead in minutes. But I've got just one more job to do." He was reaching to his belt and withdrawing a knife and from the way he looked at me, I knew what he intended. He was going to kill me!

I grabbed at my control star. I pressed the top prong, that should have given him an electric shock.

NOTHING HAPPENED!

I hit the center and pressed the top again. It should have thrown him into a trance.

NOTHING HAPPENED!

"Lombar Hisst," said Captain Stabb, "gave me orders that if you fouled up I was to kill you out of hand."

THE UNKNOWN ASSASSIN HAD BEEN CAPTAIN STABB!

He raised the blade to plunge it into my chest.

The expression on his face froze.

He suddenly folded up over a pilot seat, a long Knife Section knife protruding from his back!

Someone had thrown it through the airlock!

Chapter 3

Footsteps.

Somebody was coming.

I was trying to get at my gun.

"Just sit there quietly, Gris. I can see in there but you can't see me."

HELLER'S VOICE!

His ghost!

Oh, Gods. I began to shake with every bone.

"Unfasten that gunbelt and throw it out the door."

Moaning, I did just that.

"Put your hands high in the air."

I did that quickly. I was facing front. I did not dare turn and look. I did not know what seeing a ghost would do to my psyche.

A light footstep behind me.

Suddenly a piece of line went around my wrists. They were snapped down. Coils of line went around my body and I was wrapped to the pilot seat and tied.

More footsteps. In the pilot viewports I could see the reflection of the ghost going back through the passageways, kicking open doors, ready to fire if anyone else was there.

Another voice. "So you were trying to get me killed, just like you did my partner, Terb."

RAHT!

I looked sideways. There he was in solid flesh, his mustache bristling out on either side below his nose. He was holding a gun on me!

"Traitor!" I rasped.

"Oh, no, Gris. You're the traitor. When you lured that beautiful woman to her death, you turned my stomach. And ordering me to murder a Royal officer! You must be crazy!"

"Then he's not dead? He's not a ghost?"

Raht gave a nasty, squeaky laugh. "He's no ghost. He's a REAL officer, the kind you never could be. When he left for Italy, I followed him. I knew he was out of range of the bugs you had on him and I told him what had been going on. He showed me his orders. From the Grand Council, too.

"So I came back here ahead of him, gave the old blind woman a note that her niece read to her, and came on through and set this all up like we planned."

"You mean he actually trusted you out there with a rifle?"

"I didn't have any rifle. Those were just flash charges I set up. I called, he came out. I ignited one by the door. Then another one by a bush. Then he fired and I ignited a third, all by remote. I simply shut off the visio switch on the activator-receiver. And your viewer went blind. Then he threw down a piece of iron so you'd think his gun had fallen and he stamped his foot so it sounded like a body and I cut off the audio switch."

"You mean, you turncoat, that you also set up this battle?"

"No, no. He did that when he knew that you were deaf and blind. He put infrared illusions all around and body heat simulators, all remote. We controlled them from way over in the woods. We were nowhere near you! Oh, he's a real officer, he is—a joy to work with one for a change. Nothing like the trash you are. Terb has been avenged!"

I was still confused. "Why did those men leap up in the air with a shriek?"

"Oh, that was his secret weapon. It found and clawed each man in turn. A remote-controlled, radio-directed cat."

Heller's voice behind me: "Get up there, Mister Calico. Sit on his chest and if he moves or speaks, hit him."

The cat sprang up into the spaceship. It sailed onto my chest. It sat there glaring balefully at me.

I opened my mouth to speak.

The cat raked my face with savage claws.

"I think he knows," said Raht, "that you had a hand in killing his mistress. I'd watch out if I were you. That's a hit cat to end them all! It scares me to death!"

I looked down into its close-up baleful eyes.

It was sort of snarling down deep.

I did not dare move.

Chapter 4

Heller said, "Let's get this battlefield cleaned up, Agent Raht. Those shots might attract visitors."

He picked up the corpse of Stabb and dragged it out through the airlock. They worked outside and I could see them making a pile of bodies. I shuddered. I was certain they were going to kill me, too.

Heller came back in. He went into the crew quarters, as I could see in the reflecting port glass. He came out lugging a trash-disintegrator unit. He carried it over to the pile and small blue lights began to glow around the bodies as buttons and bits of metal momentarily resisted disintegration.

An intermittent flash of light appeared on the track to the road-house. It grew stronger. A car! The deputy sheriffs were coming in!

Oh, thank Gods, I would be saved! They would see the space-ship and come over, and I would yell at them that I was a Federal agent and order them to arrest Heller and Raht. I even had my Inkswitch I.D. with me. I wasn't going to be exterminated here after all! I'd even have Heller on a Code break.

The car lights bored straight at the spaceship. Then they veered off and pointed toward the front of the roadhouse.

The cops jumped out on either side of their car. Heller walked up to them.

Ralph said, "Having trouble here, whitey engineer?"

They weren't even looking at the spaceship. And then I realized with a sickening comprehension that it was that (bleeped) absorbo-coat—it hadn't even reflected their car lights back to them. To all intents and purposes, the tug was invisible!

Heller was closer to them now. George said, "We heard some shots and screams."

"Wildcat," said Heller.

"No (bleep)?" said Ralph.

"Must've come down from Canada," said George.

"We missed him clean," said Heller. "He ran down the creek bed, thataway." He was pointing.

The two deputies rushed off down the creek, drawing their guns. They went right off, leaving their car lights on! I groaned. Well, maybe when they came back they'd see something unusual and rescue me.

Heller was stuffing diamonds in the gunny sack on the porch. He tied the neck and threw it in the jeep.

He and Raht went into the house and shortly began to dolly out boxes from the deep mine shaft. They piled them outside the airlock.

Heller came in and spoke to the floorplates in the passageway. It was sort of eerie how the locks were tuned to his voice. "Hold hatch, open up," he said, and the floorplates flopped back with a clang.

He lowered himself down into the limited hold of the tug. In the reflecting glass, I saw him pop back almost instantly. "What's this?" he said. He was holding a sack he'd found. He opened it and peered at the contents. "Junk stones?" It was the flawed glitter I had bought in Switzerland to fool Captain Stabb. Heller took it to the airlock and tossed it to Raht.

He went back into the hold. He came up in a moment. "What the blazes?" He was carrying something heavy. He went to the airlock. "Of all things," he said to Raht. "There's about 750 pounds of gold ingots down there."

I felt like my skull had exploded. Stabb! He was the one who had stolen my first gold shipment. He'd hidden it in the tug hold, meaning probably, when he got a chance, to do away with me and steal the tug.

"Isn't that an awful lot of gold for this planet?" said Raht.

"It sure is," said Heller. "Worth about seven million dollars at current prices. We'll take it out of its boxes and you stack it on the floor of the jeep. Transfer it to my Porsche at the old lady's. She won't be able to see what it is."

I groaned again. Raht hadn't even killed the old lady. What a rotten Apparatus agent. He ought to be fired!

"That makes me nervous," said Raht. "That's an awful lot of money."

"Hand it over to my financial advisor, Izzy Epstein. He'll know what to do with it," said Heller. "Give me a hand and we'll load it."

They passed it out of the hold. Raht drove the jeep over, turned it around so the lights pointed at the house and they put the gold down on the back floorboards.

The deputies were coming back. I prayed they'd notice the black bulk of the tug and come over.

Heller went to meet them, very visible in the combined lights of the sheriff's car and the jeep.

"Didn't find him," said Ralph.

"Found his tracks, though," said George. "He's a big'un. Mind if we come over hunting him tomorrow?"

"Come ahead," said Heller. "As Maysabongo marines, you can hunt around here all you please. Just remember to wear your stars."

The deputy sheriffs went to their car. They got in. When they turned it around their headlights in the viewscreen almost blinded me!

They drove off and the bouncing haze of lights vanished from view. There was one chance gone. I still, however, had hopes. Suddenly I remembered the controls of the tug didn't work. It would be here all night and tomorrow in daylight it would be visible. A crowd would gather and I could yell to them I was a kidnapped Fed.

Heller and Raht were locking up the roadhouse.

They came back and began to pass boxes down into the hold.

Heller took the last one and turned it over and opened the wrong side.

A false bottom! So that was where he had gotten the blastgun to shoot the Antimancos with! That original cargo had had false-bottomed boxes! We had missed it on Voltar. He was taking some items out. He laid them in the airlock. Then he manhandled the rest of the box down into the hold. He was in there a while and I could hear him pulling things around, probably lashing things tight.

He came back and took up a unit he had taken from the box and handed it to Raht. "You give this to Izzy. It's a viewer-phone on a wavelength they've never heard of on this planet. I already pried the nameplates off, so tell him it's something I invented and it won't be any Code break. I'd appreciate it if you got this to him tonight. He can call me by pressing this button here. I couldn't say much over the phone from the plane as NSA monitors all those calls. I want to hear from him just as soon as possible. Got it?"

"Yes, sir," said Raht. "Won't he see you're in a spaceship?"

"I'll hold the camera low at my end. He'll only see my face and some pipes over my head. He's sort of used to me being in odd places anyway. He's already got a Voltarian time-sight in a locked box, so he's taken the security oath. Tell him that applies to this as well. We've still got an awful lot to do and he'll be pretty upset if he doesn't hear."

"Got it, sir," said Raht. I was nauseated. The traitor hadn't ever said "sir" to me.

Heller came over. He picked up the cat and set it on the instrument ledge. He said to me, "Agent Raht tells me that amongst other things you've had him on reduced pay and no allowances. Is that right?"

"Serves him right," I snarled. "He's a bungling idiot! And now that he's turned his coat, he'll sell you out too!"

Raht, in the airlock, said, "Don't you talk about being a traitor. You've broken every law in the book! All I've done is bring you to justice!"

Heller was ignoring this. He was going through my pockets even though I tried to squirm away. He found wads of paper and my wallet. I went absolutely cold. The Squeeza credit card I had recovered from Krak was in it. It had Heller's Empire State Building address written on the back. If he found that he'd know I was directly connected to his girl's death. He would murder me!

He was looking through the papers. He found a requisition blank. He filled it in, a restoration of Raht's pay and allowance with back pay. He took my identoplate and stamped it. He handed it to Raht to turn in to the New York office of the base.

Heller said to Raht, "I understand he promised you ten thousand dollars for the hit."

Raht shook his head. "No, sir, I don't want that."

"Well, here it is anyway," said Heller. He opened up the wallet and I prayed that he would miss that card. He removed ten one-thousand-dollar bills from my cash and handed them to Raht. "Buy a wreath for Terb's grave and get yourself some new clothes."

It infuriated me. I said, "I've got the laugh on you. You're not going to get out of here. This tug's controls won't operate. You're stuck!"

"Oh, thanks for reminding me," said Heller. He went out and dug around in the dirt and came back with a cylinder. It was emitting a faint buzz. He switched it off and threw it in a cabinet. "The only reason I called you in here," he said, "was I needed the tug. You landed on an engine-control cancellation coil that operated the moment you opened your airlock. You stupidly had it open already when you landed. Only the air cushion kept you from crashing. Stupid Antimancos."

"I got their I.D. plates," said Raht. "You want them?"

"Throw them in that drawer," said Heller. "They're probably false anyway. Unless I miss my guess they were ex-subofficers from the Fleet, probably under condemnation to death and grabbed by the Apparatus."

"Can you really run this tug all by yourself?" said Raht.

Heller reached down to a floorplate and pulled it up. An array of buttons and controls I had never seen before were disclosed. He was closing switches and activating it. "That captain was a know-it-all," said Heller. "Typical subofficer gone bad. I tried to tell him the day we left Voltar that in her refit I had had her totally robotized. But he didn't seem to want to listen. I thought it might come to this. She doesn't need a crew. I'll be all right."

Raht was pointing at me tied up in the star-pilot chair. "What you going to do with him?" I could see it in his eyes that he thought it would be a good idea to take me out and shoot me.

"Regulations state," said Heller, "that if at all feasible an officer found involved in crimes should be taken to the nearest base for an officer's conference trial. I'll deliver him to the base in Turkey with your evidence affidavits and mine and they can handle him."

My blood turned into slush. The Afyon base commander, Faht Bey, was just waiting for such a chance! They'd find me guilty in a second and execute me in the most painful possible way.

My wits were racing. Oh, there must be some way to get out of this!

I was facing death for sure!

Heller! Gods, how he had tricked me. And he was riding high. I did not know what he had in mind now to finish his mission but I knew it would be a catastrophe for Rockecenter and therefore Lombar. Well, to Hells with them! I had to think of ME!

Wait, wait. Suddenly I had a surge of hope.

At the Afyon base I had spread the rumor that Heller was under orders to kill them: They would shoot him if they saw him. I had taken care of that.

And Voltar? Why, Lombar hated Heller and Lombar was now in control of the entire Voltar Confederacy!

Heller was not home safe at all!

He was the one at risk.

All I had to do was con him in some way and stay alive and I would win completely in the end.

I would pretend to be cooperative. I would pretend to be his friend. I would lead him in some brilliant way straight to his doom.

My confidence began to return. I would think of something. All was very far from lost.

I almost laughed aloud. Heller and his Royal-officer ways— he'd be the dead one in the end.

Heller was bidding Raht goodbye.

Raht gave him a formal crossed-arm salute, admiration beaming from his face.

Heller closed the airlock.

He put the cat back on my chest.

Heller picked up a cordless microphone from the new controls that he had bared. "Take off and hold at altitude three hundred miles above New York," he told the tug.

It promptly and smoothly took off.

Heller went to the crew's galley and fixed himself a canister of hot jolt, which must have been his first taste of it in many months.

He came back to the other pilot chair, sat on its arm and watched the planet fall away.

Chapter 5

We were hovering at three hundred miles altitude, the lights of cities far below.

The cat sat upon my chest and glared at me, just aching to rake my face with its savage claws.

Heller had set a mate to Izzy's viewer-phone on the instrument ledge, the ball of the camera lens in it pointing past his face and up. He was waiting for Izzy's call. He was sitting in the local-pilot-maneuvering seat. He kept looking at the tug's instruments and then working a back scan of the space around.

"That's very odd," he said. "This panel is reading that there's a spaceship within a mile of us and I can't find it anywhere but in this warning light."

The breaker switch in my head! It was activating the emergency-collision light. Boltz had mentioned it. Heller must not suspect it was installed in me. He might have a hypnohelmet handy.

"Do you know if those assassin pilots took off?" asked Heller.

I was saved from discovery. And then a new inspiration hit me. Maybe in some way I could get him shot and escape. Yes, I could some way hide in the ship; he would go down the ladder and they'd see him and shoot him! "You better return to the Earth base," I answered. "The assassin pilots both took off after us. If you try to go further out than this, they'll kill you sure."

"I've got a job to do," said Heller. "I don't see their ships. This panel must be faulty." And he turned the warning light off.

"You'll get me killed," I said. "Those flying cannons can make nothing out of this unarmed tug."

"Get you killed?" said Heller. "That's a very attractive idea. The only reason you're alive right now is that you were too much of a coward to come out and fight when the others did. I told Raht you wouldn't."

"You're insulting me!" I said.

The cat raked me and I yelped.

"Don't push it, Gris," said Heller. "It was a very sad route that took you from an Academy man downhill to the 'drunks.' I never knew anyone could sink so low. I don't know what else you did to sabotage this mission or why you did it. And I'm not likely to forgive your luring the Countess Krak to her death. It's only regulations that I should return you to trial that keeps me from tossing you out that airlock."

I went giddy with the idea of falling three hundred miles and burning in the reentry to atmosphere—if I lived that long.

"It's no news to me that you are a fool," said Heller. "I knew that, that day in Spiteos. You requisitioned a blastick, obviously to kill poor Snelz. And you stood right there and let me swap an unloaded one for it with a simple sleight of hand, and you went right down and tried to fire it at Snelz.

"You tried to break me with some obvious thudder dice and didn't even know all you had to do was heat them up with shaking and they wouldn't work.

"We conned you left and right and I thought you were just a sort of demented idiot. I underrated you. You've got a vicious streak a light-year wide and a twist that ought to put you in an asylum.

"You must realize that from the first I have never been under your orders. If you recall, a combat engineer of the Fleet operates on his own cognizance. Under the authority of the Grand Council, I have been in charge of this mission from the first."

I saw an out. "What if the Grand Council revokes your orders?"

"They're in force until *I* am informed officially they have been revoked."

"You and your influence with the Grand Council," I sneered. "You and your (bleeped) code to Captain Roke!"

He looked at me. "Ah, so you *were* the one that ordered my suite raided at the Gracious Palms! You were looking for the platen! Raht didn't mention it. Well, there is no platen, Gris. The code contains only personal anecdotes that only he and I would know."

I kept very quiet. He did not know Captain Tars Roke had been sent to exile on Calabar. Let him dream. If he ever returned to Voltar, he was dead.

Somehow I must stay alive. My feet were hurting me. "If you want to deliver a prisoner that isn't dead, you better get me to a doctor. I'm probably coming down with gangrene or lockjaw."

"That would be a blessing," said Heller. "But what's the matter?"

"My feet. They got infected and have had no care. I'll probably die on you unless you get me to the Earth base."

He sighed. You weren't supposed to kill prisoners on their way to a trial. You were supposed to deliver them alive.

For a fleeting moment I thought he would take the tug to Turkey, for he was standing up.

He lifted the cat off my chest. He began to unwind the ties that held me to the star-pilot seat.

He stood back. "Strip," he said.

For a wild moment I wondered if I should take a chance. There was no gun in his hand. Maybe if I lunged . . .

Just in time I realized he was laying a trap. He wanted an excuse to shoot me.

Shaking, I began to get out of my clothes.

"Phew!" he said. "Blazes, Gris, don't you ever bathe? The air was starting to clean up after the Antimancos, and now smell it."

"It smells all right to me," I said defensively.

"It would to a 'drunk,'" said Heller. "Look at that."

The cat was sneezing!

Heller eyed me with contempt. "Now, pick up those clothes, all of them, and dump them in that disintegrator. No, not your wallet, idiot."

Weakly, I surrendered it. He might find that Squeeza credit card, and that would lead him to discover that I had first kidnapped and then killed the Countess Krak. I felt quite ill.

I threw my ski suit in the disintegrator and followed it with my other clothes. I was naked except for the bandages on my feet.

He wasn't even pointing a gun at me. He herded me into the crew's shower and made me bathe, even wash my hair.

That done, he made me limp into the small crew first-aid room and lie down on the table. He yanked straps tight across my throat and hips and knees.

He got out a pair of cutters and I was afraid he was going to torture me. But he was only cutting the bandages off my feet.

"That's pretty bad," he said. "Festered. Whatever were you walking in?"

"Goat dung," I said.

He put on a pair of surgical gloves. It was obvious to me now that torture would begin.

He was holding up one foot and looking at the sole.

He said, "Watch him, cat," and went out. I heard him rummaging in a toolbox. I knew he was getting pincers to pull out my toenails and fingernails one by one and make me talk.

He came back in. He had a couple of small portable instruments. One had a label on it: *Metal Analyzer.* It had a light. He clicked it on and passed it over the suppurating sole of my foot. He looked at its dial.

"That must have been a very funny goat," he said. "It apparently fed on a diet of copper."

"What?" I said.

"The soles of your feet are full of little tiny slivers of copper. Small as powder, but slivers all the same. Copper is a deadly poison."

A shock went through me. "Prahd! He must have dusted it on the gauze bandages the first day!"

"Prahd Bittlestiffender?" said Heller. "The young cellologist back on Voltar? The one who must have put the bugs in my eye and ear?"

I must watch what I said. I shut my mouth tightly. And then I began to seethe with rage. Prahd had thought it would drive me back and beg to get treated and, under blackmail of making me pay the *kaffarah* to the violated wives and other things, he would remove the poison barbs, after I had paid.

Heller was working with the other device he had brought. "No, it didn't happen that far back," he said. "This is very recent."

I had a sudden idea. One that might work. "Prahd is at the Earth base. We could fly in and get him to remove those bugs from your head. We could start right now."

He wasn't answering. He was adjusting a dial. It said Paramagnetic, Diamagnetic, Ferromagnetic, on its switches.

"You're lucky," he said. "This copper is alloyed with iron. I think I can get them out."

He was passing the device over the soles of my feet and ankles, very slowly. He looked at it from time to time. The plate on it was getting covered with a reddish metallic fuzz. He wiped the plate off with a cloth and kept at it.

"Prahd must really have it in for you," he said. "But there's no mystery in that. But if he'd pull a trick like that, the only way I'd let him touch me again would be if somebody was holding a gun on him."

He made several more passes. He got no further splinters. He opened a cabinet and got out a neutralizing solution and, using a paint brush, painted my feet and ankles. Then he got some hull putty, sterilized it with a light and kneaded cell-growth cream into it. He put it on my feet so that I had a sort of cast on each one.

Then I suddenly realized his motive in all this: He was making my feet so heavy I would fall faster when he threw me out of the airlock. I recoiled into myself.

He was picking up the first device. "Now let's see if you got any on your hands or anyplace else."

He turned it on. He moved it toward my upper body. I froze in horror. If that detector had certain wavelengths it would show up the tattoo on my chest. That imprint under the right kind of light would make my breast read ROCKECENTER FAMILY SPI!*

---

* *This is the correct spelling. See "Spi" in the Key.*—*Translator*

According to regulations, when a spy was caught red-handed, he could be executed by any officer. All Heller had to do was see that thing and I wouldn't go to trial. He would be totally within his rights to just shoot me!

I watched the light in horror. He was playing it over my fingers. He found a few splinters and with the other device removed them.

My pupils dilated with terror as I watched the onward sweep of that light. He was examining the skin on my stomach.

I silently mouthed a prayer. I tried several Gods and even Jesus Christ. I was inches from death.

The light swept higher.

It played upon my chest.

I closed my eyes tightly. Probably the last thing I would know would be a bullet crashing through my brain.

He had found something on my chest!

I opened one eye. He was reaching for something. I knew it would be his gun.

I looked down.

The light was playing squarely on the spot of the tattoo!

It wasn't glowing.

The light he was using was not the right kind!

I had won my reprieve!

I wondered which God had granted it.

He was picking up a splinter with the other device.

He went to a cabinet and took out a disposable spacer's fatigue suit and threw it at me.

Devils, but that had been a close call! My heart just now resumed beating.

He undid the straps. I wrestled into the suit and stood up. He was motioning for me to go back to the flight area. And I discovered then what he had been up to: Each foot, with that putty now hardened, must have weighed thirty pounds! I could scarcely make my way.

He made me sit in the star-pilot chair. He had a pair of wrist shackles now. He fastened them around and through the arms of the seat and then put them on me.

A sudden unreasoning anger took hold of me. How dare he treat me this way? I was his superior officer. I could wriggle out of any charge he brought against me. After all, Lombar Hisst now controlled the whole Voltar Confederacy!

I had to solve the predicament I was in. He didn't know he was dealing with the next Chief of the Apparatus!

"You can't do this to me," I flared. "I've only done my duty."

He looked at me and for the first time I saw real scorn. "Duty? You don't know the meaning of the word, Gris. You think that indulging your own greed and self-aggrandizement comprises duty? Don't sully the word by saying it. Duty has to do with meeting one's moral obligations. I don't see the slightest trace of morality in you. Get one thing straight: You're only sitting there so the cat and I can keep an eye on you. I can put you in suspension with one shot from the medical chest. Would you rather have that?"

I shook my head. But I still seethed. One way or the other, I would get the better of him yet!

Chapter 6

Heller was fiddling with some connection terminals in the overhead. He had a small wire from the viewer-phone leading up to some clips and he was shifting it from one clip to the next, looking back at the unit whose mate he had given to Izzy.

"Come on, Izzy," he said somewhat impatiently. "I don't think there's anything wrong with these exterior beam antennas, but I better check."

He went to the area where he'd emptied out some items and came back with a portable Earth TV set. He hooked up a wire from it to the overhead clips and turned it on. It was an evening talk show. Senator Twiddle was being interviewed.

"So you see, the increase in the price of gasoline," said Senator Twiddle, "is a very good thing for the American economy. It encourages sitting home and watching TV and so will restore American family life."

"I understand," said the interviewer, "that Octopus Oil is raising its price at the pump again. How will this benefit people, Senator?"

"Make them more industrious," said Twiddle. "They will have to work overtime to afford enough gas to get them to work. Sloth is the enemy of the American Dre——"

Heller had turned it off. "Hm. The antenna is all right even if the message isn't." He transferred the lead from the viewer-phone to another exterior antenna clip.

And there was Izzy! "Oh, dear, I hope I haven't broken this thing."

The cat jumped up on the ledge and studied the screen alertly. Izzy's horn-rimmed glasses had slid down on his beaked nose.

"Meow," said the cat.

"Oh, dear, yes," said Izzy, "I have broken it. Now I'm connected to the cat. Mr. Hopjoy, are you sure Mr. Jet told you the right buttons to push? First we got an abstract painting done with wires and now we've got the cat."

He was talking to agent Raht, whose face was visible over his shoulder. "No, he said that button there, Mr. Epstein."

Heller sat down in the local-pilot seat. "Hello, Izzy."

"Oh, thank heavens. It's Mr. Jet. I'm afraid I'm having a lot of trouble with this new invention of yours. It seems it can call anybody but you."

"It needs more developmental work," said Heller. "Listen, Izzy, I couldn't talk to you very openly from the plane. I had to have a better means of communication."

"Well, I am awfully glad you called, Mr. Jet. Mr. Hopjoy here delivered about seven million dollars' worth of gold. It's very odd gold: it doesn't have the smelter proofings stamped on it."

"Throw it in a vault," said Heller. "Use it if you need to."

"Where are you, Mr. Jet?"

"I'm just flying around," said Heller. "Izzy, did our Wonderful Oil for Maysabongo, Incorporated, acquire options to purchase all the oil reserves of the United States?"

"Oh, yes," said Izzy. "Every oil company granted them very easily. We even got options signed on all the army, navy and air-force oil reserves from the secretary of defense. They all made the final deal very quickly: It gave them extra money and they had no idea anyone would ever exercise such options. They thought the Republic of Maysabongo must have gone crazy. Nobody could afford that much money. Yes, Mr. Jet. We have tied up options to buy every drop of oil stored in the United States. All we have to do is exercise the options and Maysabongo owns every smear of it."

"Very well done," said Heller. "Now listen, Izzy. Get your ballpoint ready. I want you to acquire options to sell every share of stock of every oil company in the world."

"WHAT?"

"Don't you think you can get them?"

Izzy looked dazed. "Oh, we can buy the options to sell all right. Any big brokerage firm can write them and the Securities and Exchange Commission will enforce that they be honored. But you're talking about an awful lot of oil company shares, Mr. Jet."

"Figure it out."

Izzy grabbed some reference books and began to look up things and write:

Octopus current shares:	$30.7 billion
Octopus Oil of Indiana:	$19.6 billion
Octopus of California:	$15.4 billion
Immobil Oil:	$14.7 billion
Atlantic Bitchfield:	$13.7 billion
Octopus Oil of Ohio:	$13.7 billion
Smell Oil:	$13.6 billion
British Crude:	$13.5 billion
Foil Dutch:	$11.8 billion
Hexaco:	$10.5 billion
Gulp:	$ 7.2 billion
Fillups:	$ 7.0 billion
Disunion Oil of California:	$ 6.6 billion
Bumoco:	$ 6.4 billion
Betty:	$ 5.9 billion

He continued to write down figures and then looked up. "This adds up to over 190.3 billion dollars. That's a lot of money, Mr. Jet."

"How much will options to sell it cost?"

"Oh, just a tiny fraction of that. But if these shares go up, we'll just have thrown our money away."

"If they all went down ten dollars a share, what then?"

"If the options got exercised, we'd make about nineteen billion dollars."

"Those shares are going to drop more than that," said Heller. "Can you do the deal?"

"Oh, yes. I can buy July options to sell. If we don't exercise them before that time, they just expire. That's only a few weeks from now. How do you know all the oil shares of every company in the world will go down, Mr. Jet?"

"I guarantee it," said Heller. "Now, listen, you let me know when you've got all that in hand. Meanwhile I have a project. Good luck, Izzy."

"Good luck, Mr. Jet."

Oh, Gods, what was I looking at? What had I just heard? This was a direct attack to ruin poor Mr. Rockecenter! Oh, Gods of Gods, was I in trouble!

I hadn't the least idea what Heller was going to do. Bomb the oil nerve center of the world, Rockecenter Plaza?

Chapter 7

Heller disappeared into his quarters for a while. The cat watched me carefully. We didn't see eye to eye. I couldn't stand to look into those baleful orbs. Did the cat know I had killed the Countess Krak? It certainly was just waiting its chance to murder me.

When Heller came back he was dressed in the fatigue uniform of the Voltar Fleet: powder blue and form-fitting—his name, *Jettero Heller, Combat Engineer*, above his left breast pocket. I could see that suppressed grief had put him under strain but he was somehow carrying on. I felt that he was very dangerous to me. He was far from his usual smiling self. He was all business, an officer going to work.

He unlocked my wrist cuffs and then chained me round and round to a pipe behind the seats. "I've no place to sit down," I said. "Is this any way to treat a prisoner?"

"Would you like to go back to New York?" he said, pointing straight down. "Just say the word and I'll open the airlock for you."

I didn't have any more to say to that.

He closed the viewports, dropping their metal shields. Then he went through the ship, closing doors by speaking to them, and I could hear the clangs and grates of more metal plates shutting down.

Fear began to rise in me. Pilots closed ports against radiation belts. Was he going to depart from the planet itself? That would attract the assassin pilots!

He came back to the star-pilot chair and threw a lever. I knew what that one was: It turned the whole ship silver on the outside to repel ray bombardment.

He went back aft and returned with the other time-sight. He fitted it into place in the crutch and tube in front of the star-pilot seat. HE *WAS* GOING TO LEAVE THE PLANET!

"Whoa!" I said, feeling the sweat break out on my forehead. "The instant the assassin pilots see you turn silver they'll be on to you like hawks."

"Oh, them," he said.

And then I knew what I was up against. He really didn't care anymore. He had turned suicidal!

I felt small screams struggling to rise in my throat. One shot from one of those flying cannons and this tug would smash like a stamped-on tin can!

He looked at his screens. "I don't see any sign of them and the warning light is broken. If you're so worried about 'drunk' ships, keep your eye on that viewer there. I have other things to do."

He picked up the tug-control microphone. "Go up fifty thousand miles and sound a gong when we are through the magnetosphere."

That also scared me. The forty-thousand-mile-wide belt around the planet was composed of deadly radiation. I hoped he'd closed the port shields tight.

The tug auxiliary engines hummed. The high-pitched whine of gravity-adjustment coils impinged upon my ears. Used to Captain Stabb's rough handling, I had expected to stagger but I didn't even feel a change in weight. The tug handled itself very well. I hoped its robotbrain wouldn't suddenly go crazy.

I stared anxiously at the viewscreen. It made me a little dizzy to watch it. It was scanning in a sphere: The Earth was there and then the moon and then black space and then the sun.

We certainly were going up very fast. The moon turned yellow-yellow. The Earth began to look like a huge liquid bubble, blue-green except where continents were red-brown.

"Where are we going?" I said fearfully.

Heller was setting up an instrument. He had it hooked to an outside scanner.

"Are you looking for the assassin pilots?" I said.

"This is a gamma-ray-sensitive electron telescope," said Heller. "I'm searching for a primordial black hole. There may be quite a few in this system close by."

"The assassin pilots!" I said.

"That's your job," said Heller. "I'm busy."

Believe me, I fixed my eyes on that spherical scanner like I was hypnotized.

Time passed.

Suddenly a gong went. It scared me half out of my wits. We were through the magnetosphere. That was a relief, anyway: I wouldn't be sterilized or burned to a crisp.

I pinned my gaze on the scanner. Those assassin ships could catch us easily enough while we were on auxiliaries. I wished we were on the big time-converter Will-be Was engines. No, I didn't—they blew up sometimes!

Heller was busy with the gamma-ray telescope.

My own eyes were wearing out, anxiously watching the scanner. Earth swam like a liquid bubble. I could see no speck in that expanse which would identify the position of the assassin in his deadly ship.

Abruptly a voice spoke. I could not credit my senses. There were only two of us and the cat in the ship. Heller wasn't talking. I wasn't talking. Was the cat talking?

I mean to tell you, it was pretty rattling.

The voice came from nowhere.

Now that I could collect my suddenly dispersed wits, I realized it was speaking Voltarian.

"Sir, I am sorry to bother you, but in spherical sector X-19, Y-13, Z-91, an unidentified flying object has just altered course and speed and is parallelling ours, range 7,091.56 miles. The picture is on screen 31. If you will forgive my interruption of your doubtless far more important and intelligent considerations, I would take it as a favor if you were to look and give me your much more valuable opinion."

THE TUG WAS TALKING!

I flinched away from the side bulkhead. Was this thing made of flesh and blood?

Heller hadn't lifted his eye from the telescope image-relay cup. "Thank you," he said. "Give me your estimate of possibilities."

"Estimate one: Friendly and coming over for a chat. Not likely. Estimate two: Curious. On its way to investigate. Estimate three: Hostile. On its way to shoot at us. My inputs are blank on the subject of Fleet vessels in the area of Blito-P3, likewise Apparatus, likewise commercial. I am afraid, sir, that I am anemic from lack of input concerning space vessels in this system. Bis, when he loaded me, mentioned primitive space efforts but none of it compares here. I am sorry, sir."

"Thank you. Riffle your recognition bank."

"At once, sir. I must advise you, however, that the range is very great as yet, though closing. My image is very indistinct."

"It's probably absorbo-coat," said Heller, still studying his telescope.

"Oh, thank you, sir. That throws out 87.9 percent of the bank. I'll scan the rest."

I stared at my viewer. I couldn't see anything. Here I had been wearing my eyes out and the (bleeped) tug had been looking all the time! Not only that, it had spotted something I hadn't. I began to seethe with rage at it. One does not like to be beaten by a silly robot! It destroys one's sense of omnipotence!

"You have somebody on my flight deck," the tug said, "who is emanating hostility. Could I advise a word of caution, sir?"

"He's crazy," said Heller, still working with his telescope.

"Yes, sir. I will add that category to the classification."

I choked down my wrath.

"You might as well add him to your memory," said Heller. "He is Officer Soltan Gris, Secondary Executive of the Coordinated Information Apparatus, en route to trial for high crimes including the ordering of the murder of a Royal officer and the sabotage of a Grand Council–ordered mission."

"How dreadful," said the tug. "I have the Penal Code references of those crimes, sir, if you want the numbers."

"Just add his picture to your bank and sound an alarm if he does anything destructive," said Heller.

I heard a click somewhere as though somebody had operated a camera. I had never felt so much a prisoner in my whole life. I was in the guts of a robot. Would it digest me?

"On this other matter," said the tug, "my forty-third subbrain has been winking for attention. On the unidentified flying object, the range has closed to 6,789.078 miles. It is not responding to a demand for recognition. It is definitely estimate three: hostile."

"Classify," said Heller.

"Flying cannon. Such vessels are used by the Apparatus as assassin ships. In the reign of——"

"Thank you," said Heller. "What do you advise?"

"That I turn on the Will-be Was main drives and we depart from this locale, sir."

For once I could agree with this (bleeping) tug!

"No, I don't think that will be necessary," said Heller.

"Sir, may I remonstrate? Fleet Intelligence Officer Bis, when he loaded me, expressly stated that my first concern was your safety. In fact, sir, he said he would enter me as a failure on Fleet engineering rolls and would not rest until he had me and all models like me junked if you came to harm while aboard me. The range is 4,506.8 miles now and closing."

"What is his effective range of fire?"

"Against a battleship, about two miles. Against such a fragile thing as me, sir, about ten miles, with slight damage to be experienced at twenty."

"We've got lots of time," said Heller.

"Oh, dear," said the tug. "I wish to also call to your attention that my fifty-seventh subbrain just reported that it's 22.7 light-years to the nearest repair yard."

"There're facilities at the Earth base," said Heller.

"No Earth base is in my recordings, sir. I will amend the

fifty-seventh subbrain instantly. By 'Earth' you mean Blito-P3, sir?"

"Yes."

"I think I've got one," said Heller. "Corky, record the coordinates I've just set on this telescope. Primordial black hole."

"Yes, sir. I have them. My twenty-third subbrain says that primordial black holes are notorious for sucking unwary vessels in, sir. Formed by the initial shock which, in theory, determined the pattern of this universe, they are suction whirlpools of magnetic force and distort time and space. The exudation of gamma rays can also be quite deadly. . . ."

"Why are you telling me this?"

"It's in Fleet Intelligence Officer Bis's loaded instructions, sir. To keep you safe."

"Where is the flying cannon now?"

"He has closed to 735.86 miles, sir. Could I, in all deference, point out that we have a primordial black hole in front of us that we are drawing closer to and an assassin ship behind us that is closing. My thirteenth subbrain has concluded this is not a safe situation, sir. Do you mind if I take over and we get the Hells out of here?"

"I'm going to shut you off and go on manual," said Heller.

"Oh, dear. But of course I realize that my piloting skill can never compare with yours. However, going up against a flying cannon with an unarmored, unarmed tug is . . ."

Heller threw a switch. The voice stopped. "Robots are too cautious," he said.

"The tug is right!" I wailed. "We'll be blown right out of space!"

"Where is this guy?" said Heller. He was leaning toward screen 31. He was buckling himself into the planetary-pilot seat, used for local maneuvering.

I looked at my chains around the pipe. I remembered what Heller had told me the very first time I had ridden in this tug. The maneuverability of such a ship was so sudden one could easily snap his neck.

"What about me?" I wailed. "If you go whipping this thing around you could smash me to pulp!"

"Good riddance," said Heller. "Sit down on the floor and hold on."

Just before he fastened his last strap, he reached up and threw the shields off the pilot viewports. A blast of savage sunlight almost blinded me.

I heard the click of Heller's last strap fastener.

The tug suddenly spun about and faced the other way.

My light-dazzled eyes could make out nothing as I looked anxiously toward the globe of Earth.

There was a sudden surge.

HELLER WAS GOING BACK TO MEET THE ASSASSIN SHIP!

We didn't even have a gun!

Yes, indeed, he had turned suicidal!

PART
SIXTY-THREE
Chapter 1

Heller sent Tug One hurtling through space.

"You're going to get us killed!" I screamed. Frantically, I looked to see if there was some way I could get the shackles off the pipe and free my wrists.

He was closing with the flying cannon at a dreadful rate. I could see the speck now, by naked eyeball, through the pilot ports. It was growing in size!

It packed an enormous gun, capable of smashing a battleship's plate to old tin. What would it do to this small space tug?

Heller began to jink. Hands rapid on the tug's local-maneuvering controls, he was sending it up and down and side to side erratically. He was changing speeds from a hundred thousand miles an hour down to fifty and back!

The gravity coils that made it possible to ride this thing were not as fast as Heller's hands. There was a lag each time and even if it was only a split second, it was enough to shake me to bits!

The cat was holding on to the star-pilot seat with every claw. Even its skin looseness was apparent in these sudden surges and slows.

"Yow!" said the cat.

"Don't be concerned," Heller said. "This tug is all engines and made to do this sort of thing. That flying cannon has to pivot his whole ship to aim and shoot. I think we'll be too quick for him."

"You THINK?" I cried. "Oh, Goddess of the Seventh Sphere, prepare to take me to your breast and hold me there in peace."

"Shut up!" said Heller. "If you're going to pray, the Devils are more likely to listen to——"

WHAM!

The first shot from the assassin ship exploded to our right, a blossom of green fire, blinding bright against the ink of space. It whipped behind us.

A readout screen said the lethal vessel was only fifteen miles away.

WHAM!

The tug jarred as a shot above us barely missed.

The assassin pilot was eight miles ahead.

WHAM!

Something seemed to pound against our hull below.

The assassin was two miles below.

The tug stood on its nose. Made to push and tow enormous weights, unfettered it was like a chip in a hurricane under Heller's hands.

WHAM!

The shot was short by five hundred yards. We flashed through the blossom.

I felt like I was caught in a pinwheel. Our motions were far beyond what gravity coils could handle.

Black space.

The sun gone by in a streak.

A sudden glimpse of the moon.

"YOW!" said the cat, holding on.

Oh, horned Devils of the Sixteenth Hell, please receive me and don't let me move again for an eternity! Anything I had ever done did not deserve being in the hands of a Voltar Fleet combat engineer bent on suicide!

The tug seemed to be skidding sideways.

Abruptly the slew stopped.

STRAIGHT IN FRONT OF US, NOT TEN YARDS AWAY, WAS THE PORT SIDE OF THE FLYING CANNON!

Heller hit a throttle.

CRUNCH!

The butting bow of the tug, its wide arms made to push ships, thudded straight up against the flying cannon's hull!

I stared in horror through the viewport.

The flight deck of the assassin ship was not ten feet in front of our viewports!

The tug's nose was hard against the vessel.

There was a rending grind of metal as the killer ship tried to accelerate away!

The assassin pilot was right there, red gloves and all! He was glaring into our very viewports!

He shook his fist!

His copilot fired the gun to give them recoil to try to shake loose.

The tug was pressing against the other vessel's side, holding tight as a leech.

Heller's hand slammed against the throttles.

The assassin pilot's brutal face went white as chalk.

He was being thrust sideways.

He couldn't get free.

Heller's hand reached over for the Will-be Was main drives. He pushed.

The tug leaped ahead!

A terrible sound of rending metal transmitted through our hull.

The inertia of the flying cannon's weight fought against the tug's acceleration.

SCREEECH! BONG!

The assassin ship disintegrated.

Heller flipped the tug upside down.

Through the viewport I could see the squashed hull, shedding fragments.

Two pale pink mists were all that was left of the assassin pilots, exploded by the vacuum of space.

"You all right?" said Heller. I thought he was talking to me. I started to answer and then realized that his question was aimed at the cat.

"Yow," said the cat.

"I'm sorry," said Heller. "But you'll just have to get used to it now that you are a member of the Voltar Fleet."

Chapter 2

We were drifting in black space amidst the wreckage of the assassin ship. The Earth was a liquid ball below, fifty thousand miles away.

Heller threw on the robot's switch. "Check any hull damage, Corky."

"You should not have shut off my voice. I could have given you some pointers."

I looked around. I wasn't able to tell where the tug's voice was coming from. It was sort of spooky.

"Longitudinal seams entirely sundered, engines cracked, ammunition magazine——"

"Corky," said Heller, "NOT the flying cannon. Check your own damage."

"Oh, I am sorry, sir. The question was inadequately specific—meaning no criticism, sir. Please advise if you wish the data verbal or in printout form on your desk in the aft salon."

"Heavens," said Heller, "is it that extensive?"

"I am not used to working with you yet, sir. Your wish is necessary on certain matters. A question of substantive preference. My input expressly states that I am to make you happy if at all possible. Could I have an answer, please? My twenty-second subbrain is on hold."

"Verbal and printout," said Heller. "But let me have the data, please."

"There are two small scratches on the butting arms, sir. One is

3.4 inches long, 1/16 of an inch wide. The other is 2.7 inches long and 1/8 of an inch wide. Yard cost will be 2.7 credits."

"Is that all?"

"Well, yes, sir, but 'Is that all?' is inadequately descriptive. The absorbo-coat is breached and enemy detection gear will reflect from it. I suggest that this matter be handled at the earliest opportunity so that I can execute my actual purpose of preserving you from harm."

"You're a chatterbox," said Heller.

"Chatterbox . . . chatterbox . . . chatterbox . . . No, sir. I don't have any such part, sir, and all gears are firm. I am a Mark XIII humanoid-approximation robot manufactured in——"

"Thank you," said Heller. "Any data you have on current ship condition is required."

"Yes, sir. I am fine, sir. How are you?"

"Fine," said Heller. "Is that end of data on ship condition?"

"There is another datum on hold in the eighty-fifth idling memory. I will give you that, sir. Two locational bugs were installed in me, one on the nose, the other on the tail, while I was idle."

"Ho, ho," said Heller. "So that's how the assassin pilot found me. Is there any sign of the other flying cannon?"

"I have no ships on my screens, sir."

"Very good. Take over control. Stay alert for the second ship. Proceed at low speed toward the coordinates of the black hole earlier recorded from the telescope. Don't make sudden divergences from course. I will be working inside and outside of the ship."

"Yes, sir. I am engaged on controls now, sir."

We began to move in relation to the scattered debris of the flying cannon.

Heller pointed at me and told the cat, "Watch him." He then went to a locker and began to get out a pressure suit. He inspected it with care and then he put it on.

He got some tools, a paint brush and paint squirter. He went into the airlock and closed it behind him.

I could hear his magnetic boots clumping on the hull, the sound carried through the metal.

Then I got an awful start. His face appeared on the other side of the viewport, looking into the flight deck.

People in space helmets always look so unearthly, it makes one think of monsters. And to me, Heller was a monster anyway. He had plotted ceaselessly to do me in, he had murdered in cold blood the Antimanco crew, he had just shaken me up like dice in a cup with his insane, suicidal attack on that assassin pilot and here I was, chained to a pipe like some wild animal, completely at his mercy.

I must think of something and do something to get myself out of this. It would only be justice to do Heller in. Somehow I must still accomplish it. I was pretty certain that I could.

Chapter 3

After about half an hour he came back in through the airlock and got out of his pressure suit.

He came back to the flight deck. He had two objects in his hand. He tossed them at me and they rattled against the bulkhead. "You knew those bugs were there, I am sure," he said. "Sitting on that secret could have cost you your life."

"I didn't think it was important," I said. "The fact that you have taken these off won't prevent the second pilot from finding us. They can spot the spacial turbulence of your drives. The moment you go near that planet again, the other one will pick us up." I had a sudden wild idea. "Why not just deliver me to Voltar?"

I scarcely dared breathe, watching him. If I could con him into taking me back home, I would be free and clear. Lombar Hisst hated him and Lombar, unbeknownst to Heller, now controlled even the Emperor.

"You're the least of my worries," said Heller. "I've got other things to do. I've got to get ready for this black hole."

I shuddered. That could be dangerous. "What do you care about this planet Earth anyway?" I said. "Why don't you just go home and forget it."

"It's a pretty planet," said Heller. "If I don't complete my mission, it will become uninhabitable. In another century or less, it will be so chewed up it won't even support life. Don't you care what happens to five billion people?"

"Riffraff," I said.

He raised his eyebrows. "Well, I guess one sees in others what he finds in himself," said Heller.

I seethed at the insult. Didn't he realize that he was talking to the future Chief of the Apparatus? Oh, I'd get even with him before this was over!

He opened a door into the engine rooms and propped it back. From where I was chained, I could watch him. He was doing something very peculiar indeed. On Voltar, an enormous spare time-converter drum had been put in the tight space. They had even opened the top of the hull to get it in. He had a wrench and he was working at the entry port into the huge drum.

The sign clearly said it mustn't be touched, that it would blow your hand off if you even reached in. And he was unbolting it.

"You'll blast us apart!" I shouted.

He didn't pay me any heed at all. He got off the big plate and calmly reached in!

I flinched as I waited for his arms to disintegrate.

They didn't.

He was pulling out a large object in wrappings. He carried it to the pilot deck and stripped it.

A LASER CANNON!

Oh, the sneaky Devil! That wasn't a time-converter spare at all! It was simply a way to put aboard equipment and hide it from the view of everyone.

He opened some plates in the overhead. He slid the laser cannon on to already prepared mounts. He shoved its nose into a forward space that would open if it fired.

He went back and got a second device. I did not know what it was. He bolted it in place beside the cannon.

"Why didn't you install that before we had to fight the assassin ship?" I wailed.

"Oh, these devices aren't cannon, exactly," he said. "They wouldn't have done much to that ship."

I blinked. They certainly looked like cannons. He was connecting them up to a set of controls on the panel that resembled firing controls.

He fastened down the plates in the overhead and the two devices were no longer in view.

Then he went back to the drum and began to take out what looked like the slats of a dismantled cage. He carried these to the airlock, where he stacked them up. He added some other items to that pile. Then he put the cover back on the drum.

He closed up the engine rooms and sat down at the telescope eyepiece.

"Now that," he said, "is a very nice primordial black hole. Corky, speed yourself up and get your scanners going on target object. Input all data into banks and calculate."

The tug did a forward surge.

"Are you going to shoot that black hole?" I said. The man was clearly insane. "It would drink up every round. You might even shoot us through the thing into another universe!"

"Oh, those devices up there aren't for the black hole. I'm just getting things ready," said Heller.

What was he up to? If I had some clue as to his plans, maybe I could make him do something so I could get him.

"Well, what do you need a black hole for?" I asked.

"Fuel," said Heller. "Cheap fuel. They'll need hardly any oil when I am done."

Oh, Gods, he was going pell-mell to do in Rockecenter! Didn't he realize that any solution to the energy problem would ruin the Rockecenter monopoly? I certainly had to think of something that would WORK!

"You hungry?" he said casually. I thought he was talking to me and then I realized he was addressing the cat.

"Meow," said the cat.

"Keep an eye on the prisoner, Corky," said Heller.

I railed at my shackles. First I was being watched by a cat and now I was being guarded by a robot tug! Was there no end to this calculated program of degrading me?

I could hear Heller down the passageway. "Now, this is the chief mate's room," he was saying to the cat. "You're promoted. Here's your pan so you can relieve yourself. And here's your pillow.

Here's your water bowl and here's your dish. Now, would you like a can of chicken or a can of tuna? All right, tuna it is."

I heard him then in the crew's galley, getting himself something to eat. He came back after a while, sipping at a canister of hot jolt. The cat came back, licking his chops. That did it.

"Aren't you going to feed me?" I said.

"I didn't know that riffraff deserved to eat," said Heller.

"You're insulting me," I said.

"I didn't think that was possible," said Heller, calmly sipping his hot jolt.

Rage burned in me. "According to regulations, prisoners must be fed!"

It worked. He handed me the hot-jolt canister.

I tipped it up.

It was empty!

"Gods, how you must hate me!" I snarled.

"Hate? That's a very strong word, Gris. One doesn't waste hate on a loathsome insect."

I gripped the canister so hard it crushed.

"Let's get one thing very clear," said Heller. "You lured my girl to her death. I am not even willing to go into the aft quarters of this ship because they remind me of her. You prate of duty and regulations: You had better cherish them. It is my duty to take you to trial. It is against regulations to kill a prisoner. Those are the only reasons you are alive, Gris. But I don't hate you. A thing has to amount to something to be hated. Now shut up, for I have work to do."

The cold, dispassionate contempt in his voice had been like an icy knife searching out my vitals. A new and horrible thought struck me. If he knew that I had personally killed the Countess Krak, even his sense of duty would not restrain him. I had not fully appreciated how much danger I really was in. Oh, I had better get myself out of this. I furrowed my brow in heavy concentration. I might never live even to get to trial!

Chapter 4

He said to the tug, "Keep an eye on your clocks so we don't accidentally collide with this thing."

"Yes, sir."

Fear stabbed me. "Is that the only way you're going to know before we hit? How could you read it on that telescope if there's a time shift?"

"This telescope has a miniature time-sight element in it, but they also leak some gamma rays direct. You seem awfully nervy."

"I am."

"Good," he said heartlessly. "Maybe you'll get the idea how other people feel when you put them in terror."

I ignored his moralizing. The Hells with how other people felt. Once you got to worrying about that, you never could serve in the Apparatus. Or live with yourself either. I lifted my head to see through the pilot ports. Nothing but black sky and, a long way off, something that might be an asteroid.

"Sir," said the tug, "I think I'd better brake down from fifty thousand miles an hour."

"Oh, Gods," I said. "Don't have a breakdown out here!"

"Sir, do you wish me to record the remarks of that hostile prisoner, Gris?"

"Store them in transient memory," said Heller. "He won't be with us long—or in this universe either, for that matter. Come down to easy braking speed."

"Yes, sir. I read that we may be only 203.4 miles from the black hole."

"Good. Keep comparison with your universal absolute clock and brake the instant we cross the time band."

"Yes, sir. I have a flashout here from my 123rd subbrain concerning the prisoner, Gris. It is reading purple: solution. It has been working on the problem. May I give it to you, sir?"

"Go ahead."

"In compliance with the purpose to keep you safe, it is recommended as follows: Prisoner guilty of capital crimes including the ordering of your death. List of bases does not include Blito-P3. A legal point could be stretched and we could plead we were unaware of the existence of an officers' conference at Blito-P3. Solution: On arrival at black hole, use him as a test and pitch him through to some other universe. Holding for acceptance of solution."

I glared all around me. Even this tug had turned against me! And what a sadistic tug it was! A monster!

"The idea has merits," said Heller. "However, the answer is negative."

"Sir, please reconsider. His brain waves show extreme hostility. If he is going to some other universe as you say, I see no reason to postpone the matter. Your negative is incompatible with the purpose on which I run and is therefore illogical."

"Store it for future reference. How close are we now to the black hole?"

"About thirty miles, sir."

Seconds ticked off. "Stand by for time shift, sir. I am braking hard."

Suddenly there was a dreadful physical wrench. My brain flashed and my heart skipped. The identical sensation one got when entering the gates of Palace City on Voltar. Blast, I hated it!

"The black hole is just three miles in front of us, sir. I am holding."

I stood up. I looked through the viewports. I couldn't see anything.

"There's nothing out there," I said.

Heller was slamming and locking the viewports.

"Well, you'd be doing pretty good to see it," said Heller. "It's no bigger than a proton. That's one of the reasons they never find these primordial black holes. The other one is we're now thirteen minutes in the future. Haven't you ever been in and out of Palace City?"

"I've been there," I said defensively. I needn't tell him that every time my Academy class went, I had been in punishment drill instead. The only time I'd ever entered Palace City was that dreadful day when Lombar had managed to seize control of this fateful mission to Blito-P3. All Heller's fault for surveying the place.

"Data," said Heller.

"Yes, sir. I'll also duplicate it on printout. Mass, 7.93 billion tons. Expected longevity before final explosion, 2.754 billion years. Exudation, 5.49 billion megawatts. Space sphere warp, 10.23 miles in diameter."

"Thank you," said Heller. "Turn around, tail to it. Engage traction towing beams. Set a course for Blito-P3. Engage Will-be Was main engines. When all ready, begin towing. Gong me when we are eight hundred miles above planetary surface so I can assist in adjusting its orbit."

"Yes, sir." And the tug got busy complying with the orders.

Soon the subdued thunder of the enormous power plant began to vibrate through the ship. Heller checked the instruments to make sure all was progressing well.

I relaxed a little bit. It had suddenly occurred to me that, being thirteen minutes in the future, we were quite invisible to the remaining assassin pilot. And I was just about to relax when it suddenly flashed across my wits that once we had separated from this tow and were back in normal space, we would be sitting ducks.

Heller seemed oblivious of this. He unrolled a set of plans and began to study them.

He went back to the big converter drum and began to haul out more parts. He piled these in the airlock.

Then he climbed into a scarlet antiradiation suit. Its face mask made him look diabolical to me. A Manco Devil in truth! I cowered against the pipes. Oh, Gods, why couldn't I think of something bright that would get rid of him once and for all? I must! I must! I must!

He was now climbing into a pressure suit as a second covering. When he put the helmet in place, the mirror dome reflected everything around in twisted distortion. The cat looked fifty feet long. The pilot chairs appeared all out of shape. I looked like I was a little speck cringing in some distant closet. It matched the unreality which saturated my poor, abused mind.

Heller went into the airlock and closed it. Then he opened the outer door. He left it open and I could see through the inner door ports. He had a long safety line on himself. He set up a rudimentary bench that simply sat on empty space. He began to get to work assembling something.

He had left the plans inside, pinned across the pilot port. They were very curious.

It looked like a huge umbrella. Just below the mantle was a sort of cage. Below that, what would be halfway down the handle, was a big ring marked CONVERTER. And at the bottom was a huge ring that said WEIGHTS.

I looked out through the inner ports. He was putting the mantle together. It was nothing more or less than a sectional mirror which, assembled, would have great size.

He got that done and put together the next item, which looked like a cage: It had a lot of prongs pointed toward the center. He fastened it on a rod which went to the peak of the mantle.

Next he assembled the plate which was labelled, on the plans, CONVERTER.

That done, he hung the weights on the bottom of the rod.

He put a couple safety lines on the rig. He moved his bench and tools into the lock. He checked to make sure that the rig was simply drifting along with us, well off the hull. He closed the outer airlock door and came in.

He disrobed and hung the suits up and then went aft.

Hours passed. The cat looked like he was asleep in the pilot chair but all I had to do was twitch and he opened a baleful eye.

I hit my head with my knuckles. I must think of some way to get out of this. Didn't I realize I was going to my death?

The cat snarled.

Chapter 5

Heller came back on the flight deck. He had shaved and bathed and changed his clothes. Aside from the rather gloomy pallor he now wore, he looked rested.

"Corky," he said to the tug, "we don't want that mass to overshoot. Are you braking?"

"Yes, sir. I have a compression beam on it now and we have been slowing down for the last three hours."

"Good," said Heller. He fished a piece of paper out of his pocket and read some coordinates and speeds to the tug. It was at that moment that I realized with some horror that he was not wearing ordinary fatigue clothes: he was wearing a scarlet coverall the Fleet uses when near radiation.

"Is this ship alive?" I stammered.

"No, Corky is just a robot."

"Please! You don't get my meaning. Is the ship alive with radiation?"

"All this maneuvering will be eight hundred miles above the surface," he said. "That is within the magnetosphere, what the Earth people call the Van Allen belt. It ends about six hundred miles above Earth. We're orbiting this two hundred miles higher since there's never any orbiting traffic there. The space around the outside of the ship just now is pretty hot. That's why we're silver and have all the ports closed."

"Hey, wait a minute," I said. "You must be suspecting leaks or you wouldn't be in hot coveralls. I'm totally unprotected! Are you trying to sterilize me?"

"Thanks for calling it to my attention," said Heller. He picked up the cat and went to the chief mate's room and when he came back, the cat was wearing a scarlet blanket.

"You're absolutely heartless!" I snarled.

"I didn't know you cared," said Heller. But he unchained me from the pipe and took me to one of the engineer's cabins and let me go to the toilet. He fed me some standard emergency rations, throwing them down on the table like he might have for a dog. It emphasized more than anything else that my life was very much at risk: He might take it into his head any minute to simply cut my throat.

He gave me a disposable radiation coverall. I put it on even though I suspected he had cut holes in it or rubbed the insulation off.

He took me back to the flight deck and chained me to the pipes once more. I crouched there, trying to figure some way out of this.

He began to have conversations with Corky about orbital direction and velocity and after quite a while the big Will-be Was main engines went off and the planetary auxiliaries began to drum.

More conversations with Corky and then suddenly the auxiliaries went off. The silence was eerie.

Heller clicked every viewscreen live. There was Earth, looking awfully big. We were right above a red-brown area. But the views appeared a little strange, sort of wavy.

He checked coordinates, and by consulting a map that appeared on one screen, he located Los Angeles and then Las Vegas and then finally Barstow. His finger travelled east to a desert area marked Devil's Playground. He turned to another screen and with a pass of his hand enlarged the view directly below. What a desolate desert it was! All rocks and sand. Unlike so many other places, there was no cloud cover here. He passed his hand again and the image jumped larger. A cluster of what seemed to be newly constructed buildings. Directly in the center of the screen was a large black area.

He then got to work. Reading the screens, he cast the safety lines off the umbrella he had built. Like threading a needle, he passed a tension beam through the cage that was just below the mantle.

Then he began to work compression beams and tension beams and the whole rig moved around to the back of the ship.

He pushed it further and further astern, enlarging its image bit by bit.

Suddenly the whole thing shivered. It made a sudden movement. The concentric, in-pointing bars of the cage all went into place.

"Got it," he said with a sigh of relief.

"Got what?" I said. I couldn't see anything.

"Got the black hole in the middle of the cage without losing the whole rig. All right, now let's see if it also works as a motor." He picked up a control plate and began to touch buttons on it. Small jets seemed to come from the center out through one or another of the rods.

"That's fine," he said. "Its position can be adjusted."

"With what?" I said.

"There's an automatic sensor for these coordinates. It's in the lowest ring of weights. Excess energy from the hole can be poured through the rods and made to move the whole rig very slowly up or down or back and forth. It's got to stay in position for the next few million years, orbiting right above this spot in the Devil's Playground."

"What is this thing?"

"A concentrating mirror. Energy from the black hole inside the cage is reflected down, passed through the converter ring and hot-spotted on that pile on the Earth's surface. The lowest ring of weights uses Earth gravity to keep it upright. There is a sensor for coordinates in the weight ring that adjusts position." He watched it for a bit. "Good. We're through here."

He threw a bunch of switches that turned off all beams. "Corky, take us out of this and into normal time, five hundred miles above surface."

"You're going to leave that there?" I said. "Somebody might run into it!"

"Nobody's travelling thirteen minutes in the future," he said. "Not on this planet. They won't even see it in a telescope. And if any probe blunders into it, didn't you see the sign on it?" He was pointing at a screen.

There *was* a sign! It was all around the mantle. It was in English and it said:

POWER FOR PEOPLE, INC.
No Trespassing
Hands Off
HIGH VOLTAGE

We experienced the sudden flash and grind of a shift back into normal space. I always hated it.

The viewscreens looked more normal. The Pacific Ocean spread vastly below. It seemed, from the shadow west of Hawaii, that it must be morning in Los Angeles.

Heller was busy with the viewer-phone. Izzy's face appeared.

"Oh, thank heavens, Mr. Jet. We were getting so worried. I hope nothing serious caused the delay."

"I just ran into something," said Heller, "but pushed it out of the way. Is the chief engineer of Power for People there?"

"Dr. Phil A. Mentor is right in the anteroom. He's been sleeping there! I'm so glad you are all right, Mr. Jet. I will get him at once."

Shortly, a Vandyke-bearded man was on the screen. I suddenly recognized him from the Countess Krak's classes.

"Is your ferromagnetic pile in place?" said Heller.

"Yes, Mr. Jet. Exactly according to your design."

"It should be hot now," said Heller.

Dr. Mentor was reaching for a phone. It evidently was a lease line as he didn't make any call. An excited voice was coming through the earpiece and spilling into the viewer-phone. "Devil's Playground Observation Post One."

"Is your pile hot?" said Mentor.

"Jesus Christ, yes, chief. Hot or something. The whole God (bleeped) thing just disappeared right on schedule. Somebody left a truck in there and it vanished, too!"

"Very good," said Mentor. "Are the time step-down capacitors functioning?"

"I'll check. We got so excited when the pile vanished——"

"Check those capacitors," said Mentor.

After a moment, the excited voice came back. "Yes, sir. There's a stream of microwave power pouring out! They've got it beamed into the sky at the moment."

Mentor looked into the screen. "Anything else you want to know, sir?"

"No, that's fine. Let Izzy in there."

Izzy moved in front of the screen. "I'm so glad it's working. Congratulations, Mr. Jet."

"Thank you. How are you coming with the contracts?"

"Well, some of the cities seem rather skeptical but they'll come through as soon as we have one getting all the microwave power it needs straight into its mains. I think we are quite safe to begin construction of the microwave-mirror relay systems to deliver the power. It won't suddenly run out, will it?"

"Not for the next few million years," said Heller. "You're all okay on that, then?"

"Oh, yes. Just business routine. I think ratepayers will be delighted at a penny a kilowatt. I'm assigning industrial rate at a quarter of a cent. There is one problem, though: It's going to be a problem reinvesting all our profits, as this isn't costing us anything but installation and maintenance."

"I'm sure you're up to that," said Heller.

"Well, yes," said Izzy. "But there is one more thing. Mr. Rockecenter is not going to be very happy when the oil and coal contracts start getting cancelled left and right."

"I suppose he won't," said Heller. "Now, have you gotten all the options to sell the oil-company stock?"

"Options to sell in hand," said Izzy. "I included on my own

initiative a lot of national and small oil companies, too. We have options to sell practically every share of oil stock in the world."

"Good," said Heller. "My next project is to make it go down."

"Well, it will certainly fall, with this cheap microwave-power network."

"True. But when I say 'down,' I mean *down*," said Heller.

"It averages eighty to a hundred dollars a share right now," said Izzy. "How 'down' do you think 'down' should be?"

"About fifty cents to a dollar," said Heller.

"Oy!" said Izzy. "Mr. Rockecenter will be broke broke."

"That's the idea," said Heller. "Broke plus broke equals bankrupt. So what I want you to do now is obtain an additional set of options to buy all the oil shares in the world at one dollar."

"WHAT?"

"You heard me. Your sell options will go for a fortune. Then, when the bottom is out, your buy options will put you in control of every oil company in the world."

"Oy," said Izzy. "Our dream of corporations running the planet is going to come true! I hope Fate isn't listening in on this conversation."

"We'll make it come true somehow," Heller reassured him.

"Mr. Jet, just selling cheap power to cities won't drive the stocks that low."

"I know it won't. But this next project will. Anything else, Izzy?"

"Yes, Mr. Jet. Don't do anything dangerous. I worry."

"Oh, it's all very calm where I am," said Heller. "Bye-bye."

The viewer-phone went blank.

My wits were in a hurricane. (Bleep) this Heller! That black-hole microwave-power system would be the end of Octopus! Cheap power for all of Earth? Unthinkable! What ruin it spelled for poor Mr. Rockecenter!

Suddenly I remembered that the Russians had long ago perfected satellite killers. I began to try to figure out how I could get free and get the Russians to locate and blast that contrivance and black hole he had put in the sky.

Oh, would THAT solve my problems! I would be the hero of the hour!

Somehow, some way, I must get myself out of this! The situation was utterly intolerable for Rockecenter, for Hisst, for me. I could rescue everything if I just put my wits to it. But how was I going to do it?

Chapter 6

Heller addressed the tug, "Any sign of that other assassin pilot?"

"No, sir. I've been checking ever since we returned to normal time. But I would advise extreme caution, sir. I have turned us back to total absorption of any and all waves. But I must bring to your attention that if we go speeding about, we will leave a magnetic wake that can be spotted. I severely . . . sincerely . . . severely . . . sincerely—incorrect nuance. Urgently. I urgently counsel that we just lie still."

"Override, negative," said Heller. He got out a book. "Enter these coordinates in your itinerary data bank and then plot a sequential course to them." And he began to read a long series of exact spacial positions all over Earth: North America, the Caribbean, South America, Australia, Asia, the Middle East, Russia, Central Europe, Europe, Alaska and Canada—it went on and on and on.

What was he up to now?

Finally he finished and the tug said, "I have all of them, sir. They are strung now into sequential numbered positions."

"Go to position one," said Heller.

"That is Watson, California," said the tug. "Just below us."

"Aim the bow at it," said Heller. He was lifting the radiation shields off the ports. The tug giddily tipped up. Five hundred miles below, the Los Angeles area was a smudge of yellow smog.

Heller adjusted his screens. Magnification of the middle one showed that we were pointed straight at an oil refinery!

"Just hold there," he told the tug. He reached over to the viewer-phone and buzzed it. The worried face of Izzy came on.

"Just checking," said Heller. "Have you got the buy options yet on all the oil shares in the world at one dollar?"

"Good heavens," said Izzy. "They think we're insane—that we're wasting our option money. But, yes, our brokers are phoning in right now. Please hold."

He chattered into another phone. Then he came back to ours. "Yes—they think we've lost our minds, but we've got them. Mr. Jet, how could it possibly fall to that?"

"You'll see," said Heller. "Bye-bye."

He returned to his magnified view of the refinery below. He was checking a floor plan. "Atmospheric pipefill," he said. He made a couple of tiny adjustments to the position of the ship.

Then his hands went out toward the firing control of the laser cannon he had lately installed.

"NO!" I cried in desperation. "Don't blow up the refineries!"

His finger pressed the firing button. The gun overhead made a brief whirr.

I watched in horror. The enlarged picture of a part of a refinery, I thought, would burst into flame.

I waited.

It didn't!

"Corky, position two," said Heller.

"That's Wilmington, California," said the tug. And we moved.

Heller did the same thing as before.

I could see no change below.

"Position three," said Heller.

"That's Long Beach, California," said the tug.

Heller repeated his actions.

"Position four," said Heller.

"That's El Segundo, California," said the tug.

Heller went through his same drill.

"Say, what the Hells is going on?" I said. "Aren't you going to blow anything up?"

"I wish you'd make up your mind," said Heller. "Half an hour ago you were telling me I shouldn't."

"Please tell me what you are doing."

He glanced at me. "Everything they do in a refinery first passes into what they call the atmospheric pipefill from the crude-oil tanks. From the pipefill it goes on through every other process in the place: jet fuel, diesel fuel, virgin naphtha, you name it. All I'm doing is putting a false radiation charge in the metals of the pipefills. It will register like mad on a Geiger counter but it actually doesn't affect another thing. You're not going anywhere, so there is no reason not to tell you that Izzy has the device that nulls the wave."

He turned away and went back to work, and between him and the tug, they systematically did the same thing to every blessed oil refinery in the whole world.

It took a day and a half to cover them all.

Then Heller caught some sleep. We were over Canada now, having been everywhere else above the globe.

I crouched there thinking, what a strange thing to do. He wasn't actually destroying anything at all. It seemed very impractical to me. Certainly not an Apparatus textbook procedure. He might be a Royal officer, but he would certainly never qualify for a real organization like ours. No explosions! What an oversight!

Bathed and shaved and in fresh clothes, he came back to the flight deck. He fed the cat and then he fed me. He chained me back up to the pipe and sat down in the planetary-pilot chair. He buzzed Izzy and gave him a phone number and told him to ring it and, when he had the party, to hold the instrument close to the viewer-phone.

Izzy told the party that someone wanted to speak with them. He put the telephone where he had been told.

"This is Wister," Heller said.

"Oh! Oh, dear Wister—what a wonderful surprise! I will always be eternally grateful to you, you know."

MISS SIMMONS!

"And I will always remember you," said Heller. "Listen. I have something you will be very interested in. Did you know that every oil refinery in the world is registering as radioactive on Geiger counters?"

"NO!"

"Yes, it's a fact. I think you should get field teams out at once and check it. Every time you go near one of them a Geiger counter will click its head off!"

"GOOD HEAVENS!"

"Will you check that for me?" said Heller.

"Oh, good Lord! If that is true, Wister, the Antinuclear Protest Marchers in every land will rise in a howling storm!"

"That's what I hoped," said Heller. "Demonstrations everyplace."

"Oh, you'll have them, Wister. And thank you, thank you, thank you, you dear boy! THE (BLEEPARDS)!"

She hung up.

"Oy!" said Izzy.

"Yes," said Heller. "Double oy. The oil shares will go down like a rocket in reverse. When they get near bottom, sell. And use the cash for Maysabongo to exercise their contracts for every drop of oil in reserve in the U.S. Then in July, purchase every oil company in the world for a song."

"Oh, Mr. Jet, our every dream is coming true! I just hope Fate doesn't intervene."

"I'll try to see it doesn't," Heller said. "Bye-bye."

"Now I'll take care of the last small bit of this program and the mission will be done," said Heller.

"Done?" I cried aghast. "For Gods' sakes, what more could you do?"

"Oh, this last is just a little thing. The south pole has a tendency to wander over the sea. I have to give the globe a little tap to straighten up its rotation. Corky, take off for the planet Saturn now."

Saturn?

My head was in a whirl indeed.

All I could think of, really, was that he had just set motions in train which would utterly smash Octopus and all the other oil companies. Not even their massive control of news could quash the panic that would ensue. Rockecenter, unless I got loose, was through!

I reviewed how I could remedy this catastrophe. Actually all I had to do was get Rockecenter to put a satellite killer on to that umbrella device, bomb the Empire State Building, atom-bomb the Republic of Maysabongo out of existence and announce to the waiting world that their refineries were NOT radioactive. Yes, I could handle this.

But now for some mysterious reason we were heading for Saturn.

HOW COULD I GET LOOSE?

Chapter 7

Heller was dropping radiation shields again so we could pass once more through the magnetosphere. I could hear the planetary drives winding up higher and higher. I was chained very close to their partition just back of the flight deck and the sound began to hurt my ears.

"I don't think these auxiliaries are meant to run this fast," I said fearfully.

"Oh, stop worrying. They take this ship up to the brink of the speed of light. They sound just fine to me."

They would, I grated to myself. Oh, Gods, why did I ever get involved with anyone from the most insane corps of the Fleet, combat engineers? No wonder their average service life was only two years. Heller was long overdue, having gone three or more times that. And on top of that he was a speed maniac. "What's the hurry?"

"There's no sense dawdling around. What with acceleration and braking, it will take us hours as it is." He glanced at a readout that was whirring too fast for me to read. "Saturn, right now, is 782,617,819 miles away. It's not at minimal distance. The closest it ever gets to Earth is about 740,000,000 miles."

"Why Saturn?" I said.

Heller shrugged. He indicated the viewscreens with his hand. "You don't see any comets, do you?"

Comets? Saturn? Now I knew he was crazy.

I made another try. "If you leave this fast, that other assassin ship is certain to spot our turbulence and even if they don't get us on a scope, they'll be waiting for our return."

"True. They won't be able to follow us. They haven't got the speed we have."

"No, no. You don't understand. If we *return,* they'll be lying in wait for us. They can find us even with the locators gone."

It had been on the tip of my tongue to say that this proved he should go to Voltar right now. That would put me home perfectly safe, as Lombar would have him grabbed on sight and I would be freed. But even as I opened my mouth to speak, a sledgehammer thought hit me: The actions this Devil had just set in train spelled utter ruin for Rockecenter.

If I went home and left that mess, Lombar Hisst would have me exterminated so slowly it would take months. It would be quite different if I could come galloping in and cry "I had to return so I could save your life," or something like that. I had no excuse whatever to go back except that I had been captured. Lombar wouldn't like that.

No, I must think of some way to get free and undo the fiendish and diabolical work of Heller. I could not go back and leave Earth with no Rockecenter, clean air, cheap fuel and happy riffraff. Heller a total success? It was unthinkable!

I crouched down and thought harder.

He told the cat and the tug to keep an eye on me and went aft.

Earth, seen on the scopes, was dwindling like a ball thrown away. I realized suddenly that we were going to go through the asteroid belt with, to all intents and purposes, no pilot. It froze my wits.

Then I saw the time-sight dial slowly turn all by itself. It spooked me. Was this tug really some sort of a ghost? I couldn't figure out where its voice came from and Heller had even stopped using a microphone to speak to it.

Oh, more than ever, I made up my mind, I had to get off this thing.

But even more than that, I had to warn Rockecenter before it was too late. Even now that (bleeped) Faht Bey might be turning Black Jowl loose. Supposing I should go back to Voltar and simply tell Lombar, "Well, my friend, I have just had the whole Earth base seized." Yes, there was no doubt of it. Lombar would react, and not favorably at all.

How the HELLS could I get out of this mess?

Some time later we began to brake and perhaps a half an hour after that, Saturn was in view.

I had never seen the planet before. It was immense. We were coming in at an angle to the rings and I stared at those strange circles. The outer two were very bright and the one nearest us seemed thinner.

Heller came back to the flight deck.

The tug had slowed now almost to a stop. "I'll take over, Corky," Heller said.

"Sir, could I warn you that the gravity is very strong. I am continuing to brake. We are also quite near one of its moons and a new volcano seems to be erupting on it."

Heller looked at it and it was a colorful sight. But then, the whole place was colorful: The planet itself was yellowish but near its equator seemed pastel green, and there were patches of reddish brown. But it looked very dangerous.

"You're not going to try to land on it," I said.

Heller snorted. "The surface is gas. Be quiet while I figure this out."

I had no faintest notion what he was figuring out. He was passing a scope down the outermost ring. It seemed to be made up of thousands, millions, billions of massive particles tumbling in slow motion, a circular parade.

Heller put the tug quite close to the outermost ring and travelling with the rotation of the whole body at the same speed so that we appeared motionless except for the tiny movement of the stars beyond in the black sky. I was surprised that I could see star motion at all. This planet must be rotating on its axis more rapidly than Earth.

"Corky, turn your traction beams on. Full power. We're going to take too big a bite and then shed some if we have to cut it down in size."

"Bite of what?" I said.

"Ice," said Heller. "Those particles are ice. It will never miss a few billion tons."

"We came all the way out here for ice?" I said.

"Certainly. We could have gotten some from a comet if one had happened to be handy, but actually this is purer stuff. We don't want too many stones."

"What in Heavens' names are you going to do with it?" I said.

"Use it to tap the poles straight, of course," said Heller. "You don't want the poles drifting over water again. It would flood Earth."

"You mean you are adding water to stop flooding?" Good Gods, now I knew he was insane.

"A few billion tons of water is nothing. Water is awfully heavy stuff. What we're taking wouldn't even make a small mountain. Lock on, Corky."

The vibrations of the traction engines were added to the whine of gravity coils.

"Escape velocity is twenty-two miles per second," said Corky. "I recommend we do half a planetary rotation. That's five hours and seven minutes."

"All right," said Heller. "Carry on."

The Will-be Was time drives went on with a fearful initial roar in the center of the ship.

Heller was watching a rearward screen. At first there was very little change in the outermost ring, to which we were lying very close. Then I saw a hairline gap. As the seconds turned to minutes it began to widen.

Very, very fractionally, the planet face began to move rearward.

About fifteen minutes later, I said, "We're going to leave a hole in that ring."

"It'll fill in," said Heller. "Proportionately speaking, we're taking almost nothing."

He thought it was nothing. The whole sky behind us seemed to be filled with ice!

"Some astronomer on Earth is going to see this," I said.

"Oh, I doubt it. And if he did, he'd just think it was some new comet."

"Well, the last assassin ship is going to see it, and they'll know better."

"You worry too much," said Heller.

"I'm almost dead from worry," I said. "Why don't you let me lie down in a bunk and sleep?"

He ignored me.

Time ticked on. The vast amount of ice was creeping further and further from the ring and planet face. The Will-be Was drives droned and pounded.

The tug was right. It did take more than five hours to pull that huge mass free of Saturn's gravity and into space.

It was travelling faster and faster now, glaring white in the light of the distant sun, sharply outlined against the ink of space.

Heller and the tug calculated the course for Earth.

Whatever else was wrong and whatever else I had to solve, one fact was clear as terror to me. The assassin ship couldn't possibly miss us. And it was lying in wait.

Chapter 8

The giant Will-be Was time drives thundered in the diminutive hull, the traction motors whined. Billions of tons of silvery ice were dragged for millions and millions of miles across the ink of space. Once during the voyage it had gotten up to half the speed of light. Then the tug had turned around and braked it for a while, reducing its speed. Now we were in front of it once more, the bulk of the distance behind us, travelling at a much slower velocity but still far out and beyond the orbit of Earth's moon.

Heller was busy calculating things like Earth rotation and its coordinates in its orbit around the sun. He adjusted speed a couple of times and then seemed satisfied with the angle of approach.

Earth had ceased to be just another bright spot and was assuming shape. The shadow of its twilight zone was now becoming very plain.

Heller waited until we were about four times the orbit of the yellowish moon away from Earth and then put his clipboard down. We and the ice mass were travelling very fast.

"Check these figures, Corky," and he read them off. "How does that strike you?"

"Well, sir, it isn't going to strike ME. The mass will hit the north pole of the planet at an angle of thirty-three degrees in the direction southward on east longitude 36.5. By gyroscopic precession, it will tend to shift the spin of the internal core slightly and move the magnetic poles closer to the Earth's axis."

"And your conclusion on the effect of this?" said Heller.

"It will cure the tendency of the southern pole to wander over the water, thus melting the place and causing continental submergences. The liability is that it will probably hit some polar bears."

"Thank you. Please verify the approach again."

"Well, sir, I think it will require a final downward twitch of six million foot-pounds of thrust just before we disengage at the top of the planet's atmosphere. There will otherwise be a slight cushion effect. What about the polar bears, sir? Should I send out a warning?"

"They're extinct," said Heller. "There isn't any life worth mentioning at the north pole."

"Thank you, sir. I will amend my survey data. Sir, my 124th subbrain is reading red. There is some magnetic turbulence straight ahead about half a million miles from the planetary surface. It is on viewscreen thirteen."

There it was! A coil of disturbance.

THE ASSASSIN SHIP!

It was rising far above the Earth's surface to meet us!

"Blast," said Heller. "I didn't expect him this soon." He picked up a microphone. He spoke into it. "Calling Apparatus vessel."

There was no answer. He verified that he was on Apparatus intership frequency, limited range. "This is Tug One, the *Prince Caucalsia*, Exterior Division. I have a tow. I do not wish to be interfered with."

There was no answer.

Heller tried again, "Apparatus vessel, this is Jettero Heller, Grade X, Voltar Fleet, operating under orders of the Grand Council. You are directed to reverse your course and forgo interference with this tow."

No answer! And there should have been. We were returning to the planet, and leaving it was all they were supposed to prevent.

And then it dawned on me that that assassin pilot and his mate had also received orders to kill Heller!

The ship just kept on coming right up to meet us.

"Oh, blast!" said Heller. "I can't abandon this tow! That crazy idiot is going to cause a catastrophe!"

He had hung up the mike. He switched all controls to manual. I expected him to disengage from the ice mass so we could flee.

He didn't! The bullheaded idiot was going to go on with his project!

We didn't even have a gun!

The assassin ship was coming very fast now on the screens. Heller flipped up the viewport covers. There the deadly vessel was! Slightly to our left. Very visible to the eye: he was so contemptuous that he hadn't even switched his silver coating off.

Except for turbulence, we ourselves must be invisible to him. But he had us spotted by the nearness of the tow behind us.

Heller reached for our overhead, adjusted a dial and threw a switch. He put a thumb on the firing panel. I couldn't imagine what he was doing. We didn't have a real cannon.

Abruptly, about a thousand yards ahead of us, another ship appeared!

It rattled me.

It looked just like Tug One!

The second barrel he had put up there!

It was obviously an electronic illusion projector, so common in Voltar celebrations and displays.

To the assassins, it must have looked like the tug had simply turned its silver coat on!

The deadly ship was off to our left. It was turning.

IT FIRED!

The shot was well above the illusion.

IT FIRED AGAIN!

The shot was below the illusion.

ANOTHER SHOT!

Flame burst right in the middle of the illusion tug!

Heller threw a switch.

The illusion vanished!

For a breathless span of time I thought we had gotten away with it.

If we had luck, the flying cannon would now turn away and depart for the planetary surface, thinking it had done its job.

Please go, I prayed silently. Please be fooled and leave us alone.

Suddenly I realized what was wrong. He must have seen that no debris had resulted from the shot! Either he or his instruments thought that he had missed!

He was turning, and even though he was ten miles to our left, I could almost look down his cannon barrel. His instruments had found our turbulence again!

A FLASH!

The tug bucked.

WE WERE HIT!

Suddenly the Will-be Was main drives shrieked into a high whine.

It was as if a slingshot had been released and we were the pellet!

We vaulted across the black sky in a sickening cartwheel.

Corky's voice: "Damage! Damage! Our traction engines are disabled! We have lost our tow!"

The planet's distant surface was hurtling up at us.

Heller's hand slapped the throttles of the main drives shut. He yanked the planetary auxiliaries wide open.

We were braking at full throttle!

The Earth steadied to the same size for three consecutive seconds and then again began to grow smaller.

Heller was cuffing the controls around.

We faced now toward the vast white bulk of the tow.

An explosion bloomed off to our right.

The assassin ship was firing.

It was now visible to the right of the tow.

With the auxiliaries, Heller jinked toward the explosion spot.

Another explosion flashed to our left.

"Blast him," said Heller. "He's a better gunner!" He was slewing to the left.

I knew then that we were up against the lead assassin pilot. Yes, he was the better gunner. He was an expert at killing ships that sought to flee battle. This unarmed, unarmored tug would be nothing for him.

The flying cannon was near the hurtling mass of ice.

Heller made the tug leap far to the right.

A shot exploded just where we had been a split second before.

Heller dived. He hauled up suddenly. And just where we would have gone, fire bloomed!

"He's too good," said Heller. "And he's only firing at turbulence!"

We shifted skyward. The assassin ship was only a mile away. I saw its cannon wink.

Heller's hand closed on his firing pin.

An illusion of the tug appeared to the right of the flying cannon, between it and the ice tow.

The assassin ship turned toward it!

On other screens I could see that we were hurtling down at the top of Earth, the battle travelling at the dizzy speed of advance of that ice mass.

The cannon fired!

The shot went through the illusion and sprayed thousands of tons of ice about.

Heller maneuvered the tug.

The illusion seemed to be closing on the flying cannon.

The assassin pilot fired again. More ice tonnage flew.

The illusion seemed to be broadwise to the other vessel. It seemed to be closing with it sideways!

The flying cannon must have thought that all it had to do was push its muzzle against the tug and shoot.

It charged the illusion!

Heller twitched his controls.

The illusion must be blanking off the entire forward view of the assassin ship! But we were seeing it sidewise.

The flying cannon instruments and viewers must have been all involved with the illusion. He was depending on instruments and otherwise flying blind!

The assassin ship hurtled at its target!

Heller shifted the illusion to keep the assassin ship's nose headed at it and the instruments concentrated on it.

Suddenly I realized that the illusion was penetrating the edge of the ice mass!

The assassin ship made one more charge.

A HUGE GOUT OF ORANGE AND GREEN FIRE!

The flying cannon had plowed straight into the ice mass and exploded!

Ice and flaming chunks of debris made a sphere of their own, close beside the racing mass of frozen water.

Billions and billions of tons of ice were hurtling straight at Earth, out of control.

Chapter 9

"Oh, Lords," said Heller, "there it goes without its last correction!"

He was looking at the ice mass. Then he looked at the planetary surface. Through the viewports I could make out what must be Canada and Greenland and, over the curve, what must be Sweden, Finland and the north edge of European Russia.

"Quickly, Corky. Damage?"

"Nothing internal," the tug said. "The aft cable ends of the traction beams are totally fused. One mustn't even turn the traction motors back on or they'd explode."

"Time to repair?" said Heller anxiously.

"You don't have the tools aboard."

Heller watched the ice mass. I knew he must be considering some idiotic move like trying to butt it. Butt billions of tons of loose ice? We'd just get buried in it.

He looked at Earth again. "That's going to miss the north pole! Is there no way to give it downward deflection?"

"Bombs. We don't have bombs," said Corky. "My thirty-fourth subbrain says you could butt the planet. But this conflicts with my purpose to protect you from harm. All we would do is explode. The relative mass of our impact and the planet mass are incompatible. Correction. Incomparable. Sir, you are now approaching the magnetosphere and have your pilot antiradiation plate open. Please close it."

Heller didn't move. He was looking down at the top of Earth and the hurtling mass of ice. "Oh, Lords," he breathed.

The vast, glistening expanse of ice was closing rapidly. It now had about a hundred thousand miles to go. We were pacing beside it. Our digitals read three hundred miles a second, eighteen thousand miles a minute. Another clock was running backwards: It said there was 5.555 minutes to go.

Heller drew a long sigh. He looked over at the ice. He looked at the planet surface. He looked at his instruments.

"Well, it's a good thing we had it slowed down," he said. "There's nothing I can do."

He worked the controls and we drew off.

The great ice mass raced ahead. It was plunging at an angle toward a spot beyond the north pole.

It was going to strike a glancing blow but it would be a blow all the same.

The seconds ticked by into minutes.

I knew the TV would be alive. I wished he would turn it on. This thing would have been spotted within the last hour. There must be bulletins every minute on this "comet" that had suddenly appeared up in the sky. It must be eyeball visible from northern Canada and maybe even England now.

It was closing with ferocious speed, fifteen times that of the average meteorite. It certainly was not on target for the north pole! It was going to miss it and hit at a flatter angle.

Sweden and Finland? No, they were slightly to the right of it.

It was daylight where it was going to hit. And it was going to strike land.

Heller shifted the tug closer and to the left.

The ice mass struck the upper atmosphere. Racing, it began to change its form. At thirty miles a second it had not long to go.

It missed Finland.

It seemed to be spreading out, its mass tumbled by the resistance of air.

Ahead of it I could see now what appeared to be a large inland lake, blue in the brown of Russia. Some of it would hit that lake.

In slow, slow motion as it appeared from on high, it was racing down the last few miles.

IT STRUCK!

It seemed to generate an enormous flash like electricity!

An instant later, the mass seemed to have quadrupled in size! A piece of it had hit the lake!

Like a scythe it was sweeping onward!

Travelling at a low angle, it was levelling everything in its path. MOSCOW!

One second there was a city.

The next, there was only jumble!

The scythe swept on!

Waves of cloud were racing ahead, southward. They were growing less and less as they progressed toward the Black Sea.

Dust and debris were settling below.

And then I saw what it had done.

The recoil had flattened Leningrad.

Everything that was European Russia had been levelled!

That whole nation was no more!

I moaned.

Even worse, there went all of Rockecenter's uranium profits, with the removal of the threat of atomic war!

Oh, Gods, was I in trouble now!

PART SIXTY-FOUR
Chapter 1

If I went home now, the second Lombar heard about this he would have me exterminated.

There was no doubt of that in my mind now. If ever I needed to be brilliant and think fast, it was NOW, NOW, NOW!

Heller was sitting there in the pilot seat. He seemed to be praying.

We were holding at about three hundred miles above Russia. From this point I could see Turkey on the horizon to the south.

Suddenly, at long last, I had an idea!

"Oh, God of peoples," said Heller, "forgive me."

I took immediate advantage of his mood, although I certainly couldn't understand why anybody would be sorry about wiping out a hundred million riffraff. "The tug is disabled," I said. "You cannot go directly home."

"It's just the towing equipment," he said. "I could probably make it."

"No, no," I said. "You shouldn't put yourself at risk."

"Are you recommending all of a sudden that I go to the Earth base?"

I tried to keep the gleam out of my eyes. I had the whole plan now. It was audacious beyond belief.

"I have certain information," I said. "It is very vital to you. If I divulge it, will you give me your word as a Royal officer to take me home and turn me over there for trial?"

"If it's worth anything," he said.

"Oh, it is!" I said. "You saw that that assassin pilot wanted to kill you, even though he knew who you were."

"That's true," he said.

"You'll be interested to know that at the Earth base they think you are a spy who was sent down to kill them. They will try to execute you on sight."

"I could figure that out for myself," he said.

"But you don't know this," I replied. "There is a secret way to get in."

He looked at me, puzzled. But I knew I had him. If I could just get him to the outer gate of the villa and ring that bell, he would be shot down. And even if that missed, I could get him to my secret room and sound the alarm there, and when we went down that tunnel the assembled base personnel would riddle him!

"And why should I want to sneak in?" said Heller.

And here came the very cream of my idea! "Give me a piece of paper and a pen."

He did. I wrote on it and folded it.

"The information on this is so vital to you it will change your whole life. Promise me that if I give you this sheet and you act on it, you will return me to Voltar."

He thought a moment. "For trial," he said. "I will promise that."

"Good enough," I said. And I handed him the paper.

He opened it. He went white as a sheet!

I had had the idea that would end all ideas. I had written

THE COUNTESS KRAK IS ALIVE
IN A CELL AT THE EARTH BASE

What an inspiration—especially since she was dead! What genius to use a corpse to lure someone in!

And if we got that far, I had that planned, too. Somewhere between here and there, I would secrete a weapon. He would see her body and in that moment when his attention was off me, I would kill him, for he would be in shock.

I was so bemused by my cleverness I did not hear what he said. He had to repeat it. "You are lying!"

"No," I said. "I am telling you the truth. Some information came to us that her plane would be sabotaged by some terrorists, and we picked her up at Rome airport and flew her to the base. She is alive and well, though of course in detention."

He did not say anything for a while. He was obviously in shock. Oh, how well this was working out!

"You'd better have some proof of this," he said.

I had that all worked out, too. I had my wallet. I opened it. I handed him a piece of paper. It was the Squeeza credit card—her card with the Empire State address written on the back of it.

He looked at it. He recognized it. His hands were shaking.

He could hardly talk. Then he said, "All right. We will go."

I was nearly delirious with joy—hard put to keep it from showing on my face.

I could get him now. Of that I was sure. And then I could somehow wipe out his power company, Chryster, Okeechokee and blow up the Empire State and Izzy before those options could function. There would be repercussions with Rockecenter, but I could say proudly, "All is well, for I killed the man and your empire is intact." I would be restored to favor. I could release Black Jowl. And I still would become the next Chief of the Apparatus.

And all in all, I was absolutely amazed at my own genius. Whoever before had used a dead woman as a lure? Only a brilliant Apparatus officer would ever think of that!

Chapter 2

I think that Heller was dazed a bit, not only by my pretended news concerning the Countess Krak but also because of the destruction the assassin pilot had angled the tug into.

We had to wait for sunset. He would not let me turn the TV on. I was very sure it was full of juicy bulletins concerning the demise of Russia. Rockecenter's PRs would be rushing the media to blare how he insisted upon vast relief expeditions. But nobody need bother. There was little if anything left alive in European Russia. Probably Sweden would just move in to pick up any loot left lying around and annex the place. The so-called satellite countries would throw off the yoke and probably right this minute were murdering the Russian troops who had kept them in line and fattened off them. World power had certainly shifted. Rockecenter must be going crazy trying to figure out how to keep international tensions up now. I said as much.

"They can't blame any other nation," Heller said. "Every astronomer in the northern hemisphere plainly saw what they thought was a natural cataclysm. The planet won't destroy itself with atomic war now and that's the only benefit from this. So shut up. I don't want to hear about it."

He was doing some calculations but his mind was not on it and his eyes kept straying to the sun indicator as we hovered there, five hundred miles above Turkey.

The tug spoke up about midafternoon. "My thirty-third subbrain has calculated that the inner core of the planet will now spin slightly more true to the axis. It will take many years longer to achieve because the blow was so glancing. I have the figures. Do you want them?"

"No," said Heller, his eyes upon the clock.

About six, with shadows growing long below, Heller went aft. He returned later to the flight deck. He was dressed in black. He had a kit bag over his shoulder.

He unchained me and took me to an engineer's quarters. He let me pick out some of the Antimanco engineer's clothes which were still hanging there.

While I was still changing, he went to the crew's galley to get me something to eat.

It was then I found something.

I could not believe my luck!

The jacket I was putting on had a hidden knife! It was about five inches long and very sharp. It lay flat against the left rib cage!

When Heller brought me back a plate and canister, I carefully schooled myself to continue to look bland.

"There's a field nobody uses," I said, "about three miles from the base. It is in a fold of the mountain and innocent of rocks. It belongs to the base but the soil is worn out and it is not leased to tenants. They are giving it a rest. If we land there after dark, we only need to walk over the shoulder of a hill and we will be on a road that goes right past the villa. And it, too, is not much used. I can get you in there but you have to take my advice and do what I say."

He was only half listening. He was looking up the passageway toward a clock. I knew what would be on his mind. Every part of him wanted to believe me but part of him was also saying that it might not be true. He looked rather white around the eyes. His hands were shaking slightly.

I was careful not to exhibit any satisfaction over his state. What a brilliant bomb I had thrown into him! My whole situation was reversed. He was not even being careful!

Darkness crept across the land below.

Heller, on the flight deck, carefully located the field and fed in its coordinates.

Finally the Earth went black under us.

"Here we go," said Heller, and he reached for the controls.

I could scarcely breathe. In only a couple of hours I would be free to wipe out the hopes of Earth for cheap fuel. Rockecenter must be saved!

Very shortly now, Heller's corpse would join the lifeless body of the Countess Krak.

Chapter 3

We landed with a whisper in the dark.

Heller, at the airlock, put the cat back inside. "You stay here and guard the ship." The cat sat down and he shut the airlock in its face.

We went across an open field and began to climb the shoulder that separated us from the road.

"We must be very quiet," I said. "When you see me stop and listen, you must stop, too."

"You stay ahead of me," said Heller. "Walk fast."

I walked along. I was desperately thinking of how I could get behind him. All it would take was just one stab. He was mortal like any other man and he seemed too impetuous for caution. And I had other ways to get him, too!

We descended the slope of the shoulder and came to the road. There was no traffic.

We went along the footpath beside the road. We passed the ill-fated copse where I had had so many women in the car. We came at length within reach of the villa gate.

Everything was quiet inside. There was the glow of a single light burning in the garden and some yellow splashes from the windows of the staff hut.

I held up my hand to stop him. "There's a secret lock to open the bars," I said. I reached up on the pillar and pressed the staff alarm.

Urgent lights would be flashing in their quarters now.

I silently opened the gate.

Heller pushed me ahead of him. He had no idea at all he was walking into a trap.

I saw something moving in the bushes beside the walk.

Musef and Torgut!

Ah, bless them! They would be ready, as they had been for Black Jowl.

Heller stopped. I glanced back. He was looking around. But he was not looking toward that spot that had moved.

SUDDENLY TWO FLASHLIGHTS CAME ON!

One from the right! The other from the left!

They were drilling straight at Heller's face!

Below them were the muzzles of guns!

Suddenly a scream.

"The D.E.A. man!" cried Musef.

There was a clatter.

A lead pipe had fallen to the walk!

The flashlights were weaving a wild pattern as they went away.

They got to the wall.

They went up and straight over the top, barbs and glass and all!

"Run for your life!" Torgut was bellowing in the field beside the villa.

The rush of frantic footsteps faded away.

I was stunned.

"What was that all about?" said Heller.

I thought fast. I was swallowing my disappointment. "We must have surprised some robbers at work," I said.

But I was very far from through. All I had to do was get to my secret room, step on a tile and sound the general alarm for the whole base. They thought he was there to kill them. I had long since made sure they believed that.

Silently we crept into the patio of the villa itself. The only sound was the fountain. We went through to my bedroom.

Now, if I worked this right, I could con him into my secret room and get my foot upon the tile.

I opened the closet passageway. Heller pushed me ahead of him. I stepped through into my secret room.

The lights were on. Krak's broken viewer still lay on the floor. My gun rack glinted invitingly. Heller, seeing it, made me step back.

I only had one pace to take so I could step on the key tile and twist it to sound the general alarm. It would not be heard in here but it would bring every man on the base into the hangar and set up every gun!

Heller was in my way!

He seemed to be listening.

Then I heard it.

Someone was coming up the tunnel from the other side of the secret door!

Heller spotted the portal.

He reached out and grabbed me by the arm to hold me still.

Yes, someone was coming. They were now at the door. It swung inward.

UTANC!

She was coming out of the hangar! How could she ever have known it existed? How could she even know about this secret room? She was carrying two bags of heroin over her shoulder!

She stopped.

And then in a draw so fast I didn't even see a blur, she had a small gun in her hand!

With a sudden yank, Heller had me in front of him.

Utanc was raising the gun!

"Oh, darling!" I screamed. "Look, look, look! It's me! DON'T SHOOT!"

In terror I watched her finger on the trigger.

I made a struggle to get free.

She looked straight at me.

SHE FIRED!

Chapter 4

I felt the bullet jar my ribs.

At the same instant I saw her big black eyes.

They were cold and ruthless!

I felt myself being hurled forward by Heller.

SHE FIRED AGAIN!

Then suddenly I was thrown to my left. Utanc's gun hand was in Heller's grasp.

With a heave he snapped her spinning into the room. She went down.

He was on her like a tiger!

The gun was in his left hand and pointing at her throat!

In this moment of his distraction, I saw the key tile not three feet away. With a sudden crabwise scuttle, I got my hand on it.

I twisted. I pressed. I had sounded the hangar alarm that would assemble the whole base.

I felt a surge of triumph. Then I saw my hand. Blood was running down my fingers. I had been hit!

The shock of the bullets vanished. The pain struck me in a red, twisting tide.

The whole room seemed to spin and upend. Items in it leaped into separate view as though unconnected with the rest. Krak's broken viewer. Heroin spilled across the floor. The door to the tunnel once more tightly shut. Utanc's heels drumming on the floor.

Heller was no longer holding a gun. He was strangling her with his left hand!

Utanc's eyes were wild! She was struggling, threshing back and forth, trying to get away.

Then I saw that Heller was doing a terrible thing. He was undressing her!

The thought surged through my pain: Gods, has he gone mad? Is this a rape?

With his free hand he tore her sleeves to bits and cast her jacket aside. His fingers stabbed under her belly band and yanked. There was a sharp rip of cloth. He tore her Turkish pants off and cast them away. His savage hand gripped her underpants and tore them into shreds!

Writhing and twisting and trying to get out from under him, Utanc was naked on the floor.

The body, every muscle taut, writhed over on its side in my direction.

Through the pink mist of pain, I could not believe what I saw. UTANC WAS A MAN!

The comprehension hit me like another bullet. And then a wave of nausea swept through me.

Ever since this creature had come, I HAD BEEN MAKING LOVE TO A HOMO!

I vomited.

Heller still held the writhing body down. The bra had been torn away, showing a hairless but male chest. He was searching under the body's back. Then he shifted his holds and one hand started down the homo's inner thigh. He yanked and Utanc screamed. He had removed a flat wallet that was taped there.

Using one knee now to hold the creature, Heller was opening the leather. He was evidently reading something. He read it again, aloud, "Colonel Boris Gaylov of the Russian KGB!"

Heller glanced in my direction. "If this was your woman, it's the Code break of all time! You've been harboring an agent of the Soviet secret service! Was this your doing?"

I vomited again.

Heller turned to the homo he was holding down. "You'd better talk and talk fast! What were you doing here?"

He had relaxed his grip on the throat and a stream of profanity—Russian, English, French—sprayed from the contorted lips.

Heller reached across the floor to where the heroin had spilled. He scooped up a handful. "If you don't talk, this is going to go down your throat!"

Utanc screamed and writhed and tried to get away.

"Russia is no more," said Heller. "You can't betray it, as it has ceased to exist. Talk!" The handful of heroin approached her mouth.

"You beast!" screamed Gaylov.

"Information!" demanded Heller, the hand holding the heroin hard against Gaylov's chin. "Did you report this base to Moscow?"

"You son of a (bleepch)!" howled Gaylov. "Russia was winning! We would have ruled the world! We had the greatest spy network man has ever seen!"

"Information!" said Heller.

Crystals of deadly heroin had reached those perverted lips. Colonel Gaylov spat them out. "I kept our whole worldwide spy network financed with heroin and money from this base. And now everything is wrecked. Go ahead and kill me!"

I had ceased to throw up. I got a grip on myself. I had turned on the alarm. The longer he spent here, the better they would be organized in the hangar. Wounded though I was, all was not yet lost.

There was more struggle from Gaylov.

"Did you report this base?" said Heller.

"Yes, yes, yes!" Gaylov snarled, spitting out heroin crystals. "I've known you were extraterrestrials since I made that silly (bleepard) there think he bought me last fall!"

Heller threw away the heroin. He was grabbing straps and lines from the rack. As he tied the secret agent up he said to me, "Every time I think I've gotten to the bottom of your crimes and can't get any lower, you always have a new surprise! They'll execute you for sure for this Code break."

I glared at him as he was taping up Gaylov's mouth. I wasn't through. In just minutes now, I was certain that he would be dead. I hated him more than ever for costing me the love of my life—Utanc! She was gone forever.

Chapter 5

Heller turned me over. He pulled back my shirt and coat. I was afraid he would spot the knife and flinched away.

"You've got a bullet in your side," he said. "And one in your arm." He found some gauze compression pads and some tape. He pressed them against the bleeding holes and fixed them in place. "I don't think any vital organ was hit and there is no arterial pumping. We'll get them fixed later. Right now, we have other things to do. Can you walk?"

I groaned. But he got me on my feet. He reached for the secret door. I was bad enough off, but I pretended I was even worse. My right hand and arm were fully operational. The knife could be swiftly drawn from its secret place in the coat lining. If I could just get behind him, if only for a moment, a sudden stab would finish him and all would be well. But I might never have to draw at all. The moment he showed his face at the end of that tunnel, a blast of fire from the crew would cut him down.

The tunnel door was open. He glanced back at the securely trussed Russian. Then he shoved me ahead of him. The door clicked behind us.

He seemed to be fumbling around in the ledge above the switches just outside the secret room door. And I remembered he had been all through this place last fall. He now had something in his hand.

He pushed me further down the tunnel.

Suddenly I realized that I, myself, was in grave danger. The moment I came to the tunnel end, a blast of fire from the hangar could cut me down. And it wouldn't be bullets. It would be slashes of deadly fire from blastguns!

Cunningly, I pretended to be weaker than I was. The tunnel end was just ahead. I was just about to be pushed into the open.

Expertly, I weaved and crumpled.

I shouted, "Kill him!"

Instantly a barrage of fire racketed!

The whole tunnel exit turned blinding orange!

I felt my jacket singe!

Something had me by the collar, dragging me back. "Well, blast you!" said Heller. "It was a trap!"

He raised his voice in that piercing, Fleet-officer, carrying pitch. "I'm armed! Don't try a rush. Is the commander of this base there?"

Faht Bey's voice through a loudspeaker in the hangar: "Throw out your guns and walk into view with your hands up!"

"I am operating on orders from the Grand Council," Heller called. "Any effort to impede their execution could bring a charge of treason. Throw down your guns and step over into view."

"We know exactly why you are here!" shouted Faht Bey. "We refuse to tamely let you execute us!"

"I have no orders to execute you," shouted Heller. "But I have a prisoner here, Soltan Gris, that I must take to Voltar."

Faht Bey gave a short, barking laugh through the speakers. "This doesn't fool us for a moment. Gris is probably holding a gun on you. He is wanted here for mortgaging this base. We have a black-jowled man in custody who has confessed. Only Gris knew how to sound that alarm. Gris! Step out into view or we will begin barrage fire!"

"Stop!" said Heller. "I've got Gris here. Are you going to listen to reason or aren't you?"

"Don't try to trick us, Gris!" shouted Faht Bey through the speakers. "We've already had an earthquake today and now you! I demand that you surrender! We promise a fair conference trial."

I wailed, "I didn't cause that earthquake! This Crown agent did!"

"So you *are* there!" cried Faht Bey. "FIRE!"

A torrent of slashing flame ripped into the tunnel mouth. Rocks fell! Stone dust swirled around the green glowplates.

"Cease fire!" shouted Heller in that high-pitched Fleet voice.

The shots ceased.

Heller yelled, "If you do not surrender at once, I'll bring half that roof down on your heads. Drop your weapons and step out where I can see you!"

The answer was a renewed storm of electric flame!

Heller was flat against the floor, up the tunnel and in back of me. I looked around to see how I could get in back of him. I had some idea I could blame the difficulties of the base on him, maybe get Utanc/Gaylov to say he put her up to it. I was in pain, my head was in a whirl, but I had not given up.

Heller had a small device in his hands—it must be what he had taken from the ledge. Amidst the swirling dust he was pushing a lever up and down.

"Blast!" he said. "The wall charges won't explode!"

Abruptly I understood what he was talking about. When he was here before, he had gone all over the inside of the hangar, saying he was testing for erosion. He had been planting charges in the walls! And when I had shot at Crobe with a needle stungun, no wonder it had brought tons of rock crashing down into the hangar—I had accidentally exploded Heller's charges! No wonder there had been so much reaction!

Gouts of fire were probing deeper into the tunnel. Heller inched backwards. He pulled me with him by the heel.

Then he did something very odd. He reached into his shoulder kit bag and got out two masks. He pushed one over my face. He put the other one on himself. Gas masks? Why?

He picked up his firing board again. It had three more switches on it. He closed them.

Muffled explosions sounded above the blastgun din.

The roof didn't come down. The firing did not slacken. What had he done?

After a moment, I saw a swirl of white smoke in a portion of the hangar I could see.

Then I heard some coughing. Faht Bey's cough joined it through the loudspeakers.

Somebody screamed, "Opium!" Another took it up!

The firing stopped.

There was the beginning rush of men trying to leave.

A white fog came swirling into the tunnel mouth.

The opium storage caverns! Heller had installed flame bombs in them last fall. Countless tons of opium were burning.

The electronic illusion which made up the hangar roof would not pass air. I had seen Heller test it!

That whole hangar was now full of a powerful narcotic— OPIUM SMOKE!

There was a sound of men falling who had been trying to run.

Then there was only the burning sizzle of flame as it ate into the opium stores.

Heller shoved me ahead.

Through the soporific mist I could see the crew. They were sprawled all about, draped over sandbags and guns, out cold.

Heller said, "Take me to that detention cell."

I still had my chance. I felt for the knife and planned how I could get him ahead of me.

Chapter 6

My brilliant idea to lure him with the corpse of the Countess Krak was about to pay off.

We made our way through the swirling white mists of the hangar and to the prison corridors. I indicated the way but Heller was pushing me in front of him.

We went up the longest passage and came to the end. The port of the door was covered and I was not giving him any chance to lift it. I knew exactly what I would do. Surreptitiously, I felt for the hidden knife in the jacket. Sick as I felt, I could still draw it and plunge it into his back if I could get behind him. And I knew he was approaching a new moment of shock.

I spun the combination. I got the door open a slit, enough to get my hand through and unlock the barred grate within.

The light in the cell was dim; most of the glowplates seemed to be broken and lay about in shattered fragments.

I swung the inner door open and then stepped back, swinging the outer door wide.

It put me behind him!

He stepped straight through into the large cell.

A shaft of light seemed to be coming from the roof.

There was something lying under it, something dark.

Heller was four paces into the cell. He stopped, staring down and ahead of him.

His back was totally exposed!

With a stealthy hand I drew the knife. I stepped forward on silent feet.

I raised the blade to plunge it into his spine.

WHONK!

Something hit me over the head!

I spun around as I fell.

A heavy book hit me again!

I was staring up into the face of a very angry Countess Krak!

Once more the book came down and I went out!

Minutes later I came to. There was no knife in my hand or even near me. My wrists were pinioned behind me, tied excruciatingly tight with what must have been wire.

Heller was sitting on the bed. He was crying!

The Countess was kneeling in front of him, smoothing his hair and gripping his hand.

"I knew you'd come," she said. "When I heard the firing I knew it must be my Jettero."

He tried to talk and couldn't.

I didn't have any gas mask on. I looked at the door and thankfully saw that it was closed. This cell had an independent air supply.

Finally he said, "I thought you were dead. These have been the awfullest days I have ever spent in my whole life. And when he told me you were still alive, I didn't dare believe him."

They were both crying again and holding on to each other.

At length Heller looked around. "What happened to the lights? What is that on the floor?"

"That's a pile of ration cartons and clothes," she said. "I was trying to stand on them and dig my way out. Several days ago a funny thing happened. There was an explosion up the air shaft. The concussion was bad and it must have knocked me out for a while. It made the hole bigger and broke most of the glowplates."

She was pointing and I looked at the air shaft where dusty air was coming in. Then I remembered that in the plan I had put hooks in the air shaft to prevent anyone climbing up it. But I had also planted explosive charges there that would kill anyone who sought to go up through it. When Ahmed had dropped the gas grenade, it had simply set off the charges and the explosion had just blown the poison vapor back out as the whole series had gone off. It had damaged the solar lights. It had also opened up the shaft. Once she had gotten the hooks loose, the Countess Krak could have climbed right up to freedom!

"I've got to get you out of here," said Heller. "Fortunately, last fall, I thought I might have to take this base. But unfortunately, part of what I set up has the place swimming in opium smoke." He took a gas mask out of his bag and gave it to her to use.

He moved over and began putting my gas mask back on.

"What are you going to do with him?" said the Countess. She picked up the knife from where it had evidently been kicked. She was looking at me. I knew exactly what was in her mind. She wanted to cut my throat.

"I gave my word I was taking him back to Voltar for trial," said Heller.

"You mean we are going home?" said the Countess.

"Just as soon as I have taken care of a couple things and repaired the tug, yes—we are going home. The mission is practically complete."

"Oh, how wonderful!" cried the Countess Krak. "And when we get home, I have the most marvellous surprise for you anyone ever heard of!"

I gasped with relief. The moment he landed on Voltar, he would be arrested on some pretext. Lombar would finish him!

And as to what she was so happy about, those Royal proclamations were forgeries and if she ever tried to present them it would mean immediate execution.

INSPIRATION!

How could I arrange that they would present those forgeries so that Lombar could have a pretext to execute them out of hand?

Oh, I was not finished. Not by a long ways!

I would get even with them yet for all the hideous things they had done to me!

Chapter 7

It was hours later and the hangar presented a very strange sight.

Heller had somehow scaled the wall and gotten the electronic-illusion mountaintop switched off and let the clouds of smoke sail into the night. For some time now the place had been full of clean air, maybe for the first time in eighty or more years.

Prahd had responded to a phone call and he had temporarily patched up my wounds.

Utanc/Gaylov was lying trussed up on a bench.

The Countess Krak was standing with a blastrifle to command the entrances in case any late callers showed up.

Heller had placed a big table in the middle of the hangar floor. Sitting in chairs around it was every officer on the base, tied hand and foot!

The rest of the crew were likewise secured, piled in rows upon the floor.

Prahd was going around to the last of the officers now, applying an oxygen respirator to their faces. Then he signalled he was through.

Heller pounded at the table top with the butt of a blast handgun, using it for a gavel. "Now, are we all awake?" he said.

Faht Bey and the other officers were staring at him. They were very aware of their hands tied behind them and tied as well to the chairs.

"Good," said Heller. "I declare the meeting opened. Now, first on the agenda is the status of this base."

"First on the agenda," said Faht Bey, "is a trial of Soltan Gris!" He jabbed his head at me.

I was propped in a chair to the side, the place they usually position a man on trial.

"No, we're going to come to that," said Heller. "You have been told, I believe, that I am here to kill you. I wish to disabuse your minds." And he took from his pocket a copy of the Grand Council orders and a copy of his own and read them, numbers and all, in a very official voice. Then he held them up so they could see their seals and signatures. "Satisfied?"

Faht Bey and the others nodded.

"Now," said Heller, "this base doesn't happen to be listed. So it doesn't exist. What goes on here is known only to the Apparatus, but it happens to include illegal dealing in contraband. I have evidence that you are shipping opium, heroin and amphetamines to Voltar. I am ending that traffic."

"You can't!" said Faht Bey.

"Oh, yes, I can," said Heller. "Under my own cognizance and as a Royal officer of the Fleet enforcing His Majesty's regulations, I am commandeering this whole base in the name of the Voltar Fleet."

"The Chief of the Apparatus would kill us!" said Faht Bey.

Heller reversed the hand blastgun and pointed it at their faces. "I think there will be some changes on Voltar when I return," said Heller. "But if there are not, you can always say you were forced to do it at gunpoint."

The officers looked nervously at that gun.

"All Voltar personnel on Earth," said Heller, "are transferred as of this moment to the Fleet with similar ranks and ratings. And you will get Fleet pay."

That stirred them. The Apparatus personnel were paid hardly anything, and Fleet pay was much more.

"Then I get paid too?" said Prahd, standing with his respirator.

"You get paid too," said Heller.

Oh, Gods, what a mess he was making! Prahd was officially dead! And many of the rest of them had nonperson status—condemned criminals, the lot!

"Do you know," said Faht Bey, "that many of us have no civil status at all?"

"I suspected that. But under the regulations of the Fleet, a Royal officer operating independently in unconquered areas can recruit and induct crews of any kind and grant them a full amnesty. Your civil rights would be restored."

They looked at him with their mouths open and then looked at one another.

Suddenly Faht Bey jerked his head at me. "That doesn't include him?"

"No, it certainly does not," said Heller.

"What's going to happen to him?" said Faht Bey. "He mortgaged this base. He's guilty of crime after crime. He doesn't go free, does he?"

"I am taking him to Voltar for trial," said Heller. He pointed at Utanc/Gaylov. "I will take that creature's testimony, and with everything else he has done, I think the courts will make short work of Soltan Gris."

They suddenly began to cheer, and even the cordwooded crew began to yell with delight. The hangar practically exploded with their joyous shouts.

At length Faht Bey looked around and shouted, "Do we accept his deal?"

The din was deafening!

"Then untie us so we can get to work!" cried Faht Bey. "We got to get this place so it looks like the Fleet!"

I glowered. Turncoats. Riffraff. After all I had done for them!

But I would have the last laugh. None of these poor fools knew that Lombar controlled Voltar now.

I must go along with this. I must pretend that I was done in. I'd even look like I was cooperating.

Heller's actions would not be condoned. They thought I was their prisoner. Actually, they were mine.

I would manage it so that I would be taking this Royal officer they were so stupidly applauding back to his death. And their own demise would soon follow! They were double-crossing Lombar Hisst, who now controlled Voltar.

Chapter 8

Just before the crack of dawn, Heller went over to the field and flew the tug in.

He brought it down through the illusion, which was back on again. Despite the extremely narrow limits of the hangar, he actually turned it horizontal and landed it on its belly over to the side.

The cat heard the voice of the Countess Krak and came out of the airlock like a launched torpedo, yowling something dreadful. The Countess Krak had been guarding me. The cat hit her in the chest and she told it hello and petted it, distracting her attention. But it didn't do me much good. I was still tied to the chair.

The whole scene was very sickening. The base personnel had been standing around, waiting for the tug to come in. I had never realized before that they were, all of them, exiles, convicted of crimes large and small and banished to this place for life. I overheard remarks like "Oh, think of seeing Modon again," and "Imagine once more being able to walk the streets of Flisten cities and not having to hide," and in general, "Oh, think of being able to go home!"

Some of them found some paint and put the symbol of the Fleet, a circle around a diagonal bar, in gold against pale blue, over the Apparatus "bottle" of their shoulder patches.

Heller was undermining this whole base!

A perfectly good lot of criminals were going completely bad!

Well, a lot of good it would do them. The REAL action was

ahead of him when he collided with Lombar's coup.

Once the tug had landed, there was a lot of talk when they saw its stern. They had hated the assassin pilots even worse than they had hated the Antimancos, and they were highly condemnatory of what had happened to the tug.

Two guards came over to relieve Krak in watching me. She went to the stern of the tug to look. She gasped and covered her mouth with her hand.

"Oh, Jettero," she said, "they could have killed you."

He was standing with the ship-repair chief. "It's just a few dented housings, dear. The cable electrode ends are just fused to the sleeves. Link here says he can repair it in just a couple of days."

"Oh, but Jettero—if it had hit the hull!" said the Countess Krak. "My, but I'm glad I have the means to get you into a safer sort of life."

"What do you mean?" said Jettero.

I knew she meant the forgeries. She thought he would be appointed to the Royal Staff at Palace City, "freed from the absences and perils of the Fleet," if he successfully completed this mission. She also thought that she would get a Royal pardon and have her family estates restored. But she was in for a terrible surprise. When she resurrected those fakes from wherever she had hidden them and tried to get the emperor to sign them, she and Heller would be seized and executed for forgery of a Royal signature.

"I can't tell you," said the Countess Krak. "It's a secret. But I can assure you, I simply do not intend to live my life with people shooting at my husband left and right! What would the children think?"

"Are there children?" said Heller.

"No, not yet, but there certainly will be. And they're entitled to a real, live father. I think we should go home as soon as possible."

The repair chief said he had the tools and could make the parts. Heller and Krak went into the ship and were gone for some time. When they came out they had changed their clothes and although what she was wearing was not too unearthly, it was obvious to me that she must have left the bulk of her wardrobe in the posh quarters in the aft part of the tug.

Faht Bey waddled up to Heller. "What do we do with the prisoners, sir?" He had never called me "sir," the rotten turncoat.

"Throw the Russian into a detention cell. Hold on to that black-jowled Grabbe-Manhattan man. We're going over to the hospital and we'll take this Gris traitor with us."

Prahd was still there and his car was out at the barracks. They prodded me along and shortly we arrived at the hospital.

It obviously wasn't their first priority but they put me in an operating room and strapped me down.

Nurse Bildirjin, my latest wife, came in. She regarded me as she would waste in a trash can. She simply banged an anesthetic mask on my face and that was all I knew about that.

It must have been midafternoon when I came to in a hospital room. I was strapped down on the bed, the cat was sitting on my chest, keeping a hateful eye on me, and Nurse Bildirjin was standing by the window.

She saw I was awake. She threw two lead pellets at me. "They missed," she said.

"Missed!" I protested. "I distinctly felt them hit me!"

"They missed any vital organ. If you had any sense of decency, you would have stood a little further to the left. Then I would be a self-respecting widow."

"You (bleepch)!" I said.

The cat snarled, lifting a set of claws to rake me.

"Would you like to see your son?" said Nurse Bildirjin.

For the first time I noticed that her stomach was flat. She must have just gotten out of confinement. I hastily counted up on my fingers. That time she had jumped me after my return from New York was definitely *not* nine months ago.

She had gone out and now she returned with something wrapped in blankets labelled Hospital Nursery. She tipped it toward me.

"Listen," I said. "It's impossible. There hasn't been enough time."

"Slightly premature," she said. "Look at him."

It was a very well-formed baby, several days old.

I blinked. My eyes are brown. My hair is brown. Nurse Bildirjin's eyes were black. Her hair was black.

THIS BABY HAD BRIGHT GREEN EYES!

It had straw-colored hair.

IT EVEN LOOKED LIKE PRAHD!

I snarled, "That baby must have been conceived the very first night that that doctor arrived here!"

She smiled at me enigmatically. "Well, it just might have been if you hadn't refused to let him be paid."

I groaned. Prahd was getting his own back.

"And as it is," said Nurse Bildirjin, "your son will be quite wealthy when you choose to honor your dowry and let the bank have enough money to pay it."

"I'll see you in Hells first!" I raged.

The baby started to cry. The cat raked me.

Nurse Bildirjin looked meaningfully at my covered crotch. "Then I guess I'll just have to advise Doktor Muhammed that you need another operation."

I cringed. I knew what she meant. They would make me into a eunuch!

"All right," I said, knowing that I lied, "I will see it is paid."

But it was right at that moment that I added to my plan. I would go home and deliver Heller and Krak to Lombar. Then I would come back and undo all the damage Heller had done by providing cheap fuel. And last, for dessert, I would see that every Turk connected with this hospital and this base died horribly! Including Nurse Bildirjin and this (bleeped) baby!

Chapter 9

I spent a very sleepless night. The cat had been replaced with two guards from the base who simply sat, rifles across their knees, looking at me, saying nothing.

Young Dr. Prahd Bittlestiffender, alias Doktor Muhammed Ataturk, came in. He was carrying a pan of instruments. He made a motion to the guards and they went outside the door, making sure I knew they were still there, one on either side.

Prahd closed the door firmly and then said the most outrageous thing that I have ever heard. "I am your friend."

I snarled. If I hadn't been strapped down, I would have torn his throat out!

"Now, don't be so upset," he said. "I have had a very trying day and a half. You have no idea how nervous it makes one, attempting to operate under the muzzle of a blastgun."

"Who made the mistake of not shooting you?" I said.

"Let's not be so antagonistic, shall we? Royal Officer Heller kept a huge revolver trained on me while I removed the two bugs from the head of the Countess Krak, and when she was up and around again she held a rifle on me while I operated on him. The visio and audio bugs you had me install in them are now gone. And I'm glad of it. They are very nice people, you know, not at all like some others I could name."

"So how does this make you my friend?" I said savagely.

He didn't answer.

He unbuckled a strap and moved my arm so he could get at my side. He was working with the cups that covered my wounds, checking them. One was on the inside of my left arm, the other had plowed along my left rib cage. He injected a healing catalyst into them. It stung like blazing fire!

He put cups back on the holes and fastened them in place. He strapped my arm down once more.

He looked at me. "Friendship takes many forms," he said. "Just this morning I kept you from getting into more trouble."

"I can't be in more trouble than I am in!" I grated.

"Oh, I think that is entirely possible," said Prahd.

There was a certain look in his eye which boded no good. I braced myself.

"Do you recall my putting something in your skull for you?" he said.

I stiffened further. "Well, you didn't really tell me what it was," said Prahd. "But I have the distinct impression it is something you don't want known."

I began to sweat. He was talking about the breaker switch that prevented any hypnohelmet on this base from working on me. Without it, the Countess Krak could turn me into putty!

"They questioned me," said Prahd. "They wanted to know if I knew of any other bugs on anybody. Now, yesterday you made another empty promise to Nurse Bildirjin. I don't believe you have any intention of handling the various compensations of health funds or the dowry. I don't think you are even going to repair the mosque you blew up."

"You're talking about millions of U.S. dollars!" I snarled.

"No, I am talking about that thing I put in your head. You see, Officer Gris, I did not tell Officer Heller or the Countess Krak anything about it."

"Blackmail!" I said. "You swine!"

"Well, it takes one to know one, doesn't it?" said Prahd, gathering up his instruments. "Or shall I put it another way: I have learned a great deal serving in the Apparatus. You have been an excellent instructor."

"So you are not going to tell them about this thing in my head so long as I . . ."

"Meet your proper obligations," said Prahd. "Frankly, I haven't the least idea what it is. I only know you. So I will continue to cover it under the heading of a professional confidence. Officer Heller is quite sincere in trying to straighten out the mess you made, and now that I am a Fleet doctor I consider it my duty to help him all I can."

His green eyes were so bland, he was so self-righteous about it that I would have strangled him had I been able.

"So you're going to tell him!" I snarled.

"So I am NOT going to tell him. You, for once," said Doctor Prahd, "are going to honor your obligations. And that will help everyone. Agreed?"

I couldn't speak because of the way my teeth were gritting. I managed, finally, a nod.

He was satisfied and left.

The dismal day wore on. It was made even worse when, in early afternoon, a songbird got in a bush outside the window and whistled and sang with great abandon. He knew I was in there and he was just mocking me.

Then disaster struck again.

THE COUNTESS KRAK!

She came in all breezy, hair in a modish fluff, dressed in a pale blue suit that matched her pale blue eyes. The only thing which marred her was a healing cup on her eyebrow. She wasn't wearing brass-heeled boots but she was carrying a carton.

The guards went out and she placed the box on the foot of the bed. "A brand-new one," she said. "Just for you." And she lifted out a hypnohelmet and began to check its controls.

It was the first real evidence I had that Prahd actually had not told them about the thing he had put in my head, for Heller would have been able to figure it out. He had already seen an emergency light turn on mysteriously in the tug. And if she was going to put that helmet on me, she certainly didn't know it wouldn't work, for I had fixed every one of them on this planet. The breaker switch in my head kept them from hypnotizing me.

She made no excuses. She simply plopped it on my head and turned it on.

"Sleep, sleep, pretty sleep," she said.

I closed my eyes and pretended the helmet was doing its job.

"Now, Soltan, you will answer my questions truthfully. What happened to the suggestions I gave you last year that you would be unable to hurt Jettero?"

I knew how to act my part. I muttered, "Slum City."

"You will tell all."

"I was ill and I went to a doctor in Slum City. He said I had been hypnotized and he found the suggestion and nullified it."

"Ah," said the Countess Krak. "And how is it you could harm me?"

"I did as little as I could. I saved you from a plane terrorists sabotaged. I was keeping you safe from them." I didn't even dare open an eye to see how she was taking it. There was a long pause.

"All right," she said. I could hardly keep from showing my elation. She was buying it!

"Now, listen to me carefully. The things the hypnotist in Slum City told you are now false. Hereafter you will be very careful not to hurt Jettero or myself in any way. You will tell us everything you know that will help us. If you do not, you will feel awful and get terrible headaches. Do you understand?"

"Yes," I said in a very muffled way.

"You will also not try to escape us. If you do try, your legs will feel like they are in flames. Understood?"

"Yes," I said.

"Now, Jettero is being good enough and kind enough to try to straighten out some of the things you have done on this planet. You are under direct and explicit orders to do everything he tells you to do. Understood?"

"Yes," I said, but I didn't like this. If I backed down on something she would know this helmet had not worked.

"If you fail to do what he tells you to do, you will at once start vomiting. Understood?"

"Yes," I muttered, secretly writhing. (Bleep) her! She had led me into a trap!

"Now, you will feel much better when you awake. You will be determined to help Jettero straighten out your life. You will now forget that these were my suggestions and think they are your own. Now, as to your wounds, they will heal rapidly. When you awake you will think that is why I hypnotized you. The wounds will heal rapidly. You will thank me for helping you. Understood?"

"Yes."

She turned off the helmet and removed it. She said, "Wake up now."

I carefully kept the fury I was feeling out of my voice. I said, "Thank you for helping me."

She put the helmet away and left.

I cursed a steady stream for minutes. Trapped! I had to obey Jettero Heller or they'd know the helmet didn't work and she would simply stamp me into a mangled mess.

They were all against me. Prahd, the base, the people of Turkey, even the songbird outside the window.

I swore a savage oath to every God I knew of, including Jesus Christ, that I would get even with them all, every one!

They all thought I was powerless. What they didn't know was that I was backed and had at my call the whole Voltar confederacy, if only I could get Heller and Krak home.

Far into the night I turned and twisted. And then, very late, I came to a decision. I would be very cunning while we still remained on this planet. I would pretend to go along with whatever Heller said. I only hoped that it did not prove too much for me to bear. I must do anything I could to get him to Voltar.

Little did I know the suffering he planned for me the very next day! It was to prove completely every bad thing I had ever thought of him!

PART SIXTY-FIVE
Chapter 1

I could tell by the window that an early June dawn was barely breaking, and yet I was being gotten out of bed.

I knew they were up to some deviltry, because they would not talk.

Heller was there. He had on a stylish Panama hat, a summer-weight flannel business suit, a blue silk shirt and a dark blue polka-dot bow tie. I could tell from the boxback cut of the jacket that he had an automatic holstered in the rear of his belt. He was carrying a gray suede attaché case. He was just watching.

Two guards and a nurse were dressing me. They had brought over a conservative, dark blue suit and ensemble from my wardrobe. I protested. "This is cruelty. I am a wounded man and need my rest!" That was the third time I had said it and they still didn't stop.

Finally they shoved me out into the corridor. Heller nudged me along.

In the lobby I beheld Faht Bey. He was dressed in Western business clothes. He didn't even say good morning.

Heller pushed at me to make me go out the front door.

I stopped dead still on the steps.

There stood my Daimler-Benz with the red eagles on the door!

"So you've even taken over my car!" I said.

Heller just nudged me to get in.

I looked back of us. The two guards and Faht Bey were climbing into a nondescript car from the base. Heller nudged me again and I climbed into the Daimler-Benz and sat down.

He climbed in and sat beside me. And then something happened which infuriated me. Those two scoundrels Ters and Ahmed were sitting in the front seat. Ahmed turned around and winked at Heller!

"That man doesn't deserve any amnesty!" I snapped. "He's much more guilty of upsetting this area than I am! He raped the women! He even brought that agent in!"

"We've already discussed it," said Heller. "You're the one who gave the orders."

The injustice of it bit like a whip. Never mind. I'd tell Lombar and Ahmed would be shot.

We rolled out onto the main road. Faht Bey and the other car followed.

"Where are we going?" I demanded.

"You seem to have made quite a mess around here," said Heller. "You owe what they call *kaffarah* to a lot of villages; you owe the construction of a new mosque; and you signed some things, amongst them a bounced bank order for a dowry, on the Piastre National Bank. The manager of the local branch says nobody can make heads or tails of your finances. So we're going to call on a man who might be able to: Mudur Zengin in Istanbul."

I slid far down in my seat. The last man I wanted to see was Mudur Zengin. Teenie had said he was furious with me.

It quite spoiled my trip. I couldn't even think of ways to escape, I was so involved with trying to figure out what I might say to Mudur Zengin. I must owe him an absolute fortune in monies advanced by his bank.

We passed through the summer countryside of Turkey, but I saw none of it. We battled traffic through Uskudar on the Asian shore of the metropolis, but I gave it no heed. We crossed the Bosporus, but I was unmindful of the thick traffic below us on the water. We honked our way along Kemeralti Street in Beyoglu and still I cringed. We threaded a passage across the Golden Horn on the Galata Bridge and, wending through the hundreds of towers and minarets, were all too soon in front of the Piastre National Bank. I was exhausted from nearly three hundred miles of dread.

It was going to get worse.

Mudur Zengin said he would see Faht Bey, but when we all trooped into his office and he saw me, he looked like he was going to throw us out.

Heller took the initiative. He looked around the ornate room and pulled three chairs up to the carved desk. "Do you mind if we sit down?" he said.

"I have no business with this man!" said Zengin, looking hard at me.

Heller pushed me into a chair and sat down himself. Faht Bey took the third.

Mudur Zengin still stood. He was shaking angrily.

"We're trying to straighten out his affairs," said Heller.

"The devil couldn't do that!" Mudur Zengin said. He only sat down so he could support his elbow and shake a finger at me. "Do you have any idea what this man has done?" He waited for no answer. "He had a princely allowance: He squandered it all and ate into the capital. He let a concubine run wild with credit cards and never said a word. He left the bank responsible for paying those bills and then he even bought a yacht. He went sailing gaily across the seven seas, having a marvelous time. We financed the yacht, we paid for all its expenses—we even helped him sell it for five times its value—and then he went running off and let the deal fall through."

"I think there's some possibility of straightening all this out," said Heller.

"You do?" said Mudur Zengin. "But not with this one! He committed the highest, greatest crime you could commit!" He sat back, disdain curling his lips. "When he mortgaged his property, HE WENT TO ANOTHER BANK!"

Heller said, "Certainly there is some way——"

"After an insult like that?" said Mudur Zengin. And he made a gesture like he'd gotten something nasty on his hands.

"I think," said Heller, "that you know Faht Bey."

"Yes, we do business with the companies he represents. I am very sorry and surprised to see him mixed up with such a man as *this!*" And he indicated me.

"Well, Faht Bey and I are his family advisers," said Heller. "We came in just a little late on the scene."

"You certainly did!" said Mudur Zengin.

"Could you answer a question?" said Heller. "Could you tell me why your bank went on advancing money to pay his bills?"

"That is very simple," said Mudur Zengin. "Down in his safety-deposit box, this fool has stacks of gold certificates just lying there, losing money every day, drawing only a small percent. He wanted to leave them there. But someday he would have to come in and open that box and we would be waiting there with a claim. And if he died, its contents would have gone to probate and we would have collected."

I groaned. I had not thought Heller would learn of that box!

"Now, that is very interesting," said Heller. "I'm afraid that this Sultan Bey neglected to mention it to us. Now, you spoke of a mortgage. What if we were to obtain evidence that it was forged and produce the confession of the person who forged it?"

Mudur Zengin shrugged. "It would be typical of the Grabbe-Manhattan Bank in their international dealings. If you produced such proof, the mortgage would be declared null and void and Grabbe-Manhattan would be hauled up for conspiracy to defraud if they knew it was forged."

Heller glanced at his watch. "It is 11:30 now. In the interests of your own bank, could we ask for an interview with you after lunch?"

"Only for the sake of my other directors," said Mudur Zengin. We left and he didn't stand or see us to the door.

"Well, Soltan," said Heller when we got outside, "I see that you have not been entirely frank with us."

The car was parked in a lot now. Heller pushed me in and told Ters and Ahmed to go take a walk. He shut the door and got an instrument from under the bar. It was a viewer-phone with tape. He pushed the buttons.

"Right here," said the Countess Krak, as her face came on the viewer.

"All set," said Heller. "Put a helmet on that Russian spy and get a confession that he forged that mortgage. Get it witnessed by available Turks. Put him back in detention for future trial data on Gris and then transmit the whole confession through to me here as a valid document. Then put a helmet on that black-jowled Forrest Closure, blank him out about the existence of the base and tell him that Grabbe-Manhattan will find itself in criminal court if it pushes the matter further. Got it?"

"Yes, dear," said the Countess Krak.

Lucky them. Lucky me. I wasn't at the base where my head installation would cancel those helmets. It was a close call. My own future plans depended utterly on keeping that fact secret. They must not know that Lombar controlled Voltar.

Faht Bey had found a restaurant and he came and collected Heller. They went off and left me with the guards, who made me eat some junk they brought, sitting in the base car.

Heller and Faht Bey came back about 1:30 and Heller went to the Daimler-Benz and tore off the transmission facsimile sheets and had another word with Krak.

Pushing me ahead of him, Heller took me to the bank. But he didn't take me up to the office. He took me down to the safe-deposit section. I tried to balk. I intended to come back to this planet in a blaze of glory. I certainly did not want to be without funds!

We stood in front of the guard and clerk. "He wants his box," said Heller.

They shoved a card at me to sign.

Never did a hand and arm go so dead. If I signed it, I would be broke!

Heller was looking at me curiously. Did he suspect a hypno-helmet was inoperative on me? My life depended on keeping that fact hidden.

"Well, sign it!" said Heller.

It was very painful. I had to sign the card.

The clerk opened the bank's side of the box and left. The bank guard edged up watchfully. I opened my side of the combination. I plopped the cover back.

All those lovely gold certificates!

But Heller reached past me. He picked up a slip that was lying on top. He read it, the receipt for gold. "Aha!" he said. "Contraband gold from Voltar! Absence of proofmarks noted. Just like those on the tug. This gives me, as a Fleet officer, authority to seize the lot. And this receipt will look just great at your trial." He put it in his pocket.

I felt physically ill.

He reached over and emptied the box. He made a hurried count. He whistled. "Nearly a quarter of a billion dollars! So this is why Apparatus officers don't squawk about low pay. Contraband drugs, illegal gold——"

"You were going to make some yourself!" I snarled.

"Ah, but that is the operative word: *make* some. From these weights, those ingots are straight from Industrial City, Voltar. But I shouldn't bait you, Soltan. You may just have solved a lot of problems."

I contemplated seizing the certificates and trying to run. But the bank guard was standing there. And outside, the two armed men would shoot me in the legs, painfully.

Heller was propelling me with a certain grip on my elbow.

Shortly we were again in the office of Mudur Zengin. He was no less frosty than before.

Heller handed him the confessions. There were *two* of them.

We sat and Mudur Zengin read the first with increasing interest. Then he looked at Heller with amazement.

"This is incredible," said Mudur Zengin. "A Russian spy received orders from Rockecenter himself via Moscow to forge a mortgage to the best opium-growing property in Afyon!"

"That's what he says," said Heller. "And Faht Bey can produce said Colonel Boris Gaylov at any time with his full KGB credentials if it comes to any trial."

"Good heavens!" said Mudur Zengin. He leaned back. "I see why he is confessing. Russia is no more and he has no place to go. Why, that's almost worth the hurricane of wind and earthquake we had here the other day."

He picked up the other confession and read it with his eyes

going rounder and rounder. "Good heavens! This confession by Forrest Closure, head of their International Mortgage Division, states that he received direct orders from Delbert John Rockecenter himself to forge a mortgage to that prime opium land, and that the Russian and he cooked up a cock-and-bull story about a mountain there containing an extraterrestrial base for flying saucers to get Rockecenter interested. Why, heavens, if this got out, Rockecenter would be the laughingstock of the whole banking community. Oh, this is rich!"

"So what do we do?" said Heller.

"Well, young man, that would all depend on whether I decided to cooperate."

Heller laid the gold certificates on the desk. I noticed the bank guard had followed us up to make sure we didn't leave the building with them.

Mudur Zengin shrugged. "We would have come into possession of our rightful share of these anyway," he said, letting them lie there.

"Well," said Heller, "our misguided friend here has certain debts." He handed over a list.

Zengin looked at it. "Well, a small amount of these funds invested could provide a *kaffarah* out of the interest and feed the poor of the named villages. The dowry is simply covered with cash. The antidisease campaign could be handled through a trust of invested funds to do that. I'm not surprised at all about the mosque. The Squeeza credit-card bills were paid by our bank and he owes us, all told, something above five million dollars."

"How much would be left?" said Heller.

Zengin counted my precious gold certificates. He waggled a pencil around. He hit a calculator a few licks.

"About 232 million," said Zengin.

"And if I turned this over to your bank," said Heller, "to make it into a trust fund, could you turn the money earned by it over to Faht Bey here so he could run his businesses?"

"Well, you make it very attractive. That much money under our control would let us dominate Istanbul banking and even drive

Grabbe-Manhattan out of our operating area. It would give Faht
Bey here about four million a month free and clear to run his
businesses, and that's far more than he has ever run through his
accounts. But I don't know." And he was looking with a frown
at me.

"Mr. Zengin," said Heller. "Faht Bey, whom you know, would
have this young man's power of attorney in perpetuity to regulate
all these funds and to have all contact with your bank about this
money."

Zengin was frowning at me. "Powers of attorney can be
revoked."

"Possibly I have not been entirely frank with you," said Heller.
"I did not give you my identity."

"No, you did not," said Zengin.

"I," said Heller, "am an officer of the Crown. The matter is
completely secret. But I am taking Sultan to a country very far
away. He will be tried and, with the evidence we have, he will be
sentenced for life or executed. I can assure you that you will never
lay eyes on him again."

"Really?" said Mudur Zengin, his jaw dropped. He looked at
Faht Bey.

"He is just what he says," said Faht Bey, indicating Heller. "He
is a very capable and trusted officer. As a matter of fact, Sultan Bey
is under arrest right this minute. We are not troubling Turkish
authorities with the matter, but Sultan will be gone from this
country in a matter of days, never to return."

Mudur Zengin began to smile. Then he began to laugh. Then
he reached forward and grasped Heller by the hand and rose,
pumping it. He put his arm around Heller's shoulders. "Sir," he
said, "consider me your lifelong friend!" Emotion choked his voice.

An hour later, practically awash with Turkish coffee and their
pockets full of cigars of the finest blend, Faht Bey and Heller
paused by the car. The time had been taken up by clerks and bank
attorneys drawing up all sorts of papers that Heller had made me
sign. They hadn't given me any coffee and Zengin's praises of
Heller were acid in my ears.

Heller was making sure Faht Bey had all the papers in his stuffed briefcase. "There you go," Heller said. "Now you've got ten times the finance you ever had, and all without even touching filthy drugs."

Faht Bey was looking at him with worshipful eyes. He gave him a crossed-arm salute. It was sickening!

Heller, in the car, before he called our drivers, buzzed the viewer-phone. The Countess Krak's face promptly showed.

"Business all went well," he said. "The confessions turned the tide."

"What are they going to do with them?" said the Countess Krak.

"Mudur Zengin is putting the copies of the confessions in his vault. He's just going to show a corner of them if the matter ever comes up. There won't be another whisper about flying saucers." He laughed. "Oh, you dear, you really are the most. Implicating Rockecenter himself was the master touch."

"Now, Jettero," she said, "you are inferring that you have a dishonest future wife. It just so happens that every scrap of those confessions is the living truth. I even have Rockecenter's orders in his own handwriting here, and copies of all of Forrest Closure's files, in case it ever comes up again."

"It won't," said Heller. "And forgive me for doubting you. You always do so splendidly. Do you want anything from Istanbul? An emerald necklace or something?"

"I don't want anything from this planet," said the Countess Krak.

"All right," said Heller. "We're coming home."

I sat seething in the car. He had taken my base, he had taken my car, he had taken my gold certificates. Before he left Istanbul he bought her an emerald necklace in spite of her refusal. And it was only because he didn't think of it that he didn't take the money for it out of my wallet.

Riding back to Afyon, I could hardly restrain myself. Oh, yes, he was going home.

He was going home to Lombar Hisst—and his death!

Chapter 2

The next day at the base, the cruelty of them toward me continued and even intensified. I could tell from the attitudes of those about me that they were taking a sadistic pleasure in abusing one whom they thought could not defend himself. I submitted to the abuse only so they would not suspect what I had planned for them.

In the morning the Countess Krak took it into her head—or had been asked by Heller—to collect all the evidence that would hang me.

She said, "When we turn you over to the court, we want to make sure the justiciary has all the evidence. While I was in that cell, I had ample time to read the *Voltar Confederacy Combined Compendium Complete*, including all the Codes. It was very thoughtful of you to put that in there. Voltar law is very straightforward and no nonsense. But you have been associated with Earth and my recent experience has shown that anyone knowledgeable in its so-called justice can find loopholes by the ton. Jettero, for some reason, wants you to have a fair trial. You will claim, of course, that there are a lot of loopholes. And the biggest of them is that 'you didn't have your records' and 'all the evidence is hearsay.' Faht Bey has several teams out collecting sworn affidavits on things you have done. So we're going to dig into the dustbins you call your files and assemble them, and if you have any defense at all, you sure better find it."

I was quite sure there wouldn't be any trial of me. The trial of them, by Lombar, would be quite swift. And as to their affidavits, I fully intended to come back here with a Death Battalion and wipe this nest of traitors out.

But under her piercing eye, lest she suspect that they didn't really have me at all, I let myself be propelled by two guards into the secret room of the villa and under their watchful glare got to work.

Things were hidden under piles of other things; boxes of recorded strips were covered with dust, paint and *sira*. My logs were so badly scribbled even I had trouble making them out—reading my own handwriting was not a skill I had acquired any facility in.

The dust grew thick in the air and after a while she got restless and began to wander around the villa.

The bug in Utanc's room was working very clearly and I heard her in there. She had found the two little boys crying under the bed. She didn't speak any Turkish and they spoke nothing else and she couldn't make much sense out of the blubbering she got for answers, so she went and got Karagoz and Melahat, both of whom spoke English, and tried to get to the bottom of what was wrong.

The villa headman and the housekeeper were pretty embarrassed. The Countess Krak listened in growing horror and disgust.

It seemed that Gaylov had made the two little boys into catamites, and each night and sometimes in the day had practiced many sexual perversions with them to satisfy his lust. They knew all along that Utanc was a man but hadn't told anybody.

All this talk of homosexuality was making me very ill and the guards had to keep nudging me to keep me working at the records. So I was not prepared at all for the way it all wound up.

The Countess Krak couldn't believe it, but it seemed that what the little boys were upset about was that they weren't getting it anymore, now that Utanc had disappeared.

Krak, on an embarrassed via of Melahat and Karagoz, tried to argue them out of it. But what she got was even worse. The two small boys said that unless their mothers let them go find Utanc they were going to run away and find other men to sleep with, and if they were prevented from doing that they were going to kill themselves the very first chance they got!

By this time both Karagoz and Melahat were in tears, the little boys were in hysteria and the Countess Krak was in rage.

"This perverted planet!" cried the Countess Krak. "It's just as if they never *heard* of normal sex!"

The two little boys were dragged away and I could hear the Countess going through Utanc's things and giving orders to the staff to pack the whole room up into trunks for storage.

After a time she came in and glared at me. "While you're at it," she said, "you better dig up all the evidence of how you got mixed up with Gaylov. There are thirty-two statutes in the penal codes relating to homosexuality."

"There's homosexuality in the Confederacy!" I flashed.

"Not with children, you filthy brute."

"Wait a minute!" I flashed. "I didn't have anything to do with that! I *hate* homos!"

"You better be ready to prove it!" said the Countess and stalked off.

The injustice of it was like vinegar in my veins. I began to dig harder, assembling my records. Then I paused. How the Hells did you prove you were *not* a homo? It was almost impossible to prove you were *not* anything. The only evidence you could collect was that you *were* things. You could never show a court an *absence* of anything. You couldn't walk up to the judge and say "Here is a list of the cars I have *not* stolen." The judge would just say, "All you had to do was omit from the list the cars you *have* stolen: guilty as charged!" Justice was totally one-sided. There was no such thing as negative evidence.

And just that moment my eye lighted upon the packet of photographs of me and Teenie. There I was, into her from behind: lying evidence of *sodomy!* And children? Here was the lying evidence of *rape of a minor!*

One of the sentries tittered.

I made a hasty motion to tear them up.

The other one stopped me. "I wouldn't do that, if I were you, Gris. We have to attest you didn't destroy any evidence."

I began to sweat. I hadn't turned those little boys into

catamites. These photographs were absolute lies. The toils of the law felt like whips as they wrapped around me in my imagination. I could be hanged for things I had NOT done!

I steadied myself. I made a plan right there and then to surreptitiously destroy such things as these photographs the very first chance I got and to pick up things which would only incriminate others, just in case. It gave direction to my work which promptly paid off. I found myself holding the copy of the contract Ahmed, the taxi driver, had made concerning the buying of Utanc. It cheered me up. Ahmed was the criminal in this case, not me. And right under that was a pile of strips from the Heller and Krak bugs that I was sure would show them plotting relentlessly to depart from the careful instructions they had been given by me, their mission handler, and doing all sorts of other things. I, after all, was also under orders here. I DID have evidence that would demonstrate a colossal conspiracy to ruin me.

I got down to my task of collection.

But after three more hours of it, I began to feel very put upon. Why bother to collect all this? It just showed their general cruelty to me.

After all, there would be no trial of ME. My task was to deliver Heller and Krak into the hands of Lombar. One glance at those forgeries of the Royal signature would be followed by one command: "Execute them!" And given Lombar's hatred of Heller personally and his hatred of the aristocratic class of Krak and everything it stood for, that command would be very swift.

I would have to pretend I was going along with this charade that I would be brought to trial.

But I didn't have to like it.

Chapter 3

That afternoon the cruelty became extreme.

They put me on public display!

The Countess had seen that all the records I could gather fitted in a bag with a shoulder strap and she had hung it around my neck, and because she had to go to other parts of the base for affidavits—and, I knew, to talk about me behind my back—she had dumped me in the hangar, lashed to a chair, close beside the hull of the tug where Heller was working.

Clerks and workmen and repair crew all seemed to be finding errands that took them across the hangar floor, and although the two guards on either side of me told them time and time again to keep moving, they would stop and stare. They would whisper to each other behind their hands and once I overheard an old clerk say, "You can tell a lot from faces: look at that scowl." I would have answered that that horizontal mark was NOT a scowl but came from falling on a skateboard, but the guard, before I could get out two words, told me to shut up.

It was pretty dreadful. Out of those two hundred crew, there were many I had never seen before. I wondered if there had been a special excursion from the New York office.

It was hard to get Heller's attention. He was helping fit the last sleeves in the tug repairs. He had time to tell the cat it was a great cat when it came swaggering over to show him a rat it had caught, but he didn't have any time to help fend off the glares his suffering prisoner was getting.

I finally convinced a guard that he should tell Heller it was urgent that I talk to him.

Heller came over and I said, "What am I? Some kind of a circus freak? I feel like a monstrosity Crobe turned out! Why are you keeping me out here in the open?"

"Well, it's not from any joy in your company," he said. "I gave you my word to deliver you to Voltar for trial. There are several hundred Turks and about two hundred crew that have expressed varying degrees of desire to kill you. Your guards asked permission to keep you in sight of the Countess or myself."

"What?" I said.

A guard said, "They respect the officer and his lady too much to start a fight in their presence. And we also don't want to succumb to the temptation of killing you ourselves. Now stop bothering Officer Heller. We could have told you that."

Of course, they had just made it all up to frighten me. My treatment of these people had been just what such riffraff deserved. But it showed me the futility of expecting humane treatment.

Prahd came around and checked my wounds right in public, and people thought they had not been serious enough and were very disappointed when he pronounced me well. But they cheered when he told Heller I could travel any time.

About four o'clock, an electronics man who had been working inside the tug came out carrying a viewer-phone. "Sir," he said to Heller, "this thing keeps ringing. It's on an Earth band and it's got *Me Only* chalked on its glass." Heller took it and the man gave him a crossed-arm salute. This (bleeped) crew was certainly putting on airs!

Heller found a toolbox, saw that nothing but black hull was behind him and sat down. He pushed the answer button.

"Oh, thank heavens, Mr. Jet," said Izzy. "I finally reached you."

"Something wrong?" said Heller.

"No, I just wanted to tell you that everything's all right. That's what makes me nervous. The wonderful news that Miss Joy was all right after all couldn't help but whet the appetites of Fate. How is she? Is she still all right?"

"She's just splendid, Izzy, as always. I'll ask her to call you this evening and you can see for yourself."

"Oh, that will be wonderful. But I don't deserve it."

"So, how are things?"

"Well, bad news first. When Russia blew off the map, of course that killed all threats of international holocaust, so the price of gold went down. I was going to sell that weighty lot you gave me but it's only worth about six million now. Do you think I should hold on to it?"

"That's up to you," said Heller. "Is Russia that bad?"

"Oy, Mr. Jet. Russia ain't. And every one of its satellites has thrown off the yoke. It just shows you that there's a God in the heavens after all."

Hastily Heller said, "How are the options?"

"All right. I'll get around to the good news, now. Oil shares are going down like the Black Friday of 1929. We could already net five billion on the sell options. Brokers are ringing the phone to pieces trying to deal but we're holding on. Miss Simmons is doing the greatest job you ever heard of. They tried to shut her off the media and her people took to the streets in every country with loud hailers. People won't touch radioactive gasoline or oil and Maysabongo is exercising its buy-reserves options, so that's shut off. Our oil-shares buy options are just sitting there waiting to take over every oil company."

"What is the last date for all these options?" said Heller.

"The shares are all July options. The last real operative date is the Monday before the first Saturday following the third Friday in July. That's because brokers close them out a week earlier than the actual date on the options so they can clear their books."

"That's confusing," said Heller.

"Well, I know," said Izzy. "But if you don't keep such things confusing, then how could people in the know win?"

Heller looked at his watch. "That Monday, then, is only about thirteen days away. So everything is going fine, then."

"Right on schedule, Mr. Jet."

"Well, you've got it all under control, then. I won't be seeing you for a while, Izzy."

"Oh, no! Did I do something to displease you?"

"Of course not," said Heller. "It's just that I have some other duties I must attend to."

"What if something goes wrong?"

"We've discussed all this. You have Rockecenter, Junior, for a front name. And you are perfectly capable of handling any corporate angle anybody ever heard of. You have never fooled me for a minute, Izzy Epstein."

"Oh, dear!" said Izzy in dismay.

"Oh, by the way," said Heller, "you can close the condo."

"Oh, NO! I *have* done something wrong! You are *mad* at me!"

"No, I am not!"

"I refuse to close the condo!"

"At least lay off the staff," said Heller.

"You'll need them when you get back!" wailed Izzy. "They had the whole place full of flowers to celebrate Miss Joy's safe return! DON'T LEAVE US, MR. JET!"

Heller looked upset. He tried to speak a couple of times and couldn't. Then he managed, "I'll call you later, Izzy."

Heller turned it off and put the viewer down. He wandered away, looking very unhappy.

Faht Bey was just coming out of the tunnel into the hangar and approached him. "You don't look very cheerful, sir."

"It's kind of hard to leave," said Heller. "But I can't wait around another thirteen days when there's no reason."

"It's the lady, isn't it, sir?" said Faht Bey. "She seems awfully anxious to get home, and I don't blame her a bit, after all she's been through."

"No," said Heller, "it isn't just the lady. My job here appears to be done and I want to get my report in as soon as possible. His Majesty and the Lords should know what is going on. Something smells."

"I quite agree, sir. I've thought it for years. Link, the repair chief, just told me that the tug will be ready by sunset. What last-minute orders do you have for me?"

"Well, all right," said Heller. "Let's start with those three old freighters over there." He pointed across the hangar where three battered hulks about the size of the *Blixo* had been shunted long ago against the wall and stood festooned with litter and dust. "I was into them this morning, and with some work they will still fly. Get them fully operational."

"That shouldn't take long," said Faht Bey.

"Now, any freighters coming in here should simply be stopped and held. Do not permit them to load drugs or depart."

Faht Bey visibly shuddered. "They'll object."

"Look," said Heller. "When I get home, I will report this whole matter to His Majesty or other authorities and tell them what I have done and why. In such cases it is just a formality: Nobody really cares much what happens on an unconquered planet. They almost always back up combat engineers in matters of creating or taking over bases. In any case, you have my appointment in writing and I promise you faithfully that if anything goes wrong I will bail you out."

"That's good enough for me, sir," said Faht Bey. "You see, I and most of my men here hate handling drugs. Have you noticed that none of us take them? They're pretty awful!"

"Amen to that," said Heller. "I've had some experience with how they ruin people."

"There is another thing," said Faht Bey. "What will we do with these criminals whose identities we are supposed to change?"

"Well, a promise is a promise," said Heller. "You don't need enemies. Finish them up. Just don't accept any more."

"Good," said Faht Bey. "Can you give me a hint as to what the operating policy of this base should be?"

"Make friends," said Heller. "Get Earth doctors trained fast in disease eradication. Get Prahd to pass on what he knows about drug rehabilitation. Help the farmers around here to shift their crops over to something less deadly."

Faht Bey was laughing. "You mean actually run the school?"

"Why not?" said Heller. "Of course, the Fleet or His Majesty may have other orders for you. They may even order you to evacuate the place. Who knows? But it's best to let the future take care of itself."

"Sir," said Faht Bey, "we'd leave this desolate plateau in a minute if we had the chance."

"Well, life is never all sweetbuns and pink sparklewater. At least someday you can go home."

"Thanks to you, Officer Heller. You've been a breath of life itself. I and all my men will bless you to the day we die."

I almost vomited at this praise of that (bleeped) Heller. And as to the day they died, I'd come back here with a Death Battalion and make that as soon as possible!

I began to think of all the rotten things Heller had done that I now had to undo. Just knocking out his microwave-power unit was no longer enough. Yes, one could bomb Ochokeechokee and Detroit and the Empire State Building. But that probably wouldn't be enough. In addition to a Death Battalion to handle this base, I would have to requisition an Apparatus Flying Raid Squadron, obliterate all existing military bases and—those that refused to capitulate—seats of government. It would not have to be a major invasion, for we had a puppet potential.

I could just see Rockecenter now. There he was, all ragged and forlorn, huddling in an alley amongst the garbage cans, and I would come up to him, splendid in a full-dress Voltar uniform, flanked by good criminal Apparatus aides, and I would say, "Delbert, do you remember me?"

He would gasp and grovel and say, "Good God! Inkswitch, my family spi!"

I would say, "No less, Rockie, old boy. I've come to put you back on the throne of Earth, the place from which you fell."

And he would be babbling his gratitude while an aide supported his head to give him water and another bathed his wounds.

Then together, arm in arm, we would walk forth, deaf to the

piteous screams of the maimed and dying, and treat the riffraff to a holocaust the like of which had never been seen before.

And out of the gutters that ran with blood, Miss Pinch's pale hand would rise up and she would cry, "Forgive me, Inkswitch! Forgive me, for I did not know. . . ."

Somebody was shaking me.

"Wake up." It was Heller's voice. "Get in the tug. The sun is setting and we are leaving for Voltar within the hour."

I smiled. That was all I needed to make my dream come true.

Chapter 4

Aboard the speeding tug, for three solid days, I lay strapped down in a gimbal bed.

It was sheer torture: The Will-be Was time drives were roaring flat-out for the first half of the trip, driving us to the brink of extinction, and roaring flat-out for the last half of the trip, braking us down. Sparks were flying off everything, and amidst the crackle and din, one didn't know from one minute to the next whether the vessel would blow up. I hate space travel, and especially in that (bleeped) tug.

The cabin I occupied was to starboard and immediately aft of the bridge, and every time the door opened, I craned my neck to see if anyone was on watch.

The Countess Krak, dressed in a black spark-insulator suit, had come in from time to time to feed me and check my bonds, and never once had I seen anybody in a pilot chair. My whole conclusion was that I was not only in the hands of speed maniacs but that they were also insane. There are all kinds of things to run into between stars and, I had to conclude, they had simply left it up to the robot tug to avoid them. It put me on the verge of a nervous breakdown, complete with froth.

But now the Will-be Was drives had died and we were on planetary auxiliaries, slowing down even more for the last small part of the trip.

The Countess Krak came into my cabin wearing an ordinary

powder-blue space coverall. She gave me some hot food and was about to leave.

I said, "I'm going crazy in here."

She shrugged. "All right. I'll leave the door open." That was all the sympathy I got. But she did prop it back.

Heller, now that there wasn't any danger or need of watchfulness, was sitting in the planetary-pilot chair.

The Countess Krak sat down in the now-unused star-pilot chair. "How many miles to go?"

He didn't answer and she had to repeat the question.

"Oh, not too long. Only a few thousand miles," said Heller. "We'll shortly cross the outer defense perimeter of Voltar."

"You seem very pensive," said the Countess Krak.

"Well, yes. I was thinking of your safety. You are still a nonperson, you know. I wish to put you in a hiding place before I officially report back in."

"Do you think that is necessary?" she said.

"Well, I'll be frank," said Heller. "This whole mission started in a very peculiar way. They made me a prisoner in Spiteos. And after the attacks by the Apparatus assassin pilots I have been sort of leery of the whole thing. Fleet Intelligence Officer Bis and I decided to go through with it and see if we could find out what the Apparatus was up to. And I did find a secret base that nobody knew about but the Apparatus, and probably very few of them. But I don't have the whole story. There could be fireworks and I don't want you in the middle of it, not with your status. Why, I don't even know what's going on right this minute in Voltar."

"Are we in Homeview range?" said Krak. "Maybe we could learn something from a news broadcast."

He switched one of his screens to domestic bands and Homeview music came in.

I was being very alert indeed. I had not known that he and Fleet Intelligence had been suspicious. I had the sudden sensation that my enemies had multiplied. I suddenly recalled the awful threat Fleet officers had made to me at their club concerning what they'd do if anything happened to Jettero Heller. The stupid fools made an idol of this man simply because he had been a racing pilot and an athlete and had done more than fifty volunteer missions. So he was a Fleet hero.

Well, Lombar Hisst, as Apparatus Chief, was a man of sense. He hated the Fleet, he hated Heller personally, and he wasn't a man to be checked by a little undeserved popularity. He'd make short work of Heller. My job was to get Heller into his hands.

Suddenly I was distracted from my problems by an announcer saying, "And now it is our privilege to give you a replay of a selection from a popular musical of Hightee Heller, the darling of the spaceways, the sweetheart of billions of adoring fans."

Hightee Heller, Jettero's sister, reputed to be the most beautiful woman in the 110 planets of the Voltar Confederacy, came on the screen.

Back of her was a large ensemble of dancers and a chorus.

She sang "Bold Prince Caucalsia" and the company got on a silly-looking boat and sailed off into the sky.

Heller and Krak, the silly idiots, both applauded her just as though she could hear them.

"Well," said Heller, "I've still got a family, anyway."

"You'll have a bigger one if we can get things straightened out," said the Countess.

"That's why I must play the return so carefully," said Heller. "Nothing bad must happen to you. Here's the news."

There were some shots of a park being dedicated on some planet, then a discovery of a new species of bird on Flisten and some other like items.

A shot of some tanks being flown across a mammoth river came on. The announcer said, "Rebel forces on the planet Calabar have been under heavy pressure during the past week from new Apparatus units recently flown into the area." It was followed by a shot of an officer who looked upset. "Army Corps Commander Zog has been deposed for his failures to make progress against the rebels."

The Army corps commander said, "The adherents of the rebellious Prince Mortiiy have the advantage of an unknown number of bases throughout the hundred-thousand-foot mountain ranges of Calabar. These peaks are honeycombed with caves. It has been my consistent opinion that massive frontal assaults are far too costly. I am tendering my resignation to the Lord of the Army Division."

The announcer said, "A spokesman for the Lord of the Army stated today that the court martial of Zog is a certainty. The Grand Council deplores the fact that this rebellion is now entering its fifth year and has taken its suppression out of the hands of the Army and turned it over to the Exterior Division Apparatus forces." Lord Endow came on, dribbling and drooling a bit, reading a prepared statement nearsightedly. "It is time we . . . er . . . ended . . . ah . . . this unseemly . . . well . . . irrational adherence to the Prince Mortiiy. . . . Er . . . well . . . we just can't go on countenancing . . . yes, countenancing . . . a whole planet's population insisting on supporting . . . er . . . hmmm . . . Prince Mortiiy. I am proud . . . happy? No . . . elated?—what *is* this word here?" An Apparatus officer came on suddenly. "Lord Endow wishes to state that he is determined to kill the enthusiasm of the population for Prince Mortiiy with fire and lightning and put a rapid end to this revolt."

"Well, well," said Heller. "So they pulled the Army off the lines there and the Fleet is not participating. Those Apparatus 'drunks' will just begin systematic looting. Calabar's a nice planet, you know—fantastic scenery. I was there once as a cadet and we couldn't get over how big everything was. And how beautiful."

"The women, too?" said the Countess.

Heller laughed. "None like you, darling."

He wouldn't be laughing, I told myself smugly, if he knew that his influential friend on the Royal staff, Captain Tars Roke, had been demoted and removed to Calabar.

My thoughts, however, began to wander, for it seemed the Apparatus was taking a pretty large role. Intended for matters exterior to the confederacy, originally, it was taking an internal role more heavily than ever. It must be getting large increases of men and equipment, for it had never been very big. Being its chief was going to be a pretty large job.

There were some other news items and then the announcer said, "Concern for the health of His Majesty, Cling the Lofty— Long Live His Majesty and the Voltar Dominions—was greatly diminished today by the optimistic announcement by his spokesman, Lombar Hisst, that with plenty of rest he can be expected to survive many years."

"Hold it!" said Heller. "What *is* this? Lombar Hisst—a *spokesman* for Cling the Lofty?"

"That's impossible!" said the Countess Krak. "Hisst is just a gutter rat! He isn't a nobleman! He's violating court protocol. I know! I had a lot of time to read that *Compendium*. That function should be performed by the Lord of Empire."

"There *is* something wrong," said Heller.

I seethed. My whole stake lay in getting him to an Apparatus base. Confound those Homeview people for arousing their suspicions! I knew that Lombar had control of things. But they mustn't!

"Dear," said Heller, "maybe you'd better talk to the prisoner and see if he can shed any light on this."

I cringed. It was almost as if he had been reading my mind!

Krak promptly got up, opened a carton, came in, and without so much as a "with your permission," plopped a hypnohelmet on my head!

She turned it on. She said, "Has Lombar Hisst been up to something?"

"Oh, no," I said in a properly muffled voice, not affected by the helmet at all, "Lombar is just an efficient public servant and he has to cover up for Lord Endow."

She thought for a moment. "Were you acting on Lombar Hisst's orders when you sabotaged this mission?"

"No," I said. "That is what I am afraid of. That I will be found out. It was all my own idea. I am jealous of Heller."

"You don't know of any changes in the government?"

"No. Nothing is wrong. My most recent communications just showed everything as usual."

She told me to just lie there and not see or hear anything. She went back to the flight deck a dozen feet away.

"Dear," she said, "he says nothing is wrong. I think it is safe to land. And we can go straight to Spiteos."

"*Spiteos?*" said Heller, thunderstruck. "*Why?*"

"Dear," said the Countess Krak, "I left some papers there. They are quite vital to our future."

"Lady," said Heller, "Spiteos is Lombar Hisst's terrain. You've been hinting at this for months. I think you'd better tell me all."

"Well, I'm sure it will be all right now to tell you. The mission is over." And she proceeded to tell him all about the Royal proclamations I had had forged. One still had to be signed, but when it was signed, it would restore her identity, titles and lands. The other had to be endorsed at the end of the successful mission and it would give him a Royal post and no more suicidal combat-engineer assignments.

Heller was amazed. "You saw these things?"

"Yes, and they are entirely authentic. You mustn't forget that other people think you are valuable, too! We only have to present them to His Majesty for their final signatures."

"Where are they?" said Heller.

"I hid them at Spiteos," said the Countess Krak.

"Oh, I don't know," said Heller. "Let's face it. You are a nonperson. You do not have any civil status at all. If they laid hands on you and you didn't have these papers, they could just imprison you again. It's too awfully much a risk. I just went through too much when I thought I had lost you to even discuss the matter further. When you're two hundred years old, gray-haired and toothless and I've been dead for decades, you can bring the matter up again. But not before. That's it. That's final. That's all there is to it. You are *not* going near Spiteos! FINISH!"

"Oh, Jettero."

"No, I mean it! I am NOT going to lose you again!"

"Jettero, you are always telling me that all life is, is a series of consecutive risks joined together with hairs stood on end."

"I didn't say that."

"Well, the way you live, you probably think it. This isn't

something one should throw away. It means you can have a much better life and it means that I can marry you. This isn't something you throw away. You sit right there."

The Countess Krak came back in. She picked up the helmet microphone. She said, "Are there any other copies of those documents anywhere?"

I had been holding my breath. But now, like a brilliant blueflash, an idea came to me that had such certainty of success that I was in instant awe. The whole plan came to me, just like that! I could not only escape them but I could also get them captured.

I was hard put to keep the elation out of my voice. I forced it to be muffled. I lied, "Yes. The exact same documents, perfect duplicates, are under the floor of my office at Section 451."

When she took the helmet off it was almost all I could do not to split my head in half with a grin.

Heller and Krak had delivered themselves straight into my hands!

Chapter 5

He passed us through the defense perimeter in the outer reaches of Voltar by giving the number of a patrol craft. I had expected that he would use my identoplate but he didn't even ask me for it.

I wondered where we were going. I had thought that he would land at the hangars of the Apparatus Space Section, of course, the point where we had taken off. By craning my neck I could see that we were over a high plateau. That wasn't even the main Fleet base! Where was he taking us?

It seemed to be late afternoon on the ground. But we were not near enough to make out much detail.

Then he did another crazy thing. A challenge came up to us from whatever was below and Heller said, "*Upward Strike,* requesting permission to land."

Upward Strike? That was the last of the original intergalactic battleships, 125,000 years old. A museum piece!

We came down like a plummet in Heller's usual landing style: fast and sudden.

We were tail first, bow toward the sky. It put me upside down and I hung there, standing on my head. Then my gimbal bed belatedly reversed and I was being held down, standing up and staring out the suddenly opened port.

WE WERE TOTALLY SURROUNDED BY FLEET MARINES!

They stood with weapons ready—they even had a motorized field piece.

Heller threw open the airlock.

A hailer blared out, "Give us your recognition at once!" I knew that voice. It was Commander Crup.

We were at Emergency Fleet Reserve.

Heller yelled down from the entry port, sixty feet above the ground, "I thought that would get you!" He was laughing.

"Blazing comets!" yelled Commander Crup. "It's Jettero Heller! Jet, boy! You scared us half to death! We didn't see it was Tug One until the last two seconds. You could've gotten yourself shot!"

"I didn't want to put it on the communication channels that I was arriving here. And I wanted a guard of marines. I've got a prisoner I promised to bring home for trial. I've got to deliver him to the Royal prison."

"Who?"

"Remember that Soltan Gris?" said Heller.

"A 'drunk'?" said Commander Crup. "Well, it's about time somebody arrested him. What about Tug One? It's an Apparatus vessel now."

"I'm transferring it to independent duty on my own cognizance. I've had a bellyful of 'drunks.' "

"Who hasn't?" said Commander Crup. "Get the ladder out and you can get down."

"Good," shouted Heller. "And if old Atty is around, I want to see him, too."

Oh, this was boding no good for me. Those Fleet marines looked deadly. I waited anxiously to see what was going to happen.

When they got the ladder, Heller went down it in a long slide. Then he ran over and he and Commander Crup swatted each other on the back. The marines stood alertly, eyeing the tug, and I knew they were slavering in the hopes of getting a shot at a "drunk." I began to sweat.

Old Atty, once Heller's racing repair chief and a watchman now, came tearing up in a triwheeler and pumped Heller's hand and wiped his eyes.

Fleet reunion! I had forgotten how many friends Heller had. Next he'd probably take me to his palatial quarters at the officers' club and let the younger men beat up on me for sport.

They were grouped around Heller down there. Then Crup rushed off and a Fleet marine sergeant rushed off and Atty rushed off. They all looked very businesslike. What was Heller up to?

It struck me that nobody elsewhere had the least idea we were back. I prayed I could still make my idea work. Everything depended on delivering Heller to Lombar, and here he was surrounded by Fleet, the mortal foes of the Apparatus.

The marine sergeant came back and handed Heller a bag and Heller scaled the ladder and gave it to the Countess Krak.

Then old Atty returned with a truckload of fuel rods, followed by an atmosphere-and-water truck.

Then a civilian airbus jumped the fence and Commander Crup got out and talked with Heller.

Suddenly, I heard a step in my door and glanced hastily sideways and got the impression of a Fleet marine beside me. I felt a surge of fear. They had come to get me! I felt the buckles of the gimbal bed part and looked up.

I WAS STARING INTO THE FACE OF THE COUNTESS KRAK, DRESSED AS A FLEET MARINE!

Her hair was tucked under the combat helmet. The tan, high-collared tunic was darker than the slight tan of her face. She had done something with makeup and looked like a too-handsome young space soldier.

So that was how he was going to hide her. I overcame my terror of being so close to her and filed the information away.

PART
SIXTY-SIX

Chapter 1

"Now, Soltan," Krak said. "No tricks. When does your office close?"

A surge of hope raced through me. I didn't show it in my face. "Six," I said.

"That's sunset," she said. "And there won't be anyone there?"

"Nobody. They dive for home."

"Now listen carefully. We're taking you there to get the duplicates of those Royal proclamations. If you even so much as quiver, we'll break your legs. Understood?"

I nodded, careful not to look eager. This was going exactly per my plan.

She had a marine electric dagger in her hand. She put the satchel of my records over my head. That was what I wanted, too.

"When we've got those proclamations," she said, "we are delivering you to the Royal prison. Remember that I did not give my word that you would arrive there alive. The price is your cooperation in delivering those documents."

"You'd kill me?" I said.

"After your trying to murder Jettero? I saw it, remember. You don't deserve a trial. So do you go along quietly and help? Or do I find out right here how effective this electric dagger is?"

She had it on. I could hear it whirr. But I tried to hide a smile. She was playing the game exactly as I wished.

She prodded me down the ladder. I went the sixty feet to the ground and two Fleet marines took hold of me and marched me roughly to the civilian car.

The driver was a marine and beside him sat another, holding a needle handgun pointed straight at me.

I got in the back. Heller sat on one side of me, Krak on the other.

Heller waved to Crup and we vaulted into the sky.

All Voltar spread out below in the waning sun. We passed around the main Fleet base and began to mingle with the sky traffic. The driver was identifying us with his own identoplate, just another bunch of marines going on liberty.

As we approached Government City we bucked the outgoing evening traffic. The River Weil wound a golden track around the cliffs where the offices of Section 451 perched in decay.

Then qualms began to hit me.

I was as tense as a string about to break. Could I pull this thing off? My life depended upon it and so did Heller's death.

If it didn't work, they would deliver me to the Royal prison. That was the province of the Justiciary of Voltar and not even Lombar could tamper with the decisions of those grim judges. In the Domestic Police prisons, the Apparatus could spirit away criminals after they had been sentenced, but not the Royal prison. Stern tradition guided the justiciary there, for it housed only the most notorious criminals, those with crimes against the state. If they locked me in there under charges, not even Lombar could get me out.

This was a very risky thing.

Lombar had better appreciate all the dangers I was suffering on his behalf.

We came in slowly, making sure that the office was now closed. Old Bawtch, the chief clerk there, was dead. I had ordered him killed along with the two forgers. So there was no risk that they would be around to expose the invalidity of what we had come to pick up.

It was dusk. "Looks like they've all gone home," the marine driver said.

"Go ahead and land," said Heller.

The driver chose a place between two parked airbuses and killed the engine.

Heller got out and looked around. There was nobody in sight. The building was locked. He was carrying a shoulder kit bag and he got out an instrument. He went up and down the wall tubing with it. He located what I knew to be the central communications conduit of the place.

With two suction cups he fixed a field coil over the area. It would give the circuits the appearance of still being alive. No alarm would trigger.

Then, with a pair of snips, he cut the conduit apart. No alarm would go off and nobody could make a call out of that building now.

I was praying soundlessly to every God I knew that my trick would work.

Heller beckoned to the two marines. They already had guns pointed at me. "This is the prisoner's office. We are going in here to collect some papers. But he also might get the idea of laying his hand on a weapon. This is also Apparatus territory and he might get the idea his friends will rescue him before we can get him to the Royal prison. So at his first suspicious move, shoot to stun."

Heller motioned to me and I pushed my identoplate against the lock.

Inside, the place was its old, musty, dark, cluttery self, redolent with what sarcastic people are prone to call "drunk stink." I had no time to look around: under the prod of guns, I went through to my old office in the back.

Heller set a lamp down on a side table. Nothing had changed: dust was thick; there was even an empty hot-jolt can just where I had left it so long ago.

Oh, office of bitter memory and pain, office of nightmares and overwork, office of travail—I had not missed it even a little bit.

My private toilet door was closed.

"Well, where are they?" said the Countess Krak.

Of course, there were no duplicates of those Royal forgeries. I said, "Oh, don't think I am unwilling to cooperate. I am just trying to remember exactly which floorboard I have to lift." It really didn't matter which one I addressed first: there was ample blackmail material under each and every separate one of them, for I had been collecting career data for all my years in the Apparatus. It's the only way one could get along and get his way.

I managed to look a little distracted. I gripped my lower abdomen and made a face. Then I started to bend over to lift a board. I got it partially up. One could see there were papers under it. I dropped it. "No, that's not the one. I don't want to tear the whole place up . . ." I grimaced harder. "If I only didn't have my mind on having to go to the toilet . . ."

"What?" said Heller.

"I've got diarrhea," I said. "It's the increase of gravity. A spacer like you wouldn't notice it, but weighing one-fifth more now has got my system upset. If you let me go to the toilet, maybe I could concentrate." Holding my lower abdomen with one hand, I pointed at the toilet door with the other.

Heller gestured to a marine. "Check it out."

The marine opened the toilet door, played a light around the place, grimacing at the cluttered stink. He shined the light at the window and went over close to it to look down at the River Weil flowing darkly five hundred vertical feet below. The window was the kind that seals and never opens. He came out.

Rather hurried, to keep up the pretense, I went in. I looked back at the Countess Krak and closed the door.

Silently I slid the bolt shut.

Carefully I found the secret catch that opened the side wall. It worked smoothly and quietly. The ladder was there to the hatchway above.

I reverently thanked Bugs Bunny for the inspiration he had been in my life.

The glass in the square window was silent-break. I hefted my bag of records. I swung it at the window.

There was not even a tinkle.

The jagged edges that remained were very convincing.

I stepped back through the secret side wall and closed it behind me.

On silent feet I went up the ladder.

With hushed fingers I opened the upper hatch.

I stepped out into the starlight.

I closed the hatch behind me.

Without a sound, I crept over to an irregularity in the roof and crawled under the eave to be hidden from overfly view.

A ventilation pipe was close to hand that opened into the lower office, so I took my head well away from it.

I SHOUTED A DWINDLING SCREAM!

A silent second from below.

PANDEMONIUM!

The sound of someone trying to open the toilet door!

The crash of a gun butt against the lock!

The rip of a shattered bolt!

"HE'S GONE!"

The sound of a chair as it overturned. A rush of feet.

Then a voice, which was coming through the shattered window as somebody looked down: "That's hundreds of feet straight down!"

"Do you see a body?"

"Shall I call the river patrol?"

"Nothing can live in those rip currents."

"Do you see any sign of a ledge or a rope?" asked Heller.

"Just straight down, sir. Here's my light."

From up the ventilation pipe, the voice of the Countess Krak: "Oh, the poor dumb fool. He committed suicide rather than face a trial."

"Well, can't say as I blame him," came Heller's voice. "His execution was inevitable."

Krak: "Well, let's find the proclamations. That's what we came for."

Sound of boards being lifted. Rattle of papers. More boards.

Marine: "Still no sign of anything down there in that river, sir."

Heller: "Give us a hand with this search."

Krak: "Maybe they're behind the walls."

More boards. Sound of filing drawers opening and closing.

Marine: "Blazing (bleepards), look at this stuff, sir. He must have had blackmail on half the people in the Apparatus."

Other marine: "That's how the 'drunks' operate."

Marine: "What do we do with this stuff, sir? The disintegrator isn't working."

Heller: "They were apparently the prisoner's personal files. He's probably dead but the investigation isn't over, so grab some cartons and we'll hand them to Bis of Fleet Intelligence. No reason to leave them lying around to wreck people, even 'drunks.' "

Krak: "I'm going to look in the outer-office files."

A lot more paper rustling. Then the sounds of boards being put back and jammed in place with boot heels.

Krak: "There're no proclamations in the outer-office files. Just trash. Oh, blast, where could those things be?"

Heller: "He could have been lying."

Krak: "Not the way I got the information. Have we looked under every board?"

Heller: "Every one."

Krak: "Oh, blast!"

Heller: "What did you do with all the affidavits and confessions?"

Krak: "They're in my case in the airbus. What's that got to do with it?"

Heller: "They might contain some clue to this."

Krak: "No. The proclamations were not even mentioned. They're of no use to us now. The prisoner is dead. Oh, blast! Well, there's only one thing to do: get the originals at Spiteos."

Heller: "Oh, no!"

Krak: "Oh, yes! I know they exist and I know exactly where they are. You can slip in there with the tug and we can have them in two minutes!"

Heller: "Dear . . ."

Krak: "No, Jettero. There is too much at stake in this. We should go right back and get the tug——"

Heller: "Dear! That means you could be putting yourself straight into the hands of Lombar Hisst!"

Krak: "Nonsense. You just let down a ladder. I'll go down and pick them up in a flash and we'll be gone. I know you can do it. And our whole lives depend upon it! We don't have to stop at the Royal prison now, so we can return directly to the field. You're always doing far more dangerous things for much less reason. So let's go."

Heller groaned. Then he said, "All right."

I heard them putting the office back together. Then I heard them loading cartons.

The front door clicked shut.

Their airbus took off while I made myself small under the eaves.

I was hugging myself with ecstasy. It was even better than I had ever hoped for!

Krak and Heller were delivering themselves straight into the open jaws of death!

Chapter 2

When I knew that I was absolutely safe, I lifted the roof hatch, crept down the stairs, went through the secret door and back into my office.

I tried a switch. The lights were off because of the cut conduit. I found a hand light in a drawer and turned it on. They had done a pretty good job of putting it all back together.

I thrilled with exhilaration. I was out of their vicious hands.

But now I must make my call.

A few short words with Lombar Hisst and the whole situation would be saved!

Guns trained on the spot where the tug would arrive, one fusillade and they'd plunge a mile straight down into the chasm at the fortress edge. An unarmed, unarmored tug—nothing to it!

I grabbed a communications unit.

It was dead.

I rushed into the outer office and stabbed my identoplate at the huge computer console that should connect with everybody.

Nothing happened!

Heller had severed all the conduits and not put them back!

Well, all right. I would rush out to a street message center and place the call through civilian circuits.

Swiftly I sped into the night.

The dull light of a message center loomed. I eagerly dived in.

I reached in my pocket for coins.

I came up with a Turkish five-kuras coin.

It didn't work.

I fished out a U.S. quarter.

It didn't work.

I found a U.S. Lincoln penny and tried to force it in the slot.

I banged on it and made it jam.

Frantically I looked through my wallet and clothes.

NOT A SINGLE BIT OF VOLTAR MONEY!

I looked around on the floor in case somebody had dropped a fraction-of-a-credit coin. Very bare.

Let's see. Ske. Yes. Ske, my old driver, might be living near. . . .

No. He wouldn't be living at all. I had given him counterfeits and they would have executed him by now.

Meeley! My old landlady. Only a few blocks from here!

No. She would be dead, too, for I had paid her with money that would get her exterminated and no questions asked.

The area was all dark. There were no people around. I had no friends anyway.

What to do? What to do? What to do? I had to get word to Lombar and fast!

A police station!

No, Heller might have told the "bluebottles" about it and they might just pick me up for him.

My airbus!

But I didn't know where it would be stored or even if it was still allocated to me.

I looked wildly around. And then I had it. An airbus sat beside a building. I would steal it!

I crept up to it. Nobody was around.

LUCK!

The door was unlocked!

I slid in.

LUCK!

It had no drive-control locks.

LUCK!

It started instantly.

I took off straight up with a roar, leaping into the night. I looked down. Not even a head had come out of a window that I could see.

Now, where was I?

Over to my right was the place where Lombar had his town office. I dived in that direction.

Not even a light there.

I veered off to the left toward a place where Lombar stayed while he was in town, a sort of ramshackle palace.

Completely dark, not even any guards.

Well, to me that could only signify one thing: LOMBAR HIMSELF WAS AT SPITEOS!

Luck again!

Oh, indeed, this was my lucky night!

I vaulted up into the traffic lanes. Below me Government City spread out. I went higher. Slum City in one direction, Pausch Hills in another. My eye fell on the dark masses of the mountains. Beyond them lay the Great Desert. Beyond that lay Camp Kill and Spiteos!

I did a hasty calculation. The distance Heller had to travel to get back to Emergency Fleet Reserve was not as great as the distance to Spiteos but he would cover the distance to his target with the tug. And he drove and flew awfully fast.

This was going to be a near thing.

But I was on my way!

Chapter 3

Some small fires were burning at the camp. Beyond it Spiteos, the black castle, lay like a blot upon the ground. The mile-deep chasm against the white desert sand looked like a knife scar in the planet surface.

In the distance I saw no signs of gunfire yet. I really doubted if he could get in there unobserved, absorbo-coat or no. Nobody knew of the existence of Spiteos except a few in the Apparatus: They guarded it thoroughly and carefully, and to blandly fly in there and land on it I considered impossible. No such ships ever came near it. The challenge would be instant, gunfire would be inevitable.

I felt I was in time.

I got a challenge. An airbus at night would be very suspect. With fifteen thousand troops at the camp below Spiteos, they had lots of sentries, lots of time, no traffic to mention.

I pushed my identoplate against the screen.

The screen flashed:

Hold where you are!

Not too unusual. I clumsily gunned the airbus into a hovering stop in the sky.

The screen said:

You are not on our traffic list.

I picked up the microphone. "I've been gone. It is absolutely, utterly urgent that I see Lombar Hisst at once! This is top priority emergency!"

Hold.

Spiteos lay black and brooding in the starlight and the glow of a moon just rising. A dreadful place. One could almost hear the groans of the thousands of political prisoners buried a mile deep in its bowels.

I began to fret. I looked over at the horizon where lay Palace City, but of course it was invisible: It was powered with a black hole in the mountain behind it and was thirteen minutes in the future. I hoped that Lombar Hisst wasn't there. Time was its defense but it also made direct communications difficult.

My screen said:

Can you spot the orange flare?

I looked down. At the far edge of the camp, closest to Spiteos, an orange flare pinpointed the dark. "Yes."

The screen said:

Land there and nowhere else or we will fire.

I sent the airbus plummeting down.

The orange flare was lighting up a circle on the ground and hurting my eyes.

I made a very bad landing.

I opened the door to get out. There was a ring of Apparatus troops.

An officer was beside me, holding a hand blastgun. "Get out."

"Look, I haven't got time for this!"

"Just precautions. There have been threats against the Chief's life."

"Get me to him instantly!" I cried.

"That's right where you are going!" said the officer. "March!"

"Look," I cried, "at any instant now a tug is going to try to land on the Spiteos roof. Inform your batteries."

"A tug?"

"A tug."

"March!"

"Inform them!" I cried.

"March!"

They took me to the tunnel entrance and pushed me into a guard car. We hurtled to the first checkpoint. The sentries searched me and looked through my satchel of evidence. They pushed me back in and we roared through the long tunnel.

We came out and they escorted me into an elevator.

We went rocketing up and exited into the outer office of Lombar Hisst. There were no clerks around.

The officer made a signal on Lombar's door.

It opened.

There was Lombar Hisst!

He was as tall and as heavy and as mean looking as always, but there was a heavier scowl on his face. It made me very nervous.

"What are you doing here?" he thundered. "When I was told you wanted to land, I couldn't believe it. You're supposed to be on Blito-P3!"

"Oh, sir, there isn't time! In just minutes, Jettero Heller will be here."

"WHAT?"

"Jettero Heller, sir—the man you sent on Mission Earth."

"You didn't kill him?" said Lombar, incredulous.

"Well, no sir. He ducked."

"WHY is he coming here?" snarled Lombar.

That tone of voice terrifies me when he uses it. I opened my mouth to tell him that Heller was coming to get some forged documents. But then, with sudden wit, I checked myself. If I admitted I knew of those documents, I myself would be involved in the forgery penalties. I wound up just opening and closing my mouth several times.

Lombar's eyes went like slits. "You don't have to tell me. I know why. They're all after me!"

I tried to speak again but he interrupted me. Lombar never waited for any answers.

"Oh, that aristocratic upstart! The insolence!" said Lombar. "Coming to kill me! The effrontery of it!"

His paranoia was not about to be checked by anything I could say.

"Is he coming in a tank?" said Hisst. "No, he wouldn't get near here in a tank. He's coming in a space battleship!" Was there a flash of fear on his face?

"No, sir. Please, sir. He's coming in a tug."

"A what?"

"A space tug."

"The tug! No arms! No armor!"

At that instant, alarms went throughout the area!

The screaming howl of them hurt my ears!

HELLER HAD BEEN SPOTTED!

Hisst looked for an instant like he was going to rush back into his office. Then he checked himself.

Suddenly he rushed forward toward the elevator. I raced after him.

I knew where he was going.

There is no fighter cover at Spiteos as it would be too obvious. But Lombar Hisst had a flying cannon of his own. It was buried deep in the castle, with a tunnel for immediate release into the air. It was the most armored, most heavily built flying cannon ever made. Its gun could knock down a city and no known projectile or beam could even dent its hide.

I raced after him.

I barely made it into the elevator.

Down we went like a powered bomb.

We were in the hangar in seconds.

There sat the impregnable monster, black, big and ugly.

Lombar leaped into it and I piled into the second seat.

Lombar was pushing buttons which opened the exits. The drives of the brute roared to life.

Heller, I exulted, you will shortly be the most dead spacer anybody ever heard of!

Here we come!

Chapter 4

The tunnel walls were rushing by. Ahead I saw the stars.

We burst out upon a world of franticness.

The dull green moonlight fell upon a camp stirred up like bog beetles running madly everywhere.

Even through the window of the giant flying cannon I could hear the strident screaming of alarms.

Fifteen thousand men were pouring to their batteries of guns.

Lombar was climbing. The engines screamed. I looked wildly everywhere.

I could see no tug, no Heller, nothing!

He should be hovering over Spiteos to let the Countess off. But well away from it and looking down on it, I could see nothing.

That didn't mean he wasn't there. Absorbo-coat would not reflect any light or beam. But neither would it pass light and that tug should make a shadow against the desert sand, against the stars or moon.

All our screens were blank except for the ground below.

Then suddenly, there it was, directly above the camp! The tug! A black silhouette!

Abruptly, like a ring of blue electric flame, a thousand defense guns opened up!

Arcs of fire two miles long carved a savage geometric pattern in the sky. The apex of the two cones was the silhouette!

They must be missing!

It was still there!

The amount of fire redoubled from the ground.

Lombar, snarling so his teeth showed, turned the nose of the flying cannon in a deadly curve.

His fingers pressed the trips!

Our vessel bucked like a thing gone mad!

The screech of our missiles pierced my ears!

We must be missing!

There was no target burst of flame.

The silhouette was still there!

An illusion!

Heller was throwing a silhouette illusion of the tug above the camp!

He must be somewhere else!

I glanced out my window at Spiteos, over to our right. I could see it was very black there even with my flame-dazzled eyes.

I looked back at our viewscreens.

One was pointing at Spiteos.

There!

There was something there!

I looked closer.

A ladder! Lacking absorbo-coat, it was reflecting on our screen!

In the middle of the dangling ladder was a figure. That would be Krak!

"Lombar!" I screamed. "There! There! There!" I was pointing frantically.

He saw it.

He turned the ship.

With snarls he turned his gun controls to maximum barrage!

He pressed the trips.

The light blinded me. The savage burst almost seemed to tear the heavens up!

A second passed. Then two. Then three. I could see again.

Something was falling.

Down, down, down it went, plunging into the abyss. It had a mile to go.

It was not the tug.

It seemed that a body had been blasted! It was falling away!

Frantically I looked at the heavens.

A shadow between us and the moon! "Lombar!" I screamed. "Up there!"

Oh, where was Heller now?

I quickly added it up.

Our barrage must have dislodged Krak and sent her falling to her death.

Heller would be frothing for revenge!

"Lombar!" I screamed. "Get away from here!"

The Chief of the Apparatus was looking savagely around. The lust to kill was over him like sheen. "Where is the insolent (bleepard)?" he howled. "Royal officer! Royal (bleep)! Let me at him!" he raved.

I felt a jolt.

It was as if we had run into a wall.

Yet we were two miles above the planet surface!

I looked anxiously at the throttles. They hadn't changed.

Yet we were slowing down!

Then suddenly we started up. We rose into the sky! We were in the grip of some awful force far beyond control!

The towing tractor beams!

Heller had us gripped like any other tow.

Those things could move billions of tons, thousands of these flying cannons.

Up, up we went and then began a sickening curve.

"What's happening?" shrieked Lombar.

"He's got us in the towing grips!" I cried. "Pour full throttle on and break out! DO IT QUICK!"

Lombar was looking all around. His face was getting wild.

We swung into the beginning of a circle. We were now heading obliquely at the ground.

"They've got me!" screamed Lombar, going white.

We hit the bottom of the arc and began to climb again, and all without our power.

I was being pressed by centrifugal force against the side of my seat.

We came around the top of the arc, the moon and stars whirring by.

Down we started once more.

Lombar was howling! He sounded like an animal!

Around we went and around and around. The tug must be pivoting in a small, tight circle. It was as if we were on the end of a mile of rope.

"Turn! Turn!" I cried. "Start shooting at the pivot point!"

Lombar hit his throttles. They made us go in the same direction we were being swung!

He hit his turn controls.

They didn't work!

Suddenly our motors died.

We were in a second field, as well, that held our engines paralyzed!

The whistling scream of air going by drove terror to my soul.

We were powerless in an awful thing. We were just a pellet in a whirling sling!

We came down the arc, pointing at the ground.

SUDDENLY THE GRIP WENT OFF!

Below us stretched the desert!

We had been released! We were hurtling down at an awful speed!

The ground, moonlit, was rushing up.

The rocks and sand and bushes were suddenly too plain!

WE CRASHED!

Chapter 5

The impact must have knocked me out.

I came to in the sizzle of electric fire and the smell of smoke.

Something was lying on my legs.

The entire front panel of the ship had come off and was pinning me in the remains of the seat.

The flying cannon was a crumpled thing.

I wondered that I had survived at all. But maybe I wasn't going to: Electrical fires were dancing all along the panel back, right below my face. At any moment they could flare up and incinerate me!

My hands were bare. I could not reach anything. But this was a matter of life or death. Barehanded, screaming at the pain, I beat them out.

The green moonlight would not let me see the agonizing burns of the flesh, as I lay in shadow.

A shaft was shining in.

It hit the face of Lombar. He was lying there, head back, pinned in place with snapped cables and conduits. They made it look like he was lying in a nest of snakes.

The hull was split apart and above the creak of cooling metal I could hear the desert sounds. I lifted my head. Far off, there was Spiteos against the pale green moon. They would come for us. They had seen the crash, most certainly.

Lombar began to groan. He moved. He opened his eyes. I had moved and the moonlight was on my face. He looked at me and memory seemed to return.

His eyes went slitted. "So you were part of the conspiracy to kill me!" he said.

"No, no! I came to warn you and save your life!"

"Conspiracy to kill! You came to set me up for Heller! The two of you have been in it thick, all the time!"

"NO!" I tried to hold up my hands. "I even kept you from burning to death!"

"And all this was a ruse! You pretended to come with a warning—me, whom the angels have chosen to be king! Just so you could get me into the air and Heller could shoot me down!"

"Oh, dear Gods, no! You've got it all wrong!"

"I know who my enemies are. They are everybody. And you chose this chance to sneak up on me when I was undefended!"

Far off I could see lights dancing across the desert. Those would be ground vehicles racing to the wreck!

Lombar saw them. "As soon as they get here, that will be the end of you, Soltan Gris!"

Oh, Gods. His paranoia had him in its grip. I didn't have a chance.

Frantically I pushed at the panel that had collapsed across my legs.

I looked up at the approaching lights. They were going brighter and dimmer as they plunged over the uneven terrain. They were only half a mile away.

With strength I did not know I had, I wrenched again at the panel.

IT MOVED!

I reached out with my maimed hand to grasp the door latch. The whole side of the flying cannon fell off.

My foot was caught. Something was gripping the heel. I got my foot out of the boot.

With scrapes and tears, I moved my legs sideways.

I WAS FREE!

I leaped to the ground and ran!

Bushes whipped at my legs. Sharp rocks savaged my unshod foot. I could not go far in this condition!

My plight was extreme. Two hundred miles of impassable desert lay between me and Government City. A similarly uncrossable distance lay between me and the Blike Mountains. Nobody had ever passed through this devil-whipped desert afoot and lived to tell of it!

A dark line against the moonlit sand. A gully lined with bushes!

I plunged the few feet down the bank. I landed in agony at the bottom.

The sound of motors!

I turned around, raised myself and peered through the shrubs.

That wreck was awfully near. I thought I had gone much further!

Too late. The first vehicles were arriving. Dozens of them! Lights were playing everywhere!

Hysterically I glanced up and down the gully. I saw a large, flat stone. It lay close to a slit in the bank. I dived for it. I lay in the depression and pulled the flat stone over me. I balled up in the smallest ball I could.

A roaring voice came from the wreck. "Spread out and FIND HIM!"

The thud of running feet.

They were coming closer!

I could hear the snap and slap of guns and equipment as men ran.

More engines.

Somebody was racing around in a small ground tank. The clank of treads made the stone vibrate!

More vehicles were arriving.

I expected any moment somebody would lift the rock and I would come crawling out to be stamped upon.

Bootbeats were everywhere. They almost shook the ground.

To still my terror, I tried to think of something optimistic—like I would suddenly sizzle to a crisp and vanish. And then I did think of something: In their very numbers, they were obliterating all the tracks I might have made.

Hope trembled on the brink of my death from heart failure.

Would they miss me?

Minutes ticked away, each one an eternity.

A squad came by within feet of me. "He'd be a fool to come this way," an officer said. "Nobody can cross this desert on foot. He must have doubled back for Spiteos and we passed him in the cars."

Shouted commands and some vehicles took off in the direction of Spiteos, travelling slowly.

There was nobody in my area now. At least I heard no feet.

They were having trouble at the wreck. Some officer yelled, "This cable is wrapped around him twice. There's nothing here to cut it. Speed back to the repair shops and get the biggest pair of conduit slicers they have!"

A car roared off.

The din had diminished.

Curled in a ball, I knew I could not hold the position forever. I was far too tense. I wanted to stretch and let my nerve ends jangle. Cautiously I wriggled my arms out from underneath the stone. Nothing shot them off. Silently, I pushed the stone aside. The gully was deserted.

I wriggled up the bank and peered through the bushes.

There must be a hundred vehicles scattered around, some close to, some far from the wreck by at least a hundred feet.

Men were idling about, waiting.

A staff car arrived.

"Cutters?"

"No, they're coming."

It was a general of the Apparatus troops. He was looking into the wreck, probably at Lombar. "Sir, while we're waiting for equipment to cut you out, is there anything you would like me to do?"

"YES!" came Lombar's bellow from the twisted wreck. "Issue an immediate warrant for the arrest of Jettero Heller for attempting to murder me! Issue it to the Army, the Domestic Police! Otherwise we won't be able to get our hands on him!"

"Yes, sir. At once, sir. Get that going, Captain Bodkins. Anything else, sir?"

"Blito-P3! There must be plenty wrong there," roared Lombar. "Send a Death Battalion to that base with orders to search out any traitors that were confederates of Heller's or took his orders and exterminate them!"

"Yes, sir. Attend to that, Lieutenant Wipe. Now, is there anything else I can do, sir?"

"YES! Soltan Gris! Issue an Apparatus hunt-and-find order on him! Don't kill him! Bring him in alive! That traitor will be tortured for a month before he dies!"

Chapter 6

The last thin glimmer of hope within me died. Up to that moment, even against reason, I had clung to the despairing possibility that Lombar Hisst, once the shock of impact had worn off, might shake the hold that paranoid schizophrenia had on him and realize that I had acted to save him if I could.

But no, that was gone now.

Impassable desert lay all around me. To return to Spiteos and its torture chambers was a decision only to be made in the last throes of masochism.

I gazed forlornly at the scene which spread in the green moonlight before my eyes. Literally hundreds of troops were there. I could not begin to count the ground vehicles.

I felt there was no escape. I could not even walk!

WAIT!

If I could not walk . . .

Over to my left, not fifty feet away, stood an airbus, one of the last to come in!

Its drivers were over by the wreck.

I said a prayer.

I began to wriggle along under the cover of the gully. I glanced up from time to time, certain someone would see my head and let out a cry to the rest.

At length, I got opposite the airbus. There was twenty feet of bare ground to cover.

The light was bad. The place was thick with men.

I felt like a man must feel as he walks the last few paces to his firing squad. But I stood up.

Sauntering with great casualness, I approached the vehicle.

I reached for the door.

I opened it.

I slid under the controls.

Another airbus was coming, probably with the cutters.

I waited.

Just when it arrived, I started up.

I flew casually and slowly upward.

I headed in the direction of Spiteos.

Sudden yells below!

A fusillade of shots!

The driver of this thing must have seen his vehicle leave!

They were after me!

I slammed the throttles home.

With every inch of speed I could beat out of it, I sent the vehicle hurtling.

To where?

The Blike Mountains?

No. The game wardens would be alerted and would round me up very fast.

To Spiteos?

That was insane!

And then suddenly I knew I had a choice. Trial and a quick execution. Or capture by the Apparatus and a month of untold agony. There wasn't much choice to it!

I fled for Government City, pursued by shots, speeding air vehicles on my tail, the air alive with explosions all around.

I extinguished every light I had. I went down close to the desert floor.

My hands were killing me. The bucking turbulence of air caused by such low passage at five hundred miles an hour almost broke my wrists!

I was counting on the fact that those behind me would get my screen image messed up with the rocks and bushes and whirlwinds of this place.

The near shots were less frequent now. And then I knew why. They were counting on my interception at the other end!

The air must be alive with orders to the Government City police!

I flipped the radio to general band. There it was—the number of my airbus! A call to all bluebottles to stop that car! I flinched under the torrent of sound.

The thought of thirty days of drawn-out torture unflinched me quick. Heading low, blanking out the possibility this machine might explode from overdriving it, I hurtled at the massive bulks of the mountains that intervened between me and my goal.

A canyon yawned in the moonlight ahead. I shot into it and raced along, inches from its walls and floor.

I shot out at the top. I was between two mountain crests.

Another canyon yawned below, narrow but descending. I flashed down it.

I could feel my raw hands bleeding now. I was certain one wrist was broken. But I held on.

At better than five hundred miles an hour, I glimpsed the town pouring up at me.

There was the Royal prison on a hill, a stern and ghastly fortress, ominous in the green moonlight. But it looked like refuge to me.

Lombar could not get me out of it if I got in.

It was suddenly getting bigger. Too fast!

I put my drives in reverse. I heard the machinery break.

I crashed before the very gates of the Royal prison!

Chapter 7

Looking up at the stone arches before the clearing smoke, I did not even take time to marvel that I could move!

Something was trapping me. The bag around my neck was caught under a control stick.

I freed it.

I leaped out of the finished airbus.

Reeling as I ran, I got to the gates.

The guard!

They had their pikes lowered!

"Hold up! You can't come in here!"

"Oh, please, dear Gods!" I screamed. I glanced, terrified, over my shoulder at the sky. I faced around. I shouted at him, five feet away, "I must see a justiciary of Voltar and see him fast!"

"What is that?" a guard said, pointing at my bag. "A bomb?"

"Get out of here!" cried the other guard.

Oh, Gods, it was my last refuge anywhere!

"PLEASE!" I shrieked.

A querulous voice from a courtyard balcony.

"What's the disturbance out there?"

"Somebody wants in, Your Lordship. And that ain't never happened before!"

"What's the fellow want?"

"EVIDENCE!" I shouted. "I'VE GOT THE EVIDENCE HERE!" And I held up my bag.

The querulous voice said, "Bring him to the audience chamber.

I'll get a robe on and come down. Oddest thing I ever heard, fellow wanting to get in!"

I heard the balcony door slam.

I glanced in terror at the sky.

They were pushing me forward across the courtyard stones. They gave a signal and another guard, inside, opened a groaning door.

I was propelled forward across tiled floors and under swinging chandeliers of extinguished glowplates. The shadows of the guards were huge from nightlights on the walls.

I was thrust into a big chamber with benches all around. There was an alcove, very dark, just ahead. A door behind it opened.

Somebody turned on a light. The judge was just sitting down on a huge chair on the raised platform of the alcove.

"Seedy-looking character," said the justiciary. He was very old, very gray; the robe was crimson like blood. "Push him over here. Now, what's this about evidence?"

I raised my bag. "It's all here. Everything."

"But evidence of what?" said the justiciary. "Who are you, anyway?"

"I'm Officer Soltan Gris of the Apparatus," I said. I tremblingly offered my identoplate.

"Apparatus? Well, fellow, you don't belong here. The Apparatus has its own courts, if they ever use them. I think you've come to the wrong place."

I was terrified that they would put me out that door. By now the Domestic Police would have heard of that crash, and even though they might not know of the Apparatus alert, they would, the second they saw the identifying numbers.

"Your Lordship," I quaked. "The crimes are against the state. I'm the criminal. I am turning myself in."

"Oh, see here, now, this is very irregular," said the justiciary. A man had come through a side door, getting into his coat. His Lordship called to him. "Do we have any Royal warrant for a Soltan Gris?"

"No, Your Lordship. The only outstanding Royal warrants

unserved are against Prince Mortiiy and some of his associates. I know all the names and Soltan Gris is not one of them."

The justiciary started to lift his hand to the guards.

"Oh, please, dear Gods," I cried. "Don't put me out that door. I swear to you that I am a criminal. For the love of Heavens, arrest me!"

The justiciary frowned. "I could turn you over to the Domestic Police for creating a disturbance. Would that do?"

The bluebottles would turn me over to Lombar in a second! "Oh, Your Lordship, no! My crimes are Royal, I swear it!"

"Fellow," said His Lordship, "without a warrant and without even a stated crime, there's nothing for you here. Take him away."

"No, no!" INSPIRATION! "A Royal officer was bringing me in to you."

"Really?" said the justiciary. "Well, where is he?"

I was about to say that I had escaped. That would be bad. I was really sweating now. The servants of Hisst could be right outside that door!

"He stopped off somewhere," I cried. "I promised I would report in to you!"

"Oh, come now," said the justiciary. "I think you're just making all this up. Whoever heard of a prisoner reporting in like that?"

INSPIRATION! "Your Lordship," I cried, "I have a witness. Commander Crup at the Emergency Fleet Reserve knows I was under arrest and being brought here."

The justiciary started to shake his head. My knees were shaking. I fell on them. I cupped my hands pleadingly. "Call him— oh, dear Gods, for your hopes of Heavens, please call Commander Crup."

The justiciary was shaking his head in puzzlement at me. But he motioned to the clerk and that worthy picked up a communications instrument, and after some button punching and questions, handed it to the justiciary.

"Commander Crup? This is Lord Turn at the Royal Courts and Prison. Sorry to trouble you at such an hour but we have a rather strange situation here. A man identifying himself as Soltan Gris claims he was being brought here by a Royal officer and that you're a witness to the fact." His Lordship listened. "Well, you don't say. Who? . . . Jettero Heller? Oh, yes, the bullet-ball champion. . . . Oh, yes. I won five credits on him once. Oh, yes, a splendid athlete. . . . Well, I'm glad that straightens that out. Thank you for your courtesy. Good-bye."

Lord Turn gave back the instrument and looked at me. "Jettero Heller. Fine man. So he was bringing you here, was he?"

"Oh, yes!" I said.

"Well, Commander Crup did not know what the crime was, but I'm sure if Jettero Heller was bringing you here it would have been against the state."

"You can hold me?" I cried with joy.

"Oh, yes. We can put you in a cell. But we need something for the charge sheet. What was the crime?"

"Oh, everything!" I said. "Just everything!"

"That's pretty general," said Lord Turn. "Can't you tell me something more specific?"

"Oh, that would take hours!" I said, anxious to get actually on their books.

"Well, supposing you just write it all down and then we'll know what this is all about."

"All of it?" I said. A new inspiration hit me. A new hope dawned. "If I tell you everything, then can I expect leniency?"

Lord Turn said, "The Royal Court is always ready to be fully just. If you omit nothing and tell the truth, I will give you a very fair hearing. Clerk, have them charge him with 'Conduct against the State in contravention of Royal statutes and decrees.' Order him some medical treatment so he can write, and provide him with pens, papers and a vocoscriber, that sort of thing. Oh, yes, and put him in the tower where there is some light."

I could breathe again.

The justiciary was rising, so I stood. "By the way," he said, "did you know Jettero Heller personally?"

"Oh, yes!" I said.

"You're fortunate," said Lord Turn. "I'd like to meet him sometime myself. A great bullet-ball player. Good night."

They took me away and put me in a big cell in the tower that had tables and chairs and through the barred windows of which the lights of Government City glittered. They locked the massive door on me.

I stood staring at the sky. There were Domestic Police cars in quite close. Two Apparatus vessels hovered in the sky.

I laughed shakily. They couldn't get me here. I was a prisoner of the State, beyond even Lombar's call!

I was still laughing when a doctor came to handle my wrists and bandage my hands.

Despite the lateness of the hour, the writing materials came.

Oh, I would tell all. I had my records and my logs. I would tell everything I knew about Mission Earth.

Who knew where Heller was?

And the longer I wrote, the longer I would stay alive.

And so this is my narrative. I give it to you, Lord Turn. I do not know another blessed thing.

Be lenient.

But please don't turn me out.

Just execute me quickly!

SOLTAN GRIS

Attested that the foregoing was confessed by said prisoner:

Gummins
Tower Guard, Royal Prison

Scritch
Life Prisoner, adjacent cell

PART
SIXTY-SEVEN
Chapter 1

Needless to say, Soltan Gris did NOT get his quick execution. Had this occurred, I would never have gotten the chance to finish this story for you, for myself or for Voltar. (Long Live His Majesty, Wully the Wise!)

Instead of just bursting in upon you unannounced without so much as a trumpet blast, thus shocking your sense of proper decorum and protocol, perhaps I had better introduce myself.

I am Monte Pennwell, lately graduated from the Royal Academy of Arts. I am of average height, average coloration and, according to my mother and innumerable relatives, near and distant, a below-average chance of amounting to anything in life unless I give up the silly notion of becoming a writer of renown. How do you do?

My involvement—and, I trust, yours—in this matter of MISSION EARTH began in a quite bizarre way.

Every month, it is my duty to have lunch with my great-uncle, Lord Dohm, at the Royal Courts and Prison on the hill above Government City. These luncheons are part of a family-wide conspiracy (in which innumerable relatives take part) to get me talked to in the hope that I can be persuaded in some unsubtle way to get busy and amount to something in life, be a credit to my lineage and all that. Lord Dohm favors that I should now take up law. So every month I have to hear from him how I should run my life: He has no use for "scribblers," particularly ones who have never published anything. He means well, of course. They all do.

So I was sitting in his clerical office, waiting for him to finish a briefing on why he should lop off somebody's head. His staff were bustling about, emptying some cabinets which, it seemed, were overstuffed. They were throwing an inordinate quantity of mildew about and a shaft of late morning sunlight, swording through the towering windows, was alive with dust motes.

Suddenly I conceived a poem: I would call it "An Ode to the Dancing Air." It was already wafting through my head and I didn't have anything to write it on.

"Bumble," I said to the chief clerk—and fatal words they were—"let me have some paper, quick!"

"Young Monte," old Bumble said, "paper is expensive stuff and it's a shame to waste it." He looked down at a cart he was loading. "Here, have some scrap. The backs are blank." And he took a fistful from the moldering box and shoved it at me.

When I had finished sneezing, I looked at what I held. On every single page it was stamped Confidential: Justiciary Only. "Wait, Bumble," I said, "I don't want to get you into trouble. This is apparently a secret document."

Bumble looked at it. He shrugged. "All Royal cases are marked Confidential. A prisoner is entitled to certain privacy, at least until he is executed, and then the records are destroyed. What's the date on that document? Ah, nearly a hundred years ago. Well, you could hardly call that current business, could you? So don't trouble your busy little brain about it, Monte. This whole lot is going to the disintegrator: We need the space."

My eye had lighted on the last line of the last page. It said, "Be lenient. But please don't turn me out. Just execute me quickly! SOLTAN GRIS."

"Wait," I said. "They certainly didn't do what he requested or this document wouldn't still be here."

Bumble looked a little harassed. He peered at the big box he had taken it out of. The moldy label said Incomplete Jurisprudence, GRIS. "Well, I don't see how they could have. The rest of this is trial transcripts. But possibly they never finished trying him or those papers wouldn't be here either. Maybe a misfile. We find those now and then. But funny that it's still marked incomplete."

"How interesting!" I said. "You mean they started a trial and never finished it? Tell me more."

"Confound it, young Monte, we've got to get these drawers empty before lunch. Take the blasted box and let me get back to work."

It really had poundage. The confession itself was heavy and the rest of the papers backbreaking. However, I wrestled the moldy, dusty mess off the cart and staggered away, heading for my air-speedster in the courtyard.

Just then my great-uncle came out. "What have you got there, Monte? A hundred-pound ode? Looks like it's been rejected pretty often. Ha, ha!"

I parked the burden in a cloakroom and accompanied him to his dining hall where he regaled me with the news that he had been talking to the Chief Justiciary and they thought they could get me an appointment here as a junior clerk and wouldn't that be nice? And who knew but what, in another fifty years, I could become somebody respectable like him.

Repressing a shudder, I was then appalled to hear him say, "I was telling your mother, just last week, that if you kept insisting on this scribbler thing, and continued to refuse all the help the family is giving you, our only recourse—for your own good, mind—would be to marry you off."

"Did she have anybody in mind?" I quailed.

"Why, yes," he said, chopping off a piece of bread with a miniature headsman's axe. "The Corsa girl. She may be ugly, but don't forget, she will inherit half of the planet Modon one day."

"Modon?" I said, trying to keep my voice steady.

"Good, clean fresh air," he said. "Lots of interesting peasant revolts and different crops. The provinces are a fine, outdoor life for a vigorous young man. But I know you don't like that sort of thing, so I would strenuously advise you to accept this junior clerk appointment. It will at least keep you in town. I've always been fond of you, you know, and I don't want you to throw your life away."

The campaign was on!

I sat there, the dutiful nephew, diffidently stirring my food, well aware of my frail defenses and the perils of an overmanaged destiny. My cause seemed hopeless.

Chapter 2

Driving back to the family town estates beyond Pausch Hills that afternoon, I was in a depressed mood. My plight was cruel and the lovely spring landscape below my air-speedster had no charms.

Time was running out. I had graduated from the Royal Academy of Arts over two years ago, and to date I had not had one tiniest line of anything published. I couldn't point proudly to even a pamphlet and say, "Look, I am a writer: please let me sternly forge my way against the tides of life on my own! I will blazon my name in fire across the skies of Voltar and be a credit beyond credits to everybody's credit one day, a veritable jewel in the family's crown, if you will just let me go my own way!" But alas, I knew that the patience of my numberless uncles, great-uncles, aunts, great-aunts, cousins and second cousins was becoming strained. My days were numbered and sooner or later they would pounce with ferocity and plunge me into some ignominious post of vast respectability. And there I would be, just a cog in the relentless grinding machine of pale gray society.

Mourning my lot, I landed my air-speedster on the target in the statue park, turned it over to my mechanic and had two footmen take the dilapidated records box to my study in the west tower. They keep me relegated to the suite there, distant from other things, because I play recordings late at night and pace.

But I didn't make it. My mother, a very commanding female,

was coming down the grand staircase and spotted me seeking to duck behind a potted plant.

"Oh, there you are, Monte," she said. "I trust you had a helpful lunch. But whatever have you done to your clothes?"

I glanced down. That box had gotten me pretty moldy.

"Never mind," she said. "Just be sure that you look well for dinner. I've invited the Corsa girl and her brother." She went blithely on her way but she left me trembling. I could almost hear the mutter of the guns on the horizon as the enemy closed in for the kill.

In my study, my valet was rowing at the footmen for getting dust all over everything with that box. He is a yellow-man named Hound that served with my father on some campaign and he is very determined to bring up the son so he won't disgrace the family. His attention was distracted to me. "Look at your jacket!" he said. "You haven't been going around in public looking like *that*, have you? Here—good Heavens—get into a shower and I'll lay out some other clothes. Footmen, get that box out of here!"

"No, no!" I said. "It's valuable!"

"Valuable? It stinks just like the Royal prison!"

"That's just it!" I said desperately, blocking the footmen from carrying it out of the door. "Nearly a hundred years ago, somebody was pleading with them to execute him and they refused to! It's a miscarriage of justice. They didn't even complete his trial. It stinks!"

"Then you're going to take that junior-clerk position after all," said Hound, with some relief.

"No!" I cried. "I'm going to write an ode about it."

My valet raised his eyes to the ceiling and spread his ample hands. It was a typical gesture.

We compromised by having a couple of maids wipe the worst of the dust off and leave the container in the middle of the floor, but with a cloth under it to protect the carpet.

After I had my shower and changed my clothes I got rid of the intruders. Thinking to take my mind off my own troubles by studying those of others, I picked the thick confession off the top of the other papers, sat down in an easy chair and prepared to read. There might also be an ode in this. Some lines had already occurred to me:

> *Oh, stern prison walls,*
> *At last my heart hath . . . break? . . . broken?*
> *Bring down, bring down the headsman's axe*
> *To end . . . token? . . . broken? . . . hopeless fate? . . .*

Well, I'd get it smoother later. I better find out what I was writing about first.

I began to read the confession.

I read all afternoon. I found myself quite absorbed. The prose was military, terse, unembellished. But also it was archaic. They don't write that way these days: they just use sounds and pretty words without bothering to put any thought behind them. The intent is to build up towers of metered cloud which then avalanche down into a great thunder of nothingness. It was interesting to read something which spoke of events and scenes in a realistic way. Novel idea. Some of the early classics are like that. They tell a story that has a beginning and an end and everything: remarkable. I shall try to imitate it.

Dinner came and Hound had to dig me out and get me dressed and for four hours I had to sit at the long table and in the music salon being chatty with the Corsa girl and her brother. She weighed twice as much as me and was as muscular as a man. She talked of crops from a too-thin mouth and he talked of hunting lepertiges with cannons, and while I pretended interest, I was inwardly shuddering at the horror of being exiled to Modon and its fresh air with this pair. My mother's coy remarks and hints felt like somebody had a battering ram against my spine, pushing me off a cliff.

I was only too happy to get back to my study and continue to read the confession.

The man's villainy had been absolutely appalling. His shamelessness had no slightest twinge of conscience. He was totally convinced that he was reacting quite naturally. I had never realized that the criminal mind operated that way. I read and read.

I was actually unable to put it down. When I finally finished the confession, it was the middle of the next night.

I sat there in the midst of the yellowed vocoscriber pages.

Well, (bleep) him!

Here were TWO empires left totally up in the air, Voltar *and* Earth! Here was a whole base about to be executed to a man. Here was Jettero Heller with a warrant out for him. Here was the Countess Krak possibly dead and falling into a mile-deep chasm. And it didn't even say what happened to the cat!

WHAT THE HELLS HAD HAPPENED *THEN?*

Oh, I was pretty peeved with this criminal, Soltan Gris. Here he was, begging to be executed. Well, he ought to be executed for leaving a reader in the middle of the sky like that!

Well, there was nothing for it. I knew that before I could get to sleep I would have to get some idea at least what had happened to Voltar and Earth at that time.

I routed out Hound and, with complaints, he woke up a seneschal and they got into the tower storerooms and, with many a raise of eyes to the ceiling, got out my old school books.

Confidently I opened the unread pages of a dusty history text. It had dates on the margins to keep the student oriented and I found the comparable era.

I read: "This period was noted for its peace and calm. The orderly succession from the reign of Cling the Lofty to that of Mortiiy the Brilliant was notable mainly for its unnotableness."

Hold it. Gris had mentioned that Prince Mortiiy was revolting on Calabar. Apparatus troops had undertaken the final assault to wipe out the rebel.

I hurriedly opened up a civics text on the Voltar government. I looked in the table of divisions and departments.

THERE WAS NO SUCH ORGANIZATION AS THE APPARATUS!

I sat back. I have mobs of relatives connected to every imaginable part of the Voltar government. I had never heard any of them ever mention the Apparatus. And then I suddenly understood:

THEY WERE KEEPING THE APPARATUS *SECRET!*

Oh, but what a cover-up that was! A whole organization!

But I was far from finished yet.

I got Hound back up out of bed and made him go wake up the chamberlain and unlock the library in the south tower and bring me up all the old encyclopedias, and when the footmen had lugged these in, with many an accusing look, I began to tear through them.

I found Jettero Heller, a famous combat engineer and noted space racer and bullet-ball champion. There was no mention of his ever having been to Earth.

I sent the staff scurrying for additional volumes.

Once more I tore into pages. This time I was looking for the Planet Earth or Blito-P3.

NO SIGN OF IT!

Well, I can tell you, reader, I was a very puzzled person.

I couldn't make heads nor tails of it.

At the insistence of the seneschal and the chamberlain and Hound and accompanied by many eyes of the staff rolled at the ceiling, I went to bed.

I was quite cross with Gris.

Chapter 3

The following morning, when I awoke, despite the accusative racket Hound was making with spinbrushes and closet doors, I lay awake, on my back, looking at the ceiling.

WHAT had happened to those people?

What had happened to Izzy Epstein and Rockecenter?

Hound fell over some of the books still stacked in my bedroom and I turned to ask him if he didn't realize that writers needed quiet to concentrate, when my eye lit on one of the books that had fallen. It was *145th Deluxe Edition: In the Mists of Time, Legends of the Original Planets of the Voltarian Confederacy, Compiled by the Lore Section, Interior Division.*

Wait a minute. The Gris confession had mentioned that. I padded into my study and brought it back and, despite Hound's eyeballs going to the ceiling, plopped it down on the bed in total disregard of the fountain of dust. Aha! Here was the number in the Gris confession: Folk Legend 894. It mentioned Blito-P3.

I turned to the Deluxe Edition, feeling lucky that it was recent and not abridged. At least I could check that point.

I flipped the pages. I found Folk Legend 893. I read the number of the next one. It was Folk Legend 895.

Hold it. Back up.

FOLK LEGEND 894 WAS DELETED!

I seized the Gris manuscript. Could my eyes be playing me tricks? No, there it was: Folk Legend 894. It even quoted it, telling all about Prince Caucalsia and how he had escaped to Blito-P3!

Hound tried to distract me by making me sit down while he shaved me, but I clung to the confession with a grip of steel. I continued to thumb through it while I was dressed and all the time I was eating breakfast, looking at it, wondering about it. His descriptions of the Planet Earth seemed so real, I could not possibly imagine how he could have made them up.

My eye was wandering over a page where an investigative reporter, Bob Hoodward, had overturned the presidency. That didn't quite ring true. What was an "investigative reporter"? I tried to imagine it. Obviously, it was somebody who investigated and wrote a book about it. Yes, that must be it. But to overturn a presidency? That seemed to be laying it on rather heavy. There was no such profession as "investigative reporter" in the Confederacy. Had Bob Hoodward overturned the whole planet? No. The confession also said that he had gotten shot.

My mother interrupted my work by telling me that Corsa and her brother had been waiting on the lawn ever so long for me to come out and play bat ball. Of course I had to go and for the next hour had to watch Corsa galloping about shaking the ground while her brother broke bats. And when I got battered through a backstop by a sizzler, it was very plain to me that if I ever got pushed into marrying her and had to spend my life listening to their raucous provincial laughter whenever I fell down, life would be a very dreary thing. Modon was definitely not for me!

Showering off the sweat and turf stains, I was in the grip of desperation.

Seeking anything to get my mind off such awful fates, I returned to the subject of the confession. Wrapped in a towel, I turned over the pages of the *Mists of Time*. Yes, Folk Legend 894 was missing. Then, as I closed the book, my eye lit on its publisher. The Interior Division! It was a government book! For some reason they had seen fit to delete this reference to Blito-P3!

I stood in sudden shock. My schoolbooks were government.

The encyclopedias were government. Everything I had been examining was government printed!

If the Gris confession were true, then I WAS STARING AT THE GREATEST GOVERNMENT COVER-UP IN THE LAST MILLENNIA!

It was the first time I had suspected that the government would ever do such a thing. Believe me, reader, it shook me. I had always been brought up carefully to believe that, in government, truth, decency and honor were inseparable. Every relative I had, had dinned it into me! And I believed it myself! Could a government actually pretend something didn't exist which did? Could it be partners with a lie? Incredible!

Then I was shaken again. But this time it was by Hound, who was trying to get me into some pants.

This was the way my life was going: pushed this way and that. I was being made the victim of a tailor-made destiny that might have fitted any of them but certainly did NOT fit me!

Almost musingly, while my scarf was being tied too tight, I wondered what it would be like to be a free agent, dashing around overthrowing governments like that Bob Hoodward. It must be very satisfying. Even if you got shot.

I quivered with a sudden idea. If I were an investigative reporter and exposed the biggest cover-up of the millennia and wrote it in a book, they'd HAVE to publish it! Otherwise I could go on lecture tours and tell people that they lived under repressive censorship!

And if I published a great exposé, my name would be emblazoned across the skies of Voltar! There would be no more of this laughter behind hands because no one published my odes. There would be no more pushing of me into horrifying posts. There would be no threat of living a life battered with raucous, provincial laughter. They would have to admit that, yes, indeed, Monte Pennwell was a WRITER!

I could even hear my great-uncle Lord Dohm telling the Chief Justiciary at lunch, "You know those great reviews my nephew

Monte is getting? Well, we gave him his start right here." How proud he would be!

But wait, I had better be a little more steady on my facts. Had there been a government cover-up? Or was that copy of the *Mists of Time* just a printing error?

Chapter 4

I knew I was taking my life in my hands. My cousin, Sir Chal, is an older man and is bent on getting me to take a job as a filing clerk in the Royal Astrographic Institute, and he is a very deceptive sort of chap. He usually appears sort of dreamy and out of this world but he can come back into it fast enough when the occasion arises.

I took a grip on my nerve and flew down to their domed building south of the city. I wondered exactly how an investigative reporter would act. Casual? Furtive? Disarming? Open?

I would try furtive. I went into his outer office where they kept the files and to a clerk who has known me since I was just a little boy, I said, "Flipper, could you let me have some old charts? I want some decoration for my study. Something antique."

"Why, certainly, young Monte," he said and waved his hand to an anteroom. "Drawers 35 to 190. Just check with me to be sure you don't take the only copy we have."

I went in and fumbled about, pulling out charts. They were printed three-dimensionally on flat paper and they showed complex systems. Some were even nicely decorated with little trees and inhabitants around the borders. On one of them the planets were animated by an optical trick and even a comet could be made to sail across the sky—a real curiosity. And then I couldn't believe my eyes.

IT WAS THE BLITO SYSTEM!

And there, plain as day, was Blito-P3!

I raced straight into my cousin's office. He looked up and said, "Monte, as I live! Come down to take the filing job, I see."

I had known beforehand it would be dangerous to go in there. I hastily waved the chart. "Cousin Chal!" I said. "Here is a planet that isn't mentioned in government books. Blito-P3!"

He came down from his clouds. "What planet?"

"Blito-P3!" I said. "The one they call Earth locally! It isn't in any government text and yet here it is right here on this chart!"

He frowned. "Let me see that," he said. He looked at it. "Why, this chart is one of the old astromotion types. We haven't printed those for a thousand years!"

"It shows this planet!" I said, pointing to it and making it move around its sun. "No modern text mentions it!"

"Astromotion charts were inaccurate," he said. "They were inadequate for astrogation. They had minutes of error in them."

"Yes, but that inaccuracy wouldn't include including a whole planet in error!"

"Give me that chart," he said. It was a strange thing to say because he already had it. I didn't like the grimness in his tone.

He went out into the outer office. He said, "Who gave Monte this chart?"

"Why, I did," said Flipper.

"Flipper," said Sir Chal, "I've been thinking for some time that you need to freshen up as a professional. I'm ordering you to space-survey duty, effective at once."

Flipper looked at me accusingly.

It was quite a row. It took me an hour to get connected through to my Aunt Ble and get her to get her husband Lord Cross to catch the transfer order as it came through the Royal Personnel Office and change it to librarian on one of our family estates. I couldn't have Flipper's head rolling into my lap and staring at me with accusing eyes.

I wasn't permitted to retain the chart. But I had something else. A conviction.

THERE WAS A GOVERNMENT COVER-UP ON THE SUBJECT OF BLITO-P3!

And another conviction: Being an investigative reporter was not without perils!

But I could begin to see my name glimmer in the skies of Voltar. The nightmare of Modon faded a bit.

NOW what would I do?

Chapter 5

I sat in my air-speedster and thought about it.

I had the Gris manuscript with me. There was another clue in it but I was pretty nervous about following it up: it would be very dangerous.

My great-uncle Guz was the civilian Assistant Lord of the Fleet. He has adamant political opinions and he talks about politics by the hour. There is no stopping him. He also drinks tup by the gallon and you have to drink with him. His ideal plan for me is a position at a desk in his office receiving notables. They also drink tup. Association with Sir Guz alone would ruin anyone's health and such employment would lead to a very early demise with liver trouble.

I had the number of the original patrol craft that surveyed Earth on the first Heller trip. The Fleet slavishly keeps records of every vessel it ever had.

You realize, dear reader, that I undertook these perils for your sake.

I headed for the Fleet administrative complex in Government City.

Typical of any Fleet installation, it looked like a formation of spaceships. They are laid out on blue gravel walks and "lawns." You practically have to go through airlocks to get into the buildings.

I had figured that my great-uncle Guz, at this time of the day, would have returned from lunch. My luck was out. He was just leaving and nothing would do but that I come along and meet Admiral Blast who was departing later today for an inspection tour of all 110 Fleet planetary bases. Admiral Blast turned out also to be a great tup drinker. He thought it would be a terribly good idea for me to come along as part of his inspection party and get some idea of each of the 110 main planets of the Confederacy: I could sign on as a civilian aide and help him fend off notables. My great-uncle Guz thought it would be splendid training for my post in his office, as I would get an insight into the politics of every planet. The two of them practically had me packed up and on board before, mercifully, tup took over and they went off arm in arm singing "Spaceward Ho!"

I let my tenor fade out and I faded likewise. Two hours hence, they wouldn't remember me at all. I slipped back into the main building. I found the office labelled Fleet Vessel Logs, Archives, and walked in.

I would try the direct approach this time. "Sir Guz said I could look at some old ship logs," I said, knowing full well my great-uncle wouldn't remember anything about it one way or the other.

An old spacer with half his face burned off said, "What ship?"

I said, "Patrol Craft B-44-A-539-G."

He indicated a cubicle and I went in and sat down in front of the screen. The vessel's log began to roll off before my eyes. There was a slow button and a stop button on the console. There were also a lot of other controls.

It was speeding along toward the date I wanted. I pushed slow. THEN, THERE IT WAS!

Entry by entry, the whole cruise rolled off. It had left Voltar carrying Combat Engineer Jettero Heller, had proceeded to Blito-P3, surveyed it without landing and had returned. Fifteen weeks' worth of log and routine action.

Aha!

This was the ship Lombar Hisst, Chief of the Apparatus, had

then grabbed at the patrol base, seizing all of its crew and sending them to Spiteos.

But none of that was in the log. It simply went blank for a bit. Then suddenly there were more entries. They started with a refit and proceeded on with routine duties.

Hastily, I found a reverse button and backed it up. The blank area had a little symbol appearing beside it on the screen. It was a green spiral. I looked at the code on the machine side and it said the symbol meant "See Fleet Intelligence."

I glanced out of the cubicle at the clerk. He was busy at something else. I addressed the console keyboard. It was not too different than a library keyboard at school. I punched the green-spiral key and then fed in the patrol-craft number.

Payoff!

PATROL CRAFT B-44-A-539-G. IN A ROUTINE CHASE OF SPACE SMUGGLERS IN COORDINATES 80/45/32, FLISTEN SECTOR, FLEET CRUISE VESSEL *BAULK* DISCOVERED AND REPOSSESSED SAID CRAFT.

Aha! The reason neither Gris nor anyone else could find the crash was that that crooked Death Battalion squad had sold the vessel to smugglers! They hadn't crashed it as ordered.

Wait. There were some more symbols. I deciphered that if one wanted the battle report one should punch in Fleet Cruise Vessel *Baulk*. But if one wanted the disposition of the patrol-craft crew, one should punch in Fleet Intelligence.

I was not interested in the battle with smugglers but I was interested in the patrol craft's crew.

In the Gris narrative, he had gone to Spiteos where the crew had been imprisoned, had gotten a prostitute and had put her and poisoned food into the cell and had supposed they would shortly all be dead.

YET HERE WAS A FLEET INTELLIGENCE REPORT ON THIS CREW!

Believe me, I lost no time punching it in!

And here it came!

CONFIDENTIAL

From: Craftleader Soams, Patrol Craft B-44-A-539-G

To: Fleet Intelligence Officer Bis

SIR! *Pursuant to your request that I make a report to you in full, it is my pleasure and duty to do so.*

SIR! *When we received emergency orders to take off, we boarded our craft and went skyward. Fifteen men of the Apparatus Death Battalion suddenly emerged from hiding in the ship and overpowered us.*

SIR! *There is an Apparatus fortress two hundred miles across the Great Desert which is not on our charts. It is a black castle generally supposed to be a primitive ruin. But it is totally policed and defended.*

SIR! *The twenty of us, names attached, were incarcerated contrary to all regulations. We were stripped naked and thrown in an underground cell.*

SIR! *We would have starved to death had it not been for our skill in catching vermin.*

SIR! *We would have died of thirst had it not been for underground water leakage.*

After some days we were approached by a General Services officer, brown hair, brown eyes, who did not identify himself.

SIR! *He wanted information concerning our cruise to Blito-P3 and, in particular, data concerning JETTERO HELLER, Royal officer, who was nominally in command of the survey we undertook of said unconquered planet. In particular, he wanted to know any weaknesses of said Royal officer, Heller.*

SIR! *He tried to bribe us with food, money and then a prostitute. Recognizing that he was a "drunk,"* we told him nothing but got the bribes out of him anyway.

The prostitute was shown to us outside the cell door and we were told we could have her if we talked. One of us spacers, a pilot from Flisten, recognized the girl as a Guaop from her eye form and long fingernails. He had learned to speak Guaop as a boy. Using that language he told her not to struggle and to come in. The "drunk" pushed her through the slot as she was not very big. She was in terrible condition. Her larynx had been removed. Although she could not talk, by using hand signals for yes and no and designs drawn in the dirt, we for the first time learned where we were. See data above.

The food was suspect so we fed some to a vermin which died horribly.

The money was examined by our finance man and was found to be counterfeit.

A magic bag which did not disclose what was in it was part of the bribes. We found out how to work it.

A pass, according to the girl, had been left for her at the guard station.

We promised the girl that if she helped us we would see that she got an artificial larynx and would be sent home to Flisten. She agreed.

A knife was made for her from one of the food cans. The medical spacer fixed her up so she looked like she had a venereal disease and would not be raped by the guards.

Under our instructions, she took the poison food out and buried it at Camp Kill. In subsequent trips in she brought us metal scraps from old wrecks, concealing them in the magic bag under sexual tricks.

Weapons were made by us.

At strike hour the girl dug up the poisoned food at Camp Kill, carried it through our guardroom, dropped the bag of it in the guardroom so that it spilled. The guards there, of course, seized it and began to open it to eat. But the girl, per plan, induced the officer to come to the cell with her, saying they would now kill her and promising him, with gestures, certain favors.

The guard officer fell into our hands. He proved, under threat, very compliant.

The guards in the guardroom had eaten the food and were dead. We dragged their bodies into our cell, stripped them and donned their uniforms. We put on riot helmets to hide our faces. When the relief guard squad came, we took care of them.

The captured officer passed us and the girl out through the tunnels.

An airbus was commandeered by the captured officer and we flew to our base. As agreed, we then let him escape and I doubt he will go near the Apparatus.

Finance for an artificial larynx and a passage to Flisten for the girl were provided by our crew so there is no Fleet expense or vouchers.

Request that I and my crew be permitted to bomb Apparatus central headquarters in Government City, as they are just "drunks" and it would be no loss.

> *Respectfully, SIR!*
> *Craftleader Soams*

Endorsement 1: File with ongoing Fleet Intelligence investigation of the Coordinated Information Apparatus.

> *Endorsement 2: After any necessary medical treatment, restore crew to normal operating status.*
>
> *Endorsement 3: Negative on bombing Apparatus. Developments are being watched.*
>
> *Bis*
> *Fleet Intelligence*

I was in an instant, giddy whirl!

This compared exactly with the Gris confession!

There HAD been an Apparatus!

There HAD been a survey of Blito-P3!

There HAD been a planet called Earth!

Oh, dear me! This WAS a gigantic cover-up!

But they hadn't covered up everything!

The burned spacer said, "You got what you want in there?"

I hastily folded the printouts and put them in my case. He must not know what I had gleaned.

Oh, life as an investigative reporter could be very exciting!

I walked out casually.

I stood on the blue gravel and pondered. Where would I go next?

Then it came to me in a flash.

SPITEOS!

Chapter 6

I rushed to my air-speedster and grabbed the communications mouthpiece. I called the family estate hangar-garage and got through to my mechanic.

"Shafter," I said, excitedly, "get the old air-wagon ready. I will be home to pick it up at once."

"The air-wagon!" he wailed. "Why, young Monte, that hasn't been out of the hangar for ten years! We haven't used it since we used to take you and your chums to school!"

"Get it ready!" I said sternly. "It's going on a long trip! Now switch me over to Hound."

"Young Monte?" Hound said. "It's a good thing you called. Your mother has been on to me since noon trying to find out where you were. Didn't you remember you had a swimming date with Corsa and her brother?"

But I was filled with too much eagerness to be bothered now with that. My salvation was on its way. "Hound, throw some instruments and camping equipment and guns and things in the air-wagon right away."

"Guns?" he said. "You don't have any guns, young Monte. Besides, you can't go camping. You're supposed to go to Corsa's town house for dinner!"

"Hound," I said, "don't fail me just this once. I promise not to make you listen to my next ode. How's that?"

"Very tempting," said Hound. "But you better come home!"

I broke all speed records getting back to the estate.

And what did I run into? Oh, reader, you should appreciate what I've had to go through to get this story finished for you!

The air-wagon, pretty scruffy, was on the pad all right. But so were my mother and Corsa and her brother and Hound. The latter three were dressed in outing clothes!

"Oh, I think it's so romantic," my mother said. "There will be two moons tonight."

"I got you guns," said Hound. "Corsa's brother has them by the ton."

Shafter was in the driving seat. "I can't trust you with this old wreck, young Monte. I'll probably have to overhaul the drives in midair."

We took off, my mother waving hopefully. Corsa cuddled up.

It wasn't going quite as I planned. I doubted that Bob Hoodward could have unseated any presidents if he'd been mired down in family.

"Where we going?" asked Shafter. I sort of glared at him. I had wanted to drive to see if I could do it like Heller, with one knee. But I would make the best of it.

"Go over these hills and head out across the Great Desert," I said.

"Oh, we're going to the Blike Mountains," said Hound. "I'd better call the Earl of Mok. That's his hunting preserve. He'll want game wardens to meet us."

"No, no!" I said. "We're not going there. We're heading for Spiteos."

"Never heard of it," said Shafter, reaching for a button to turn on the panel map screen.

"You won't have," I said proudly. "It's a huge black castle left over from primitive times. It's two hundred miles straight west. You can't miss it. It's an enormous ruin, I think."

"I don't like ruins," said Corsa. "On Modon we build everything shiny new. In fact, I have some architects working on our house."

I felt a little ill. This sort of thing could go too far and it was certainly going too fast!

Her brother thought he'd better educate me on how you handled lepertiges with cannons so I wouldn't get hurt the first time out. And Corsa informed me at considerable length what you had to do about worms getting into the crops.

I felt I had received a Royal reprieve when Shafter said suddenly, "If that's it, there it is!"

I looked ahead and down. Through a dancing column of wind and dust, like purple diamonds in the slanting sun, I saw a gash that rent the ground, deadly and awful deep. Just beyond it seemed to be an area of black stone sprawled upon the desert floor.

"I don't see any castle," said Corsa.

"I thought you said there was a castle," said her brother.

There was green grass along the chasm rim and some grazing animals dotted the area.

"A herder!" cried Corsa. "Land down there so I can ask him about his flock!"

Shafter promptly landed.

I got out and before Corsa could get to him, I ran to the rustic and said, "Is this the castle of Spiteos?"

He hunched the blanket he wore as a cloak so it wouldn't fall off and looked where I was pointing. "Them black rocks?" He was chewing on a leaf and he spat liquidly in that direction. "I heard my great-grandfather call it 'Castle Rocks' once. And maybe they did look like a castle once. But there's been earthquakes, you know, and things get tumbled around."

I looked at the yawning chasm. "You ever been down into that?"

"What?" he said, aghast. "You must think I'm crazy. I had an animal fall there once and you could hear him scream for half an hour and he never did hit bottom."

Corsa had come up and she wanted to know all about the crop value of his animals and did he ever have to treat them for colic.

I went over and sat down on a large black boulder and looked at this scene. From the Gris manuscript, I could get a pretty good idea of where Camp Endurance—or Camp Kill as they called it—had been. I didn't want to go near that chasm where the Countess

Krak apparently had fallen to her death. I wondered if there were still dungeons and bones underneath this sprawl of enormous basalt.

Unable to resist the urge, since it was singing in my head, I whipped out a pad of paper and wrote:

AN ODE TO SPITEOS
Oh, grandeur fallen in decay,
You fill my soul with dread dismay.
Your broken, ruined stones that fell,
Many a dismal tale could tell.
Oh, in your blackness did you spring
Up, like some demented thing,
From some foul, fetid, screaming Hell?
Oh, Spiteos, you who speak of dead
Forgotten men fill me with dread!
I'm glad your bones again will wed
The ground on which your evil bled.
The cry of mourning is the moan
Of desert wind. Not mine!

I looked at it. Pretty good, I thought. You're in fine form, Monte.

Footsteps behind me. It was Corsa and her brother and Hound. I couldn't resist reading it to them.

RAUCOUS LAUGHTER!

When she could catch her breath, and holding her side, Corsa said, "Oh, Monte! It will be such a relief when I can cure you of this obsession with writing. I honestly don't think my stomach muscles could stand too much of this."

From that moment, I hated her with enduring passion!

I hardly heard Hound's comment, "You promised not to read me another one of them things. Shows I got to work harder impressing on you the value of keeping one's word!"

I sternly repressed the urge to write "An Ode to Those Who Have No Souls."

Very well aware that I had been born in the wrong time and the wrong place, I went over to the air-wagon.

"Get out the instruments," I told Shafter.

"Well, you didn't say what kind. But I got everything here you can analyze any motor with that's made."

"I'm not trying to analyze motors. I'm trying to detect metal under the ground."

"Metal?" he said. "You don't have to detect metal to fix a drive. That's all they're made of. Every detector I brought detects *currents*."

The possibility of any current still running in anything after a century or more, unless it was a black hole or something, was too remote.

Feeling defeated, I went away and sat down.

If my search dead-ended and I never got the uncover-up book written, my fate was sealed. Faced with clerks' desks or exile to Modon, the only possible solution seemed to be to throw myself into the chasm and have done.

I sat there in the sunset, getting bluer by the moment. I didn't have enough material. All I had was an old chart I didn't keep, a ship's log, an intelligence report and the Gris confession. They did not comprise any real evidence of or reason for such a vast cover-up. I wondered what Bob Hoodward would have done.

Shafter came over. "Oh, don't just sit there pouting. I heard you spouting and that poem wasn't that bad. Besides, I've had an idea. If you want to find metal under the ground, I can take a spare fuel rod and push it into the dirt and tap it and if there's any metal around, it will polarize the current and one of these analyzers will spot it. What you looking for, buried treasure?"

"Oh, indeed so!" I said. And priceless treasure it would be. It would buy me out of total, degraded slavery if I could find the evidence I needed!

"Then," he said, "let's get to work."

Chapter 7

I could see at once that there was going to be an awful lot of digging.

Hound said, "No, no, no! You can't dig in that suit you're wearing and if you think Shafter and I are going to do all the digging, you've got another think coming, young Monte." He called to the herdsman. "Haven't you got a village around here?"

The herdsman spat liquidly in a northerly direction. "Just on the other side of them biggest black rocks."

I asked Corsa's brother to unload the camping equipment and set it up and then scrambled after Hound, who had gone lumbering off in the indicated direction.

With many an admonition to not scuff my shoes and not fall in any obviously gaping holes, Hound led me around the mammoth pile of stones, and after about fifteen minutes of walking we came to the "village."

It wasn't a village at all. The rocks seemed to have a lot of holes in them that could be said to be caves and there were women and kids visible.

Hound, with a lot of questions to blank or wide-eyed faces, located the headman in a cavity that was mainly furnished with odors. He was gnarled and twisted and toothless, 190 if he was a day.

Aha! I thought. These were some of the prisoners that escaped during the earthquake and they stayed around!

"This tribe?" said the old man. "We're herders. We drifted in here about fifty year ago, found grass and settled down." No, he didn't know this had once been a castle.

Hound said to me, "How many holes are you going to dig?"

"How should I know how many holes I'm going to dig?"

"Well, I better make plans for a lot of holes if your record in Kid Sandpiles is any gauge. How much money have you got on you?"

I said, "Why should I have any money on me?"

Hound said, "Because I'm going to hire these men to do the digging."

"Oh."

He struck up some kind of a crass commercial bargain in which the fifty men of the village would dig.

Cautioned numerous times not to catch the cuffs of my pants on thorns, we got back to the air-wagon.

There was no sign of any pitched shelters. A bang in the distance told me that Corsa's brother was utilizing the remaining light to shoot songbirds. Corsa was busy discussing animal husbandry with the herdsman.

Hound said, "I'm going to take the air-wagon back to town and get an advance on your next month's allowance. And I'm going to get you some digging clothes. You should have told me what you were up to. Sit right there on that rock until I come back."

He and Shafter threw the camping gear out and Hound took off. I sat on the rock and wondered what it would be like to live an unmanaged life. I was certain that Bob Hoodward didn't ever have such obstacles to overcome.

Shafter was going around pushing a fuel rod in the ground and tapping it. Finally he said to me, "Young Monte, I can't tap the rod and read a meter at the same time. When I tap the rod, you walk around me fifteen or twenty feet away and watch the meter."

I did as he suggested. Almost at once I got a huge surge. Excitedly I began to tear out grass by the roots and scoop away sand. Shafter was right with me. We looked like a couple of sporting animals going down a varmint hole for the kill. Grass tufts were flying through the moonlight in one direction and sand in another.

"What are you doing?" said Corsa.

"We're going after buried treasure," said Shafter.

"Well, you shouldn't be digging this grassland up like that. You'll ruin their pasturage. Fill that hole up at once and replace the turf."

"Oh, we will, we will," I said. "Let's see what's down here first."

"Monte," she said severely, "I can see right now that you have a terrible amount to learn. When you dig up pasturage that way, you get erosion. I really sigh when I realize the terrible time I will have making an acceptable farmer out of you. You have no finer sensibilities. Cease and desist at once!"

Of course we had to stop. I went back and sat down on the rock, mourning. What the Devils had been down underneath there, giving that read on the analyzer?

The moons were well up when Hound came back. He had brought two footmen, a cook and a maid for Corsa. I got scolded because my lounge suit was now turf-stained.

They found a spring, erected inflatable shelters and belatedly we had a dinner they had brought from town.

But I was very cunning. You are lucky that I was, dear reader, for we never would have found out what happened after the Gris narrative left us in midair.

I waited until everybody was asleep. I crept out of my shelter and went back to the hole and began to dig. I was very quiet. I dug and scraped and brushed and wore my fingers to the bone.

And then, there in the green moonlight, I knelt there looking at it.

A CANNON WHEEL!

It was corroded and twisted. The rim was partially melted as from a flaming blast.

Clearly there had been a battle here!

My hopes soared.

Clearly I could put an end to the overmanagement of my life. Fame beckoned!

I came out of my trance. I rolled it over onto flat ground. I carefully filled the hole in although I couldn't find the turf.

I rolled the clumsy, battered wheel into my shelter and at last went to sleep.

A blasting bustle awoke me. I couldn't find out what it was right away because Hound had to shave me and get me into some sport clothes and proper boots and even insisted I have breakfast.

At last I got out of the shelter. The area was teeming with men from the village. They all had digging tools. They were standing around Corsa. My hopes soared. Maybe she was on my side. Then I overheard what she was saying.

She was telling them that the grazing area could be quadrupled if they dug certain trenches that would stop erosion and enlarge the spring. Certain actions, it seemed, would then create ponds from the occasional runoff of the rains.

"There's far too much spill into that chasm," she told them. "So here is your map. Now get to work."

They all went trudging off and she came over to me. "Now, I've taken care of that for you, Monte. Why don't you go find my brother and help him shoot these songbirds. They're terrible for crops."

It was my turn to raise my eyes to the sky but, of course, I didn't. Not in front of her.

Shafter and I had no choice but to follow the diggers about and hope they would hit something by accident.

Almost at once we began to hit paydirt! (That's a mining term.)

A digger threw some dirt aside and Shafter saw something glitter and was in there like a shot. He picked up something round and then said, "Blast, I thought it was a coin!" He threw it away and I picked it up quickly.

A button! It had a symbol on it that looked like a bottle—no, a fat paddle with an upside-down handle!

THE APPARATUS!

Aha! The Gris confession was no myth!

All that day I tagged around collecting things. Odds and ends of metal were evidently not unusual in this place. One of the men said they appeared on the ground every time it rained. This had been a vast encampment!

By evening I had a hoard that even included the remains of an electric whip!

Oh, I was getting warm. I didn't even mind a lecture by Corsa's brother, as he sorted out a mound of plumage, on what kind of songbird you had to get rid of first if you ever expected to get a wink of sleep. I wondered sourly to myself if Gris' ancestors had come from Modon. I wondered if my sanity could stand up to much more association with this pair.

About midnight the conspiratorial voice of Shafter woke me up. "If we're ever going to find any buried treasure," he whispered, "we're going to have to work at night. Come along. I need somebody to read the meter."

We stealthily crept out of camp. "Now, today when I went into town to get a load of grass seed," he said, "I took a look at this place from the air. If this was ever a castle, when the earthquake knocked it over, it fell due west. There's a pattern of fallen stone that looks just like a tower when you see it from above. My hunch is that if you root around over there and if it ever had a strongroom, it would lie in that mess. So let's go."

We clambered over shattered piles of black basalt under the bright green moons. This was more like the kind of thing I thought Bob Hoodward would do.

A wind had come up and it was moaning through the tumbled stones. The beginning lines of "An Ode to the Homeless Ghost" began to run through my head. I wasn't watching where I was going.

I FELL STRAIGHT DOWN!

Fifteen feet below I fetched up with a horrible thud!

Shafter's voice out in the night. "Hey, where'd you go?"

"I'm down here!" I yelled.

I could see his head above in the hole, silhouetted against the moon-hazed sky. "You shouldn't go running off that way! You could get hurt!"

"*Could* get hurt?" I wailed. "I'm smashed! Get me out of here!"

He shined a light down into the place. "Hey!" he said. "Good going! You found a room!"

I stopped feeling for broken bones and looked around. Yes, I was in what might have been a room.

Shafter got out a line but instead of hauling me up, he came down. "What's that you're lying on?" he said.

I looked.

A DOOR!

It was made out of impervious alloy and had been so covered with dust that it had taken my fall to expose it.

We uncovered it. Shafter used a disintegrator drill to remove the hinges and we managed to lay it aside. There was a gaping hole under it and when we shined in the torch, we were looking at a room lying on its side.

It had the collapsed remains of some furniture in it. We dropped down a rope into it. I righted a chair. It was an ornate antique. I thought maybe that we had gotten into some old tomb. I looked around for signs of a coffin or burial artifacts. There were only a lot of shards of glass.

"Let's see if there's any buried treasure back of these walls," said Shafter. "You read the meter. I'll get on some insulator gloves and bang this fuel rod."

Shortly the sparks were flying as he went along the walls. It made the air smell like ozone.

I was passing the meter along one wall. I got a tremendous read. Shafter rushed over to me. "Crashing cogwheels!" he said. "There must be metal back of there by the millions of tons!"

We went down the wall and found, under a cascade of stone, another door. We unburied it, disintegrated the hinges and removed it.

We were in another room.

I shined my torch. Just behind the place where I had gotten my read was the remains of a COMPUTER BANK!

"Oh, blast," said Shafter. "That isn't any treasure. My current was just energizing the electromagnetic coils. We been had!"

"No, we haven't!" I cried. I suddenly knew where we were. That antique throne chair in the other office, this door, the desks tumbled about, all compared with the Gris confession!

WE WERE IN THE TOWER OFFICES OF LOMBAR HISST!

THAT WAS HIS COMPUTER CONSOLE!

Oh, the very thing I had hoped to find!

"Quick, Shafter!" I said. "Can you get power into that thing?"

He looked at it. When the tower had crashed, the retaining bolts had held. But it was a sorry-looking mess.

"Well, why?" said Shafter.

"To get the information out of it, of course!"

"Well, Monte, I hate to have to tell you this but if there had been anything left on those recordings, it's gone now."

"What do you mean?" I wailed.

"Well, we been sending hellish jolts of electricity around to find things and it would have wiped every cell in it."

I collapsed.

What Bob Hoodward must have gone through!

If I got any more help on this project I might as well give up!

At length I climbed back up the lines we had left dangling and got outside. I sat down on a rock in the moonlight.

Prospects of Modon with Corsa and her brother or prospects of drudgery at dull desks were two types of torture it was impossible to choose between. The green haze in the sky was not emblazoned with my name. The mile-deep chasm looked very attractive. Dully, I began to compose "An Ode to a Snuffed-out Life."

Chapter 8

Listlessly, all the next day, I loafed around, not even bothering to pick up the bits and pieces the land-reclamation project was turning up.

In the first place, I had had very little sleep. In the second place, I knew down deep that it was a good thing for this herding tribe to have more water and grass and I was sort of ashamed of myself for feeling so harshly about it. The Great Desert had once been a fertile plain, 125,000 years ago or more. It had the remains of primitive canals all through it. But the civilization had been wiped out and it had all gone to dust.

I began to ruminate upon the transient nature of cultures. They could be interrupted. For the first time I wondered about our own. It was, on the surface, quite stable. What if some cataclysmic war destroyed us in a puff of flame?

Before I had gotten very far with "An Ode to Vanished Glory," in a very sad meter that fitted my mood, I suddenly had an errant thought.

Maybe there wasn't any real cover-up. Maybe Voltar had wiped out Blito-P3. Maybe it simply wasn't there anymore. Maybe it had become an awful threat!

I mentioned it at supper. I said, "Say, do you suppose some unconquered planet far from here could have developed weapons that could defeat the Voltar Fleet and wipe out the Confederacy?"

"WHAT?" said Corsa's brother. "Wipe out 110 planets? You must be crazy."

"What planet are you talking about?" said Corsa.

"It is a planet designated on our charts—or used to be—Blito-P3. The name the inhabitants use is Earth."

"Does it have people on it?" said Corsa's brother.

"Yes. I guess you could call them Earthmen."

He let out a snort of laughter. "The Earthmen are coming!" he finally managed with a bucolic guffaw.

Corsa joined in with raucous laughter.

Her brother looked up at the twilight sky. "Get under cover quick! Strange ships are in the air!"

They really laughed.

I wouldn't have felt so bad about it but the staff around joined in.

"Oh, Monte," Corsa said at last, "you'll wreck my belly muscles yet! You are such a clown!"

I was trying to explain to them that what I had meant was that Voltar might have found it expedient to wipe the planet out because it somehow could have threatened us. But they weren't listening. They had the whole staff rushing out to make sure there was no enemy fleet in the sky, and they were pretending to see strange ships and running into each other with fake cries of horror at discovering the other was an Earthman just landed. They were awfully energetic. I guess the fresh night air does that to you.

Later her brother amused himself by drawing what an Earthman must look like. He tried feelers and discarded that for horns and threw that away for blobs. Corsa gathered them up and said she couldn't wait to show them to her friends.

I retired early.

It was a good thing I did. About midnight, just when I had composed my tortured wits enough to drop off, Shafter woke me up.

I got some clothes on and followed his beckoning finger. When we were far enough from the camp to be able to talk normally, he said, "You should have told me you were looking for data banks. Is this a secret or something?"

I rued that I had not kept it more secret from that Modon pair.

"Yes, very much so," I said. "I'm trying to find out what happened after a confession I read. He left it all up in the air."

"Well, you just come along," Shafter said.

We were going to the village!

A very shadowy tribesman met us and led us onward. We went into what appeared to be a cave, stepping over bundles of hides. We went to the back.

"I couldn't stand to see you pouting," said Shafter. "So last night I followed the cables from that console. I came out here!"

He was pointing down a tunnel. I followed him. He opened a huge metal side door.

It was a vast room full of tables, benches and cabinets. Pieces of hide and working tools lay all about.

"They use it for a sort of factory to make clothes in. They had no way to get the cabinets open and didn't need them anyway."

"What is this place?" I said, playing my light down the vast expanse of grimy, age-crusted cabinets.

"The computer feeder room," he said. He threw open a cabinet whose hinges he had disintegrated. "This is the place where they prepared the memory bank of that console."

I reached in and pulled out sheaves of paper.

DOCUMENTS!

These were the originals!

RECORDING STRIPS!

These were the first-generation recordings!

"Will this do?" said Shafter.

"Oh, thank Heavens and all the Gods, yes!" I cried, my hands shaking.

"Well, that's a good thing," said Shafter, "because you just bought the place."

Chapter 9

Rape, murder and sudden death: I was looking at so many crimes at once, it was a shocking mess!

To me, raised in the belief that government is honest and does no wrong, protects its citizens and labors for the good of all, it was a terrible shock!

No wonder they hid—what were these headed, the Coordinated Information Apparatus?—from the public view!

Kidnap this one, assassinate that one, blackmail someone else. And silly crimes as well: "Poison his pet fish!" And crimes that were stupid: "Break the windows of his house so he'll think the public don't like him." But dominant were awful crimes: "Rob a bank, plant the evidence on him, make it look like suicide." "Kidnap his children and when he comes to get them back, murder them in front of his eyes." A catalogue of villainy such as I had never seen stared at me from this data bank: slaughter, arson and revenge— destruction, hungry and rampant!

How could this possibly be? Was THIS the government?

All through the night and near to dawn I sorted through this fearful hoard, staggered in reality but too fixated to let the papers drop.

"You better come away from there." A voice was at my side. "The camp and village will be up soon and they'll be wondering where you are."

"I'm halfway between the sixth and seventh Hells," I said. "I've just come on a small religious group the government harassed. The

order here says to plant a whole false file into their church with
their names forged to it. Then there's going to be a raid and they'll
all be arrested and shot. Incredible!"

"Come away," said Shafter. "Your eyes are pretty wild."

He led me off and I went to bed to fall, dumbfounded, into
fitful sleep.

Hound routed me out, scolding me for getting my clothes and
hair so thickly scummed with dirt. I didn't tell him the shape my
soul was in. I felt it was past washing.

Midmorning, dear Corsa came bounding over. How much she
looked like a farm animal, I unkindly thought. "Oh, Monte!" she
said, sitting down at the camp table, crossing her beefy legs and
emptying my canister of hot jolt, "I know you thought it would be
awfully sweet of you to buy this place for me. Here are the deeds the
village headman endorsed: aren't they quaint? Squatter's deeds,
laying claim to abandoned land. They also make you responsible for
any existing tenants. Valid enough, but really, Monte, it will cost
a fortune to clear away those old black rocks and there's hardly
enough ground here to run my pets on. I know you mean well,
Monte, but really, I sometimes wonder about your finer sensibilities.
It is very plain that you need someone strong to take you in hand."
She patted me on the shoulder and left a bruise. "But never mind,
we'll get along just fine once we're on Modon and I have the help of
my family in shaping you up."

She threw the deeds down into the sweetbun syrup and gal-
loped off.

"A fine girl," said Hound.

He would think so, I thought privately. He weighs about three
hundred pounds. I would have to weigh more than that and be
a champion wrestler to boot to handle Corsa—and now, to this
threat, she had added her family. Were they all like her brother?
Charging around breaking bats and shooting songbirds?

But I had a secret weapon. Despite the shock it gave me, I was
certain I had my hands on a cover-up to end all cover-ups. The
matter was very dicey, of course. When I saw what a government
could cover up, the task of uncovering it seemed monumental. But

somehow I would get my name blazing across the sky yet! The Gris confession was an understatement of the way things ran!

Having slept a bit in the afternoon and, although jaded from a dinner full of "The Earthmen are coming," I was able to go to bed early, sneak out the back of the shelter and go with Shafter back to the tunnels.

I saw tonight that what had preserved this area was that it had been below ground level and whatever earthquake had overturned the place had left this whole level, and probably areas below, intact.

"There's an old cellological laboratory in there," said Shafter, pointing to a door. "And right up here, there is what might have been a gymnasium or something. The tribesmen couldn't get the doors open but I took care of that."

I looked into the place. The Countess Krak's training rooms! I waded through clouds of dust that almost made a white fog in front of my lamp. Cabinets of training materials! I was looking for something—there it was! Blito-P3 materials! I opened a drawer. Aged newssheets in some strange language! Was that English? I didn't dare touch them: after nearly a hundred years they were so yellow and decayed that, even in this dry desert air, they looked like they would go to powder.

Back in the hall, Shafter said, "It's lucky the tribesmen couldn't open this next one."

I turned my light into it. An arsenal! Blastrifles, blasticks, grenades. They were in preservation boxes, all usable if you had power packs. But what was this? Hand firebombs, assassin scopes, poison, booby traps for houses, on and on. Oh, they *were* very nasty people.

"Lock that place up!" I told Shafter with a shudder as I came out.

I went back to the computer feeder room, stifled my reaction to half-rotten hides and got back to work on the files. I just want you to know, reader, what I went through to finish this job!

This night I was hopefully searching for more data about Blito-P3. After only a couple of hours, I came up with something shattering.

SURVEYS!

There were more than fifteen thousand years' worth of surveys on Blito-P3! I was amazed that Voltar had been interested in it that long. Every few years, or sometimes every few centuries, a whole survey crew had wandered through the place. They had references here and there to the Voltar Invasion Timetable. Civilizations had risen and fallen and track had been kept of them. I couldn't read the originals, of course, but the computer summary in Voltarian—the sheet they used to transmit the data into the banks—was pinned to each one.

The most massive collection of these was grouped under just one heading: Earth Government Intelligence Organizations.

The pack covered a span of about three thousand years. Strange-sounding names jumped out at you: Julius Caesar, Karl Schulmeister, Napoleon, Webber, a host of them. They seemed to get thicker as they approached later dates. They were separated into groups, and near the top, the thickest one began with *Cheka,* then, moving forward, *OGPU, NKVD, MGB,* and wound up with *Komitet Gosudarstvennoy Besopasnosti* or *KGB.* Another pack said *OSS* and *CIA* and yet another one said *FBI.* I guessed that Voltar was keeping tabs on what the potential enemy was doing. And they must be very interested, because every one of these documents was initialed by the existing Chief of Apparatus at the time of its receipt. The latest ones bore initials which I knew by now stood for Lombar Hisst.

Very, very curious: a supersecret organization Voltar didn't even admit existed, studying supersecret organizations that maybe their governments didn't admit existed either.

I glanced over my shoulder. I knew exactly how Bob Hoodward must have felt when he was about to blow the cover off something.

I put all those packs back and got into the Voltar files. I was getting a little giddy at the sheer quantity of this stuff. How was I ever going to straighten it out and extract a coherent story?

But if I could ever get through this and sort it out, I really had them! No wonder they would engage in a huge cover-up! Their hands were running scarlet with innocent blood! How could a population stand for this? What an explosion my exposé would make!

I was standing in front of a cabinet that was labelled Don't File. Ah, this should be interesting.

I reached in and the very first thing I picked up almost made my eyes pop out. It said:

> ARREST HIGHTEE HELLER AND HOLD HER. THEN BARGAIN WITH HER BROTHER AND GET HIM TO COME IN. THEN KILL THEM BOTH.
>
> LOMBAR HISST

My hands shook. I was on the trail! That was Jettero Heller's sister!

Wait a minute. Hightee Heller was still alive! I'd seen her being interviewed on Homeview not a month ago. She was in her later middle age now, graying but not too badly preserved. They had been having a festival to commemorate her songs. She had even sung a bar or two.

I wondered if she realized there had been a government plot against her life. A celebrity like that? Monstrous!

Maybe there were more details elsewhere. I looked at this vast, vast array of files—millions, billions of bits. The feeling came over me that it might take me years and years. Long before that they would have me shipped off to Modon or bolted to a dusty desk. Desperation took the place of hope.

Abruptly, as I looked back at what I held in my hand, the solution to the whole thing hit me.

Hightee Heller would know all about her brother. She would have letters, clippings, things beyond the government reach. They obviously had never dared kidnap her.

My mind was made up. I would use this scrap of paper for an entry. I would go see Hightee Heller. I would get her help.

Oh, we would blow the cover off everything!

I had Shafter lock the place up. We went back. At the crack of dawn I told them the camping trip was ended. I told the headman to take care of the place, finish Corsa's project, and shelled out the rest of my allowance so he could.

We sped back to the city.

At two o'clock that very day, using my family connections with the manager of Homeview, I walked into the drawing room of Hightee Heller's rooftop estate at Pausch Hills.

A bit gray-haired, retaining some of her beauty and very pleasant, Hightee Heller graciously told me to sit down.

"I've come to tell you there has been a plot against your life," I said.

She looked at the paper and then at me. "What are you doing?" she said.

"I'm writing the story of Jettero Heller's life."

"A writer," she said. "Well, well, you've come to the right person, Monte Pennwell. You may have to do some travelling, for his papers are all kept in the place where he was born: Tapour, Atalanta Province, Planet Manco. I can give you a letter to the museum librarian there."

"What about this threat against your life?" I said.

She went to the window and looked across at Government City. Then she said, "Are you a good fighter, Monte Pennwell?"

"I'm not sure," I said. "I never tried."

That seemed to surprise her. Then she looked at the paper. "From this, I would say that you have somehow gotten into the files of the Coordinated Information Apparatus. Have you got more than this?"

"I've got tons and tons and tons," I said. "I even own the place they're sitting in: the old fortress of Spiteos. I just bought it."

"Good Heavens!" said Hightee. She grew very thoughtful. She looked back at Government City. Then she looked at me. "You seem a nice young man. I know your family quite well. I won't give you a letter. I'll come with you. I haven't been home for a long, long time."

And that was how, with the Apparatus files, I got all the data that permitted me to finish the confession of Soltan Gris.

I hope you appreciate it. It was an awful lot of work!

It DOES contain the cover-up of all time!

And right now, with no more ado, I will get on with it and grab that Soltan Gris by the neck in midflight and tell you what really happened after that fatal day he rushed into the Royal Prison hoping to be executed quickly!

The REAL story is a stunner!

PART SIXTY-EIGHT
Chapter 1

Jettero Heller, Royal officer of the Fleet, Grade X, and member of the Corps of Combat Engineers, tried to counter the eagerness of his lady, the Countess Krak.

He did not like the idea of approaching Spiteos, heavily defended as it was, in an unarmed and unarmored tug.

Just returning from what he supposed to be the completion of Mission Earth after an absence from Voltar of ten months, he did not like the look of things.

He was still travelling on his own orders, those of a combat engineer, and these gave him very wide latitude. He didn't have to report in to the Apparatus and he had no slightest intention of doing so.

Ten months before, after he had been kidnapped by Lombar Hisst and thrown into the dungeon at Spiteos, he had found himself being pushed into a mission under the Exterior Division. His mission handler was supposed to be an Apparatus officer named Soltan Gris. What Gris didn't know was that Jet had never once supposed himself to be directed by the Apparatus.

Before they left, while outfitting the mission vessel *Prince Caucalsia*, a space tug, Jet had had a chance to talk to Bis of Fleet Intelligence.

"The 'drunks' are up to something," young Bis had said. "We can't do anything direct because we do not have the cooperation of the Lord of the Fleet. He's on the Grand Council; he's a nobleman but not a Royal officer. What it's going to take is massive evidence.

With that we can force the issue. So I wish you would undertake the mission and keep your eyes open. But stay alert. Even at the best of times the Apparatus is dangerous. So stay alive and be nimble and maybe the Fleet will have the 'drunks' dead to rights."

The mission had been dangerous enough to please even the most suicidal soul and he'd almost lost his darling, the Countess Krak.

On Voltar Homeview news, the bit that the Chief of the Apparatus, Lombar Hisst, was now the spokesman for His Majesty, Cling the Lofty, rang an alarm bell in Jet.

If, however, he reported in to Bis, his mission would be over, his orders cancelled and he would not have solved the situation of the Countess Krak.

If she continued on as a nonperson, he could not marry her. Worse, she could be picked up by the Apparatus at any time and slammed back into Spiteos or even executed.

There were these so-called Royal proclamations Gris had given her. As yet not fully validated by the signature of the Emperor, they offered an out for her. But he didn't care so much about the other one commending himself—he had them by the bale already.

Gris had given them to her to secure her cooperation in getting the mission launched. Jet didn't trust anything connected with Gris.

They had not found the duplicates in Gris' office. Gris was apparently dead now. She said she had hidden the originals at Spiteos. Dangerous!

Well, a few more hours before reporting in would make no difference. He was still operating under his own cognizance. He decided to take a chance. So he said "All right." It was a fateful decision: Even though it showed no sign of it on the surface, it was going to change the course of hundreds of billions of lives.

In the dark outside of Gris' office in Government City, they loaded up the cartons of blackmail material they had found and the two marines drove them back to Emergency Fleet Reserve.

Commander Crup met them by the parked tug. "You deliver the prisoner all right?"

"Committed suicide," said the Countess Krak.

"Well, that saves the government expense," said Crup. "I wish that could be arranged for all the 'drunks.'"

"Maybe somebody is working on it," said Jet. "Could you please see that these boxes are delivered to Fleet Intelligence Officer Bis? They were the prisoner's personal blackmail files. Tell him I'll report in a bit later when I've attended to one last detail."

Old Atty, Heller's former racing repair chief and now a watchman here, came up beaming all over himself. "We changed her water and air, we crammed her full of food and we put enough spare fuel rods in her hold to take a grand tour of the galaxies."

"She'll only be in operation a few more hours," said Jet. "I think you overdid it."

"You had a hundred thousand credits left on Mission Earth allocations. 'Drunk' money: You think I'd leave that unspent? I even got flowers for the lady!"

"But the ship will be coming right back here," said Jet. "For lay-up."

"No, she won't," said Commander Crup. "Tug One belongs to the Exterior Division now and the only reason you can come here at all is because you are on Fleet orders."

"Well, I don't want to turn a nice ship like this over to the 'drunks'!" said Jet. "They'd just strip the silver and gold and precious stones out of it and use it to throw garbage in."

"You must have been in action," said Commander Crup. "I see the tail has been repaired. That permits you to file a total-loss report and give it to the lady."

"I can't do that," said Jet. "It isn't honest."

"Oh, you," said Commander Crup. "You're dealing with the 'drunks.' What's honesty got to do with it? Look, I'll file the report for you myself. I've got your mission-order number. I'm blasted if the Apparatus is going to get anything off the Fleet! Even if they paid for it."

"No," said Jet.

"Yes," said Crup. "Lady, you've got yourself a space tug. Put it in the back yard and raise kids in it."

The Countess Krak, dressed as a Fleet marine for disguise,

blushed a blush that was visible even in the night.

They all laughed. "I see I can't keep any secrets around here," said Jet. "We've got to get going. Tonight's work isn't done. A million thanks to all of you. If all goes well, I'll invite you to the wedding."

Chapter 2

Up into the Voltar night soared the *Prince Caucalsia*. She had an appointment with destiny that none of them suspected.

It looked like a very simple thing to Jet from an operational standpoint. His only worry was for the Countess Krak.

As far as he and the tug were concerned, they could escape detection. A dull green cast of light from a partial moon made the surface of Voltar luminescent. There was the main Fleet base to the south, and beyond it, Government City. And to the west of these sparkling lights and glowing traffic streams lay the mountains which blocked off the Great Desert.

The Countess Krak had changed into an athletic suit. She stood in the passageway now behind Heller, drawing on a pair of gloves. "It's very simple," she said. "Don't look so tense. The documents are in a waterproof envelope in a crevice on the roof."

"That's a relief," said Heller. "I don't know how long I can hold above the castle undetected. Where is the crevice exactly? I know that roof."

"Right beside the exit elevator. They drilled some extra holes to install a false radiation reflector. I simply rolled the envelope up and put it in the hole. It won't take me but a second to recover it."

"The exit elevator has a dome. I can't sit down on it. We'll have to roll out a ladder and I don't like that. It has no absorbo-coat on it."

"Well, you're always telling me I'm an angel," said the Countess Krak, "but I can't fly. I'll need the ladder."

"We'll have to be very fast. I'll put the ladder in place and when I give you a signal, open the airlock outer door, kick the ladder out, go down it like a flash, get your envelope and get right back up. We're not hanging around!"

"Aye, aye, sir," said the Countess Krak in English.

Heller didn't smile. He put the ladder hooks through rings and checked the coil so it would unroll quickly. He gave her a pat on the shoulder. "Don't forget to allow for the slightly greater gravity. Once you've got the envelope, get back up into the airlock like a shot!"

He took the tug off automatic control and, somewhat anxiously, wishing it were possible for him to do this gymnast act, sent the tug hurtling the two hundred miles across the Great Desert.

Jet didn't like the presence of the moon. And he didn't like the risk of the uncoated ladder, for he was almost certain it would set off alarms.

He still had the illusion projector in the overhead. He checked it to be sure it would project an electronic illusion above the camp if the alarms went off. The image of the tug suspended in the air should attract any gunsights.

He did not know at that time that Lombar Hisst had long since parked a heavy flying cannon underground in the structure. He thought all he had to do was get in and get out, and there was nothing like the quick-maneuvering tug to do a thing like that. He could move it faster in the sky than gun controls could track it and get their heavy pieces repointed to fire. So his main interest was simply on making sure that the Countess Krak got down and got up. THAT made him very nervous. But he couldn't do the flying and the gymnastics, too.

Jet brought the tug down over Spiteos, as invisible as a ghost. He was flying very slow so there would be no air or space turbulence to spot. He was being careful not to become a silhouette against the moon.

Below him the castle brooded blackly against the greenish-glowing desert sand. The gash of the mile-deep chasm gaped close by the fortress side.

All seemed peaceful down there: A few fires burned in Camp Kill; watchlights made pools along the roads and at the barricades.

He came down to thirty feet above the castle roof, directly over the dome. His screens read no detection yet.

"NOW!" he shouted.

The Countess Krak spun the airlock wheels. She thrust back the door. She dropped the ladder out.

INSTANT ALARMS!

The strident voices of the bells brayed like things insane!

"COME BACK!" shouted Heller. "I'M LEAVING!"

But the Countess Krak was gone!

Jet jammed his thumb against the illusion on-button. The image appeared over the camp.

A savage barrage erupted!

A cone of electric fire scorched up from the camp, crossed at the illusion and stood another cone in the air above!

Heller could not leave his controls. He could not peer over the edge.

The Countess Krak had decided to take the chance. She was three feet down the ladder when the first salvo went off. She slid almost free-fall to the castle's roof.

She raced to the cache. It was all black stone. The hole, in this ink, was hard to locate.

The sudden barrage of guns helped her. With handspan measures she located the plugged-up hole. She couldn't get the rock out! She reached into her pocket. Nothing! She had no tools!

A stone! There was one lying ten feet away.

She sprang for it. It was heavy. She struggled back to the hole with it. She raised it over her head. She bashed at the rock.

The stone broke!

She seized a falling splinter of it.

The flickering fire of the barrage made it possible to see. She found a sharp edge in the splinter and used it for a pry.

The plug came out!

She could hear Jet's voice yelling urgently to her. Something new was happening.

She fished into the hole. The envelope was still there! It was stuck. She made it roll tighter and drew it out.

Jet's voice was shouting at her. She could not hear what he was saying above the din.

She shoved the envelope inside her shirt and raced for the ladder.

Up she began to climb!

Yes, there was more gravity than she was lately used to.

She got halfway to the top. Another fifteen feet to go.

THE ROAR OF ANOTHER SHIP!

She glanced back and up.

A FLYING CANNON AGAINST THE MOON!

A blast of fire went by her!

The ladder swung as though struck by a mighty hammer!

She held on.

She scrambled higher on the ladder.

A second blast of fire!

Her hands tore loose!

Something had her by the wrist!

With a mighty yank, Jet snapped her into the airlock!

With two kicks of his feet he freed the ladder hooks. The ladder fell away.

"Rise maximum!" he shouted at the tug, now on automatic.

He slammed the airlock door and spun its wheel.

They were rising violently fast.

He bent for an instant over the Countess Krak. She grinned at him. "That was a great trapeze act. But I don't think we ought to keep it in the show. I got them. But what was that?"

"A flying cannon," said Jet. "It must have been hidden somewhere. Its fire directors centered on the ladder. Your boots are scorched. Are your feet all right?"

"A bit warm."

"I hope their fire control followed the ladder down, what there was left of it."

The Countess Krak was picking herself up. "We got what we came for. Let's get out of here."

"We can't. We can outmaneuver that thing but we can't outrun it. I can't open up the Will-be Was main drives or he'd zero in on the turbulence before we were out of range." He yelled to the tug. "Where is he now?"

"We're just passing a hundred miles altitude, sir. His detectors are lashing about much lower. But that's a two-hundred-mile-range gun, sir."

"Blast," said Heller.

"I don't have any guns, sir," said the tug. "I can't blast."

"Shut up," said Heller and pushed the switch off automatic.

He settled into the local-pilot seat. "Hold on," he yelled back to the Countess Krak.

He dived the tug like a plummet. He was watching his screens. He was locating the exact position of the lethal ship and keeping his own silhouette away from its view of the moon.

He had the flying cannon dead ahead. He was jinking, to confuse its fire direction.

Suddenly he spun the tug exactly backwards to his assailant.

He hit the lever for traction towing beams.

The flying cannon was in his grip. He began to swing it like a pebble in a sling. It helped out by gunning its own engines in the same direction.

Round and round the other ship swung in a huge circle.

Suddenly Heller let it go.

He reversed the tug.

The flying cannon plummeted to the desert floor.

Sand flew, a crash resounded and the distant scream of rending metal faded away.

Heller's hand seized the local radio and turned it on.

A bedlam of voices was coming over it on battle frequency. He was listening to see if any more defense craft would be launched.

Then suddenly a voice rang out: "That was the Chief! All available rescue units, head for that crash! Urgent! Urgent! Lombar Hisst is wrecked three miles south of Camp Kill! Urgent! Urgent!"

"Well, what do you know!" said Heller. And then he looked sadly at the Countess Krak. "We're for it. I've slammed down the mighty Lombar Hisst."

"Oh, good!" cried the Countess Krak. "Hurray!"

"No, dear," said Jet. "It didn't burn and he probably isn't dead. As he is spokesman to the Emperor, our chances of getting those documents signed now are exactly zilch."

Chapter 3

They were vaulting again into the sky, too fast and too far for any retaliation from the ground. Heller anxiously watched his screens to see if turbulence foretold any intercepting spacevessels in sight.

The Countess Krak fished the proclamations out of her shirt. She opened the envelope and looked at them. The one would honor Jettero for his successful conclusion of the mission and promised him safe employment on Royal staff hereafter: He had already lived three times as long as the normal life expectancy of a combat engineer. It was time to get him into a safer post while he was still alive. The other restored her citizenship and rights: Without it she would remain a nonperson, subject to execution at a whim and with no penalty; without it she could not hope to marry. It even restored the Krak estates on Manco, once so vast but long since lost by legal chicanery.

They looked so beautiful with all their scrolls and seals and, on one, even the signature of Cling the Lofty. She did not know they were forgeries done by Gris' office. But no matter how clever they were, they would not appear in the Royal log at Palace City and anyone presenting them would be seized and executed instantly. Gris had covered his own tracks well: he had even ordered the forgers executed.

"Look at these," said the Countess Krak. "Aren't they worth some risk?"

Jet turned from his screens. He read the papers and looked

them over carefully. He saw nothing wrong. But still, they had come from Gris. "Very nice," he said. "We can hang them on the wall of a cave while we hide out."

"Oh, Jettero, our whole future depends on our bringing this off. I must insist we make an effort to get them signed."

"WHAT?" he said. "After crashing Lombar Hisst? Right this minute he must be turning the planet upside down to find us!"

"Jettero, he had no slightest way of knowing it was us. To him it was just a strange ship."

"I doubt it. The illusion I used was of a tug."

"But he doesn't even know you're home. Gris is dead. How could he guess?"

"I'll bet there's an alarm out right this instant."

"I doubt it very much," said the Countess Krak. "And an alarm of that kind wouldn't reach the palace. The guards there are Royal. They have no traffic with ordinary police matters."

"Wait a minute!" said Heller. "You are suggesting I go straight to the palace?"

"While I was in that cell, I had time to read the *Compendium* on protocol. A Royal officer always has the right of audience with the Emperor."

"Lady, it may say so but I doubt a Royal officer has called on His Majesty in the last ten thousand years."

"But it's right in the regulations. You could tell them to look it up."

"You mean I simply walk in there," said Heller, "and say 'Here, Your Majesty. Wake up! Sign on the dotted line'?"

"You've got your dress uniform. You wore it the day you left Voltar for Earth. You've even got your Fifty Volunteer Star."

"Oh, no! Look at the time of night!"

"People are always rushing up to an Emperor with bad news. You have a perfect right to rush in and say, 'Hello, hello! Good news! I knew Your Majesty was personally interested in Mission Earth. Well, ho, ho, it's all done. Sign here!' And even if the word is out for us, if we move awfully fast we can get it done before Palace City hears. And we'd be safe."

"Wow!" said Heller. "You're crazier than a combat engineer! Forget it!"

"Jettero, as your future dutiful and obedient wife, I must put my foot down firmly and insist we go ahead!"

"Oh, Lords, Gods and Devils!" said Heller. "If this is obedience, I'll take a tyrant any time!" He laughed. "But I'll show you I'm not a *male chauvinistic pig*. If you're willing to take the risk, I'll give it a try. But I want it entered in the log: 'I'm only doing this because I want desperately to marry the girl I love.' "

"Oh, Jettero." She threw her arms about his neck and kissed him.

The tug said, "Sir, Red Warning. You're in a power dive."

Chapter 4

Palace City lies just south of a mountain. The mountain contains a black hole of undetermined age. The black hole gives power to the palaces and defenses. It also puts the city, because it warps the space, thirteen minutes in the future.

Looking down on it all, especially at night, there was exactly nothing to be seen but a sort of mist.

In all the ages since it had been built, Palace City had never fallen to outside attack. Although sometimes it had changed hands due to a palace coup, it was considered impregnable, impervious to being breached.

Emperors and courtiers were used to living with the time stress: the compensation was that the place could never fall, even from riots and civil commotion. The only danger that existed was the faint chance that someday the black hole itself might suddenly reach term and itself explode with unthinkable violence. But they could live with this: the topmost government was so safe, the Emperor was so secure that only a madman would contemplate an overthrow of the realm. Revolutionaries were doomed from the start. People like Prince Mortiiy were rightly, by normal standards, looked upon as insane: Even if they won a planet or two, they could never overthrow the whole government so long as Palace City held.

This was the problem the ambitious Lombar Hisst had confronted when he heard the angels telling him he should be Emperor. The only possible way to seize the government was through a coup d'état, working from within Palace City.

And Lombar Hisst was very near to the total completion of his goal. The weapon had been drugs. And as of this night, when Jettero Heller and the Countess Krak hovered above the mist, they did not know that every single member of the Grand Council was hooked. It had begun innocently enough: The court physicians had gullibly welcomed a means to stimulate the declining energies of Lords with small amounts of amphetamines. Then, when nervous symptoms arose, they were only too happy to accept, with a touch of blackmail here and there, the balm of opium. And from opium it went to heroin. Uppers and downers had done their work. Lombar Hisst controlled the supply.

The very last Lord had been hooked months ago. It was now thoroughly extended to everyone in Palace City. All Hisst had to say was "no bag for him" and very shortly the noncompliant officer or Lord was signing, ordering and doing exactly what he was told.

The whole thing had been very smoothly done. Medical journals sang the praises of "the new miracle drugs." The grip was now extending outward to the populations.

Earlier that very night, Lombar Hisst had been at Spiteos doing inventories and allocations of speed, heroin and opium, for it was at Spiteos that these bulk drugs were received from Earth. Lombar Hisst, thanks to a law that forbade the growth or manufacture of the lethal commodities in the Confederacy, had a total monopoly.

The crown itself was inches from his grasp and each night he heard the angels sing and urge him on. Mad already, Lombar Hisst himself was on drugs. Slum-rat born, he saw nothing insurmountable to his ascension to the throne of Voltar. Such a thing had happened many times on Earth: it was his model. That it had never before happened in the Confederacy was a matter he could brush aside. With drugs he could do anything and he was winning all the way. Palace City now danced to his slightest whim. All Voltar awaited him tomorrow. And every planet of the whole 110 would soon be his.

That was the actual scene which lay below the tug that night. And Heller and Krak really knew nothing of it.

True to the reputation of combat engineers taking foolhardy risks despite forlorn hopes, Heller was going about this one in an orderly way.

Amongst the things he had gotten from old Atty was a collection of ship identifications of retired craft that were still listed as being in active, if reserve, service. He had thought he might need them to move about freely without reporting in or alerting others to the fact that he was home.

Hovering at a height of a hundred miles, inside the defense perimeter of the planet, he plugged in a repeating signal: Survey Ship *Wave*, Making Tests. Stand Clear. He had not used it over Spiteos but he would use it now. A survey ship could be testing almost anything from the concentration of moonlight to the potentials of an earthquake. Such ships were quite common in the sky; they often stayed still and people kept away from them.

Having then accounted for the fact that a vessel was hovering above Palace City, should his presence be detected, he went to his aft dressing room and got into his full-dress uniform. He then donned, over it, a technician's coverall. He picked up a pair of two-way-response radios and went back to the flight deck.

The Countess handed him the proclamations and he slid them inside his tunic. He slipped into the local-pilot seat. "Here goes everything on one roll of the dice," he said and pushed at the controls.

Down they went. Up came the mist of warped space.

There was a moment of giddiness and nausea and they were through. The cat let out a yowl; he didn't like it.

Abruptly, to their left, loomed the mountain. They were thirteen minutes in the future.

Jet listened tensely to see if there had been a Palace City alarm. His speakers were silent.

He looked ahead of them. The night-lit palaces sprawled on down the slopes; circles of lights marked the parks. He oriented himself exactly.

Then, carefully, he eased the tug over onto a shoulder of the mountain and gently landed.

He pointed straight ahead through the open pilot ports. "You see that tower down there, straight ahead?"

The Countess Krak singled out the black silhouette of the structure about half a mile away.

"That's their alert system," said Heller. He handed her one of the tiny radios. "Keep this on. When you hear me say 'Now!' push the firing pin on the dash. I'll only do it if something happens to me."

"Oh, dear," she said, "I hope it doesn't come to that."

"I trust it won't. Now, you sit tight. You've got the hardest part—waiting."

"If you step out there," she said, "won't you get a dose of radiation from the black hole?"

"Negligible, but keep the airlock closed after I leave and open it quick when I come back. This sort of operation has a lot of running in it if things get unstuck."

"Shouldn't you give me a blastrifle or something in case I have to cover your retreat?"

"You'd only attract fire. The defenses of this place internally are heavy beyond belief and, frankly, I think they must be getting awfully slack to let a survey ship land without a challenge. But the place has the liability of being sort of out of communication and, for the moment, they probably think, if they detected us at all, that somebody called us for some reason. If anybody calls you except me, say nothing. They'll think the crew has left the ship and is checking cables or reflectors or something. Just sit tight."

She watched him open the airlock outer door and drop to the ground. She began to realize that the risks might be pretty great. She had a sudden panic that she might not see him again.

He went past the front of the tug, turned back and waved and then melted into the night.

Chapter 5

Over the rocks and down the hill in blackness, Jettero Heller headed for the alert tower. The ground he was crossing was very tumbled and hard to cross: there were no paths, for nobody ever came this way. The real entrances to Palace City were a mile or more away, over on the perimeter of the eastern side.

The amount of light that glowed back from the palaces and parks gave everything a dusky glow and he was able to get along without any serious collisions with boulders, though a time or two he almost stepped off into unsuspected holes. It was rough walking.

He came to the tower. He inspected it and found a cable conduit which led toward the first palace. The path of it was marked with small stakes. He went along it: if challenged, he planned to say he was a technician making sure that it had no faults. It was also easier walking since the trench had been covered over and pounded flat.

He came to the side of the first palace. He oriented himself. The Emperor's quarters were a half mile to the south, past other palaces and parks: the structure was quite commanding, bigger than the rest.

Right here he had to make up his mind at what point he would abandon the technician role and become a Royal officer. He had not seen any guards as yet, for nobody in memory had ever tried to enter these precincts by the back door.

He decided that he had better not risk a guard seeing a technician one minute and a Royal officer the next. In deep shadow, standing against the palace wall, he removed the coveralls.

He adjusted his circular, brimless cap to the proper slant, put the gold chinstrap in its regulation place, switched the dust off his boots with a tuft of grass and looked up at the palace side. There was a large, round window about eight feet up. It was open. He gave a jump and a few seconds later he was through it.

Everything in Palace City is built in circles and the hall he was in was no exception. It was a quarters area. The doors were all closed. There was no one about. He tucked his officer's baton under his arm and, with no attempt at quietness, strode along.

He came near the front of the building. He started to exit from the front door and received an awful start. There were two guards there, lounging on blastrifles. They were NOT Palace City guards in blue and violet. They were Apparatus guards in mustard yellow!

For an instant he thought there might be an alert for him.

It was too late to turn back. He walked boldly forward, past them and down the curving steps. They looked at him oddly. They did not salute. But neither did they challenge him.

Heller headed across the circular park. His back was braced for a shot.

The statue of some statesman was ahead, bathed in light. Heller walked straight through the illuminated area looking like someone who knew where he was going and had a legal reason to be there.

Something moved on the other side of the statue.

Two more Apparatus guards!

They did not salute.

Heller crossed the remaining half of the circular park, again with an itching back.

Where were all the palace guards? Usually they stood at intervals along the walks like statues in their own right. These sloppy, dishevelled Apparatus troops sent a chill through him.

He suddenly changed his plans. He felt the need of support. He knew where Captain Tars Roke was quartered: it was not out of his way. Still striding along, baton tucked under his arm, the gold citations on his tunic gleaming, feeling like an interloper, he approached the senior officers' quarters of the Royal staff. He went up the curving staircase to the front door.

Two more Apparatus guards!

They barred his way.

"I want to see Captain Tars Roke," said Heller, "the King's Own Astrographer."

One of the guards looked toward a screen and pushed a button. A series of names rolled off. He looked back at Heller. "You must not have been around lately, spacer. There's no Roke on this list and it hasn't been changed for months."

"He was transferred to Calabar," said the other, consulting another screen. He looked up suspiciously. "What's your name?"

"Thank you," said Heller. And he turned and walked down the staircase at a military pace. His back felt like it had holes in it.

So that was why Gris had felt he could kill him safely! He had had a communication line with Roke in a code of reminiscences he knew they could not decipher since there was no cipher in it. He felt a twinge of guilt: They had removed poor Captain Roke to cut his communication line. This was adding up to something very bad.

Well, he would go it without support.

The Emperor's quarters lay just ahead, round and imposing, blazing with light.

A squad of Apparatus troops marched by, relieving guards and replacing them.

An armored vehicle, an oddity in Palace City, clanked in what appeared to be a constant tour around the imperial quarters.

Heller felt he was getting deeper and deeper into very dangerous territory. Every foot he travelled forward was one he would have to travel back. The only thing which kept him going was the belief that if he could get the proclamations signed, it wasn't likely they would then instantly shoot him.

He didn't know he was carrying forgeries which could bring about just that.

He stood on the walk, looking up at the curving, gold-and-silver-encrusted staircase that led to the imposing entrance.

Ordinarily, palace guards would be standing there every few steps, their silver helmets blazing. There were none.

Heller gave his baton a hitch and sedately went up the wide steps.

He passed through several halls of state. At this late hour they were deserted, dimly lit, their trappings faintly gleaming.

He went down a hall. He was in the Emperor's living area now: these doors must open into the rooms of Royal staff. They all must be asleep.

His bootbeats echoed far too loudly through this place. His reflection in the polished walls walked with him. It seemed to make him far too evident. Even in ordinary times an officer intruding here would have amounted to near sacrilege. He had been brought up impressed with the majesty and might of Palace City. Doing what he was doing even in daylight and for a better reason would have made him tense.

He went through a mammoth arched door and found himself in the antechamber of the sleeping quarters of the Emperor. And right there his luck ran out.

Two Apparatus officers, uniformed in black, were sitting in chairs on either side of what must be the Emperor's bedroom door.

They saw him.

They stood up suddenly.

Heller paced to the middle of the room. He eyed the pair warily. They were both big men. The one on the left was sallow, with the twisted face of a criminal. The one on the right had deeply pocked skin and a snarl for a mouth. These were hoods, not officers, despite insignia and dress.

They were armed with long electric swords! A baton was no match for those!

"What in Hells is an officer of the Fleet doing here?" the one on the left said, advancing. He had his hand on his sword hilt.

"I have urgent news for His Majesty," said Heller. "I must get to him at once."

The one on the right, still beside the door, glanced at it and back at Jet. "He must be out of his wits!"

"What's your name?" snapped the one on the left, still advancing.

Jet knew he was taking a chance. He said, "Jettero Heller, Grade X. I am claiming the Royal officer right of——"

"Heller?" The one on the left took one more forward pace peering. "By blast, it IS!"

The electric sword swept out of its scabbard in a sizzle of sparks!

The one by the door started forward, drawing.

Heller looked at the snapping shaft of the first one's sword. It was coming straight for him.

Time seemed to slow down.

That blazing length was rushing straight at his stomach! One touch of it and he would burst into flame. He could not deflect it with his metal baton.

Heller did a sidestep. He pulled in his stomach. The sword went by him.

He seized the officer's wrist.

The other man was coming, a blazing shaft in his hand.

Heller turned the first officer and, gripping the sword wrist, directed the blade straight at the rushing second man whose sword was upheld for a stroke.

The first man's sword stabbed into the other one.

The second officer's sword, sweeping down at that instant, decapitated the one that Heller held.

Flames and smoke made two blinding pillars.

Heller had jumped back, protecting his eyes from the bursting glare.

The floor was alight with fire. The room was blurred by the billowing smoke.

The tinkle of a red-hot button sounded as it bounced across the tiles.

Heller grabbed a hanging from the wall and beat out the fires.

He stopped and peered through the smoke at the hall entrance door. Had either of this pair hit a pocket alarm?

What a spot to be in! The least they would suspect was attempted assassination!

Chapter 6

His only salvation, Heller realized, was to get to the Emperor. How you could explain two dead guards, he didn't know.

He rushed to the bedroom door. It was locked!

The keys must be in that mess of ash. At the risk of a burned boot he pushed at the cremated residue. Yes, there were the keys. Red-hot!

He took a corner of the hanging he had used to put the fire out and picked up the keys. The hanging cloth scorched but he could hold on.

Hastily he tried three keys, one after the other, his fingers blistering even through the cloth. He glanced toward the hall door. No one coming yet. The fourth key turned the lock but its metal was too pliable now and it jammed. He worked it amidst oil smoke that poured out around it. The lock opened. He could not withdraw the key.

He glanced once more at the hall entrance door. Nobody yet.

He stepped into the Emperor's bedchamber and bolted the door shut behind him.

He had had no real idea what he had expected to see: probably Cling the Lofty lying asleep on a huge bed all in silver and gold. But that wasn't what he saw.

The place looked like a hospital!

The Emperor was lying on a narrow metal cot!

The place was filthy!

It stank!

There was a huddled form under a sheet. Heller stepped forward and lifted up the cloth.

Cling the Lofty, in all his public portraits, was a tall, well-formed monarch of middle age, perhaps ninety or a hundred, imperious, arrogant.

This creature here was so far from that that Heller thought for a moment he might have come into the wrong room.

There was a side table and a glowplate. Heller turned it up.

Yes, this was the same man. But he must be at least 180. He was shrunken and gray. Only wisps of disordered hair remained. The face was covered with age mottles but they were not what gave the impression: It was that he looked like someone who had starved to death: Even the outline of the few remaining teeth could be seen through the skin of the face.

As Heller peered, the man's eyes fluttered open. They were bloodshot in the extreme. A palsied hand came up. Then fear was replaced by some sort of recognition.

The voice quavered, "Are you a Royal officer?"

"Your Majesty," said Heller and was instantly on one knee.

The skeletal hand reached out, feebly raking at Heller's chest. "A real Royal officer," he said, as though it was too much for him to believe.

"At your service, Your Majesty."

"Oh, thank the Gods. At last! In the name of all my lineage, get me out of here before Hisst has me killed!"

Heller was about to speak. There was a sound of boots in the antechamber. Many! One of the officers *had* hit an alarm.

Jet gripped his radio. "NOW!" he said.

The door was bulging inward!

Apparatus guards were shouting outside.

Somewhere a siren moaned and then began to climb toward a shriek. Other signals joined it.

Heller was at the door. It burst wide!

The first guard in received the slash of the baton across his face. He flinched and his blastrifle was in Heller's hands. Its butt smashed the guard's chest in.

Heller dropped on one knee.

His finger hit the firing lever.

The bucking rifle sprayed an arc into the rushing patrol.

Flame erupted in their place.

Fragments of the patrol spattered through the room.

Heller stood up. A guard was moving. He fired once more.

There was only smoke and dismembered bodies in the ante-chamber.

The scream of gongs and sirens was deafening.

The clamor in the building increased.

Heller stepped back into the room.

He grabbed a covering and wrapped it around the Emperor. The man was desperately clawing the air and Heller suddenly realized he was making grabbing motions at a cabinet over at the side.

Heller grabbed at the cabinet and swung the doors open. It contained the crown and chains of office and a carved diamond seal. Heller swept them all into a bag that lay beside them. Cling was nodding now.

Heller picked the Emperor up, adjusted the blanket to hide the bag and ran through the antechamber.

Chapter 7

Heller carried his burdens covered up so no one could see what they were.

Streams of people were tearing out of the building, trampling one another, eyes wild.

He went down the broad stairway, carried like a chip in a storm.

Sirens and gongs were ripping the air to bits.

He tried to turn but the running mob was pressing him forward.

With great trouble he forged sideways to his left. He was suddenly out of the panicked, racing throng.

The Emperor and the symbols of state weighed close to 150 pounds and with this increased gravity after so long on Earth, he found it difficult to run. But he headed north toward the mountain.

As he turned around a building he was hit with another screaming mob, fleeing south and east. He had to back up to the wall and brace himself against their buffeting passage.

It was clear again. He began to run. He headed across a park.

Another compact mob was coming like a battering ram. He crouched down in the lee of a statue and let them tear by.

Then he was up and running again. He went around the northernmost building and spotted the conduit path. He raced up it toward the tower.

His heart was pounding and his breath was getting short. His arms were beginning to ache. Yet he still had a half a mile of uphill running to go and it lay through rocks.

Stumbling, narrowly avoiding boulders, leaping across pits, he raced upward toward the tug. He thought his lungs were going to catch fire.

The last hundred yards were agony.

He reached the airlock. The Countess Krak had it open. Her strained face was a blur in the dark.

Heller put his burdens in the airlock.

With his last breath, he shouted, "Maximum rise!"

The tug vaulted skyward.

The Countess got the airlock outer door shut. She spun its lock. She turned on a light.

"Your hands!" she cried. "They're blistered!"

Heller, slumped on the floor, nodded. "Yes," he panted, "things were pretty warm."

The nauseating twist of going through the time barrier gripped them. They went through it and the tug continued to claw for sky.

The Countess got some false skin from her bag and spread it on his hands.

"I heard your 'Now!' said the Countess, "and I pushed the firing button. Nothing happened!"

"Plenty happened," said Heller, holding his chest and trying to get his breath. "You sent a stream of false gamma straight at their alert system. It set off the alarms that tell them the mountain's black hole is about to blow up. I almost got killed in the stampede! They're probably jammed a thousand deep at the exit gates of Palace City. You did fine."

He took a couple more deep breaths. "Oh, am I out of condition."

He struggled up and got to the pilot panel, yanked out the identification of Survey Ship *Wave*, fumbled in a bag and plugged in Cruiser *Vanguard*, Routine Patrol. "Where are we?" he yelled at the tug.

"Entering lower range of outer defense perimeter," said the tug.

"Three hundred and forty-four miles altitude. Speed accelerating to fifty miles a second. No beams on us."

"We may have made it," said Heller. "But that doesn't mean much. We have no place to go."

The Countess Krak followed him back into the airlock. He was picking up the burdens he had put aboard. "Did you get them signed?"

Heller didn't answer. He made his way to the small medical room. He dropped the bag in the corner and laid the blanket-wrapped body on the table.

The Countess Krak watched noncomprehending. "I said, did you get them signed?"

Heller was strapping the body down securely and covering the wasted limbs. "No," he said.

"Oh," moaned the Countess Krak.

"Other duties got in the way," said Heller. He was feeling the aged wrist for a pulse.

"What other possible duties could be more important?" she said.

Heller pointed at the man on the table. "Him. This is His Majesty, Cling the Lofty."

"WHAT?" she peered more closely. "Oh, good Heavens! It IS!" Then she said, "He can still sign them!"

Heller shook his head. "I don't know," he said. "I didn't bring him out for that. Hisst had him a prisoner and he ordered me to rescue him." He shook his head again. "But I don't think that that was any use. He looks like he is dying."

"Oh, NO!" cried the Countess Krak.

"I'm afraid so," said Heller. "That's an awfully shallow pulse."

"Oh, nothing could be worse!" cried the Countess.

"Yes, it could," said Jet. "There's no record of his order. And when they wake up back there and find the mountain didn't blow up and it was just false gamma, they'll think I kidnapped him."

"Why? They couldn't know it was you."

"Yes, they could and will," said Heller. "I had a misunderstanding with a patrol in the Emperor's rooms. I made a very bad mistake, even if nobody alive recognized me. In the scuffle, I dropped my baton. It has my name on it."

"Oh, Jettero."

"Yes. I'm an idiot. We've committed one of the highest crimes there is against the state. And we have no place to go."

PART
SIXTY-NINE
Chapter 1

Heller called to the tug, "Where are we now?"

"Six hundred miles altitude, accelerating. We had one challenge and then no further interest. Please close your radiation port covers. We're about to enter the lower edge of the magnetosphere."

Heller went out and banged the various covers shut. "Any other dangers?" he called.

"We are going to come too close to the moon Niko if we stay on this course."

"Well, avoid it," said Heller.

"You better make up our mind where we are going," said the tug. "At this acceleration, space only knows where we'll wind up."

Heller went back into the medical room. The Countess had gotten more blankets. She was covering the Emperor up more thoroughly. "I think he's just asleep but he seems awfully restless."

Jet felt the pulse again. "His heart seems to be too faint and too irregular. He needs more help than I can give him."

He went back to the flight deck. He turned on a radio and clicked over to the police band.

Instantly, it blared out, ". . . shoot on sight. All patrols and stations, alert. A general warrant has been issued for Jettero Heller, Grade X Fleet combat engineer for the attempted murder of Lombar Hisst, Chief of the Apparatus and Minister of State. The officer is armed and desperate. The warrant states to take no chances. Shoot on sight. All patrols and stations alert. A general warrant . . ."

The Countess Krak had heard it. "How could he be sure it was you?"

Heller shook his head. "That doesn't matter now. What does matter is that I have an awfully sick man here and I can't get him any help. I wouldn't dare compromise a unit of the Fleet in this."

The Emperor was very restless, giving sudden spasmodic twitches. He flung his arm out from underneath the covers. Heller stared at it. He took hold of the wrist and turned the inside of the limb to the light.

The Countess Krak gasped. The whole inside of the arm was patterned with scars and punctures.

Heller reached for the other arm and looked at it, finding it in even worse condition.

Jet dropped the arm and grabbed a light. He pried open an eye. He examined it and stood back.

"Heroin!" he said.

"What?"

"I've seen this before. Mary Schmeck."

"Who? A woman?"

"Never mind. The poor thing died. And all for the want of a nickel bag."

The Countess Krak was puzzled. "What was all this?"

Jet ignored it. "Hisst made the Emperor into a heroin addict," said Heller. "I don't know if this is also something else. But he is sliding into withdrawal symptoms and at his age, I don't think his heart will stand it."

"Oh, the poor man! Whether he signs anything or not, don't let him die, Jettero."

He stood perplexed for a moment and then his face brightened. "Look," he said, "hold that oxygen mask over his face. I'll be right back."

He had had a solution for this. He had brought samples of heroin and opium and amphetamines with him from Earth, but he had turned them over to Crup with other evidence for Bis. But now it occurred to him that Gris had had some drugs that day he came aboard at the original departure from Voltar. He went to that cabin and opened its vaults. His hopes sank. He found nothing.

Thinking maybe that Gris had hidden them elsewhere, he went to the next crew cabin which had been occupied by Captain Stabb. None of the Antimanco cabins had been cleared out. He opened the vault.

PACKAGES!

Amphetamines, morphine and heroin!

Stabb had been hooked!

Quickly he went to the remaining vaults of other members of the Antimanco crew.

They had also been hooked!

Packing bundles of the stuff, he went back to the medical room. "I have it!" he said to Krak. "Now how, in Heavens' name, do you fix this stuff?"

"You're not going to shoot him with that poison?" said the Countess, aghast.

"It's an awfully strange way to serve the Emperor, but for the moment it's the only way to stop a slide into a very nasty state indeed. If I DON'T do it, he'll wake up and have hot and cold flashes, severe leg pains and be liable to overstrain his heart. And after that he'd run a fever and have vomiting spells and probably die."

He was trying to remember what he had read in the office of the FBI. The one thing that stuck in his memory was that Mary Schmeck would not have died had she had her fix.

He found a metal cup. He put it in a sterilizer. Then he put some water in it and boiled it over a burner. He was not at all sure he was doing this right and it was an awful chance. He did not even know the amount of heroin to use. He opened up a paper pack, verified that that was what it was. He sprinkled some into the hot water and watched the white crystals dissolve.

"Do we know what we're doing?" said the Countess Krak, for his hesitation and uncertainty were far from usual.

"No," said Heller. "We only know that if we don't do it, we may have a dead man on our hands by tomorrow. Get that blood-pressure tube and wrap it around his upper arm."

Heller got a pressure injector out of a drawer and filled its recess with the fluid.

He examined the inside of the arm for veins. There were none that had not collapsed. He signalled the Countess to remove the tube she had tied on. He told her to refasten it around the middle thigh. No veins showed up.

Heller took a deep breath. He simply fired the pressure injector at the inside of the leg.

"All we can do is hope," he said. "I don't know what tolerance he has developed. I don't know if subcutaneous injection like this will work. I don't know if I haven't given him an overdose. Watch him and keep that oxygen going."

"What a risk!" said the Countess Krak.

"Yes," said Jet, "but the biggest risk is to do nothing at all."

They hovered breathlessly.

The Emperor's restlessness gradually ceased. Was he going into a coma?

Heller felt his pulse. It was very hard to tell but it seemed to be strengthening. The breathing became less tortured and more normal.

Would it turn out to be an overdose?

The man's eyes opened. He pushed the oxygen mask away. The gaunt and sunken face was not easy to read. It was like looking at a death's head. He looked at them. He gave a long, shuddering sigh and closed his eyes.

Heller felt his pulse and listened to his breathing. "He's just asleep. I wish we could get some food into him."

"If he wakes up, I'll try," said the Countess Krak. "He needs a lot more help than this."

"Indeed, he does," said Heller, "but if Lombar Hisst has gone this far, he'll stop at nothing to get him back. And His Majesty was sure that that was certain death. Also, I don't think there's a single doctor in the Confederacy who knows how to treat drug addiction.

It's all new ground to them. We can't land on any planet in the Confederacy. . . ."

Suddenly he and the Countess Krak looked at each other. They both said it at the same time. "PRAHD!"

Chapter 2

They fled for Earth, more than twenty-two light-years away from Voltar.

Tug One, redubbed the *Prince Caucalsia,* unfettered with a tow and using its Will-be Was main drives, intended for transgalactic travel but being used within one, could put them across the space to Blito-P3 in three days. It was an advantage, Heller knew, that would give them five weeks and three days over any other craft that could make the run. If pursuit occurred—and he had no doubt that Lombar would think of Earth as a possible refuge they might use—it would take any other ship six weeks. He was buying time.

Heller and the Countess Krak stood watch-and-watch over the Emperor. The situation was not good. Cling the Lofty was bordering close to coma and communication with him was difficult.

The danger was not only to Cling's life: If he did not give evidence that he was there by his own orders, then Heller could be charged with kidnapping him. But all due respect to Heller, he was not thinking of that: His concern was concentrated on trying to save the monarch's life.

There was something else that was amiss, both Heller and Krak were sure of that. The man could barely swallow and trying to get food and fluid down him was almost impossible. His veins were so collapsed that intravenous feeding was beyond their skill. The Countess Krak sponged the aged body with water and kept the cracked lips wet. She wished she knew of some way to get nutrition into him.

Every three to six hours, when he would begin to thresh about, they would give him another pressure shot of heroin: It seemed that that was all that kept his heart going.

Haggard and worried, they came at last to the point above Afyon, Turkey, and that evening in the dark they slid downward through the mountaintop illusion and into the Earth base.

Faht Bey was there on the hangar floor, worried to see them. They had left only seven days earlier and he had supposed that all would go smoothly on Voltar. But Heller had told him that if there was trouble, Heller would bail him out. This must mean trouble.

Heller opened the airlock and shouted down, "Get me Prahd and get an ambulance and get it fast!"

Faht Bey rushed off and grabbed a phone and called. When he came back they had a ladder to the side of the tug. Heller was coming down it carrying a burden wrapped in a blanket.

"Who is this?" said Faht Bey as Heller reached the ground. "Are we in trouble?"

"Later, later," said Heller. He carried the burden up the tunnel, Faht Bey running beside him.

"Where's Gris?" said Faht Bey.

"Dead, so far as I know."

"Bless Heavens!" cried Faht Bey. "I hope it was a nasty death."

"I think so," said Heller. "Where's that ambulance?"

"Coming, coming," said Faht Bey.

When they got to the workmen's barracks, the ambulance was already there. So was Prahd. They put Heller's burden on a stretcher and soon were screaming up the road to the hospital.

"What's wrong with him?" said Prahd, pulling back the blanket.

"If I knew, I wouldn't be here," said Heller. "It's heroin addiction bordering on coma but he doesn't seem to recover. I don't think his heart will stand up to withdrawal. But there's something else."

Prahd looked at the sunken face and withered arms. "Dehydration. Extreme."

"He can't seem to swallow. His veins are all collapsed. Listen:

you've got to put him in a totally secure room and let nobody near him."

"Why?"

"Just do it," said Heller.

"I'll put him in the basement out of public view. The guards are all deaf-mutes there. Where's Gris?"

"He's evidently dead."

"Praise Allah, from whom all blessings avalanche," cried Prahd. "That's wonderful news. We're all right, then."

"Not quite. If this man dies, I'm afraid we're all in trouble."

"Who is he?"

"Never mind," said Heller.

They unloaded at the basement entrance. Nurse Bildirjin came down and with hand signs they got a tub rigged and put the sick man in it.

Prahd started working with meters and then began inserting tubes. The work was fast and furious and Heller stood by.

At length Prahd had done all he immediately could do. He came over to the worried Heller. "He's a crashed speed freak. Amphetamines."

"Then I was giving him the wrong drug!" said Heller.

"No, no," said Prahd. "He was also a heroin addict. By keeping that going you kept him out of its withdrawal, and that would have killed him, as his heart is shot. He was doing an upper-downer routine: feel low, use speed; feel too high, use heroin. You got him here alive."

"Not very," said Heller.

"He must have been nearly dead when you found him," said Prahd. "He was already pretty old and the amphetamine caused premature aging. That stuff can cause years of aging in just a few months. If he had his teeth when he started it, they're mostly gone now, too. And every gland in his body has been practically atrophied. Who is he?"

Heller didn't answer. He didn't want to load Prahd with the shock of it.

But Prahd read something from that. He went back and looked

at his blood test and other readings. He fixed his bright green eyes on Heller. "This man is not just a commoner. He's a member of the nobility, the product of very selective breeding for thousands, tens of thousands of years."

"Can you bring him around?"

"I don't know. At the very least his mind will be clouded; his vocabulary will have dropped to a few hundred words. It takes years to recover from amphetamines and he's already so old it's doubtful if he can make it."

"Can you keep him going?"

"I don't know," said Prahd.

"Basically," said Heller, "the reason he is here is humanitarian. He couldn't be left to be killed. But it's also important that he be able to talk and write."

Prahd's eyes narrowed. He went back and looked at the unconscious old man now suspended in fluid. Something seemed to tug at his memory. Suddenly he lifted the cover of the tub and turned the top of the old man's shoulder to him. He took a brush, dipped it in a liquid and drew it across the skin.

The symbol of a comet appeared.

Prahd stepped back, eyes wide with shock. "The mark they put on Royal babies!" He stared at Heller. "This is Cling the Lofty, Emperor of Voltar!"

"Yes," said Heller, "and unless you can bring him around so that he can provide evidence it was at his orders he was removed from Palace City, we'll all be executed for hiding a kidnapped Emperor."

Prahd collapsed upon a bench. He mopped his forehead with his gown tail. "What a way to become the King's Own Physician!"

Chapter 3

Back aboard the tug, the Countess Krak met Heller at the airlock. "Will he live?"

"I don't know," said Heller.

"Poor old man," said the Countess. "When will we know?"

"Not for several days. We may be in the soup but at least I can make sure this planet is all right."

"You think we may need it?"

"I doubt that. But Izzy was our friend and I better see if he is all right. I wasn't all that happy about leaving when we did and I wouldn't have except that I thought we would get home in time to alert Fleet Intelligence. We didn't."

He got out the viewer-phone and took it down into the hangar where it wouldn't be smothered by the tug. He buzzed it.

Nothing happened!

The viewer stayed blank.

It was only the end of the afternoon in New York. Izzy should be there.

In the next two hours, he tried several times again.

No result!

He went up the tunnel to Faht Bey's office and put in a long-distance call and got into a snarl through the Turkish telephone exchange. For reasons he could not make out, they could not connect him.

Heller turned to the base communication system with the base office in New York. The printouts showed they were on the job. When they realized who was on the machine they got quite excited and polite: they were very happy to be Fleet. Heller gave them the numbers in the Empire State Building and asked them to at least call on some subterfuge and ask Izzy to go into his office and respond on the viewer-phone.

He waited. Suddenly the printout began to roll.

THE NEW YORK INFORMATION OPERATOR SAYS THAT ALL THE NUMBERS YOU LISTED, SIR, ARE OUT OF SERVICE.

Heller typed back:

IS RAHT THERE?

He got a response:

NO, SIR, HE IS AT THE BASE.

Heller thanked them and turned off the machine. He went out and found Raht in the hangar crew's quarters. "Do you know of anything wrong?" he asked when greetings were over.

"No, sir. I went by there just two days ago before I came here. Everything was fine with the office. Of course, things are pretty upset in New York, just as they are here. You know, don't you, that Turkey and Sweden have both moved into the former territory of Russia and are getting ready to fight a war as to which one will annex the place. In the U.S., there's general mobilization. I don't know if it's connected with the Russian thing. When I left John F. Kennedy Airport, soldiers were all over the place. Flights were uncertain, too. Does this help?"

"No," said Heller. "That doesn't seem to connect with Izzy. He's 4F, allergies and things. You sure he was all right?"

"Saw him myself. He was running down a hall with a handful of papers, looking cheerful and busy."

"Blast!" said Heller. "What could have happened to him in just the last two days? All his phones are out of service."

"You want me to go back, sir?"

Heller shook his head. "What Earth day is this?"

"It just was Wednesday, sir."

"All his options will be up next Monday. If he's not active on them, he'll be in tons of trouble."

Heller went back to the tug and climbed aboard. He got very busy in his aft quarters. The Countess Krak came in just as he finished changing into a Western summer lounge suit.

"Listen," said Heller. "I want you to keep an eye on the Emperor and make sure that that goes along as well as it can. And keep this base in line."

"Where are you headed for?" she said in alarm.

"I'm going to have Ahmed and Ters drive me to Istanbul. I'm catching a dawn plane for New York."

"Oh, no! Is Izzy in trouble?"

"I can't be sure. I promise not to run off with any Miss Americas. I'll be back in a few days. You can reach me or leave word for me at the condo."

He was piling things into his case. Then he went to a cabinet and got out a spacetrooper collapsible sled and some bombs.

"Good Heavens!" said the Countess Krak. "You look like this is war!"

"There seems to be a lot of that hanging around. But I'm just being careful."

"Bombs? Careful?"

Heller laughed and gave her a kiss. He went to the airlock. There was suddenly an awful yowling. Mister Calico was standing on the top of the ladder and he wouldn't let Heller descend.

"He sees the clothes and bag," said the Countess Krak. "He thinks you're going somewhere and deserting him."

Heller looked at the cat.

The cat yowled forlornly.

Heller laughed, got a shoulder satchel, threw some of Mister Calico's kit in and then lifted up the cat and dropped him in it.

Heller slung the strap over his shoulder and Mister Calico put his paws on the edge and looked out, purring.

The Countess and Heller said good-bye. Heller slid down the ladder. He was on his way to more war than he had imagined!

Chapter 4

Mister Calico thoroughly enjoyed his ride to New York. Jet was travelling on non-U.S. airlines that were not too insistent on putting pets in special boxes—after Jet talked to them—and the flight attendants let him have a spare seat beside Heller, a window seat from which one could admire the various seas and mountains. He also enjoyed the food, both in flight and in a posh restaurant during their long layover in Brussels. He also enjoyed his twin bed in the deluxe hotel.

It was from Belgium that Heller tried again to phone Izzy. Service suspended, he was told. He switched the call to the condo. Balmor answered.

"Do you know where Izzy is?" Heller asked.

"Why, no, sir, Mr. Jet, but I've been wondering myself. He was up here Sunday and he was supposed to drop by yesterday to inspect some new potted trees the gardeners put in. But he didn't show. Is anything wrong?"

"I hope not," said Heller. "It would be a real mess if he had disappeared. Meet me at JFK with the Silver Spirit. I'll arrive at 2:00 P.M., your time, Friday afternoon." And he gave him the flight number.

"Oh, I am so pleased you're coming home. Is the madame with you, sir?"

"Not this trip," said Heller. "But she is fine and sends her best."

"She's such a charming girl, a real American lady. 2:00 P.M. it is, sir, at JFK."

It was in flight across the Atlantic that Heller found that the cat wouldn't be admitted unless he were held in quarantine for several months.

"It's their resistance to anybody landing," he told the cat. "They fight it with tooth and claw. But we will put our heads together."

When they debarked, Heller had the cat in the satchel, zipper closed except for a small opening so it could get some air.

The corpse at the immigration desk took Heller's passport, looked up in his secret book to see if Jerome Terrance Wister was wanted anywhere, pushed buttons with his knees, read secret screens and, giving no sign of anything, let Heller through.

The U.S. Customs hand-baggage counter was just beyond. There was a crowd jam. Some old lady had been found to be carrying some smelling salts and they were sure it was cocaine. They had her spread-eagled against a wall and were frisking her: a typical American welcome-home for Americans.

Heller, waiting in the line, bent over to tie his shoe—quite a feat since it had no laces. With the satchel scraping the floor and hidden from view by other legs, the cat stepped out.

Heller gave a whispered command, stood up and went through the handbag customs line. "Cat food?" said the inspector. "What the hell is this? You importing American cat food? Barney, open this can and see if it's full of hash."

The inspector called Barney did and came back eating it. "No drugs. Only preservatives. But two are listed as cancer-causing by the FDA. We'll have to confiscate the lot."

Heller handed over the cat food. He walked ahead. The cat followed him quietly below the counter level. He went into the baggage-retrieval area, got his grip onto the counter, got it chalked, picked it up and walked out into the lobby. The cat was sitting on a waiting-room seat, washing his face.

"You already had a criminal record as long as your tail," said Heller. "You are now an illegal alien. One day you are going to have to reform." He put the cat back in the satchel.

The place was absolutely swarming with military personnel.

Balmor was there and took his grip. Heller made him wait

while he tried another call to the Empire State Building. Service still suspended.

They went out to the parking lot where sat the Rolls. The chauffeur saluted.

"I'll go to the condo and wash up and change," said Heller. "And then you can take me downtown to the office. I think I have a lot of urgent business, the way things look."

"I hope there isn't more trouble," said Balmor from the front seat as they rode. "We were so upset about the lady. The whole staff was. And Mr. Epstein wept for days. I'm sorry Miss Joy didn't come with you. Ever since your call, we've been busy decorating the place. You'll really be surprised."

"Did Mr. Epstein keep the whole staff on?" said Heller.

"Oh, yes, sir. He wouldn't think of downgrading your home. I hope you'll be pleased with what you find, sir."

They rode for about an hour through highways jammed with military convoys and all the signs of national emergency. They eventually turned off Central Park West and drove into the underground garage.

Heller, anxious about Izzy, was first in and first out of the elevator to the penthouse. He walked across the small private lobby and opened the front door.

He walked partway across the room.

A voice said, "Stand right where you are!"

Heller whirled, eyes riveted on a leveled .45 Colt automatic!

The man who held it said, "You are under arrest!"

Two men came in from side doors. They had carbines pointed straight at Heller.

Jet sized them up. The first man was an army captain. The other two were white-helmeted military police.

Balmor walked in. He dropped the grip. "Oh, sir," he cried in horror, "I had no idea!"

"It's all right," said Heller. "Probably that bird at airport immigration alerted them."

"You're quite correct," said the captain. "Sergeant, do your duty."

A third MP came out of the library, putting a white-lanyarded revolver in his holster and taking some handcuffs out of his belt.

"Wait a minute," said Heller. "What's this all about?"

"You're an army deserter! You didn't report in when the president ordered general mobilization two days ago."

"I had a waiver!"

"That expired the instant a national emergency occurred," said the captain. "You're an ROTC graduate and you knew very well you were supposed to report for induction. This makes you a deserter. You'll get at least five years. Sergeant, the cuffs."

"Hold it," said Heller. "I was out of the country. I just got back a couple hours ago!"

"Hm," said the captain.

"That's true, sir," said the sergeant. "We got the tip-off from immigration."

"(Bleep)!" said the captain. "You're a barracks lawyer, Wister. I can tell that. You're going to make a case of this, aren't you?"

"I certainly am," said Heller.

"All that paper work!" said the captain. "Busy as I am, I just don't have time to make out some long report or appear at your trial either. I tell you what I'll do. Just as a favor, mind you, since you'll be a fellow officer. Get into your uniform and we'll take you down and get you inducted."

"I'll get your uniform pressed," said Balmor, hurrying into Heller's bedroom. He instantly came back out. "Sir!" he wailed. "They've got the whole staff in there, tied hand and foot!"

"Release them," said the captain to the sergeant. "This guy isn't any fighter, I can tell. But the country is going to need every man it's got. Get your uniform and get dressed, mister."

"After I'm inducted, what will happen?" said Heller, thinking very anxiously of Izzy.

"You're Intelligence, aren't you?" said the captain. "You'll get a chance to reconnoiter Camp Dix. And then maybe overseas. Who knows? I'm not G-2. But to be on the safe side, pack your kit. You're in the army now—or will be as soon as you raise your right hand."

"I've been away," said Heller. "Would you mind telling me what this war is all about?"

The captain sighed. "I don't know what use you'll be to Intelligence, not knowing that. But there isn't any war yet. This is just a presidential mobilization. This is Friday. War will be declared just as soon as Congress meets Monday. They're being real legal this time."

"Declared on whom?" said Heller.

"Maysabongo, you idiot! Those (bleepards) have got all our oil and the only way we can get it back is declaring war and seizing it under the Enemy Property Act."

Heller reeled.

He had gotten his first inkling of how Izzy was in trouble! He must be in the middle of this impending war!

And here he himself was, in the grip of the army, and couldn't help him!

And he knew he didn't dare stay on Earth more than another five weeks. To be here longer would be fatal to the Emperor and the base!

Chapter 5

Driving to the army headquarters in jeeps, there was far less traffic than usual on the streets.

"You're awful lucky to have a ride," the captain said. "When these tanks are empty, that's it. I don't know how we're going to fight this war on no gas."

"I thought you said we'd grab the Maysabongo supplies as soon as war was declared," said Jet.

"I said 'oil,' not gas," replied the captain. "Maysabongo has nailed down all the reserves of crude oil and even though that's seized, it won't do us much good. It's got to be refined to get gasoline and kerosene and the refineries all went radioactive. Jesus, I don't know what use they're going to make of you in Intelligence. You don't seem to have even one brain cell in your head."

"Well," said Jet, "it's a good thing Maysabongo is no bigger than a postage stamp. It won't take much gas."

"It won't take any gas at all, you dumbbell. We'll use a hydrogen bomb."

"Then why mobilize all these men?" said Jet.

"Questions, questions. It's not yours to reason why. It's just yours to do and die. Didn't they teach you anything at all in the ROTC?"

"They should have taught me to keep my mouth shut," said Heller.

The captain seemed to find this uproariously funny. "That's the spirit. Grin and bear it. True grit. I got a feeling you'll make it after all."

Heller was very far from laughing. The thought of Maysabongo, which had been friendly to him, obliterated, put a new stress on his situation.

The day was very hot: New York in July can be sweltering. He hadn't noticed it before, as the Silver Spirit had been air-conditioned, as had the condo. But riding in this open jeep, the city felt like a steam bath.

They drew up and double-parked outside the armory. Jet picked up his duffel bag and they nudged him inside. They got a receipt for him from the guards and drove away to round up other deserters.

Jet found himself in an enormous hall. They had put camp desks and folding chairs all over the drill floor. The place was crammed with perspiring people and awash with fluttering paper. The place was boiling hot.

A guard shoved Jet into a corner of the room where some medical equipment was set up. He waited and waited, watching men go through a physical examination.

Suddenly somebody asked him for his papers, somebody else told him to strip, somebody else told him to stand on a scale, somebody else told him to cough, another said to jump up and down and put a cold stethoscope against his chest and somebody else told him to get dressed.

A doctor signed some papers and a guard told Jet to go over to another part of the armory. In a mob of young men he waited and waited. Then somebody lined them all up three ranks deep and started looking at their papers.

Somebody said to Jet, "You're an officer candidate. These are enlisted inductees. You're in the wrong place."

They indicated he should go to another corner of the armory. There was a colonel there, very old, apparently very deaf, sitting at a desk with lots of orders in front of him. Jet put his papers down in front of him.

"Who are you?" said the colonel.

"Wister, Jerome Terrance, it says there," said Jet.

"What do you want?" said the colonel.

A sergeant got up from his desk and looked at the papers. "He's an officer candidate, ROTC. He's supposed to be sworn in."

"I don't care what he was born in," said the colonel.

The sergeant made a sign by raising his hand.

"Oh, *sworn* in," said the colonel. "All right, Blister, stand in front of the desk and raise your right hand."

Heller's hair stood up. As a Royal officer, taking an oath of allegiance to some other power could get him a fast court-martial.

"Repeat after me," said the colonel. And he rattled off the oath of allegiance to the United States.

Heller rattled off the oath of allegiance to His Majesty, Emperor of Voltar, in Voltarian.

The colonel threw the papers to the sergeant and got back to his own work.

"What the hell was that?" said the sergeant.

"The oath of allegiance," said Heller with a lisp.

"It didn't sound like you repeated it," said the sergeant.

"I have trouble with my tongue," said Heller, speaking in a muted way.

"Oh," said the sergeant. "Now go over there and get finger-printed and things."

Heller got into another line and waited and waited. He was getting worried. Night had fallen. Time was running and he didn't know how he was going to get out of this.

Eventually it was his turn. They rolled each finger in ink and made a card. They put him in front of a camera.

"This is a G-2," somebody said. "Henry, you got any Intelligence blanks?"

They didn't. A man went out and was gone a long time. He came back with the proper I.D. blanks for an Intelligence officer. They typed it out, put his picture and a thumbprint on it and laminated it. They gave him his I.D.

They pushed him over to another part of the armory. There was a row of typewriters along the wall. A single officer, a colonel, was sitting at a single desk in a cleared space. He was beefy and perspiring. His desk was piled two feet thick with loose sheets of paper. Men were sitting on their baggage all around. Aside from the colonel and the enlisted men at the typewriters, Heller was the only one in uniform.

Jet asked one of the waiting men, "What are we doing here?"

"We're waiting for our orders so we can be shipped off to camp." He waved a hand toward the single colonel at the single desk. "Fatty there might or might not get it sorted out tonight. You're in the army now. Hurry up and wait."

Heller glanced at his watch. It was well past midnight. Saturday was here. He had to find out about Izzy. He had to get out of this.

He looked at the colonel perspiring away at his desk. He looked at the typists along the wall.

It was terribly hot in the place. The only cooling they had was a huge fan on a column stand and it was idling away blowing air at an angle toward the ceiling.

Heller walked over to the typists. As he was in uniform, they didn't seem to mind his reading over their shoulders.

They were typing orders for drafts of men to this place and that. They were very backlogged.

Heller saw a corporal coming from the fingerprint area. He saw him put a sheaf of papers down beside the typewriter of an enlisted girl. Heller drifted over.

Heller hoped his own papers would be amongst them. Maybe he could intercept them and do something. He walked over to the girl but just as he was beside her, she got up and walked over to the colonel's desk and laid some papers down.

Jet looked at the file carbon of what she had just typed. It was a list of men being ordered to Camp Dix. The original had just been delivered to the colonel's desk. The name, WISTER, Jerome Terrance, 2nd Lieutenant, Army of the United States, headed it!

He was too late!

He hastily put the carbon in his pocket but that wouldn't solve it.

He looked around. He went over to one of the men sitting on their baggage. He said, "Look at that poor colonel. He must be dying of the heat. You're in the army now. You must learn to respect your officers and help them."

The man looked at him. "Well, yes, sir," he said doubtfully.

"See that fan?" said Heller, pointing to the stand. "Turn it off, move it in closer, point it at the colonel and turn it on again. Got that?"

"Yessir," said the inductee.

He went over, turned the fan off, and moved the stand up beside the colonel. He pointed the fan level. He turned it on.

AN EXPLOSION OF PAPERS FLEW EVERYWHERE!

The colonel slammed his arms down and tried to contain the blizzard. Then he came up like a raging bull.

The inductee who had done it scuttled off, instantly lost in the mob.

The colonel kicked the fan over with a raving curse. Papers were still flying about the armory.

Heller rushed up. "Sir, I'll give you a hand!"

He promptly began to gather papers up, his fast eye taking in every piece as he stacked it.

The enlisted men had rushed from their typewriters and were helping out and Heller had to work fast.

In five minutes all the papers had again been collected. But Heller had the one that sent him to Fort Dix. He also had the typist carbon.

He went over to a desk whose typist had stepped out for a coffee break. He rapidly retyped the draft order to Camp Dix, omitting his own name.

He put more paper in the typewriter and, using the format he saw on other orders lying there, typed a set of orders which sent WISTER, Jerome Terrance, 2nd Lieutenant, Army of the United States, to the "Anti-Saboteur Unit" as officer in charge, detached duty, on his own cognizance and to report only to the Secretary of War.

He put his own file and the carbons in the proper baskets. He went down the line of typists and collected other orders to be signed and took the lot to the colonel.

"These are urgent, sir," he said.

The colonel grunted, mopped his brow and signed the lot.

Heller took them back to the typists, put his own in his pocket, picked up his duffel bag and walked out.

Ten minutes later, he stepped into the Silver Spirit Rolls Royce.

"Are you in the army now, sir?" said the chauffeur.

"I've already fought my first campaign," said Heller. "But the Empire State Building must be swarming with saboteurs. Take me there at once!"

NOW to find out what had happened to Izzy!

Chapter 6

Driving through the deserted streets of very late night New York, Heller removed his tunic and snipped the ROTC shoulder patch away. He polished up the gold castles which represented Intelligence and burnished his single rank bars. He redonned the tunic and slipped his orders and I.D. into his side pocket.

He stopped the chauffeur on 34th Street and went forward to the Empire State Building side entrance on foot.

Two New York policemen were there, lounging on either side of the door. They looked at him suspiciously. He went on in.

At the elevators, the boy on night duty let him into the car. Jet gave the number of his floor. The boy turned around to him. "I can take you up there but they might not let you out of the car."

"Who's 'they'?" said Heller.

"New York City Police," said the boy. "They've been blocking off half of that floor since last Tuesday."

"Take me anyway," said Jet, very curious.

The boy shrugged and they shot upwards. The car stopped and the door opened.

In front of him, in the floor lobby, sat FIVE cops! Four instantly came to their feet, clubs alert. The fifth, a police captain, sat at a desk which blocked the hall that led to all of Jet's and Izzy's offices.

Heller walked up to the captain. He wanted to get into these offices and look around: maybe Izzy had left him a note. "I have to search the place," he said.

"No, no," said the captain. "Nobody gets in or out of this area."

"What's the matter?" said Jet. "A bomb alert or something?"

"Worse than that," said the captain. "A bunch of desperate criminals are holed up in the Maysabongo Legation right down that hall."

"What have they done?" said Jet.

"Littering," said the captain, "and a court injunction has denied them the use of sidewalks."

"Aha!" said Jet. "The very people I must interrogate." He held out his Army I.D. and his orders.

The captain waved them aside. "Listen, Army, these people have immunity inside their legation. So far it's just a civil matter. But we can't let you pass. Their phones are shut off, so don't try any funny business."

"I must see them," said Heller.

"Sorry, Lieutenant. That's quite impossible. We've got our orders. Nobody in or out and that means nobody, including you. Come Monday, after war is declared, army commandos will hit this place and clean it out. But up to then, no dice. That's the way it is, Lieutenant. The Maysabongo Legation is sealed off. Get lost."

Heller said, "Can't I even go into the other offices?"

"Nope," said the captain. "This whole half-floor is shut and there's cops on every entrance. So bye-bye, Army. Sergeant, escort him out of the building."

On the street again, Heller walked back and got into the Rolls.

At least he now knew where poor Izzy was!

"Take me home," he told the chauffeur.

Balmor, despite the hour, met him at the door. "Oh, sir, how opportune. Miss Joy is just this minute on the phone."

Heller walked across the salon and picked up the instrument. "I didn't get a chance to phone, dear."

"When you didn't call to say you arrived, I got worried. How are my two warriors?"

"Well, one is now in the army and the other is lying here snoring off a pint of cream."

"How dreadful!"

"Oh, cream won't hurt him. It's pasteurized."

"I mean the army."

"They wouldn't take him. Criminal record. Illegal alien. They only like to send good fellows out to be shot."

"Jettero, be serious."

"It is serious, but I'm not going to discuss it past the ears of NSA. How's the sick man?"

"He just lies there. The doctor says he is better but he doesn't seem to know where he is and he doesn't speak. That's what I'm worried about. He may not recover. What's this about the army?"

"Don't worry about that. I have it under control. I may be busy for a couple days. Love you."

"You take care of yourself, Jettero. This planet isn't worth it."

"It's the only planet we've got at the moment. Take care of things, dear."

She told him that she loved him, in an anxious voice. His hint about the National Security Agency and the inference he was about to do something had her worried.

He hung up and went to his room and changed his clothes. He put on a black summer-weight suit, black engineer boots and black engineer gloves.

He packed a shoulder-strap bag with explosives and other items. He tied the collapsed spacetrooper sled to it.

He picked up the cat's satchel, checked its items and put the cat in it.

Balmor escorted him down to the car and handed him a leather lunch case overfull with sandwiches, hot coffee and milk. "An army crawls on its stomach, sir. I don't think you've eaten since you got off the plane."

"Thanks, Balmor. The fellow who said war is hell didn't have you for a butler."

He rolled downtown in the Rolls Royce, sharing sandwiches with the cat.

Chapter 7

They stopped half a block from the Empire State Building. Heller thanked the chauffeur and told him to go home.

He shifted the two satchels to comfortable positions on his shoulders and strode along, carrying the lunch box.

He went in by another entrance than the one he had used last time. It also had police and they eyed him. He took an elevator to the floor above his own.

He walked along until he was above the Maysabongo Legation. He looked around to make sure there were no night cleaners in sight.

Expertly he opened the lock of an office door, went in and closed it behind him. He crossed it and opened a window. He verified that he was right.

He got out a spaceship safety line and hooked its quick release to a pipe.

Heller looked far down at the distant street. Two cop cars were standing there.

A swirl of mist went by his window, such was the altitude of it. He looked up: the sky was pale black above.

He swung out and dropped down.

He came opposite the legation window. It was all dark inside. He thumped on the glass quietly.

Suddenly there was Izzy's face!

Heller made a gesture of opening the window.

Izzy came out of his shock. He fumblingly obeyed.

Heller slid in. He gave the safety line a twitch and it fell into his hand. He closed the window.

A candle was being lit.

"Don't say, 'Jet, how did you get here?' " said Heller. "It will very shortly be dawn and we haven't got much time."

"Mr. Jet, how did you get here?" said Izzy, eyes round as saucers behind his horned-rimmed glasses.

In the candlelight, Bang-Bang was grinning ear to ear. Delbert John Rockecenter II was getting off a desk, popeyed.

"What's going on?" said Heller. "Did you execute the options or what?"

"Oh," said Izzy. "It is a dreadful thing. Miss Simmons has got all the refineries in the world shut down. Maysabongo exercised the options to buy all the oil reserves."

"Couldn't you pay for them?" said Heller.

"Oh, yes," said Izzy. "That was easy. We had the cash. Maysabongo controls every drop of crude oil in the tanks and on board ships. That's why they're going to declare war!"

"But didn't you make good the options to sell all the oil stock in the world? Didn't it go down?"

"Oh, it went down! It's worth almost nothing."

"Well, all right," said Heller. "You must have made billions!"

"I should say so," said Izzy. "That's another trouble. That's more cash than there is available and it will break the American banking system. They don't have 189 billion in their tills!"

"Well, didn't you exercise the options to buy in all the oil-company stock for a dollar?"

"Mr. Jet," said Izzy, "I got to tell you something. The options at the brokers will expire Monday noon. We can't get out of here. We can't phone. We can't send messengers. We're living on Maysabongo samples of coconut oil. We can't reach the brokers or the bank. We haven't exercised either the sell options or the buy options!"

"It's Rockecenter," said Bang-Bang. "He got Faustino to order the New York City Police to bottle up this place."

"He got the president of the United States to declare mobilization," said Izzy. "Sunday evening, the Swillerberger Conference of International Financiers is meeting in Philadelphia. They're ordering the president and Congress to declare war on Maysabongo Monday morning. They'll take back the oil as enemy property and we'll be out our money. They'll sell it back to Rockecenter for pennies and he'll make billions."

"But what if we owned all the shares?" said Heller.

"The money we make with the sell options will do us no good," said Izzy. "They'll keep the banking system intact by saying we're enemy-connected people and seizing all our funds. Even if we execute our buy options, all those shares will be seized and the oil companies will be sold to Rockecenter for nothing. He'll come out of this far more rich and powerful than he ever was before."

"And us guys," said Bang-Bang, "will wind up in the jailhouse as enemy agents."

"And," Izzy continued, "although I filed their 13D form with Securities and Exchange Commission, saying we were going to acquire more than 5 percent of a lot of oil companies, they claim they never saw the paper and we'll be facing Federal warrants. Oy, Mr. Jet, I have never seen such trouble!"

"Well, I can solve part of it," said Heller. "Have a sandwich and some hot coffee." And he hefted the lunch case onto a desk.

"Oy, Mr. Jet. I wish I had your nerve!" said Izzy. "My ulcers are killing me."

"What are you doing here?" said Heller to Delbert John Rockecenter II.

"I'm a conscientious defector," said Twoey. "Tuesday a bunch of men with guns shot the land yacht all to pieces. Me and the staff were down at the barns feeding pigs. They set fire to the barns, too, and shot a lot of helpless swine. We barely got away with our lives. I had just got here when they closed this place down. Let me tell you, Jerome, this being a Rockecenter son is dangerous. I think I better warn you: they don't even respect pigs! All I did was phone our father and ask him to do a commercial telling people not to eat ham. . . ."

"You phoned him?" said Heller.

"Yeah, Miss Joy left the number in the land yacht. I talk good

English now and everything. There wasn't any reason for him to blow up. Any self-respecting boar treats his kids better."

"Mr. Jet," said Izzy. "That's another thing. Bleedum, our attorney, was looking up the Rockecenter wills, and did you know that there's a ten-billion-dollar trust standing by if Rockecenter has a son? The boy would get it when he was eighteen and up to then Delbert Senior is the trustee. I don't think it's safe for either you or Twoey to be seen around. If you can get us out of here, I've got airline tickets for Brazil."

"Eat your sandwiches," said Heller. "The only flying that's going to be done right now is by me."

They had been pouring out hot coffee for themselves but they stopped and watched what Heller was doing.

Jet was assembling the spacetrooper sled. Its antigravity lifts hummed as he checked them. He verified the connections and drive power with the meter on one of its rods.

"You didn't see this," he said.

He gave the cat satchel and the other bag a hitch to get them around toward his back. He laid the two poles at the sled front on the windowsill. He opened the window and lay on the sled, belly down.

The three stared at him in astonishment.

"You guys just sit tight and stay alive," said Jet. "I'm going to see what I can do to rescue you. Bye-bye."

He wrapped his hand around the button control at the front of the right-hand pole.

The sled soared out the window and into the mist and night.

PART SEVENTY

Chapter 1

Heller launched himself into the first gray of the dawn. Unseen, flying at a thousand feet like a javelin through the whistling air, he headed southwest. The blackness and the lights of the Hudson lay below. A very faint pink strand of cloud heralded the eastern sun.

Quite unlike him, his mind was filled with misgivings and doubt. But like a gambler who stakes all on one last throw, he had to take the chance.

As he flew, he told himself his prospects did not look good. His plan was good enough, providing he could surmount one huge obstacle.

He knew he had to fight a war. It was not the war which Congress would declare on Monday. Heller's war had to be over and done with, victorious, in just slightly more than forty-eight hours.

He didn't have any troops. Rockecenter obviously owned the army and told it what to do, and additionally Heller knew that the War Department was not likely to approve the battle he must fight. And win. He knew where the troops were to be had but it was a very iffy thing: Babe Corleone!

Half a year before, due to the false publicity of J. Walter Madison, Babe Corleone had believed him to be a turncoat and traitor and a supporter of Faustino "The Noose" Narcotici. She thought Faustino had paid him to throw a race.

Faustino styled himself the *capo di tutti capi*. But Babe Corleone, who had guided the Corleone family since the death of her aged husband, "Holy Joe," despised drugs and would not deal with the Faustino mob.

She had regarded Heller as a son until the fatal rift. He wondered if he were not sticking his head into a hornet's nest now even thinking of approaching her. The wrath of the six-foot-six, statuesque, ex–Roxy chorus girl was legendary, her thirst for vengeance proverbial. When he had last seen her she had washed her hands of him and, in sackcloth and ashes, had ordered him to get out. It had made him very sad, for he was fond of Babe. He had obeyed and had not gone near her since.

But she had *soldati* and, in his extremity, Heller thought just possibly he might be listened to. He was taking a long chance.

He skirted along the New Jersey shore of the Hudson, whistling lower now, barely above the height of cranes along the wharves. If defense radar picked him up they would think he was a patrol helicopter, common on this run.

The sky was growing pinker. By its light ahead he saw Bayonne. The New Jersey Turnpike, oddly empty of cars, unreeled below. Newark Bay, a pool of growing crimson now, came to view. He banked along the western edge of Bayonne Park. He spotted Babe's high-rise. She lived in the whole top floor. It was defended like a fort, but nobody expected an approach from the roof.

Heller pressed the controls and the wind went out of his hair. He settled to a gentle, silent landing on the flat asphalt top.

It was quite light now. Daylight saving time made it 6:35. The sun would be completely over the horizon in five minutes. He had not been too soon. But what an awful hour to make a call!

He rapidly folded up the spacetrooper sled. He went to the access door, pressed his ear to it and listened. No sounds. He got out a picklock and opened the door.

Silently, he crept down the steps. He had to be very careful: He was likely to be shot, no matter who he was, coming in this way. But he could not take any chance by using the front door. It would, he thought, just get slammed in his face. He had to have a chance to state his offer.

A man was sitting in a chair by the elevator! Geovani! Babe's bodyguard!

He had his back to Heller. He was dozing. Heller did not want him to draw. Jet made a pistol out of his index finger and put it into the middle of Geovani's back. "Freeze," he said, "it's a friend."

Geovani whirled so fast he almost snapped his neck off. He stared. *Sacro scimmie!* he said. "Sacred monkeys, it's the kid! Mother of God! You almost scared me to death! Where . . . ? How . . . ?" He was looking wildly around, unable to comprehend how Heller had gotten in.

Heller put down the spacetrooper sled and took off his satchels and hung them on it. He unbuttoned his jacket and opened it. "See, I'm not heeled. Not even a knife. I've got to talk to Babe."

Geovani looked uncertain and bewildered.

A call came from behind the closed door at the end of the hall. "I hear voices. Who is there?"

The hall door opened. Babe Corleone, holding a lingerie robe about her, looked out. She had a Heckler and Koch .45 in her other hand.

She peered. "Jerome? It can't be. Jerome, is that really you?"

And then she dropped her pistol on the floor and bowed her head and began to cry. She swabbed at her eyes with the back of her hand. She said, brokenly, "Oh, Jerome, I am . . . I am so glad you got over being mad and came to me."

Heller had advanced up the hall to her. "Mad at you? I thought you were mad at ME!"

"Oh, I don't blame you for walking out," wept Babe. "I was so awful nasty. I didn't understand you were just setting up Faustino by getting him to confess he got you to throw the race. And then when I saw how it weakened him . . ."

"Weakened him?" said Heller.

"Ruined him in the gambling racket. He had to pay back all the bets and nobody would trust him anymore. The numbers rackets and everything came over to us. I don't blame you for not forgiving me and moving out and never calling again. It was just a straight Italian double-cross and I didn't understand. I have been such a stupid mother. Can you ever forgive me?"

"I didn't call because I thought you were still mad. I was never angry with you, even once," said Heller.

She suddenly threw her arms around him. "You DO forgive me then! Oh, Jerome, I've missed you so!" She put her head down on his shoulder and cried without restraint, gripping him convulsively.

After a time they sat down upon the couch but Babe still held his hand, gazing at him with a glad smile that every now and then again dissolved into tears.

Finally she turned and yelled, "Geovani, don't stand around like a (bleeped) fool. Get Gregorio up and tell the (bleepard) to look alive and get Jerome some milk and cookies! And then get him some breakfast!" She turned to Jet. "You look starved. Tired, too. Nobody has been looking after you."

"I've been pretty busy," said Heller. "Been up without sleep for quite a while. How are things going with the family?"

She made a tipping motion, back and forth, with her hand. "So-so. But things weren't the same after you left."

"I've come back with a peace offering," said Heller. "I thought even if you were still cross, you might care to listen."

"But I'm not cross with you, dear boy. And I promise never to be so awful again. You don't need any peace offering."

"Well, I think you'll be interested anyway," said Heller. "Although I've not seen him in all these months, I think I can deliver Faustino into your hands."

"You already gave us all his gambling connections. What else?"

"Faustino and the whole empire," said Heller. "The lot."

Babe's gray eyes kindled with interest. "How?"

"War," said Heller. "But I need *soldati*, all you've got. It's no trap. I'll do the risky part. And if all goes well, Faustino will be no more."

"A total wipeout? A rub of the whole Rockecenter–I. G. Barben drug empire, too?"

"Yes, I want you to be the *capa di tutti capi*. The chieftainess of all chiefs!"

Babe suddenly caught her breath. "Oh, *sangue di Cristo*, would

THAT put the mayor's wife in her place!" She turned to Heller eagerly.

He rapidly sketched out the part of his plan she had to know.

Babe balked. "I won't let you do it. It's too risky for you!"

"Less risk than you think," said Heller.

"No," said Babe. "I didn't get you back just to lose you! We have to remember that you're the only son I've got!"

Heller took a shot in the dark. "Well," he said, hoping it would awaken her nostalgia for her dead husband and hoping she would supply something he only thought existed, "You know what 'Holy Joe' used to say."

Babe nodded thoughtfully. " 'The only good enemy is a dead enemy.' You've got a point, Jerome."

"Then that settles it," said Heller.

She surged up, eyes glowing. "I'll make the calls." Then, on her feet, she checked. "But if you're going to do something like that, you need to eat your breakfast and get some sleep. No, I won't hear any argument. You sorely show all the signs of my awful neglect. Now do what your mother tells you. Where IS that (bleepard) Gregorio!"

She pushed Jerome into "Holy Joe's" still-maintained bedroom. "Now take a shower. You've got ink all over your hands." She rushed out to hurry up Gregorio and a tray.

Heller obediently showered. It was true that he still had some fingerprint ink on his fingers.

He heard Gregorio wheel in a trolley and leave.

Then Babe's voice sounded somewhere, "Geovani, you lazy son of a (bleepch), take in his baggage and help him get to bed. And then go out and get him some decent clothes. MOVE!"

Geovani handed Heller a bathrobe over the top of the shower stall, an old, ornate robe, probably the late "Holy Joe's."

Heller came out. A breakfast sat under silver warming covers. He opened the satchel and let the cat out. The action did not seem to surprise Geovani: he was oversaturated with surprises.

Jet sat down and began to eat scrambled eggs, feeding some to Mr. Calico.

"Cristo," said Geovani, "you sure turned the lights on. I'm glad you came back, kid. She's been moping around for half a year. It's good to see her at high roar. She's out there talking on three phones at once! From what she's saying, it sounds like a full-fledged gang war. What are we going to attack?"

Heller smiled. "You'll find out tonight."

Chapter 2

Heller awoke, much refreshed, feeling he had caught up with what they call on that planet "jet lag." Of course, a spacer seldom cares what time he sleeps, for all his days in flight are apt to be out of phase with the planets he visits.

The cat was nowhere to be seen. Jet pushed a bell to tell people he was awake.

Geovani came in. He was holding up a tuxedo on a hanger. It was a summer-weight suit of the blackest black with an indigo velvet flared collar. "She told me to get you some clothes, but they didn't have much that I liked. Now, this little article will fit you like a glove, tailor-made for one of the executives. He never picked it up: He got shot. It's got a black silk shirt, black bow tie, black cummerbund and black pearl studs. Ain't it a beauty?"

"It would be the first time I ever went to war in a tuxedo," said Heller.

"Yeah, but I know you," said Geovani. "You got class. You slept the clock around almost. You musta been shooting a lot of guys to get that tired. It's 6:00 P.M. and Babe had Gregorio fix you a dinner that'll make the table legs crack. Real Italian food, the kind you like."

Heller got up, did a fast shave and shower. He got into the tuxedo: It did fit well, airy and cool.

"Now, that's what I call tradition," said Geovani, handing him a black Homburg hat. "Give you a Tommy gun and you couldn't tell the difference between you and "Holy Joe's" old rumrunner mob. Except for the modern cut, of course. Babe will love it."

Heller went out. Babe was at the table already, waiting for him. She was dressed in a beige silk safari suit with a wide collar and ruby buttons, suitably attired for a war. She looked at him with a glad smile, admired his appearance and got him seated. She was quivering with excitement, practically radiating it. She stacked his plate with antipasto.

The cat had apparently made friends. He was sitting at the table behaving himself, though he had already emptied his silver bowl of cream.

"Are all the arrangements made?" said Heller.

"Of course," said Babe. "Now, eat a good dinner. You look thin."

Heller was talking around a mouthful of antipasto. "And they'll all be there?"

"I know those (bleepards)," said Babe. "Every Saturday night around 11:00 P.M., they been meeting for an after-show dinner and their payoff—for the last ten years. And they're meeting tonight. I verified."

"And they're never armed?"

"In the presence of Faustino? You must be kidding, Jerome. Of course, bodyguards will be outside the door and the building will be full of *soldati*. They're the ones you have to be careful of. They're always on the alert on Saturday night. Faustino himself will be heeled, of course. You wouldn't think he could shoot the way his fat overlaps his eyes but he can, so you watch it. If it comes to him or you, make sure it's him. Gregorio! Bring in some more antipasto!"

Heller didn't know if he could get around what he had.

"Eat your dinner," said Babe. "You're thin as a rail! Listen, I got good news for you. Con Edison has had to shut down all its oil generating plants. The only power they're able to get into the Big Apple now is coal and hydroelectric. There'll be no floods on the buildings and no street lights. How's that for a break! Now, enjoy your dinner, you've got plenty of time. 'Holy Joe' always used to say there was nothing like going to war on a full stomach unless it was getting stuffed at Sardine's afterwards."

Gregorio brought in a steaming side dish of spaghetti but Heller knew better than to eat much of that. Immediately came the entrees of lasagne and ravioli. And then Heller was inundated with fettucini, rigatoni, chicken cacciatore, manicotti, veal parmigiana and finally linguine with both red and white clam sauce. All these were special Italian dishes served on that planet. When he was served vast blocks of spumoni, an Italian ice cream, he could hardly open his mouth.

Babe then went into the salon and put on a piece of music called "The Ride of the Valkyries," a wild, bombastic symphony, and said, "That's to aid your digestion. Now, just sit down and relax. Sunset isn't until after 8:00."

Heller sank into an easy chair. He could hardly move. Babe sat perched upon the couch, quivering with excitement. Although she was middle-aged, she still retained much of her Roxy showgirl beauty. A proud and deadly glitter was in her eyes. "Oh, we'll fix that Faustino."

After a while, Heller said, "Let's fix our timetable." And he took a pad and wrote it out. He handed it to her.

She looked at it. Then suddenly her smile froze. "Wait a minute, Jerome. This says, when I see you come out of the *window*. The way I understood it, you were going to land on the roof in a helicopter and after you'd done your thing, you were just going to wait with your hand on Faustino's collar for our frontal assault. That was dangerous enough for you. I thought you were going to lower yourself down into the banquet room through the ventilation system."

"Well, it is kind of a helicopter. I just didn't give you the details."

"This is mad! I'm not going to have you diving out windows! No, Jerome. If you insist on this, the whole thing is off. You might FALL!"

"I'll have a safety line," said Heller.

"Oh, I don't like it. Maybe I should hire you a stunt man!"

"There isn't time now," said Heller.

"Well, that's true. What's this 'spacing of booms'? It says 'Tenth boom.' Then it says . . . Oh, Jerome. You be careful with explosives. Can't I get you a good explosives man? Where's Bang-Bang?"

"He's sort of out of circulation," said Heller. "Now don't you worry about me, Mrs. Corleone. You just follow that timetable and it will go off as smooth as silk."

"Well, all right. But I've known silk to snag. However, I will be a good general. I will use your orders. It gives me goosebumps, the thought of you climbing out a thirty-fifth story window. Now, don't you fall, you hear me?"

"I promise," said Heller.

"Oh, how I wish 'Holy Joe' was here. How he would have loved this! Faustino, no less! I can hardly wait to see the face of the mayor's wife!"

Chapter 3

They left Bayonne after dark in Babe's high-powered, bullet-proof limousine. The New Jersey Turnpike, when they joined it, was a wasteland of concrete, deserted of all traffic due to the absence of fuel. Geovani had had no problem with that: They had their own emergency supplies. He was burning up the road, delighted to do a hundred miles an hour with nothing else in sight. Not even the cops could chase him, as they had no gas either—though it was doubtful if they would have, knowing the car.

To their right, the city of New York was not visible at all, though the summer night was clear. Heller could not ever remember seeing it that way: Only a few beacon lights, red sparks, gleamed as aircraft warnings on the taller towers and buildings.

He made out, at last, the beacon light on the top of the Empire State Building. The top thirty-two stories of the building, usually lit, were dark, probably for the first time since a bomber had crashed into it nearly a half a century before. "We'll get to you later," Heller told it silently, but he wondered how his imprisoned friends were doing there. That lunch case hadn't contained all that much. They would have finished it by now.

He asked Babe if he could use the phone and called the condo. Balmor answered.

"Did she call?" said Heller.

"Oh, yes, sir," said Balmor. "She left a message that there was no change in the person. Do you have a message if she calls again, sir?"

"Tell her I'm working and that I'm fine. And give her my love."

He rang off and found Babe looking at him. "Who was that?" said Babe. "Some girl? It's very important that you marry well, Jerome. You must introduce her to me."

"Oh, you'd approve of her," said Heller. "She's from the same country as that Prince Caucalsia I told you about. The one that belongs at the top of your family tree."

"Really?" said Babe.

"Oh, yes," said Heller. "And she's blond, tall, blue-eyed except when they are gray, very beautiful, talented, educated. She's also an aristocrat."

"Jerome!" said Babe, looking at him. "You're in love!"

Heller laughed. "I plead guilty. And she'll love you, too, when she meets you. Who wouldn't?"

Babe smiled and then began to laugh. "Oh, Jerome—no wonder you forgot your mother for a while. But it's all right. What I couldn't bear was thinking you were mad at me. Now, here's what we will do. As soon as we have finished this war, I'll have a big reception. I'll present her to all the people who matter and if she's as beautiful as you say, we'll be the envy of everybody! Now, let's see: The Waldorf-Astoria Hotel is a little bit old-fashioned but the ballrooms are quite nice. Or should we use the Plaza? Maybe the Grand Hyatt. No, I know. Madison Square Garden! Are you engaged yet?"

"Well, not formally. It's just an understanding between us."

"Ah! If I approve of her, we'll have an engagement party! What's her name?"

Heller, the Fleet officer, would not lie about his girl. He said, "Her passport says her name is Heavenly Joy Krackle. But her real name is the Countess Krak."

"Good heavens! A COUNTESS! And not snooty or anything?"

"She's the soul of charm. You'll love her!"

"Very good, then. That's settled. An engagement party at Madison Square Garden! Choruses from five musicals! The best bands! Champagne! Imagine it: love and war! Oh, Jerome, I'm so glad you have come back!"

They were entering the Holland Tunnel. Babe stopped making notes of the list of guests and put it firmly aside. "I better get my mind on this timetable or we'll be fleeing for our lives to our estates in South America. But promise me faithfully one thing, Jerome."

"What's that?"

"Don't fall!"

Chapter 4

Thanks to the dizzying speed Geovani had driven and the empty, dark streets of lower Manhattan, the limousine arrived early on the scene. They parked beside a small, dark park.

Further to the south, a quarter of a mile away, lay the police headquarters, seen only as a faint blue emergency light. Nearer to hand but unseen were the U.S. Court House and the New York County Court House. To their right and close by on the Bowery lay the dim, unlighted bulk of the Narcotici mob building. The high-rise of Total Control, Inc., was black glass and chrome but one was hard put to even make it out against the murky stars.

Heller, with an infrared flashlight and a lens over his eye, was scanning one final time the plans of the building that Babe had gotten him that day.

There was a sound of footsteps approaching and Babe looked up alertly. She slid her window down and a face appeared, half seen. *"Mia capa?"* It was Signore Saggezza, *consigliere* of the Corleone family.

"All set?" said Babe.

"Mia capa," said Saggezza, "can I not caution you against this thing and call it off before it is too late? Even 'Holy Joe' would have thought a thousand times before he attempted it."

"I know it is your duty, *signore,* to guide us safely through the storms of life," said Babe, "but can the chatter and answer my question. All set?"

"The good God watches over the completely mad with a special providence," said Signore Saggezza. "I just hope he isn't looking the other way tonight. Here's your report: The only power they've got is emergency on one elevator. It's a hot night and there's no air conditioning, so they've got windows open. See that glow up there on the thirty-fifth floor? They're using candles in the banquet room. The city officials are all there; the last one just went in five minutes ago. Our units are all in position. But I must warn you that you are not the only one who sees that this power blackout is an opportunity: Faustino has every *soldat* in his mob inside and watching every door. There's also an army tank unit parked in Tompkins Square about a mile and a half from here and they're likely to come running if there's any firing. The police station is only a quarter of a mile south of here."

"Fix their police cars," said Babe.

"All handled, *mia capa,* but police have feet. This whole thing is quite mad. I also ordered your jet to stand by at Newark in case you have to run for it. Are you still determined?"

"*Signore,* an opportunity like this comes once in a lifetime," said Babe. "The curtain is going to go up."

"Then here's your radio," said Saggezza, "and may the good God have mercy on our souls." He handed the FM walkie-talkie through and vanished in the dark.

Heller reached over and handed her a two-way-response radio. He showed her where the button was.

"I'm in business," said Babe. "Bring on your war!"

Heller said, "Zero your stopwatch. Now start it." He pushed his own.

He got out of the limousine, got his satchel straps on his shoulders and lifted the spacetrooper sled.

"Good luck," said Babe.

With a wave of his hand he trotted off into the darkness of the park.

Working rapidly and unseen, he assembled the sled. He lay down on it, making sure he did not squash the cat in its satchel. He wrapped his fingers around the rod controls.

Up into the night he soared.

Delicately manipulating the controls, he edged sideways to the building as he climbed. It was a fifty-five-story building and it was so dark he almost missed the top.

The gleam of chrome was to his hand. He made the sled hover. He reached into his bag and brought out a handful of round objects. Working with one hand, he looked at their numbers. He found one that said *1* in a glowing numeral. He pushed it against the chrome. He glanced at his watch. He gave the blob a twist.

So much for the top floor.

He dropped down two floors. He found a blob that said *2*. He pressed it against the chrome building side.

Lower he went, two more floors. He fixed a number *3*.

Down and down he went, pausing each time, pushing in another one.

Finally he planted a number *10*.

He glanced at his glowing watch.

The ground was absolutely black below, more than thirty-five stories down.

He edged the sled along at the same level and then found what he was looking for: the window of Faustino's office.

A single candle was burning on a table, hardly enough to show up the murals of Sicily all along the walls. There was a steel canopy, a dome like a sunshade, over a chair. The chair was empty. Beyond, the door to the banquet hall was closed.

Heller, hovering on the sled before the window, reached into the satchel and took out a disintegrator gun. He threw its switches to ON, carefully keeping it away from the sled. It buzzed with a quiet hum.

Flying the sled with one hand and holding the gun on the window, he played the energy on the glass. The edges curled away. In a workmanlike fashion, he made the glass vanish without disturbing the visible alarm cables all around the frame.

The candle on the table guttered from the admitted current of night air.

Heller flew the sled through.

He turned it off and laid it to one side.

He took quick steps over to the door and listened. He could hear the laughter and the clink of the night supper in progress.

With the flick of a switch, he narrowed the beam of the disintegrator gun to a pinpoint. He made a hole through the door and put the gun away.

Heller looked into the hall. Despite the narrowness of the aperture he could see quite well.

The city officials of New York were sitting at a U-shaped table, half a hundred of them. The whole center expanse of the floor was empty.

Then he received his first setback.

The head of the table was NOT backed to this door. It was all the way at the other side of the room!

Faustino was sitting clear over there! A hundred and more feet away! The U of the table was open to the office door!

Somehow he had to get to the other side of that room! He couldn't just open this door as he thought might be possible and grab Faustino by the collar. To do that he had to get across more than a hundred feet of open floor!

By the light of candles, Faustino was making a speech. Something about the great success of the Civic Betterment League. What he was saying was getting guffaws and applause every few words. He was enormously fat, better than three hundred pounds. His face was so puffy he didn't even seem to have eyes: a balloon with a hole in it that opened and closed for a mouth.

Heller glanced at his watch. Time would be critical.

He took the cat out of the satchel and fixed the tiny radio in its ear. He made the other preparations with it. He put the tiny cat transmitter between his teeth and, talking with his mouth barely open, told the cat what to do.

He laid his hat down on a chair. He took off his satchels and put them by the sled. He neated up his tuxedo and bow tie. He blew out the office candle and opened the door a crack.

Then he went to the office hall door and looked out.

Two guards were standing at the banquet door with riot guns. There was no route in that way.

Heller went back to the door that led to the banquet room. There was nothing for it. He would have to take a chance.

He gripped the office door and slowly pulled it open. Then he pushed it with a ferocious rush. He blocked it from slamming with his foot.

The blast of air burst like a gale into the room!

All but one candle went out!

Heller, low down, was on his hands and knees and through the door like a black shadow.

Startled curses rang through the dark.

Lighters shortly began to flash. The candles were getting relit.

But Heller, on his hands and knees, was well around the back of the U-table. Speedily he crawled until he came silently back of Faustino.

Somebody got up to stare at the office door and made as if to approach it.

Faustino was still on his feet. "Naw, naw," he said. "Sit down. It was just the wind. Be calm, be calm. I was saying, gentlemen, that this week, we have never had such a high sale of street drugs. The nervous tensions of the coming war have upped consumption immeasurably. And now, thanks to your splendid cooperation, I must announce a DOUBLE BONUS to you all!"

Faustino bowed to the applause. Then he was holding up an envelope, "To the Mayor, a princely reward this Saturday! Behold . . ."

"Now, march!" Heller whispered into the transmitter, mouth closed.

There was a sizzle of sputtering at the other end of the room. Instead of beholding the uplifted envelope, all eyes turned to the office door!

The cat walked into the banquet hall.

He was towing a black, round sphere which slid along behind him.

He was dragging it by holding the fuse in his mouth.

The end of the fuse was throwing sparks!

A startled gasp of horror went through the assemblage.

Sedately the cat marched forward toward the middle of the U.

Its eyes were pale green orbs in the candlelight.

The sparks trailed across the floor.

"A BOMB!" came the concerted scream.

Faustino snapped a hand into his coat, grabbing for a holstered gun in some insane effort to shoot the cat.

But Heller's hand darted and had the gun.

Heller's other hand had Faustino by the collar.

"IT'S GOING TO EXPLODE!" screamed Heller.

Some officials had been trying to leap over the table to get at the fuse. But at Heller's yell, they abandoned it.

There was a crush and a rush at the door.

All were leaving but Faustino—and Heller held him firm.

Chapter 5

The cat stood in the middle of the floor, still holding the cord. It was only a sparkle cord that ignited at the end when it was squeezed and it was stuck into the mouth of a black ball.

Heller dragged Faustino's hands behind his back and looped a tie cord around his wrists. He boosted the man over the table and from behind him, gave him a shove toward the office.

"Drop it now," said Heller to the cat. "Come on!"

They banged through the office door. Faustino seemed to stumble. He fell beside the steel canopy.

"Guard him!" shouted Heller to the cat. He turned to bolt the door to the banquet room. He turned on a small pocket light so he could see.

There was a yowling from the cat. Heller whirled.

Faustino had rolled himself under the canopy!

The cat was on top of him, clawing.

Heller started to move.

CRASH!

The steel canopy came down!

Faustino had triggered something! The man and cat were obscured!

Heller grabbed at the canopy edge. He tried to lift it. It would not budge!

He dived for his satchel.

He could hear men coming up the hall.

He dived for the hall door and bolted it from within.

Heller raced back and got the satchel open. Palming the disintegrator gun, he leaped to the canopy. Working at an angle so as not to hit the cat, who might be underneath, he tried to make a hole in the steel.

A voice in the banquet hall. "It's not a bomb! It's a fake!"

There were now men at both office doors! Shoulders and boots were thudding at them!

The steel was armor alloy and very resistant. Heller stepped up the beam strength of the gun. He had made only a little hole!

A shotgun blasted at the hall door lock!

Heller banged a shot at it with Faustino's gun!

He glanced at his watch. The glow told him he was almost out of time.

He wasn't making progress fast enough getting through the canopy. He shined his light through the slot he had cut.

EMPTINESS!

No Faustino! No cat! No floor!

He could make out the outlines of a spiral chute going down!

A shotgun blasted again at the door.

Heller grabbed his satchels.

He threw himself on the spacetrooper sled.

The shotgun roared again!

Heller hit the controls.

The sound of the door bursting in.

The sled started out the window.

Another shotgun blast!

Something tugged at his heel!

He shot out into the dark night!

THE FIRST EXPLOSION WENT!

It sounded just like lightning had struck close to hand, a blasting, cracking roar that filled the night!

The sled bucked and twisted.

It plummeted earthward from thirty-five stories high.

THE SECOND EXPLOSION WENT!

Convulsively, Heller gripped the sled controls. The ground was coming up, unseen, but it must be very near!

He got the sled into a climb.

THE THIRD EXPLOSION WENT!

The sled slewed.

Heller got it straightened out.

A tree straight ahead!

Heller zoomed over it.

At least he knew where the ground was now.

He settled the sled vertically and played his light down.

He landed.

THE FOURTH EXPLOSION WENT!

He was behind Babe's lines, half a block from the building.

Quickly he collapsed the sled and lashed it to his satchel.

He started to run forward, toward the building.

"Stand where you are!"

A flashlight hit him in the face.

"It's the kid!" said somebody else. "Don't shoot him." Corleone men, part of the ring around the building.

Heller was worried about the cat. "Let me through! I've got to get back there!"

"Naw, naw, kid. You stay here! They're pouring out of there like rats from a sinking ship."

THE FIFTH EXPLOSION WENT!

It was like a nearby crack of lightning but no flash or flame. The explosions were coming from the building top, progressing down where he had planted each of them.

A rush of running feet from the building. A crash and a yell.

Three more Narcotici men had slammed into the fishnets strung across the streets.

Corleones gathered them up, disarmed them and shunted them over to a group where they were quickly tied.

THE SIXTH EXPLOSION WENT!

"Jesus, what are those things?" said a Corleone to Jet. "There ain't any flame or debris. Sounds like a whole God (bleep) floor goes up each time."

Heller could have told him that they were matter-vibration-intensifying bombs used by Voltar combat engineers to create diversions at point B when they were really quietly blowing up point A. They did not transmit their sound directly into the air but only through matter molecules. They didn't destroy anything except perhaps an eardrum if you were inside the place. But Heller said, in Italian, "Who knows? The wrath of Gods, perhaps."

THE SEVENTH EXPLOSION WENT!

When its *crack* ceased echoing, Babe's voice came over somebody's walkie-talkie. "*Signore!* What's the count now?"

"Five hundred and thirty-six, *mia capa*," crackled back.

"Couple hundred to go," came Babe's voice. "Stay on your toes! Has anybody seen Jerome?"

THE EIGHTH EXPLOSION WENT!

Heller grabbed his two-way response radio. "I'm on the ground, Mrs. Corleone. I'm okay. I'm at Station Six. Please tell the men to let me through. I've got to get back to the building."

THE NINTH EXPLOSION WENT!

A dozen Narcotici men, running in panic from the building in the dark, hit the net near Heller. They were jumped on promptly, disarmed and carted aside.

Babe's voice. "Station Six. Don't let Jerome through until after you've launched the general assault."

"Yes, yes, *mia capa*."

THE TENTH EXPLOSION WENT!

A hissing series of orders sizzled near Jerome. The same sound, more distant, was coming from other stations all around the encircled building.

A sudden shout from half a thousand throats, "CORLEONE!"

A rush and thunder of feet moving forward in the blackness.

The general assault had begun.

A blaze of gunfire flamed.

"You can go now, kid," said a voice near Heller.

Heller rushed forward. It was not quite as dark. Gun flashes coming from lower windows and those replying gave the night a fitful, jerking light. Most of the assault force was inside now but those in view were seen like sudden still pictures as a rifle went.

Somebody yelled, "Army tanks rolling south, half a mile! Mop this up fast!"

Heller sized up the building. There had been no spiral chute on the plans. The basement under this section of the structure, below Faustino's office, was all furnaces.

He went up to the outer wall, pressing in against it. He edged along. He must be now directly below Faustino's office. The side of the building was made of huge, black blocks of stone here, flanking the street.

Gunfire was rolling inside where diehards were holding out. He heard the thud of a grenade.

He was looking for a manhole cover, some telltale.

AN ARCED SCAR ON THE PAVEMENT!

It began at the bottom edge of one of the black stones and curved in a perfect arc across the sidewalk. At some time this stone had swung open and a bit of debris had been under it, making the mark.

There was a vertical line where the stone joined another in the outer wall. Heller took his disintegrator gun and widened the crack. He took a bar and forced it in and pried.

It *was* a door!

Once more he applied the disintegrator gun to the crack. The inside bolt latch vanished.

He shoved the bar in further.

The door reluctantly opened!

He shined in the light.

There was the cat!

He was sitting on the tied Faustino's chest!

Faustino tried to turn toward Heller's light.

"Save me!" he screamed.

The cat hit him.

"I got it, Mister Calico," said Heller. "You've done great tonight!"

Heller grabbed Faustino and got him to his feet. "Corleone!" he yelled over his shoulder. "To me!"

The firing around the building had died. Two men sprinted over to Jet. He thrust Faustino into their hands. "Rush this guy to Babe direct!"

They shoved Faustino out and pushed him along the sidewalk. Heller reached back in to pick up the cat.

When he emerged he was hit in the face with a spotlight!

A TANK!

Heller let the cat jump away and held his arms high and wide. He walked directly to the tank.

The tank's machine guns were trained on his chest.

An officer was standing in the turret, covering him with a .45. By the light from inside the turret, Heller saw the silver eagle of a colonel.

"What the hell's all this?" roared the colonel.

"May I identify myself, sir?" called Heller.

"Advance easy or I'll shoot!"

Heller, arms held wide, sprang up on the tread.

"Reach in my side pocket, sir." He made a brief indication which one.

The colonel looked at the tuxedo and then, holding the .45 wide, pulled the papers out.

"Lieutenant Wister of Army Intelligence, sir," said Heller. "Rounding up Maysabongo saboteurs. The men you see are my unit in mufti."

The colonel scanned the I.D. and then the orders. "Why wasn't I informed?" he said.

"All hush-hush," said Heller. "But we got them before they could blow up the whole city."

"The vicious (bleepards)!" exclaimed the colonel. "A (bleeped) good thing you did! Loudest explosions I ever heard in my life! Are you sure you got them all?" he added, looking around.

"We're just mopping up," said Heller.

There was a thunder of feet on the street behind them.

COPS!

Police Inspector Grafferty, blowing from his run, came into the tank's lights. "You're all under arrest!" he bellowed.

The colonel stiffened. He stared down at Grafferty. "This is an army operation!" he roared. "How dare you interfere!"

Grafferty's eye suddenly caught sight of Heller. "WISTER!" he shouted. "Colonel, I know this man! He's a criminal!"

The colonel glared at him. "So now you're calling army officers criminals, are you! Get the hell out of this operation before I turn my guns loose on you!"

Grafferty quailed. He hastily withdrew and gave an urgent signal to the cops to leave with him.

Heller saluted. "Sir, I've got to get the prisoners to the stockade, so please excuse me if you will."

"Of course, of course," said the colonel. "You seem to have done very well." He glanced at the orders before he handed them and the I.D. back. "I'll commend you to the secretary of war."

"Oh, that's awfully nice of you, sir," said Heller. "But I am just doing my duty."

"Splendid, Wister. You'll mention me as assisting? I'm Colonel Boots."

"Of course, sir," said Heller.

"Very good, Lieutenant. I'll get my unit back to the park. Carry on."

Heller trotted off around the building. Things were quiet now. The mobs of captured Narcotici men were gone. The fishnets had disappeared. There was only an old Corleone *soldato* left picking up cartridge empties.

Heller got to the limousine and opened the door. Faustino was lying on the floor, tied up very thoroughly. The cat had evidently followed the mobster, for Mister Calico now sat on a jump seat, ready in case a claw rake was needed.

Babe was sitting there with her radios. She looked up with a glad smile when the door light came on.

Before she could speak, Saggezza's voice came over. "*Mia capa,* all computers have been taken. All Faustino's notebooks are in our hands. No data banks or books have been damaged. I am putting men throughout the building. The whole operation is in our hands."

Babe said, "Splendidly done, *signore.* We have the fat one right here, so that's the end of them complete."

Heller said, "Did you get the New York Chief of Police?"

"And every other official of the city, including the mayor. They're over there behind those bushes blubbering for their lives."

"Well, please have that police chief told that he must phone and have the guard taken off the Empire State Building at once."

"Of course, Jerome. Anything you want. The whole city is ours!"

Not yet, thought Heller privately. This could still rebound like a comet return unless I can finish it before Monday.

Chapter 6

Two hours later, Izzy, Bang-Bang and Twoey were celebrating their joyous deliverance from the Empire State Building by eating anything and everything Heller could stuff into them at Sardine's Restaurant.

When there was nothing left to consume but the tablecloth, he sent them home to get rested and cleaned up with orders to meet him in the morning at the condo.

The battle was not over. The hardest part was just ahead: Rockecenter. And in this one, Heller was very short of troops.

From Army Intelligence Headquarters, Heller learned that Rockecenter was at his Pokantickle Estate, north of Hairytown. The place was being guarded by a regiment of hastily mobilized New York National Guard under the command of a major general, no less.

Heller also learned that Rockecenter would leave there this Sunday afternoon and drive to Philadelphia. There he would join the Swillerberger Conference of International Financiers, which he thoroughly controlled, and Sunday night, the president of the United States would be summoned before this private body. Then, on Monday, the president would address Congress in Washington and formal war would be declared on the Republic of Maysabongo.

Jet knew that he was now up against the powers that ruled Earth. The preparation he could do on this one was pretty thin at best, but he had better get on with it.

He returned to the condo through a dark New York. He got on

some coveralls and went to work on the old cab. Using a Voltarian light he turned its color to olive drab, then, using a spray can and brush, he gave it white army insignia and numbers.

While he worked, the radio battered him with war hysteria, not the least of which was news that Maysabongo saboteurs had attempted to blow up the New York City Hall but had been foiled by an army tank unit under Colonel Boots. Motorists were also being warned to keep off major highways and leave them clear for the army: a safe enough order since there wasn't any gas. People were also being requested to stay alert for Maysabongo partisans who might be planning to blow up railroads, airfields and convoys, and to report such information to the army.

Much martial music was also on the airways. The country was obviously girding up its loins for battle. Heller knew that, with a lot of luck, he might be able to prevent it. Nobody else seemed to be trying.

About 8:00 A.M., he dressed in a clean uniform. Then he loaded a khaki-colored shoulder bag with the tools of the trade of a Voltar Fleet combat engineer—mainly bombs.

Bang-Bang Rimbombo showed up. He was dressed in his ROTC uniform and Heller made him remove the shoulder patch so he would look like an army driver.

Izzy Epstein arrived, hollow-eyed and worried.

Delbert John Rockecenter II got there, upset because he couldn't have the time to go out and see to his surviving pigs in New Jersey.

They set off, looking very official, for Pokantickle Hills, twenty-three miles or more to the north. There were no cars on the road. All the traffic lights were off. The old cab, now running not on gas but on a carburetor that converted asphalt into oxygen and hydrogen, had lots of speed and pep. Bang-Bang, having no cars to run into, had them at the gates of the estate by nine.

A vast array of New York National Guard met their eyes. It was camped and parked all over the lawns and soldiers were drilling and marching around everywhere.

The gate was a formidable barricade. A whole squad with pointed and cocked rifles blocked the way, combat ready.

An officer, web-cross-belted and helmeted, stepped up to the car. The National Guard was determined to confront the Regular Army with a snarl.

"Get out and get your hands up!" said the officer.

"No, no," said Heller. "This is a family matter." He turned around to Twoey. "Give me your driver's license." Twoey handed it over. "We're here to get his father's permission for him to join the army."

"Delbert John Rockecenter, Second!" said the officer, looking at the license and then at Twoey. "Jesus Christ, I'm sorry!" He hastily grabbed a pad from his belt and scribbled a pass with the word *FAMILY* in block letters and slid it under the windshield wiper. "Open the gates, men, we got orders not to interrupt the household." He saluted Heller.

They drove on up the winding drive past tents, troop carriers, motorcycles, field pieces and two tanks.

"I am not going to join the army!" said Twoey with determination. "They shoot pigs!"

"You shut up," said Heller. "Let me do the talking."

"All right, brother," said Twoey, "but don't you go getting me in any army!"

They drew up before the front entrance to the house. Everything was oversize. So were the two National Guardsmen who stood on either side of the door.

Heller handed his shoulder satchel to Bang-Bang. "You just sit tight out here."

Izzy and Twoey and Heller got out and walked up the steps. An officer appeared. He glanced at the pass under the windshield wiper: the word *FAMILY* could be read fifteen feet away. He said, "Sorry, but orders are that everyone be searched." He frisked them for weapons and found none. He looked into the briefcase Izzy was carrying, saw nothing but papers and gave it back. He saluted and had an enlisted man open the door.

The three walked into an enormous living room heavily

furnished with outdated, enormous furniture. Huge, enlarged photographs of severe-looking Rockecenters glared down at them.

Voices were coming through a closed door of another room. Heller walked up to it, opened it, shepherded the other two in and closed it behind them.

It was a study, huge, out-of-date. French doors opened out of it on to a side drive.

Delbert John Rockecenter was standing like an angry vulture back of the desk.

Bury, his attorney from the firm of Swindle and Crouch, was standing unhappily against the far wall, his prune face aggrieved.

"And that's very plain to me!" Rockecenter was saying. "You did NOT do your job! I ought to turn you over to Miss Agnes and get her to electric-shock some sense into you! If you had taken any precautions at all, I would not have to be making a long, tiresome drive to Philadelphia just to see that nincompoop of a president! I am sick of doing your work! I should terminate both you and your firm! And I mean terminate! You're all against me anyway!"

Bury had caught sight of Heller. He was staring. He went white. "WISTER!"

Rockecenter would have gone on talking but it began to be borne in upon him that he had lost his listener. He glanced with annoyance at the group which had entered. "Tell the general," he said to Heller, "that I am not leaving yet." He turned back to Bury. "I am not through telling you what I think of you! And I will remind you, Bury, that what I think is important! LISTEN TO ME!"

Bury was making little stabbing points at Heller, "Sir, that's your . . . sir, that's the fuel man. . . . Sir, oh, my God!"

"Fuel man? Fuel man?" said Rockecenter. "What are you gibbering about now?"

"Perhaps I had better explain," said Heller. "We have come to make you a fair offer that can settle all this oil trouble, Mr. Rockecenter."

"Who is this?" Rockecenter asked Bury. "What's he talking about?"

"Sir, that one in uniform is Jerome Terrance Wister!"

"And this," said Heller, "is Mr. Israel Epstein. He controls the companies that own the microwave-power setup, Chryster Motors, gasless carburetors, gasless cars—and he controls, as well, all the U.S. oil reserves now possessed by Maysabongo."

Rockecenter sat down very suddenly. He stared at Izzy. Then he said, "The Jew. You're that (bleeped) Jew!"

Heller said, "I think you two can make a deal that will make everybody happy."

Rockecenter was still staring at Izzy. Then his eyes went slitted and a look of cunning came over his face. "Do I understand that you own the patents of that carburetor and those cars and that microwave-power setup?"

"Companies that I can control do," said Izzy. "They're right here." He opened his case and took them out, advanced and put them on the huge desk.

Bury instantly shifted over behind Rockecenter and inspected them. He whispered something to the effect that they were valid.

"You mean," said Rockecenter to Izzy, "that you are willing to turn these over to me in exchange for peace?"

"Not exactly," said Izzy. "Turn them over to you, yes, but there is something we must have in return."

"Oh," said Rockecenter, seemingly disappointed. Then he glanced sideways at Bury and looked again at Izzy. He smiled a slight, strange smile. "So what do you want in return, Jew?"

Izzy said, "We have certain options we will exercise tomorrow that will put us in possession of billions and also the shares of every oil company. You may have 49 percent of the money and 49 percent of the shares."

"That's giving me even more," said Rockecenter. "So there's something crooked afoot here."

Izzy said, "Mr. Rockecenter, you once had a wife. You also had two sons."

Rockecenter looked like he had been shot.

"According to earlier family wills," continued Izzy, "a son of yours would receive a ten-billion-dollar trust fund. You are trustee of that fund. What we want you to do is recognize Delbert John Rockecenter II as your son."

"I am withdrawing any rights I may seem to have," said Heller.

"This allegation is preposterous!" blustered Rockecenter.

"The documents are right here," said Izzy and drew out copies and passed them over.

Rockecenter stared at them, stricken. The Wall Street lawyer scanned them. Bury whispered something in his ear. Heller only caught a phrase that Miss Agnes had botched it.

"We want," said Izzy, "that acknowledgment. We also want you to pass over that trusteeship, for your son here is now the required age. We also want you to make a will leaving him your entire estate, appointing me executor."

"And if I do this thing?"

"The oil companies can have these patents, the U.S. will have its oil. The refineries will get back in operation. . . ."

"They can't!" said Rockecenter. "The protest marchers claim they're radioactive! They won't let them open!"

"I will promise to see that they are decontaminated and gotten back into operation," said Heller.

"It's all propaganda anyway!" said Rockecenter. "So what's a little radiation in people's tanks? Riffraff anyway!"

"I can also call the marchers off," said Heller.

Rockecenter sat back. "You're pretty smart, Jew. If I only have 49 percent of the oil companies, you will control their boards and policies. I'll have to resign from everything!"

"That's a little more drastic than was intended," said Izzy. "But let me point out that you would be the wealthiest man in the world."

"And if I say no?" said Rockecenter.

"Why then," said Heller, "I'm afraid Mr. Bury here will be defending you in court on a charge of conspiracy to murder your wife and son. I'm sorry to put it so bluntly. And all the rest of this will also go to court and you'll lose anyway."

"That's blackmail!" said Rockecenter.

"That's murder," said Heller coolly. "And when you add it up with millions of other murders in the name of war, millions of babies dead from your abortion programs and hundreds of millions of lives ruined with inflation just so you can make a quick buck with oil, I wonder that they haven't hanged you a hundred million times over. I'd be glad to hold the rope myself!"

"No, no," said Izzy hastily. "This is a business conference."

"Well, this bird has caused me a lot of trouble," said Heller. "What he calls business is just banditry on a planetary scale. He's just a pirate and I don't like looking at him or talking to him. I disagree completely with the generosity of your offer, Mr. Epstein."

"Mr. Wister," said Izzy, "please stand over to the side, there, and let me continue these negotiations. Mr. Rockecenter can recognize a profit when he sees it."

A scowl drew in the prune wrinkles of Bury's face. He knew he was looking at the good-guy–bad-guy conference approach. He bent toward Rockecenter to whisper some advice but he didn't get a chance to utter it.

Rockecenter whispered at him and then looked at Izzy with a sly expression.

"Jew," said Rockecenter, "I'm afraid we'd have to call in attorneys to draw up such a deal. We——"

"No, you wouldn't," said Izzy, opening his case. "You have Mr. Bury here and our attorney Bleedum was up half the night typing all this out."

One by one, Izzy laid the assignments of patents to the oil companies on Rockecenter's desk. Then he laid out the transfer of Maysabongo oil. Then he drew out the assignment of 49 percent of the sell-option profits and followed it with an assignment of 49 percent of the oil-company shares. Then he laid out the document assigning the trust. Then he laid out a will.

Rockecenter and Bury read them.

Rockecenter said suddenly, "All right. I will sign them. Mr. Bury is a notary. We will execute everything right now."

"And call off the war?" said Heller.

"Of course," said Rockecenter. "You can even have my sacred word on that. When we're through, I'll just ring the president and that will be that."

Chapter 7

Rockecenter drew the pack of assignments and contracts to him. Smiling slightly, he rapidly began to sign on every signature place. He finished straight on through to the will and scrawled his name on it with a flourish.

"Now, Jew," he said, pointing to Izzy, "it's your turn."

Izzy grabbed the pack, bent over, adjusted his spectacles and began to sign.

"Now you," said Rockecenter to Twoey when Izzy was done. "There's a document here relating to the trust that requires your signature."

Twoey shuffled forward and scrawled his name.

Rockecenter looked at Heller, then at Bury. "Doesn't he need to sign a quitclaim?"

Bury nodded and went to his attaché case and got out a blank form. He brought it over to the desk.

"Now," said Rockecenter, "Bury, as a notary, will need your I.D. to verify your signatures, so lay your wallets out right here." He tapped the middle of the desk.

All three put their wallets there.

Bury looked at them and the signatures. He got busy with notarial stamps and worked down through the pile. Rockecenter whispered something to him.

The Wall Street lawyer got to the last sheet. It was Heller's quitclaim. "You've signed this Jerome Terrance Wister." He finished notarizing it. "But I am going to have to have one signed Delbert

-331-

John Rockecenter, Junior, from you also. I'll get another blank."

He walked around Heller and went to the wall where his attaché case lay. He reached in and handed Heller the second quitclaim.

Heller bent over to fill it in and sign it.

He had his eye on the top of a solid silver inkwell.

In distortion, he saw Bury draw!

Behind his back, the gun came out like a striking snake!

Heller whirled. His hand shot up!

He caught Bury's wrist, forcing it toward the ceiling!

THE GUN WENT OFF!

Heller bent the arm into a smashing blow!

He made the clenched gun strike Bury's head!

The scalp parted to the bone!

"HOLD IT!" came a shout.

Heller whirled.

The library doors had slammed open.

THERE CROUCHED AN INFANTRYMAN WITH A BA-ZOOKA!

TWO MORE SOLDIERS HAD THEIR RIFLES ON HEL-LER!

Bury fell to the floor behind the couch, blood pouring from his head.

He had taken the gun with him!

Heller stood there, unarmed. The soldiers were too far away to rush.

Rockecenter stood, with a sharp, crazy laugh. He scooped up all the papers. He scooped up their wallets. He reached down and grabbed a huge steel briefcase. It had a circular dial combination. He opened it. The only thing that made it different from a safe was that it had a handle.

"You think I'd keep my word on a crazy deal like that? All I wanted from you was the patents! Now we can nullify and hide this work and keep the world on profitable oil." He peered over at Bury on the floor. The man appeared to be dead. "I'll take the rest of this along to keep it out of plotting hands." He stuffed the papers and wallets and all Izzy's papers into the case, got them out of the way of the beveled, fitted edges, closed it and spun the combination.

A major general came rushing in, followed by a squad.

"General," said Rockecenter, "hold this riffraff until I return. Then, as we will be at war, we'll have work for a firing squad!"

Has Rockecenter
foiled the entire plan?

What will Hisst do
to retaliate?

Find out in
MISSION EARTH
Volume 9
Villainy Victorious

About the Author
L. Ron Hubbard

Born in 1911, the son of a U.S. naval officer, the legendary L. Ron Hubbard grew up in the great American West and was acquainted early with a rugged outdoor life before he took to the sea. The cowboys, Indians and mountains of Montana were balanced with an open sea, temples and the throngs of the Orient as Hubbard journeyed through the Far East as a teenager. By the time he was nineteen, he had travelled over a quarter of a million sea miles and thousands on land, recording his experiences in a series of diaries, mixed with story ideas.

When Hubbard returned to the U.S., his insatiable curiosity and demand for excitement sent him into the sky as a barnstormer where he quickly earned a reputation for his skill and daring. Then he turned his attention to the sea again. This time it was four-masted schooners and voyages into the Caribbean, where he found the adventure and experience that was to serve him later at the typewriter.

Drawing from his travels, he produced an amazing plethora of stories, from adventure and westerns to mystery and detective.

By 1938, Hubbard was already established and recognized as one of the top-selling authors, when a major new magazine, Street and Smith's *Astounding Science Fiction,* called for new blood. Hubbard was urged to try his hand at science fiction. The red-headed author protested that he did not write about "machines and machinery" but that he wrote about people. "That's just what we want," he was told.

The result was a barrage of stories from Hubbard that expanded the scope and changed the face of the genre, gaining Hubbard a repute, along with Robert Heinlein, as one of the "founding fathers" of the great Golden Age of Science Fiction.

Then as now he excited intense critical comparison with the best of H. G. Wells and Edgar Allan Poe. His prodigious creative output of more than a hundred novels and novelettes and more than two hundred short stories, with over twenty-two million copies of fiction in a dozen languages sold throughout the world, is a true publishing phenomenon.

But perhaps most important is that as time went on, Hubbard's work and style developed to masterful proportions. The 1982 blockbuster *Battlefield Earth,* celebrating Hubbard's 50th year as a pro writer, remained for 32 weeks on the nation's bestseller lists and received the highest critical acclaim.

"A superlative storyteller with total mastery of plot and pacing."—*Publishers Weekly*

"A huge (800+ pages) slugfest. Mr. Hubbard celebrates fifty years as a pro writer with tight plotting, furious action, and have-at-'em entertainment."—*Kirkus Review*

But the final *magnum opus* was yet to come. L. Ron Hubbard, after completing *Battlefield Earth,* sat down and did what few writers have dared contemplate—let alone achieve. He wrote the ten-volume space adventure satire *Mission Earth.*

Filled with a dazzling array of other-world weaponry and systems, *Mission Earth* is a spectacular cavalcade of battles, of stunning plot reversals, with heroes and heroines, villains and villainesses, caught up in a superbly imaginative, intricately plotted invasion of Earth—as seen entirely and uniquely through the eyes of the aliens that already walk among us.

With the distinctive pace, artistry and humor that is the inimitable hallmark of L. Ron Hubbard, *Mission Earth* weaves a hilarious, fast-paced adventure tale of ingenious alien intrigue, told with biting social commentary in the great classic tradition of Swift, Wells and Orwell.

So unprecedented is this work, that a new term—dekalogy

(meaning ten books)—had to be coined just to describe its breadth and scope.

With the manuscript completed and in the hands of the publisher and all of his other work done, L. Ron Hubbard departed his body on January 24, 1986. He left behind a timeless legacy of unparalleled story-telling richness for you the reader to enjoy, as other readers have, time and again, over the past half century.

We the publishers are proud to present L. Ron Hubbard's dazzling tour de force: the *Mission Earth* dekalogy.

"I AM ALWAYS HAPPY TO HEAR FROM MY READERS."

L. Ron Hubbard

These were the words of L. Ron Hubbard, who was always very interested in hearing from his friends, readers and followers. He made a point of staying in communication with everyone he came in contact with over his fifty-year career as a professional writer, and he had thousands of fans and friends that he corresponded with all over the world.

The publishers of L. Ron Hubbard's literary works wish to continue this tradition and would very much welcome letters and comments from you, his readers, both old and new.

Any message addressed to the Author's Affairs Director at Bridge Publications will be given prompt and full attention.

BRIDGE PUBLICATIONS, INC.
1414 North Catalina Street
Los Angeles, CA 90027